CLIVE CUSSLER

HarperCollins*Publishers*

HarperCollins*Publishers*
77–85 Fulham Palace Road,
Hammersmith, London W6 8JB

www.harpercollins.co.uk

This paperback edition 2005
1

Previously published in paperback by Grafton 1990
Reprinted 20 times

First published in Great Britain by
HarperCollins*Publishers* 1993

Copyright © Clive Cussler Enterprises Inc. 1990

The Author asserts the moral right to
be identified as the author of this work

ISBN 978-0-00-788422-3

Set in Sabon

Printed and bound in Great Britain by
Clays Limited, St Ives plc

To the men and women of our
nation's intelligence services,
whose dedication and loyalty
are seldom recognized.

And whose efforts have saved
American citizens from more
tragedies than can be imagined
and never revealed.

DRAGON

Dennings' Demons

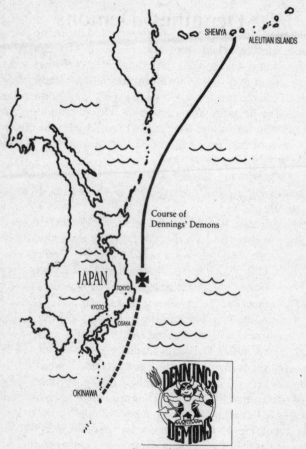

SHEMYA

ALEUTIAN ISLANDS

Course of
Dennings' Demons

JAPAN

TOKYO

KYOTO

OSAKA

OKINAWA

Insignia of Dennings' Demons

August 6, 1945
Shemya Island, Alaska

The devil clutched a bomb in his left hand, a pitchfork in his right, and smirked impishly. He might have appeared menacing if it wasn't for the exaggerated eyebrows and the half-moon eyes. They gave him more of a sleepy gremlin look than the fiendish expression expected from the ruler of hell. Yet he wore the customary red suit and sprouted regulation horns and long forked tail. Oddly, the clawlike toenails of his feet were curled over a gold bar that was labelled *24 K*.

In black letters above and below the circled figure on the fuselage of the B-29 bomber were the words *Dennings' Demons*.

The aircraft, named for its commander and crew, sat like a forlorn ghost under a sheet of rain driven southward over the Aleutian Islands by a wind from the Bering Sea. A battery of portable lights illuminated the area beneath the open belly of the plane, casting wavering shadows from the ground crew on the glistening aluminium body. Flashes of lightning added to the haunting scene, stabbing the darkness of the airfield with disturbing frequency.

Major Charles Dennings leaned against one of the twin tyres of the starboard landing gear, hands shoved deep into the pockets of his leather flight jacket, and observed the activity around his aircraft. The entire area was patrolled by armed MPs and K-9 sentries. A small camera crew recorded the event. He watched with uneasy trepidation as the obese bomb was delicately winched into the modified bomb bay of the B-29. It was too large for the bomber's ground clearance and had to be hoisted out of a pit.

During his two years as one of the top bomber pilots in

Europe, with over forty missions to his credit, he had never laid eyes on such a monstrosity. He saw it as a gigantic overinflated football with nonsensical boxed fins on one end. The round ballistic casing was painted a light grey, and the clamps that held it together around the middle looked like a huge zipper.

Dennings felt menaced by the thing he was to carry nearly three thousand miles. The Los Alamos scientists who assembled the bomb at the airstrip had briefed Dennings and his crew the previous afternoon. A motion picture of the Trinity test explosion was shown to the young men, who sat stunned in disbelief as they viewed the awesome detonation of a single weapon with the power to crush an entire city.

He stood there another half hour until the bomb-bay doors were swung closed. The atom bomb was armed and secure, the plane was fuelled and ready for takeoff.

Dennings loved his aircraft. In the air he and the big complex machine became as one. He was the brain, it was the body, a unity he could never describe. On the ground it was another story. Exposed by the shining lights and beaten by the rain that became sleet-cold, he saw the beautiful ghostlike silver bomber as his crypt.

He shook off the morbid thought and hurried through the rain to a Quonset hut for his crew's final briefing. He entered and sat down next to Captain Irv Stanton, the bombardier, a jolly round-faced man with a great walrus moustache.

On the other side of Stanton, his feet stretched out in front of him, slouched Captain Mort Stromp, Dennings' co-pilot, a complacent southerner, who moved with the agility of a three-toed sloth. Immediately behind sat Lieutenant Joseph Arnold, the navigator, and Navy Commander Hank Byrnes, the weapons engineer, who would monitor the bomb during the flight.

The briefing led off with an intelligence officer unveiling a display board showing aerial photographs of the targets. The industrial section of Osaka was the primary target; the

12

backup, in case of heavy cloud cover, was the historical city of Kyoto. Directional bomb runs were advised as Stanton calmly made notes.

A meteorology officer displayed weather charts and predicted light headwinds with scattered clouds over the targets. He also warned Dennings to expect turbulence over northern Japan. Just to be on the safe side, two B-29s had taken off an hour earlier to scout ahead and report visual assessments of weather over the flight route and cloud cover above the targets.

Dennings took over as polarized welder's goggles were passed around. 'I won't give you a locker-room pep talk,' he said, noting the relieved grins on the faces of his crew. 'We've had a year of training crammed into one short month, but I know we can pull this mission off. In my humble opinion you're the best damned flight crew in the Air Force. If we all do our jobs, we may well end the war.'

Then he nodded at the base chaplain, who offered a prayer for a safe and successful flight.

As the men filed out toward the waiting B-29, Dennings was approached by General Harold Morrison, special deputy to General Leslie Groves, head of the Manhattan bomb project.

Morrison studied Dennings for a moment. The pilot's eyes showed a weariness around the edges, but they glowed with anticipation. The general held out his hand. 'Good luck, Major.'

'Thank you, sir. We'll get the job done.'

'I don't doubt it for a second,' said Morrison, forcing a confident expression. He waited for Dennings to reply, but the pilot had gone silent.

After a few awkward moments, Dennings asked, 'Why us, General?'

Morrison's smile was barely visible. 'You want to back out?'

'No, my crew and I will see it through. But why us?' he

repeated. 'Excuse me for saying, sir, but I can't believe we're the only flight crew in the Air Force you'd trust to fly an atomic bomb across the Pacific, drop it in the middle of Japan, and then land at Okinawa with little more than fumes in the fuel tanks.'

'It's best you know only what you've been told.'

'So we can't give away top secrets if we're captured and tortured?' Dennings said evenly.

The general's eyes turned grim. 'You and your crew know the score. Each of you were issued a lethal capsule of cyanide.'

'Open wide and swallow, should any of us survive a crash over enemy territory,' Dennings recited coldly. 'Why not jettison the bomb at sea? At least we'd stand a chance of being picked up by the Navy.'

Morrison shook his head solemnly. 'The slightest possibility of the weapon falling into enemy hands is unthinkable.'

'I see,' Dennings murmured. 'Then our other choice, if we're hit by flak or fighters over the Japanese mainland, is to ride it down and detonate rather than waste it.'

Morrison stared at him. 'This is not a kamikaze attack. Every conceivable measure has been carefully planned to safeguard the lives of you and your crew. Trust me, son. Dropping "Mother's Breath" on Osaka will be a piece of cake.'

Dennings almost believed him; for a brief instant he came within a hair of buying Morrison's convincing line, but he read foreboding in the older man's eyes and voice.

' "Mother's Breath." ' Dennings repeated the words slowly, without tone, as one would repeat the name of some unspeakable terror. 'What warped soul came up with such a cockamamie code name for the bomb?'

Morrison made a resigned shrug. 'I believe it was the President.'

*

Twenty-seven minutes later, Dennings gazed past the beating windscreen wipers. The rain had increased, and he could see only two hundred yards through the wet gloom. Both feet pressed the brakes as he ran the engines up to 2200 rpm's. Flight Engineer Sergeant Robert Mosely reported number-four outboard engine turning over fifty revolutions slow. Dennings decided to ignore the report. The damp air was no doubt responsible for the slight drop. He pulled the throttles back to idle.

In the co-pilot's seat to the right of Dennings, Mort Stromp acknowledged the control tower's clearance for takeoff. He lowered the flaps. Two of the crew in the waist turrets confirmed the flap setting.

Dennings reached over and switched on the intercom. 'OK, guys, here we go.'

He eased the throttles forward again, compensating for the tremendous torque by slightly advancing the left engines over those on the right. Then he released the brake.

Fully loaded at 68 tons, *Dennings' Demons*, her tanks filled to their filler caps with over 7,000 gallons of fuel, her forward bomb bay holding a six-ton bomb, and carrying a crew of twelve, began to roll. She was nearly 17,000 pounds overweight.

The four 3,350-cubic-inch Wright Cyclone engines strained at their mountings, their combined 8,800 horsepower whipping the 16.5-foot propellers through the wind-driven sheet of water. Blue flame erupting from exhaust manifolds, wings enveloped in a cloud of spray, the great bomber roared into the blackness.

With agonizing slowness she picked up speed. The long runway stretched out in front of her, carved out of the bleak volcanic rock and ending at an abrupt drop eighty feet above the cold sea. A horizontal bolt of lightning bathed the fire trucks and ambulances spaced along the runway in an eerie blue light. At eighty knots Dennings took full rudder control and advanced the right engines to their stops. He

15

gripped the wheel grimly, determined to get the *Demons* in the air.

Forward of the pilots, in the exposed nose section, Stanton the bombardier apprehensively watched the runway rapidly diminish. Even the lethargic Stromp straightened up in his seat, his eyes vainly attempting to penetrate the darkness ahead for the change in black where the runway ended and the sea began.

Three quarters of the runway passed, and she was still glued to the ground. Time seemed to dissolve in a blur. They all felt as though they were flying into a void. Then suddenly the lights of the jeeps parked beside the end of the runway burst through the curtain of rain.

'God almighty!' Stromp blurted. 'Pull her up!'

Dennings waited another three seconds and then he gently eased the wheel toward his chest. The B-29's wheels came free. She had barely clawed thirty feet out of the sky when the runway vanished and she struggled over the forbidding water.

Morrison stood outside the warmth of the radar hut under the downpour, his four-man staff dutifully standing behind him. He watched the takeoff of *Dennings' Demons* more in his mind that his eyes. He saw little more than the lurch of the bomber as Dennings thrust the throttles forward and released the brakes before it was lost in the dark.

He cupped his ears and listened to the engine's pitch diminish in the distance. The uneven sound was faint. No one but a master flight mechanic or an aircraft engineer could have caught it, and Morrison had served in both capacities during his early Army Air Corps career.

An engine was slightly out of tune. One or more of its eighteen cylinders was not firing continuously.

Fearfully, Morrison listened for some sign the bomber was not going to lift off. If *Dennings' Demons* crashed on takeoff, every living thing on the island would be incinerated within seconds.

Then the radar man shouted through the open door, 'They're airborne!'

Morrison exhaled a tense sigh. Only then did he turn his back on the miserable weather and walk inside.

There was nothing to do now but send a message to General Groves in Washington informing him that Mother's Breath was on her way to Japan. Then wait and hope.

But down deep the general was troubled. He knew Dennings. The man was too stubborn to turn back with a bad engine. Dennings would get the *Demons* to Osaka if he had to carry the plane on his back.

'God help them,' Morrison muttered under his breath. He knew with dread finality his part of the immense operation didn't stand a prayer.

'Gear up,' ordered Dennings.

'Am I ever glad to hear those words,' grunted Stromp as he moved the lever. The gear motors whined and the three sets of wheels rose into their wells under the nose and wings. 'Gear up and locked.'

As the airspeed increased, Dennings dropped the throttle settings to save on fuel. He waited before beginning a slow and gentle climb for altitude until the airspeed touched 200 knots. Unseen off the starboard wing, the Aleutian Island chain slowly curled northeast. They would not sight land again for 2,500 miles.

'How's that number-four engine?' he asked Mosely.

'Pulling her share, but she's running a tad hot.'

'Soon as we hit five thousand feet, I'll drop her back a few rpm's.'

'Wouldn't hurt, Major,' Mosely replied.

Arnold gave Dennings the course heading they would maintain for the next ten and a half hours. At 4,900 feet Dennings turned control over to Stromp. He relaxed and stared into the black sky. No stars were in sight. The plane was feeling the turbulence as Stromp threaded it through the ominous mass of thunder clouds.

When they finally cleared the worst of the storm, Dennings unbuckled himself and climbed out of his seat. As he twisted around, he could see through a port window below the tunnel leading to the waist and tail section of the plane. He could just make out a piece of the bomb suspended in its release mechanism.

The crawl tunnel had been narrowed to receive the immense weapon into the bomb bay and was a tight fit. Dennings wiggled through past the bomb bay and dropped down on the opposite end. Then he swung open the small airtight door and slipped inside.

Pulling a flashlight from a leg pocket, he made his way along a confined catwalk running the length of the two bomb bays that had been modified into one. The weapon's huge size made for an incredibly snug fit. Its outer diameter measured less than two inches away from the longitudinal bulkheads.

Hesitantly, Dennings reached down and touched it. The steel sides felt ice cold to his fingertips. He failed to visualize the hundred thousand people it could burn to cinders within a short second, or the ghastly toll from burns and radiation. The thermonuclear temperatures or the shock wave from the Trinity test could not be sensed in a black and white movie film. He saw it only as a means of ending a war and saving hundreds of thousands of his countrymen's lives.

Returning to the cockpit, he stopped and chatted with Byrnes, who was running through a schematic of the bomb's detonation circuits. Every so often the ordnance expert glanced at a small console mounted above his lap.

'Any chance of it going off before we get there?' asked Dennings.

'Lightning strike could do it,' answered Byrnes.

Dennings looked at him in horror. 'A little late with a warning aren't you? We've been flying through the middle of an electrical storm since midnight.'

Byrnes looked up and grinned. 'We could have gone up just as easily on the ground. What the hell, we made it, didn't we?'

Dennings couldn't believe Byrnes's matter-of-fact attitude. 'Was General Morrison aware of the risk?'

'Better than anyone. He's been on the atomic bomb project from the beginning.'

Dennings shuddered and turned away. Insane, he thought, the operation was insane. It'd be a miracle if any of them lived to tell about it.

Five hours into the flight and lighter by 2,000 gallons of expended fuel, Dennings levelled the B-29 off at 10,000 feet. The crew became more upbeat as the dawn's orange glow tinted the eastern sky. The storm was far behind them, and they could see the rolling swells of the sea and a few scattered white clouds.

Dennings' Demons was cruising to the southwest at a leisurely 220 knots. Thankfully, they had picked up a light tail wind. Full daybreak showed them alone in the vast emptiness of the North Pacific Ocean. A solitary aeroplane going from nowhere to nowhere, Bombardier Stanton mused as he gazed absently out the windows of the nose.

Three hundred miles from Japan's main island of Honshu, Dennings started a slow, gradual climb to 32,000 feet, the altitude at which Stanton would release the bomb on Osaka. Navigator Arnold announced they were twenty minutes ahead of schedule. At the current rate of speed, he figured they should be landing at Okinawa in a shade under five hours.

Dennings looked at the fuel gauges. He suddenly felt cheerful. Barring a hundred-knot headwind, they should make it with four hundred gallons to spare.

Not everyone was wallowing in good cheer. Seated at his engineer's panel, Mosely studied the temperature gauge of engine number four. He didn't like what he read. He routinely tapped the dial with his finger.

The needle twitched and wavered into the red.

He crawled aft through the tunnel and stared through a port at the underside of the engine. The nacelle was streaked with oil and smoke was trailing from the exhaust. Mosely returned to the cockpit and knelt in the narrow aisle between Dennings and Stromp.

'Bad news, Major. We're going to have to shut down number four.'

'You can't prod her along for a few more hours?' asked Dennings.

'No, sir, she can swallow a valve and catch fire at any minute.'

Stromp looked over at Dennings, his face sombre. 'I vote we shut four down for a while and let it cool off.'

Dennings knew Stromp was right. They would have to maintain their present altitude of 12,000 feet and nurse the other three engines to keep them from overheating. Then restart number four during the ascent to 32,000 feet and the bombing run.

He hailed Arnold, who was bent over his navigator's board tracing the flight path. 'How long before Japan?'

Arnold noted the slight drop in speed and made a swift calculation. 'One hour and twenty-one minutes to the mainland.'

He nodded. 'Okay, we'll shut number four until we need it.'

Even as he spoke, Stromp closed the throttle, flicked off the ignition switch, and feathered the propeller. Next he engaged the automatic pilot.

For the next half hour everyone kept a wary eye on number-four engine while Mosely called out the temperature drop.

'We have a landfall,' announced Arnold. 'A small island coming up about twenty miles dead ahead.'

Stromp peered at it through binoculars. 'Looks like a hot dog sticking out of the water.'

'Sheer rock walls,' observed Arnold. 'No sign of a beach anywhere.'

'What's it called?' asked Dennings.

'Doesn't even show on the map.'

'Any sign of life? The Nips could be using it as an offshore warning station.'

'Looks barren and deserted,' answered Stromp.

Dennings felt safe for the moment. No enemy ships had been sighted, and they were too far from shore to be intercepted by Japanese fighters. He settled down in his seat and stared unseeing at the sea.

The men relaxed and passed around coffee and salami sandwiches, immune to the droning engines and the tiny speck that appeared ten miles away and 7,000 feet above their port wingtip.

Unknown to the crew of *Dennings' Demons*, they had only a few minutes to live.

Lieutenant Junior Grade Sato Okinaga saw the brief glint from the reflected sun below him. He banked and went into a shallow dive for a closer inspection. It was an aircraft. No question. A plane from another patrol, most likely. He reached for the switch to his radio, but hesitated. In a few seconds he'd be able to make a positive identification.

A young and inexperienced pilot, Okinaga was one of the lucky ones. Out of his recently graduated class of twenty-two, who were rushed through training during Japan's desperate days, he and three others were ordered to perform coastal patrols. The rest went into kamikaze squadrons.

Okinaga was deeply disappointed. He would have gladly given his life for the Emperor, but he accepted boring patrol duty as a temporary assignment, hoping to be called for a more glorious mission when the Americans invaded his homeland.

As the lone aircraft grew larger, Okinaga didn't believe what he saw. He rubbed his eyes and squinted. Soon he could clearly make out the ninety-foot polished aluminium fuselage, the huge 141-foot wings, and the three-storey vertical stabilizer of an American B-29.

He stared dumbfounded. The bomber was flying out of the northeast from an empty sea, 20,000 feet below its combat ceiling. Unanswerable questions flooded his mind. Where had it come from? Why was it flying toward central Japan with one engine feathered? What was its mission?

Like a shark knifing toward a bleeding whale, Okinaga closed to within a mile. Still no evasive action. The crew seemed asleep or bent on suicide.

Okinaga had no more time for guessing games. The great winged bomber was looming up before him. He jammed the throttle of his Mitsubishi A6M Zero against its stop and made a circling dive. The Zero handled like a swallow, the 1,130-horsepower Sakae engine hurtling him behind and beneath the sleek, gleaming B-29.

Too late the tail gunner sighted the fighter and belatedly opened fire. Okinaga squeezed the gun tit on his control stick. His Zero shuddered as his two machine guns and two twenty-millimetre cannons shredded metal and human flesh.

A light touch of the rudder and his tracers ate their way into the wing and the B-29's number-three engine. The cowling ripped and tore away, oil poured through holes, followed by flames. The bomber seemed to hover momentarily, and then it flipped on its side and spun toward the sea.

Only after the choked-off cry of the tail gunner and his short burst of fire did the *Demons* realize they were under attack. They had no way of knowing from what direction the enemy fighter had come. They barely had time to recover when the shells from the Zero ate into the starboard wing.

A strangled cry came from Stromp. 'We're going in!'

Dennings shouted into the intercom as he fought to level the plane. 'Stanton, Jettison the bomb! Jettison the goddamn bomb!'

The bombardier, wedged against his bombsight by the centrifugal force, yelled back. 'It won't fall free unless you straighten us out.'

The number-three engine was blazing now. The sudden loss of two engines, both on the same side, had thrown the plane over until it was standing on one wing. Working in unison, Dennings and Stromp struggled with the controls, fighting the dying aircraft to an even keel. Dennings pulled back on the throttles, levelling out but sending the bomber into a flat, sickening stall.

Stanton pulled himself to an upright position and popped open the bomb-bay doors. 'Hold it steady,' he yelled futilely. He wasted no time adjusting the bombsight. He pushed the bomb release button.

Nothing happened. The violent twisting motion had jammed the atomic bomb against its tight quarters.

White-faced, Stanton struck the release with his fist, but the bomb stubbornly remained in place. 'It's jammed!' he cried. 'It won't fall free.'

Fighting for a few more moments of life, knowing that if they survived they must all take their own lives by cyanide, Dennings struggled to ditch the mortally wounded aircraft in the sea.

He almost made it. He came within two hundred feet of settling the *Demons* on her belly in a calm sea. But the magnesium in the accessories and crankcase on number-three engine flared like an incendiary bomb, burning through its mounts and wing spar. It dropped away, ripping away the wing control cables.

Lieutenant Okinaga slipped the Zero off one wing, spiralling around the stricken B-29. He watched the black smoke and orange flame curl from the blue sky like a brush stroke. He watched the American plane crush itself into the sea, followed by the geyser of white water.

He circled, searching for survivors, but saw only a few

23

bits of floating debris. Elated at what was to be his first and only kill, Okinaga banked around the funeral pyre of smoke one last time before heading back to Japan and his airfield.

As Dennings' shattered aircraft and its dead crew settled into the seabed a thousand feet beneath the surface, another B-29 in a later time zone and six hundred miles to the southeast set up for its bomb run. With Colonel Paul Tibbets at the controls, the *Enola Gay* had arrived over the Japanese city of Hiroshima.

Neither flight commander was aware of the other. Both men thought only their aircraft and crew were carrying the first atomic bomb to be dropped in war.

Dennings' Demons had failed to make its rendezvous with destiny. The stillness of the deep seabed was as silent as the cloud that settled over the event. The heroic attempt by Dennings and his crew was buried in bureaucratic secrecy and forgotten.

PART ONE
Big John

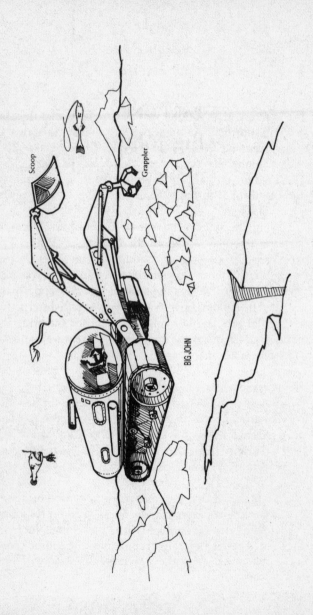

Scoop

Grappler

BIG JOHN

1

October 3, 1993
Western Pacific Ocean

The worst of the typhoon had passed. The mad thrashing seas had subsided, but the waves still climbed the bows and came green and leaden over the decks, leaving a welter of foam behind. The thick black clouds broke apart and the wind died to a gusty thirty knots. To the southwest, shafts of sunlight broke through, painting blue circles on the tumbling swells.

Braving the winds and spray, Captain Arne Korvold stood on the open bridge of the Norwegian Rindal Lines passenger-cargo liner *Narvik* and aimed his binoculars at a huge ship wallowing dead in the whitecaps. She was big, a Japanese auto carrier by the look of her. Her upper works stretched from blunt bow to a perfectly squared stern, like a rectangular box laid horizontal. Except for the bridge and the crew's quarters on the upper deck, there were no ports or windows on her sides.

She seemed to have a ten-degree permanent list but rolled to twenty as the swells smashed into her exposed port broadside. The only sign of life was a wisp of smoke from her stack. Korvold grimly noted that her lifeboats had been launched, and a sweep of the restless sea failed to find any sign of them. He refocused the binoculars and read the English name spelled out beneath the Japanese characters on the bow.

She was called the *Divine Star*.

Korvold returned to the comfort of the central bridge and leaned into the communications room. 'Still no response?'

The radio operator shook his head. 'Nothing. Not a peep since we sighted her. Her radio must be closed down. Impossible to believe they abandoned ship without a distress call.'

27

Korvold stared silently through the bridge windows at the Japanese ship drifting less than a kilometre off his starboard rail. Norwegian by birth, he was a short, distinguished man who never made a hurried gesture. His ice-blue eyes seldom blinked, and his lips beneath the trimmed beard seemed constantly frozen in a slight smile. Twenty-six years at sea, mostly in cruise ships, he had a warm and friendly disposition, respected by his crew and admired by the passengers.

He tugged at his short greying beard and swore quietly to himself. The tropical storm had unexpectedly swung north onto his course and put him nearly two days behind schedule on his passage from the port of Pusan, Korea, to San Francisco. Korvold had not left the bridge for forty-eight hours and he was exhausted. Just as he was about to take a welcome rest, they sighted the seemingly derelict *Divine Star*.

Now he found himself faced with an enigma and a time-consuming search for the Japanese car carrier's boats. He was also burdened with the responsibility of 130 passengers, most seasick to the gills, who were in no mood for a benevolent rescue operation.

'Permission to take a boarding crew across, Captain?'

Korvold looked up into the sculpted Nordic face of Chief Officer Oscar Steen. The eyes that stared back were a darker blue than Korvold's. The chief officer stood lean and as straight as a light pole, skin tanned and hair bleached blond from exposure to the sun.

Korvold didn't immediately answer but walked over to a bridge window and gazed down at the sea separating the two ships. From wave crest to trough the waves were running three to four metres. 'I'm not of a mind to risk lives, Mr Steen. Better we wait until seas calm a bit.'

'I've taken a boat through worse.'

'No hurry. She's a dead ship, dead as a body in the morgue. And from the look of her, her cargo has shifted and she's taking on water. Better we leave her be and search for her boats.'

'There may be injured men over there,' Steen persisted.

Korvold shook his head. 'No captain would have abandoned ship and left injured crewmen behind.'

'No captain in his right senses maybe. But what kind of a man would desert a sound ship and lower boats in the midst of a sixty-five-knot gale typhoon without sending a Mayday signal?'

'A mystery all right,' Korvold agreed.

'And there's her cargo to consider,' Steen continued. 'Her waterline indicates a full load. She looks capable of transporting over seven thousand automobiles.'

Korvold gave Steen a shrewd look. 'You thinking salvage, Mr Steen?'

'Yes, sir, I am. If she's totally abandoned with a full cargo, and we can sail her into port, our salvage claim should be equal to half her value or better. The company as well as the crew could share in five or six hundred million kroner.'

Korvold considered for a few moments, a tantalizing thought of greed wrestling with a deep feeling of foreboding. Greed won out. 'Pick your boarding crew, and include the assistant engineer. If there's smoke from her funnel, her machinery must still be in working order.' He paused. 'But I still prefer you wait for the water to settle.'

'No time,' Steen announced flatly. 'If her list increases another ten degrees, we may be too late. I'd better go quickly.'

Captain Korvold sighed. He was going against his better judgement, but it also occurred to him that once the *Divine Star*'s situation was known, every salvage tug within a thousand miles would come full speed toward their position like tow-truck operators flocking to a highway accident.

Finally he shrugged. 'When you're assured none of the *Divine Star*'s crew is on board, and you can get her under way, report back and I'll begin a search for her boats.'

Steen was gone almost before Korvold finished speaking. He assembled his men and was lowered down into the swirling water within ten minutes. The boarding party consisted of himself, and four seamen; the assistant chief engineer, Olaf Andersson; and the communications man, David Sakagawa, the only crewman on board the *Narvik* who could speak Japanese. The seamen were to probe the vessel while Andersson examined the engine room. Steen was to take formal possession of the auto carrier if it was found abandoned.

With Steen at the helm, the double-ender launch ploughed through the heavy seas, struggling over the crests of the waves that threatened to swamp her before plunging down into the troughs. The big Volvo marine engine growled without a miss as they bore down on the auto carrier with the wind and sea astern of them.

A hundred metres from the *Divine Star* they discovered they weren't alone. A school of sharks circled the listing ship as though some inner sense told them it was going to sink and maybe leave behind some tasty scraps.

The seaman at the wheel slipped the boat under the stubby bow on the lee side. It seemed to them the *Divine Star* was going to roll over on them with each wave that broke against her hull. When the great ship rolled down, Steen heaved up a light nylon boarding ladder with an aluminium grappling hook on one end. On the third try the hook caught on the top edge of the bulwark and gripped.

Steen scrambled up the rope ladder first and over the side. He was quickly followed by Andersson and the rest. After assembling beside the huge anchor winches, Steen led them up a fire escape-like stairway that was attached to the windowless forward bulkhead. After climbing five decks, they entered the largest bridge area Steen had ever seen during his fifteen years at sea. After the small, efficient wheelhouse on the *Narvik*, this one looked as vast as a gymnasium, and yet the impressive array of electronic equipment filled only a small section in the middle.

It was empty of life but littered with charts, sextants, and other navigation equipment that spilled from open cabinets. Two briefcases lay open on a counter as if their owners had just left the room for a short time. The exodus appeared to be bathed in panic.

Steen studied the main console. 'She's fully automated,' he said to Andersson.

The chief engineer nodded. 'And then some. The controls are voice operated. No pushing levers or giving helmsmen course instructions here.'

Steen turned to Sakagawa. 'Can you turn this thing on and talk to it?'

The Norwegian-born Asian leaned over the computerized console and silently studied it for several seconds. Then he pushed a pair of buttons in quick succession. The console's lights blinked on and the unit began to hum. Sakagawa looked at Steen with a slight smile. 'My Japanese is rusty, but I think I can communicate with it.'

'Ask it to report the ship's status.'

Sakagawa rattled off Japanese into a small receiver and waited expectantly. After a few moments a male voice answered in slow, distinctive tones. When it stopped, Sakagawa stared at Steen blankly.

'It says the sea cocks are open and the flood level in the engine room is approaching two metres.'

'Order it to close them!' snapped Steen.

After a short exchange, Sakagawa shook his head. 'The computer says the sea cocks are jammed open. They can't be shut off by electronic command.'

'Looks like I've got my work cut out,' said Andersson. 'I'd better get down there and get them turned off. And tell that damned robot to start the pumps.' While he spoke he motioned for two of the seamen to follow him, and they disappeared down a companionway on a dead run toward the engine room.

One of the remaining seamen came up to Steen, his eyes

31

wide in shock and face as white as plaster. 'Sir . . . I found a body. I think it's the radioman.'

Steen hurried into the communications room. An almost shapeless corpse sat in a chair hunched over the radio transmitter panel. He might have been a human when he stepped on board the *Divine Star*, not now. There was no hair, and but for the fully exposed teeth where the lips had been, Steen couldn't have told whether he was looking at the front or back. The pathetic abhorrence looked as though his skin had been blistered off and the flesh beneath burned and partially melted.

Yet there wasn't the slightest indication of excessive heat or fire. His clothes were as clean and pressed as though he'd just put them on.

The man seemed to have burned from within.

2

The horrible stench and the shocking sight staggered Steen. It took him a full minute to recover. Then he pushed the chair with its hideous owner off to one side and leaned over the radio.

Fortunately the digital frequency dial was labelled in Arabic numerals. After a few minutes of trial and error, he found the correct switches and hailed Captain Korvold on the *Narvik*.

Korvold answered immediately. 'Come in, Mr Steen,' he replied formally. 'What have you discovered?'

'Something sinister has happened here, Captain. So far we've found a deserted ship with one body, that of the radio operator, who was burned beyond recognition.'

'Is there fire on board?'

'No sign. The computerized automated control system shows only green lights on its fire warning systems.'

'Any indication as to why the crew took to the boats?' asked Korvold.

'Nothing obvious. They seem to have left in a panic after attempting to scuttle the ship.'

Korvold's mouth tightened, his knuckles turned ivory as he squeezed the phone. 'Say again.'

'The sea cocks were turned and jammed open. Andersson is working to close them now.'

'Why on earth would the crew scuttle a sound ship with thousands of new cars on board?' Korvold asked vaguely.

'The situation must be viewed with suspicion, sir. Something on board is abnormal. The body of the radio operator is ghastly. He looks like he was roasted on a spit.'

'Do you wish the ship's doctor to come over?'

'Nothing the good doctor can do here except perform a post-mortem.'

'Understood,' replied Korvold. 'I'll remain on station for another thirty minutes before I leave to search for the missing boats.'

'Have you contacted the company, sir?'

'I've held off until you're certain none of the original crew is alive to challenge our salvage claim. Finish your investigation. As soon as you're satisfied the ship is deserted I'll transmit a message to our company director notifying him of our taking possession of the *Divine Star*.'

'Engineer Andersson is already at work closing the sea cocks and pumping her dry. We have power and should be under way shortly.'

'The sooner the better,' said Korvold. 'You're drifting toward a British oceanographic survey vessel that's holding a stationary position.'

'How far?'

'Approximately twelve kilometres.'

'They're safe enough.'

Korvold could think of little else to say. At last he said simply, 'Good luck, Oscar. Make port safely.' And then he was gone.

Steen turned from the radio, his eyes avoiding the mutilated body in the chair. He felt a cold shudder grip him. He half expected to see the spectral captain of the *Flying Dutchman* pacing the bridge. There was nothing as morbid as a deserted ship, he thought grimly.

He ordered Sakagawa to hunt up and translate the ship's log. The two remaining seamen he sent to search the auto decks while he systematically went through the crew's quarters. He felt as though he was walking through a haunted house.

Except for a few bits of scattered clothing, it looked like the crew might return at any minute. Unlike the mess on the bridge, everything seemed lived in and ordinary. In the

34

captain's quarters there was a tray with two teacups that had miraculously failed to fall on the deck during the storm, a uniform laid out on the bed, and a pair of highly polished shoes side by side on the carpeted deck. A framed picture of a woman and three teenage sons had dropped flat on a neat and clean desk.

Steen was hesitant to pry into other men's secrets and their memories. He felt like an uninvited intruder.

His foot kicked something lying just under the desk. He leaned down and picked up the object. It was a nine-millimetre pistol. A double-action Austrian Steyr GB. He pushed it into the waistband of his trousers.

The chiming of a wall-mounted chronometer startled him, and he swore he felt his hair rise. He finished his search and beat a quick path back to the bridge.

Sakagawa was sitting in the chart room, his feet perched on a small cabinet, studying the ship's log.

'You found it,' said Steen.

'In one of the open briefcases.' He turned back to the opening pages and began to read. ' "*Divine Star*, seven hundred feet, delivered March sixteenth, nineteen eighty-eight. Operated and owned by the Sushimo Steamship Company, Limited. Home port, Kobe." On this voyage she's carrying seven thousand, two hundred and eighty-eight new Murmoto automobiles to Los Angeles.'

'Any clues as to why the crew abandoned her?' Steen asked.

Sakagawa gave a puzzled shake of his head. 'No mention of disaster, plague, or mutiny. No report of the typhoon. The last entry is a bit odd.'

'Read it.'

Sakagawa took a few moments to be sure his translation of Japanese characters into English was reasonably correct. 'The best I can get out of it is: "Weather deteriorating. Seas increasing. Crew suffering from unknown illness. Everyone sick including Captain. Food poisoning suspected. Our passenger, Mr Yamada, a most important company director, demands we abandon and sink ship during hysterical outburst. Captain thinks Mr Yamada has suffered nervous breakdown and has ordered him placed under restraint in his quarters." '

Steen looked down at Sakagawa, his face expressionless. 'That's all?'

'The final entry,' said Sakagawa. 'There is no more.'

'What's the date?'

'October first.'

'That's two days ago.'

Sakagawa nodded absently. 'They must have fled the ship shortly after. Damned funny they didn't take the log with them.'

Slowly, unhurriedly, Steen walked into the communications room, his mind trying to make sense out of the final log entry. Suddenly he stopped and reached out to support himself in the doorway. The room seemed to swim before his eyes and he felt nauseous. Bile rose in his throat, but he forced it down. Then, as quickly as the attack came, it passed.

He walked unevenly over to the radio and hailed the *Narvik*. 'This is First Officer Steen calling Captain Korvold, over.'

'Yes, Oscar,' answered Korvold. 'Go ahead.'

'Do not waste time on a search effort. The *Divine Star*'s log suggests the crew left the ship before they were struck by the full force of the typhoon. They departed nearly two days ago. The winds would have swept them two hundred kilometres away by now.'

'Providing they survived.'

'An unlikely event.'

'All right, Oscar. I agree, a search by the *Narvik* will be useless. We've done all that can be expected of us. I've alerted American sea rescue units at Midway and Hawaii and all vessels in the general area. Soon as you regain steerageway we'll resume course for San Francisco.'

'Acknowledged,' Steen replied. 'I'm on my way to the engine room to check with Andersson now.'

Just as Steen finished transmitting, the ship's phone buzzed. 'This is the bridge.'

'Mr Steen,' said a weak voice.

'Yes, what is it?'

'Seaman Arne Midgaard, sir. Can you come down to C cargo deck right away? I think I've found something – '

Midgaard's voice stopped abruptly, and Steen could hear the sounds of retching.

'Midgaard, are you sick?'

'Please hurry, sir.'

Then the line went dead.

Steen yelled at Sakagawa. 'What button do I push for the engine room?'

There was no reply. Steen stepped back into the chart room. Sakagawa was sitting there pale as death, breathing rapidly. He looked up and spoke, gasping the words with every breath. 'The fourth button . . . rings the engine room.'

'What's wrong with you?' Steen asked anxiously.

'Don't know. I . . . I feel . . . awful . . . vomited twice.'

'Hang on,' snapped Steen. 'I'll gather up the others. We're getting off this death ship.' He snatched the phone and rang the engine room. There was no answer. Fear flooded his mind. Fear of an unknown that was striking them down. He imagined the smell of death pervading the whole ship.

Steen took a swift glance at a deck diagram that was mounted on a bulkhead, then leaped down the companionway six steps at a time. He tried to run toward the vast holds containing the autos, but a nausea cramped his stomach and he weaved through the passageway like a drunk through a back alley.

At last he stumbled through the doorway onto C cargo deck. A great sea of multicoloured automobiles stretched a hundred metres fore and aft. Amazingly, despite the buffeting from the storm and the list of the ship, they were all firmly in place.

Steen shouted frantically for Midgaard, his voice echoing from the steel bulkheads. Silence was his only reply. Then he spotted it, the oddity that stood out like the only man in a crowd holding aloft a sign.

One of the cars had its hood up.

He staggered between the long rows, falling against doors and fenders, bruising his knees on the protruding bumpers. As he approached the car with the open hood, he shouted again. 'Anyone here?'

This time he heard a faint moan. In ten paces he had reached the car and stared frozen at the sight of Midgaard lying beside one tyre.

The young seaman's face was festered with running sores. Froth mixed with blood streamed from his mouth. His eyes stared unseeing. His arms were purple from bleeding beneath the skin. He seemed to be decaying before Steen's eyes.

Steen sagged against the car, stricken with horror. He clutched his head between his hands in helplessness and despair, but noticing the thicket of hair that came away when he dropped them to his sides.

'Why in God's name are we dying?' he whispered, seeing his own grisly death mirrored by Midgaard. 'What is killing us?'

3

The deep-sea submersible *Old Gert* hung suspended beneath a large crane that sat on the stern of the British oceanographic vessel *Invincible*. The seas had calmed enough to launch *Old Gert* for a scientific probe of the seafloor 5,200 metres below, and her crew were following a tight sequence of safety checks.

There was nothing *old* about the submersible. Her design was the latest state of the art. She was constructed by a British aerospace company within the past year and was now poised for her maiden test dive to survey the Mendocino fracture zone, a great crack in the Pacific Ocean floor extending from the coast of Northern California halfway to Japan.

Her exterior was a complete departure from other aerodynamic submersibles. Instead of one cigar-shaped hull with a pregnant pod attached beneath, she had four transparent titanium and polymer woven spheres connected by circular tunnels that gave her the appearance of a jack from a child's game. One sphere contained a complex array of camera equipment, while another was filled with air and ballast tanks and batteries. The third held the oxygen equipment and electric motors. The fourth sphere, the largest, sat above the other three and housed the crew and controls.

Old Gert was built to withstand the immense pressures found at the deepest parts of the world's seabeds. Her support systems could keep a crew alive for forty-eight hours, and she was powered to travel through the black abyss at speeds up to eight knots.

Craig Plunkett, the chief engineer and pilot for *Old Gert*, signed the last of the check-off forms. He was a man of forty-five or fifty, with greying hair combed forward to cover his baldness. His face was ruddy and his eyes a medium brown with a bloodhound droop. He had helped design *Old Gert* and now treated her as his own private yacht.

He pulled on a heavy woollen sweater against the expected chill from the cold bottom water and slipped his feet into a pair of soft fur-lined moccasins. He descended the boarding tunnel and closed the hatch behind him. Then he dropped into the control sphere and engaged the computerized life-support systems.

Dr Raul Salazar, the expedition's marine geologist from the University of Mexico, was already in his seat adjusting a bottom sonar penetrating unit.

'Ready when you are,' said Salazar. He was a small dynamo with a huge mass of black hair, his movements quick, black eyes darting constantly, never staring at any one person or object for more than two seconds. Plunkett liked him. Salazar was the kind of man who accumulated his data with a minimum of fuss, made the right decisions without clouding the facts, and was accustomed to engineering a deep-sea probe from more of a business viewpoint than an academic project.

Plunkett glanced at the empty seat on the right side of the sphere. 'I thought Stacy was on board.'

'She is,' answered Salazar without turning from his console. 'She's in the camera sphere making a final check on her video systems.'

Plunkett bent over the tunnel leading to the camera sphere and found himself staring at a pair of sweat-socked feet. 'We're ready to launch,' he said.

A feminine voice accompanied by a hollow tone came back, 'Be finished in a sec.'

Plunkett eased his feet under his control panel and was settling into his low half-reclining seat when Stacy Fox wiggled her way backwards into the control sphere. Her face was flushed from working nearly upside down.

Stacy wasn't what you'd call disturbingly attractive, but she was pretty. Her long, straight blonde hair fell around her face, and she often tossed it back with a brief shake of the head. She was slim and her shoulders were broad for a woman. The crew could only speculate about her breasts. None had ever seen them, of course, and she always wore loose-fitting sweaters. But occasionally, when she yawned and stretched, her chest gave an indication of firm substance.

She looked younger than her thirty-four years. Her eyebrows were thick, her eyes wide apart, irises reflecting a soft pale green. The lips above a determined chin easily parted in a bright, even-toothed smile, which was almost constant.

Stacy was once a golden California beach girl, majoring in the photographic arts at the Chouinard Institute in Los Angeles. After graduation she migrated around the world recording marine life that had never been captured on film. Twice married, twice divorced, with one daughter living with her sister, her presence on board *Old Gert* to photograph the deep ocean was actually a cover for a more demanding assignment.

As soon as she gained her seat on the right side of the sphere, Plunkett signalled an okay. The crane operator nudged the submersible down a slanted ramp through the ship's open stern and gently lowered it into the sea.

The chop had died, but the swells still rolled past from one to two metres high. The crane man timed the entry so *Old Gert* touched a wave crest and continued into the trough, where she settled and rose in perfect sequence with the swells. The lift cables were electronically released, and several divers made a last-minute check of the exterior.

Five minutes later the surface controller, a jolly Scot by the name of Jimmy Knox, reported to Plunkett that the sub was cleared for descent. The ballast tanks were flooded, and *Old Gert* quickly passed under the sparkling sea and began her trip to the bottom.

Though *Old Gert* was the newest submersible off the drawing boards, she still descended by the old tried and true system of filling ballast tanks with seawater. For rising to the surface, variable-sized iron weights were dropped to increase buoyancy, because current pump technology could not overcome the opposing pressures at great depths.

To Stacy, the long fall through the vast liquid void came like a hypnotic trance. One by one the spectral colours from the scattered light on the surface faded until they finally vanished into pure black.

Except for their separate control consoles mounted around the inner diameter of the sphere, they had an unobstructed 180-degree view ahead. The transparent polymer with the thin threading of titanium made vision equal to that of the resolution on a large-screen television set.

Salazar paid no attention to the blackness or the occasional luminescent fish that swam outside, he was more concerned about what they would find on the bottom. Plunkett monitored the depth and the life-support instruments, watching carefully for any bugs as the pressure increased and the temperature dropped with every passing moment.

The *Invincible* carried no backup submersible in case of an emergency. If disaster unexpectedly occurred and they somehow became wedged in rocks or the equipment malfunctioned, preventing *Old Gert*'s return to the surface, they could jettison the control sphere and allow it to sail to the surface like a giant bubble. But it was a complex system never tested under high-pressure conditions. A failure here and they had no hope for rescue, only the certainty of death by suffocation and a lost grave deep in the eternal night of the abyss.

A small eel-like fish slithered past, its luminous body giving off flashes of light as though a stream of traffic was passing around a series of curves. The teeth were incredibly long in proportion to his head and fanged like a Chinese dragon's. Fascinated with the interior light of the submersible, it swam up to the control sphere unafraid and cast a ghostly eye inside.

Stacy aimed her battery of still and video cameras and caught it in seven lenses before it was gone. 'Can you imagine that thing if it was twenty feet long?' she murmured in awe.

'Fortunately blackdragons live in the depths,' said Plunkett. 'The pressure of deep water prevents them from growing more than several centimetres.'

Stacy hit the exterior lights, and the blackness was suddenly transformed into a green haze. The void was empty. No life was to be seen. The blackdragon was gone. She turned off the lights to conserve the batteries.

The humidity rose inside the sphere, and the increasing cold began to seep through the thick walls. Stacy watched the goose bumps rise on her arms. She looked up, clutched her shoulders with her hands, and made a shivering gesture. Plunkett caught the signal and turned on a small heating unit that barely held off the chill.

The two hours it took to reach the bottom would have passed tediously if everyone hadn't been busy at their own jobs. Plunkett found a comfortable position and watched the sonar monitor and the echo sounder. He also kept a wary eye on the electrical and oxygen-level gauges. Salazar kept busy plotting their probe grid once they reached the bottom, while Stacy kept trying to catch the denizens of the deep off guard with her cameras.

Plunkett preferred the strains of Johann Strauss for stereo background music, but Stacy insisted on using her 'new age' music in the cassette player. She claimed it was soothing and less stressful. Salazar called it 'waterfall' music but went along.

Jimmy Knox's voice from the *Invincible* sounded ghostly as it filtered down on the underwater acoustic telephone.

'Bottom in ten minutes,' he announced. 'You're closing a bit fast.'

'Righto,' replied Plunkett. 'I have it on sonar.'

Salazar and Stacy turned from their work and stared at the sonar screen. The digital enhancement showed the seabed in contoured three dimension. Plunkett's gaze darted from the screen into the water and back again. He trusted the sonar and computer, but not ahead of his own vision.

'Be on your guard,' Knox alerted them. 'You're dropping alongside the walls of a canyon.'

'I have it,' returned Plunkett. 'The cliffs plunge into a wide valley.' He reached for a switch and dropped one of the ballast weights to slow the descent. Thirty metres from the bottom he dropped one more, giving the submersible almost perfect neutral buoyancy. Next he engaged the three thrusters mounted on the outer ends of the lower spheres.

The bottom slowly materialized through the jade gloom into a broken uneven slope. Strange black rock that was folded and twisted into grotesque shapes spread as far as they could see.

'We've come down beside a lava flow,' said Plunkett. 'The edge is about a kilometre ahead. After that it's another three-hundred-metre drop to the valley floor.'

'I copy,' replied Knox.

'What are all those wormy rocks?' asked Stacy.

'Pillow lava,' answered Salazar. 'Made when fiery lava strikes the cold sea. The outer shell cools, forming a tube through which the molten lava keeps flowing.'

Plunkett kicked in the altitude-positioning system that automatically kept the submersible four metres above the bottom slope. As they glided across the scarred features of the plateau, they spotted the trails of deep crawlers in scattered pools of silt, perhaps from brittle stars, shrimp, or deep-dwelling sea cucumbers that lurked in the darkness beyond the lights.

'Get ready,' said Plunkett. 'We're about to head down.'

A few seconds after his warning, the bottom dropped away into blackness again and the sub nosed over and fell deeper, maintaining its distance of four metres from the steep drop of the canyon walls.

'I have you at five-three-six-zero metres,' echoed Knox's voice over the underwater phone.

'Righto, I read the same,' replied Plunkett.

'When you reach the valley floor,' said Knox, 'you'll be on the plain of the fracture zone.'

'Stands to reason,' Plunkett muttered, his attention focused on his control panel, computer screen, and a video monitor now showing the terrain below *Old Gert*'s landing skids. 'There's no bloody place left to go.'

Twelve minutes passed, and then a flat bottom loomed up ahead and the sub levelled out again. Underwater particles swirled by the sphere, driven by a light current like flakes of snow. Ripples of sand stretched in front of the circular lit pattern from the lights. The sand was not empty. Thousands of black objects, roundly shaped like old cannonballs, littered the seabed in a thick layer.

'Manganese nodules,' explained Salazar as though tutoring. 'No one knows exactly how they formed, although it's suspected sharks' teeth or whale ear bones may form the nucleus.'

'They worth anything?' asked Stacey, activating her camera systems.

'Besides the manganese, they're valued for smaller quantities of cobalt, copper, nickel, and zinc. I'd guess this concentration could run for hundreds of miles across the fracture zone and be worth as high as eight million dollars a square kilometre.'

'Providing you could scoop it up from the surface, five and a half kilometres away,' Plunkett added.

45

Salazar instructed Plunkett on what direction to explore as *Old Gert* soared silently over the nodule-carpeted sand. Then something gleamed off to their port side. Plunkett banked slightly toward the object.

'What do you see?' asked Salazar, looking up from his instruments.

Stacy peered downward. 'A ball!' she exclaimed. 'A huge metal ball with strange-looking cleats. I'd guess it to measure three metres in diameter.'

Plunkett dismissed it. 'Must have fallen off a ship.'

'Not too long ago, judging from the lack of corrosion,' commented Salazar.

Suddenly they sighted a wide strip of clear sand that was totally devoid of nodules. It was as though a giant vacuum cleaner had made a swath through the middle of the field.

'A straight edge!' exclaimed Salazar. 'There's no such thing as prolonged straight edges on the seafloor.'

Stacy stared in astonishment. 'Too perfect, too precise to be anything but manmade.'

Plunkett shook his head. 'Impossible, not at this depth. No engineering company in the world has the capability to mine the abyss.'

'And no geological disturbance I ever heard of could form a clean road across the seabed,' stated Salazar firmly.

'Those indentations in the sand that run along the borders look like they might match that huge ball we found.'

'Okay,' muttered Plunkett sceptically. 'What kind of equipment can sweep the bottom this deep?'

'A giant hydraulic dredge that sucks up the nodules through pipes to a barge on the surface,' theorized Salazar. 'The idea has been tossed around for years.'

'So has a manned flight to Mars, but the rocketry to get there has yet to be built. Nor has a monster dredge. I know a lot of people in marine engineering, and I haven't heard even a vague rumour about such a project. No mining operation of this magnitude can be kept secret. It'd take a surface fleet of at least five ships and thousands of men working for years. And there is no way they could pull it off without detection by passing ships or satellites.'

Stacy looked blankly at Salazar. 'Any way of telling when it happened?'

Salazar shrugged. 'Could have been yesterday, could have been years ago.'

'But who then?' Stacy asked in a vague tone. 'Who is responsible for such technology?'

No one immediately answered. Their discovery did not fit accepted beliefs. They stared at the empty swath with silent disbelief, a fear of the unknown trickling down their necks.

Finally Plunkett gave an answer that seemed to come distantly, from outside the submersible. 'No one on this earth, no one who is human.'

4

Steen was entering into a state of extreme emotional shock. He stared numbly at the blisters forming on his arms. He trembled uncontrollably, half mad from the shock and a sudden abdominal pain. He doubled over and retched, his breath coming in great heaves. Everything seemed to be striking him at once. His heart began beating erratically and his body burned up with fever.

He felt too weak to make it back to the communications compartment and warn Korvold. When the captain of the Norwegian ship received no replies from his signals to Steen, he would send another boarding party to see what was wrong. More men would die uselessly.

Steen was drenched in sweat now. He stared at the car with the raised hood and his eyes glazed with a strange hatred. A stupor descended over him, and his crazed mind saw an indescribable evil in the steel, leather, and rubber.

As if in a final act of defiance, Steen took vengeance against the inanimate vehicle. He pulled the Steyr automatic he'd found in the captain's quarters from under his waistband and raised the barrel. Then he squeezed the trigger and pumped the bullets into the front end of the car.

Two kilometres to the east, Captain Korvold was staring through his binoculars at the *Divine Star* when she blew herself out of existence, vaporizing in the final blink of his eyes.

A monstrous fireball erupted with a blue brilliance whose intensity was greater than the sun. White-hot gases instantly burst over an area four kilometres in diameter. A hemispherical condensation cloud formed and spread out like a vast doughnut, its interior quickly burned out by the fireball.

The surface of the sea was beaten down in a great bowl-like depression three hundred metres across. Then an immense column consisting of millions of tons of water rose into the sky, its walls sprouting thousands of horizontal geysers, each as large as the *Narvik*.

The shock wave raced from the fireball like an expanding ring around Saturn, speeding outward with a velocity approaching five kilometres a second. It struck the *Narvik*, pulping the ship into a formless shape.

Korvold, standing in the open on the bridge wing, did not see the holocaust. His eyes and brain had no time to record it. He was carbonized within a microsecond by thermal radiation from the explosion's fireball. His entire ship rose out of the water and was tossed back as if struck down by a giant sledgehammer. A molten rain of steel fragments and dust from the *Divine Star* cascaded the *Narvik*'s shattered decks. Fire burst from her ruptured hull and engulfed the shattered vessel. And then explosions deep in her bowels. The containers on her cargo deck were tossed away like leaves before a gust from a hurricane.

There was no time for hoarse, tortured screams. Anyone caught on deck flared like a match, crackled, and was gone. The entire ship became an instant funeral pyre to her 250 passengers and crew.

The *Narvik* began to list, settling fast. Within five minutes of the explosion she rolled over. Soon only a small portion of her bottom was visible, and then she slid under the agitated waters and vanished in the depths.

Almost as suddenly as the *Divine Star* evaporated, it was over. The great cauliflower-shaped cloud that had formed over the fireball slowly scattered and became indistinguishable from the overcast. The shimmering fury of the water calmed, and the surface smoothed but for the rolling swells.

*

Twelve kilometres across the sea the *Invincible* still floated. The incredible pressure of the shock wave had not yet begun to diminish when its full force smashed into the survey ship. Her superstructure was gutted and stripped away, exposing interior bulkheads. Her funnel tore from its mountings and whirled into the boiling water as the bridge disappeared in a violent shower of steel and flesh.

Her masts were bent and distorted, the big crane used to retrieve *Old Gert* was twisted and thrown on one side, the hull plates saucered inward between her frame and longitudinal beams. Like the *Narvik*, the *Invincible* had been beaten into a formless shape that was almost unrecognizable as a ship.

The paint on her sides had blistered and blacked under the fiery blast. A plume of black oily smoke billowed from her smashed port side and lay like a boiling carpet over the water around her hull. The heat bored right through anyone exposed in the open. Those below decks were badly injured by concussion and flying debris.

Jimmy Knox had been thrown violently into an unyielding steel bulkhead, bouncing backward and gasping for air as if he was in a vacuum. He wound up flat on his back, spread-eagled, staring up stunned through a gaping hole that appeared as if by magic in the ceiling.

He lay there waiting for the shock to pass, struggling to concentrate on his predicament, wondering in a fog what had happened to his world. Slowly he gazed around the compartment at the bent bulkheads, seeing the heavily damaged electronic equipment that looked like a robot with its guts pulled out, smelling the smoke from the fires, and he felt the hysteria of a child who had lost his parents in a crowd.

He looked through the slash above into the bridge housing and chart room. They had been gutted into a tortured skeleton of deformed beams. The wheelhouse was a smouldering shambles that was now a crypt for burned and broken men, whose blood dripped into the compartments below.

Knox rolled to his side and groaned in sudden agony caused by three broken ribs, a twisted ankle, and a sea of bruises. Very slowly he pushed himself to a sitting position. He reached up and adjusted his glasses, surprised they had remained perched on his nose during the incomprehensible devastation.

Slowly the dark curtain of shock parted, and his first thought was of *Old Gert*. Straight from a nightmare he could see the submersible damaged and out of contact in the blackness of the deep.

He crawled across the deck in a daze on hands and knees, fighting back the pain, until he could reach up and grasp the receiver to the underwater telephone.

'*Gert?*' he burst out fearfully. 'Do you read?'

He waited several seconds, but there was no reply. He swore in a low monotone.

'Damn you, Plunkett! Talk to me, you bastard!'

His own answer was silence. All communications between the *Invincible* and *Old Gert* were broken. His worst fears were realized. Whatever force had battered the survey ship must have travelled through the water and mangled the submersible that was already subjected to incredible pressures.

'Dead,' he whispered. 'Crushed to pulp.'

His mind suddenly turned to his shipmates, and he called out. He heard only the groan and screech of metal from the dying ship. He moved his eyes to the open doorway and focused on five bodies sprawled in untidy, stiff attitudes like cast-off display mannequins.

He sat fixed in grief and incomprehension. Dimly he felt the ship shudder convulsively, the stern slipping around and sliding beneath the waves as though caught in a whirlpool. Concussions reverberated all around him. The *Invincible* was about to take her own journey to the abyss.

The urge to live surged within him, and then Knox was scrambling up a slanted deck, too dazed to feel the pain from his injuries. Charging in panic through the door to the crane deck, he dodged around the dead bodies and over the devastated steel equipment that sprawled everywhere. Fear took the place of shock and built to a tight, expanding ball inside him.

He reached the twisted remains of the railing. Without a backward glance, he climbed over and stepped into the waiting sea. A splintered piece of a wooden crate bobbed in the water a few metres away. He swam awkwardly until he could clasp it under one arm and float. Only then did he turn and look at the *Invincible*.

She was sinking by the stern, her bows lifting above the Pacific swell. She seemed to hang there for a minute, sailing toward the clouds as she slipped backward at an ever increasing speed and disappeared, leaving a few bits of flotsam and a cauldron of churned water that soon subsided into a few bubbles tinted in rainbow colours by the spilled oil.

Frantically Knox searched the sea for other members of the *Invincible*'s crew. There was an eerie hush now that the groans of the sinking ship had passed. There were no lifeboats, no heads of men swimming in the sea.

He found himself the only survivor of a tragedy that had no explanation.

5

Beneath the surface, the shock wave travelled through the incompressible water at roughly 6,500 kilometres per hour in an expanding circle, crushing all sea life in its path. *Old Gert* was saved from instant destruction by the canyon walls. They towered above the submersible, shielding it from the main force of the explosive pressure.

Yet the submersible was still whirled about violently. One moment it was level, the next it was tumbled end over end like a kicked football by the turbulence. The pod containing the main batteries and propulsion systems struck the rocklike nodules, cracked and collapsed inward from the tremendous pressure. Fortunately, the hatch covers on each end of the connecting tube held, or the water would have burst into the crew's sphere like a pile driver and mashed them into bloody paste.

The noise of the explosion came over the underwater telephone like a thunderclap almost in unison with the express-train rumble from the shock wave. With their passing, the deep returned to a beguiling silence. Then the calm was broken again by the screech and groan of tortured metal as the ravaged surface ships fell through the deep, buckling and compressing before plunging against the seafloor in great mushroom clouds of silt.

'What is it?' Stacy cried, clutching her chair to keep from being thrown about.

Whether from shock or radical devotion to his work, Salazar's eyes had never left his console. 'This is no earthquake. It reads as a surface disturbance.'

With the thrusters gone, Plunkett lost all control of *Old Gert*. He could only sit there in helpless detachment as the sub was tossed across the field of manganese nodules. Automatically he shouted into the underwater telephone, skipping all call sign formalities.

'Jimmy, we're caught in unexplained turbulence! Have lost our thrust pod! Please respond!'

Jimmy Knox could not hear. He was fighting to stay alive in the waves far above.

Plunkett was still trying desperately to raise the *Invincible* when the submersible finally ended her erratic flight and struck the bottom on a forty-degree angle, coming to rest on the sphere surrounding the electrical and oxygen equipment.

'This is the end,' Salazar murmured, not really knowing what he meant, his mind mired in shock and confusion.

'The hell it is!' snapped Plunkett. 'We can still drop ballast weights and make it to the top.'

He knew as he spoke that releasing all the iron ballast weights might not overcome the added weight of the water within the shattered pod, plus the suction from the muck. He activated the switches, and hundreds of pounds of dead weight dropped free from the submersible's underbelly.

For a few moments nothing happened, then centimetre by centimetre *Old Gert* pulled herself from the bottom, rising slowly as if pushed by the hushed breaths and pounding hearts of the three people inside her main sphere.

'Ten feet up,' announced Plunkett after what seemed an hour but in reality was only thirty seconds.

Old Gert levelled out and they all dared to breathe again. Plunkett futilely kept trying to contact Jimmy Knox. 'Jimmy . . . this is Plunkett. Talk to me.'

Stacy stared so hard at the depth metre she thought the glass over the dial would crack. 'Go . . . go,' she pleaded.

Then their worst nightmare burst on them without warning. The sphere holding the electrical and oxygen equipment suddenly imploded. Weakened by its impact into the seafloor, it gave up its integrity and was crushed like an egg by the merciless pressure.

'Bloody hell!' Plunkett gasped as the sub dropped back into the silt with a jarring bump.

As if to drive home the terrifying reverse, the lights blinked out and snapped the sphere into a world of pure ebony. The malignancy of the stygian blackness is a horror only the totally blind experience. To those with sight the sudden disorientation curses the mind into believing unspeakable forces are approaching from beyond in an ever tightening circle.

At last Salazar's hoarse voice broke the silence. 'Mother of Jesus, we're finished for good.'

'Not yet,' said Plunkett. 'We can still make it to the surface by jettisoning the control sphere.' His hand groped over his console until his fingers touched a particular switch. With an audible click the auxiliary lights came on and relit the interior of the sphere.

Stacy sighed with relief and briefly relaxed. 'Thank heaven. At least we can see.'

Plunkett programmed the computer for an emergency ascent. Then he set the release mechanism and turned to Stacy and Salazar. 'Hold tight. It may be a rough trip topside.'

'Anything to get the hell out of here,' grunted Salazar.

'Whenever you're ready,' Stacy said gamely.

Plunkett removed the safety peg from the release handle, took a firm grip, and pulled.

Nothing happened.

Three times Plunkett feverishly ran through the routine. But the control sphere stubbornly refused to detach from the main section of the sub. In desperation he turned to the computer to trouble-shoot the cause of the malfunction. An answer came back in the blink of an eye.

The release mechanism had been twisted and jammed by the angled impact with the seabed, and there was no way to repair it.

'I'm sorry,' Plunkett said in frustration. 'But it looks like we stay until rescued.'

'Fat chance of that,' snapped Salazar, wiping the sweat that poured from his face with the sleeve of a down ski jacket.

'How do we stand on oxygen?' asked Stacy.

'Our main supply was cut off when the pod imploded,' replied Plunkett. 'But our emergency canisters in this unit and the lithium hydroxide scrubber to remove our exhaled carbon dioxide should keep us sucking air for ten to twelve hours.'

Salazar shook his head and gave a defeated shrug. 'Every prayer in every church of the world won't save us in time. It'll take a minimum of seventy-two hours to get another submersible on site. And even then it's doubtful they could lift us to the surface.'

Stacy looked into Plunkett's eyes for some small sign of encouragement, but she found none. He wore a remote and distant look. She got the impression he was saddened more by the loss of his precious submersible than he was at the prospect of dying. He came back on track as he became aware of her stare.

'Raul is right,' he said tautly. 'I hate to admit it, but we'll need a miracle to see the sun again.'

'But the *Invincible*,' said Stacy. 'They'll move heaven and earth to reach us.'

Plunkett shook his head. 'Something tragic happened up there. The last sound we heard was a ship breaking up on her way to the bottom.'

'But there were two other ships in sight when we left the surface,' Stacy protested. 'It might have been either one of them.'

'It makes no difference,' Plunkett said wearily. 'There is no way up. And time has become an enemy we cannot defeat.'

A deep despair settled in the control sphere. Any hope of rescue was a fantasy. The only certainty was a future salvage project to retrieve *Old Gert* and their bodies long after they were dead.

6

Dale Nichols, special assistant to the President, puffed on his pipe and peered over his old-style reading spectacles as Raymond Jordan entered his office.

Jordan managed a smile despite the sickly sweet tobacco fumes that hung in the office like smog under an inversion layer. 'Good afternoon, Dale.'

'Still raining?' asked Nichols.

'Mostly turned to drizzle.'

Jordan noted that Nichols was under pressure. The 'protector of the presidential realm' was an efficient operator, but the thicket of coffee-brown hair looked like a hayfield in a crosswind, the eyes darted more than usual, and there were tension lines in the face Jordan had never seen before.

'The President and the Vice President are waiting,' said Nichols quickly. 'They're most anxious to hear an update on the Pacific blast.'

'I have the latest report,' Jordan said reassuringly.

Though he was one of the five most powerful men in official Washington, Jordan was not known to the general public. Nor was he familiar to most bureaucrats or politicians. As Director of Central Intelligence Jordan headed the National Security Service and reported directly to the President.

He lived in a spectral world of espionage and intelligence, and there were very few outsiders who were aware of the disasters and tragedies from which he and his agents had saved the American people.

Jordan did not strike a stranger as a man with a brilliant intellect who possessed a photographic memory and was conversant in seven languages. He seemed as ordinary-looking as his men and women in the field. Medium height, late fifties, healthy head of silver-grey hair, solid frame with slight paunch, kindly oak-brown eyes. A faithful husband to his wife of thirty-seven years, they had twin daughters in college, both studying marine biology.

The President and Vice President were engaged in quiet conversation as Nichols ushered Jordan into the Oval Office. They turned instantly and faced Jordan, who observed that they were as uptight as the President's special assistant.

'Thank you for coming, Ray,' said the President without fanfare, nervously motioning to a green couch beneath a portrait of Andrew Jackson. 'Please sit down and tell us what in hell is going on out in the Pacific?'

Jordan always found himself amused by the painful uneasiness that gripped politicians during an impending crisis. No elected official had the seasoned toughness and experience of career men such as the Director of Central Intelligence. And they could never bring themselves to respect or accept the immense power Jordan and his counterparts possessed to control and orchestrate international events.

Jordan nodded to the President, who towered a good head above him, and sat down. Calmly, with what seemed to the others agonizing slowness, he set a large leather accountant's style briefcase on the floor and spread it open. Then he pulled out a file as a reference.

'Do we have a situation?' the President asked impatiently, using the formal watchword for an imminent threat to the civilian population, such as a nuclear attack.

'Yes, sir, unfortunately we do.'

'What are we looking at?'

Jordan glanced at the report purely for effect. He'd already memorized the entire thirty pages. 'At precisely eleven-fifty-four hours, an explosion of great force took place on the

North Pacific, approximately nine hundred kilometres northeast of Midway Island. One of our Pyramider spy satellites recorded the flash and atmospheric disturbance with cameras and recorded the shock wave from clandestine hydrophonic buoys. The data was transmitted directly to the National Security Agency, where it was analysed. This was followed by readings from seismographic array stations linked to NORAD, who in turn relayed the information to CIA technicians at Langley.'

'And the conclusion?' the President pushed.

'They agreed the explosion was nuclear,' he said calmly. 'Nothing else could be that massive.'

Except for Jordan, who seemed as relaxed as if he was watching a soap opera on television, the expressions of the other three men in the Oval Office looked positively grim at the abhorrent thought that was finally thrown out in the open.

'Are we on DEFCOM Alert?' inquired the President, referring to the scale of nuclear readiness.

Jordan nodded. 'I've taken the liberty of ordering NORAD to go immediately to a DEFCOM-Three Alert with standby and staging for DEFCOM-Two, depending on reaction by the Soviets.'

Nichols stared at Jordan. 'Are we airborne?'

'A Casper SR-Ninety recon aircraft took off from Edwards Air Force Base twenty minutes ago to verify and collect additional data.'

'Are we certain the shock wave was caused by a nuclear explosion?' asked the Vice President, a man in his early forties who had only spent six years in Congress before being tapped for the number-two job. The consummate politician, he was out of his depth on intelligence gathering. 'It might have been an underwater earthquake or volcanic eruption.'

Jordan shook his head. 'The seismographic recordings showed a sharp pulse associated with nuclear detonations.

The reflection from an earthquake goes back and forth for a longer length of time. Computer enhancement confirms that fact. We should have a good idea of the energy in kilotons after the Casper collects atmospheric radiation samples.'

'Any guesses?'

'Until all the data is in, the best guess is between ten and twenty kilotons.'

'Enough to level Chicago,' Nichols murmured.

The President was afraid to ask the next question, and he hesitated. 'Could . . . could it have been one of our own nuclear submarines that blew up?'

'The Chief of Naval Operations assures me none of our vessels were within five hundred kilometres of the area.'

'A Russian maybe?'

'No,' Jordan replied. 'I've notified my USSR counterpart, Nikolai Golanov. He swore all Soviet nuclear surface ships and submarines in the Pacific are accounted for, and quite naturally blamed us for the event. Though I'm one hundred percent sure he and his people know better, they won't admit they're in the dark as much as we are.'

'I'm not familiar with the name,' said the Vice President. 'Is he KGB?'

'Golanov is the Director of Foreign and State Security for the Politburo,' Jordan explained patiently.

'He could be lying,' offered Nichols.

Jordan shot him a hard look. 'Nikolai and I go back twenty-six years together. We may have danced and shined, but we never lied to one another.'

'If we aren't responsible, and neither are the Soviets,' mused the President, his voice gone strangely soft, 'then who is?'

'At least ten other nations have the bomb,' said Nichols. 'Any one of them could have run a nuclear bomb test.'

'Not likely,' answered Jordan. 'You can't keep the preparations a secret from Global Bloc and Western intelligence gathering. I suspect we're going to find it was an accident, a nuclear device that was never meant to go off.'

The President looked thoughtful for a moment, and then he asked, 'Do we know the nationality of the ships in the blast area?'

'All the details aren't in yet, but it appears that three vessels were involved, or at least innocent bystanders. A Norwegian passenger-cargo liner, a Japanese auto carrier, and a British oceanographic ship that was conducting a deep-bottom survey.'

'There must have been casualties.'

'Photos from our satellite before and after the event show that all three ships had vanished and were presumed sunk during or immediately after the blast. Human survivability is very doubtful. If the fireball and shock wave didn't get them, the heavy radiation will in a very short time.'

'I take it a rescue mission is planned,' said the Vice President.

'Naval units from Guam and Midway have been ordered to the site.'

The President stared at the carpet steadily, as if seeing something. 'I can't believe the British were secretly conducting a bomb test without notifying us. The Prime Minister would have never gone behind my back.'

'Certainly not the Norwegians,' said the Vice President firmly.

The President's face made a mystified expression. 'Nor the Japanese. There's no evidence they ever built a nuclear bomb.'

'The device might have been stolen,' suggested Nichols, 'and clandestinely transported by the unsuspecting Norwegians or Japanese.'

Jordan shrugged offhandedly. 'I don't think it was stolen. I'm willing to bet a month's pay an investigation will prove it was deliberately being carried to a scheduled destination.'

'Which was?'

'One of two California ports.'

They all looked at Jordan in cold speculation, the enormity of the whole thing growing in their minds.

'The *Divine Star* was bound from Kobe to Los Angeles with over seven thousand Murmoto automobiles,' Jordan continued. 'The *Narvik*, carrying a hundred and thirty passengers and a mixed cargo of Korean shoes, computers, and kitchen appliances, sailed from Pusan for San Francisco.'

The President grinned mildly. 'That should put a small dent in the trade deficit.'

'Good God,' muttered the Vice President, shaking his head. 'A frightening thought. A foreign ship smuggling a nuclear bomb into the United States.'

'What do you recommend, Ray?' demanded the President.

'We despatch field teams immediately. Preferably Navy deep-sea salvage vessels to survey the sunken ships and learn which ship was transporting the bomb.'

The President and Nichols exchanged knowing glances. Then the President stared at Jordan. 'I think Admiral Sandecker and his ocean engineering people at NUMA are better suited for deepwater operation. I'll leave it to you, Ray, to brief him.'

'If I may respectfully disagree, Mr President. We can keep a tighter security lid on the event with the Navy.'

The President gave Jordan a smug look. 'I understand your concern. But trust me. The National Underwater and Marine Agency can do the job without a news leak.'

Jordan rose from the couch, professionally annoyed that the President knew something he didn't. He made a mental note to dig at his first opportunity. 'If Dale will alert the admiral, I'll leave for his office immediately.'

The President extended his hand. 'Thank you, Ray. You and your people have done a superb job in so short a time.'

Nichols accompanied Jordan as he left the Oval Office to head for the NUMA Building. As soon as they were in the hallway Nichols asked in a low voice, 'Just between you and me and the furniture, who do you think is behind the bomb smuggling?'

Jordan thought for a moment and then replied in an even, disquieting tone. 'We'll know the answer to that within the next twenty-four hours. The big question, the one that scares the hell out of me, is why, and for what purpose.'

7

The atmosphere inside the submersible had become rank and humid. Condensation was dripping from the sides of the sphere, and the carbon dioxide was rising into the lethal range. No one stirred and seldom spoke, to conserve air. After eleven and a half hours, their life-preserving oxygen supply was nearly gone, and what precious little electrical power was left in the emergency batteries could not operate the CO_2 scrubbing unit much longer.

Fear and terror had slowly faded to resignation. Except for every fifteen minutes, when Plunkett switched on the lights to read the life-support systems, they sat quietly in the dark, alone with their thoughts.

Plunkett concentrated on monitoring the instruments, fussing with his equipment, refusing to believe his beloved submersible could refuse to respond to his commands. Salazar sat like a statue, slumped in his chair. He seemed withdrawn and barely conscious. Though he was only minutes away from falling into a final stupor, he could not see the point in prolonging the inevitable. He wanted to die and get it over with.

Stacy conjured up fantasies of her childhood, pretending she was in another place, another time. Her past flew by in fleeting images. Playing baseball in the street with her brothers, riding her new bicycle Christmas Day, going to her first high school prom with a boy she didn't like but who was the only one who asked her. She could almost hear the strains of the music in the hotel ballroom. She forgot the name of the group, but she remembered the songs. 'We May Never Pass This Way Again' from Seals and Crofts was her favourite. She had closed her eyes and imagined she'd been dancing with Robert Redford.

She cocked her head as if listening. Something was out of place. The song she heard in her mind wasn't from the mid-1970s. It sounded more like an old jazz tune than rock.

She came awake, opened her eyes, seeing only the blackness. 'They're playing the wrong music,' she mumbled.

Plunkett flicked on the lights. 'What was that?'

Even Salazar looked up uncomprehendingly and muttered, 'She's hallucinating.'

'They're supposed to be playing "We May Never Pass This Way Again", but it's something else.'

Plunkett looked at Stacy, his face soft with compassion and sorrow. 'Yes, I hear it too.'

'No, no,' she objected. 'Not the same. The song is different.'

'Whatever you say,' said Salazar, panting. His lungs ached from trying to wrest what oxygen he could from the foul air. He grabbed Plunkett by the arm. 'For God's sake, man. Close down the systems and end it. Can't you see she's suffering; we're all suffering.'

Plunkett's chest was hurting too. He well knew it was useless to prolong the torment, but he couldn't brush aside the primitive urge to cling on to life to the last breath. 'We'll see it through,' he said heavily. 'Maybe another sub was airlifted to the *Invincible*.'

Salazar stared at him with glazed eyes and a mind that was hanging on to a thin thread of reality. 'You're crazy. There isn't another deep-water craft within seven thousand kilometres. And even if one was brought in, and the *Invincible* was still afloat, they'd need another eight hours to launch and rendezvous.'

'I can't argue with you. None of us wants to spend eternity in a lost crypt in deep ocean. But I won't give up hope.'

'Crazy,' Salazar repeated. He leaned forward in his seat

and shook his head from side to side as if clearing the growing pain. He looked as though he was ageing a year with each passing minute.

'Can't you hear it,' Stacy uttered in a low croaking voice. 'They're coming closer.'

'She's crazy too,' Salazar rasped.

Plunkett held up his hand. 'Quiet! I hear something too. There *is* something out there.'

There was no reply from Salazar. He was too far gone to think or speak coherently. An agonizing band was tightening around his lungs. The desire for air overpowered all his thoughts save one; he sat there and wished death to come quickly.

Stacy and Plunkett both stared into the darkness beyond the sphere. A weird rat-tailed creature swam into the dim light coming from inside *Old Gert*. It had no eyes, but it made a circuit of the sphere, maintaining a distance of two centimetres before it went on about its business in the depths.

Suddenly the water shimmered. Something was stirring in the distance, something monstrous. Then a strange bluish halo grew out of the blackness, accompanied by voices singing words too garbled by the water to comprehend.

Stacy stared entranced, while Plunkett's skin crawled on the back of his neck. It had to be some horror from the supernatural, he thought. A monster created by his oxygen-starved brain. There was no way the approaching thing could be real. The image of an alien from another world crossed his mind again. Tense and fearful, he waited until it came nearer, planning on using the final charge of the emergency battery to switch on the outside lights. A terror from the deep or not, he realized it would be the last thing he'd ever see on earth.

Stacy crawled to the side of the sphere until her nose was pressed against its interior. A chorus of voices echoed in her ears. 'I told you,' she said in a strained whisper. 'I told you I heard singing. Listen.'

Plunkett could just make out the words now, very faint and distant. He thought he must be going mad. He tried to tell himself that the lack of breathable air was playing tricks on his eyes and ears. But the blue light was becoming brighter and he recognized the song.

Oh, what a time I had with Minnie the Mermaid
Down at the bottom of the sea.
I forgot my troubles there among the bubbles.
Gee but she was awfully good to me.

He pushed the exterior light switch. Plunkett sat there motionless. He was used up and dog-weary. Desperately so. His mind refused to accept the thing that materialized out of the black gloom, and he fainted dead away.

Stacy was so numbed with shock she couldn't tear her eyes from the apparition that crept toward the sphere. A huge machine, moving on great tractorlike treads and supporting an oblong structure with two freakish manipulator arms on its underside, rolled to a stop and sat poised under the lights of *Old Gert.*

A humanlike form with blurred features was sitting in the transparent nose of the strange craft only two metres away from the sphere. Stacy closed her eyes tightly and reopened them. Then the vague, shadowy likeness of a man took shape. She could see him clearly now. He wore a turquoise-coloured jumpsuit that was partially opened down the front. The matted black strands on his chest matched the dark shaggy hair on his head. His face had a masculine weathered, craggy look, and the mirth wrinkles that stretched from a pair of incredibly green eyes were complemented by the slight grin on his lips.

He stared back at her with a bemused interest. Then he reached down behind him, set a clipboard on his lap, and wrote something on a pad. After a few seconds he tore off a piece of paper and held it up to his view window.

Stacy's eyes strained to focus on the wording. It read, 'Welcome to Soggy Acres. Hang on while we connect an oxygen line.'

Is this what it's like to die? Stacy wondered. She'd read of people going through tunnels before emerging into light and seeing people and relatives who had died in the past. But this man was a perfect stranger. Where did he come from?

Before she could match the puzzle pieces, the door closed and she floated into oblivion.

8

Dirk Pitt stood alone in the centre of a large domed chamber, hands shoved into the pockets of his NUMA jumpsuit, and studied *Old Gert*. His opaline eyes stared without expression at the submersible that sat like a broken toy on the smooth black lava floor. Then he slowly climbed through the hatch and dropped into the pilot's reclining chair and studied the instruments embedded in the console.

Pitt was a tall man, firm muscled with broad shoulders and straight back, slightly on the lanky side, and yet he moved with a catlike grace that seemed poised for action. There was a razor hardness about him that even a stranger could sense, yet he never lacked for friends and allies in and out of government who respected and admired him for his loyalty and intelligence. He was buoyed by a dry wit and an easygoing personality – a trait a score of women had found most appealing – and though he adored their company, his most ardent love was reserved for the sea.

As Special Projects Director of NUMA he spent almost as much time on and under water as he did on land. His main exercise was diving; he seldom crossed the threshold of a gym. He had given up smoking years before, casually controlled his diet, and was a light drinker. He was constantly busy, physically moving about, walking up to five miles a day in the course of his job. His greatest pleasure outside his work was diving through the ghostly hulk of a sunken ship.

There was the echo of footsteps from outside the submersible, footsteps crossing the rock floor that had been carved smooth under the curved walls of the vaulted roof. Pitt slewed around in the chair and looked at his longtime friend and NUMA associate, Al Giordino.

Giordino's black hair was as curly as Pitt's was wavy. His smooth face showed ruddy under the overhead glow from the sodium vapour lights, and his lips were locked in their usual sly Fagin-like smile. Giordino was short, the top of his head came just up to Pitt's shoulder line. But his body was braced by massive biceps and a chest that preceded the rest of him like a wrecking ball, a feature that enhanced his determined walk and gave the impression that if he didn't come to a halt he would simply walk through whatever fence or wall happened to be in his path.

'Well, what do you make of it?' he asked Pitt.

'The British turned out a nice piece of work,' Pitt replied admiringly as he exited the hatch.

Giordino studied the crushed spheres and shook his head. 'They were lucky. Another five minutes and we'd have found corpses.'

'How are they doing?'

'A speedy recovery,' answered Giordino. 'They're in the galley devouring our food stores and demanding to be returned to their ship on the surface.'

'Anyone brief them yet?' asked Pitt.

'As you ordered, they've been confined to the crew's quarters, and anyone who comes within spitting distance acts like a deaf mute. A performance that's driven our guests up the walls. They'd give their left kidney to know who we are, where we came from, and how we built a livable facility this deep in the ocean.'

Pitt gazed again at Old Gert and then motioned a hand around the chamber. 'Years of secrecy flushed down the drain,' he muttered, suddenly angry.

'Not your fault.'

'Better I left them to die out there than compromise our project.'

'Who you kidding?' Giordino laughed. 'I've seen you pick up injured dogs in the street and drive them to a vet. You even paid the bill though it wasn't you who ran over them.

70

You're a big softy, my friend. Secret operations be damned. You'd have saved those people if they'd carried rabies, leprosy, and the black plague.'

'I'm that obvious?'

Giordino's teasing look softened. 'I'm the bully who gave you a black eye in kindergarten, remember, and you bloodied my nose with a baseball in return. I know you better than your own mother. You may be a nasty bastard on the outside, but underneath you're an easy touch.'

Pitt looked down at Giordino. 'You know, of course, that playing good samaritan has put us in a sea of trouble with Admiral Sandecker and the Defense Department.'

'That goes without saying. And speaking of the devil, Communications just received a coded message. The admiral is on his way from Washington. His plane is due in two hours. Hardly what you'd call advance notice. I've ordered a sub readied to head for the surface and pick him up.'

'He must be psychic,' mused Pitt.

'I'm betting that weird disturbance is behind his surprise visit.'

Pitt nodded and smiled. 'Then we have nothing to lose by raising the curtain for our guests.'

'Nothing,' Giordino agreed. 'Once the admiral gets the story, he'll order them kept here under guard until we wrap up the project anyway.'

Pitt began walking toward the circular doorway with Giordino at his side. Sixty years in the past, the domed chamber might have been an architect's vision of a futuristic aircraft hangar, but this structure covered no aircraft from rain, snow, or summer sun. Its carbon and ceramic re-inforced plastic walls housed deepwater craft 5,400 metres beneath the sea. Besides *Old Gert*, the levelled floor held an immense tractorlike vehicle with an upper body housing shaped similar to a cigar. Two smaller submersibles sat side by side, resembling stubby nuclear submarines whose bows and sterns had been reattached after their centre sections were removed. Several men and one woman were busily servicing the vehicles.

Pitt led the way through a narrow circular tunnel that looked like an ordinary drain pipe and passed through two compartments with domed ceilings. There were no right angles or sharp corners anywhere. All interior surfaces were rounded to structurally resist the massive outside water pressure.

They entered a confined and spartan dining compartment. The one long table and its surrounding chairs were formed from aluminium, and the galley wasn't much larger than the kitchen on an overnight passenger train. Two NUMA crewmen stood on each side of the doorway keeping a tight eye on their unwelcome guests.

Plunkett, Salazar, and Stacy were huddled at the opposite end of the table in muffled conversation when Pitt and Giordino entered. Their voices stopped abruptly, and they looked up suspiciously at the two strangers.

So he could talk with them at their own level, Pitt planted himself solidly in a nearby chair and glanced swiftly from face to face as if he was an inspector of police examining a lineup.

Then he said politely, 'How do you do. My name is Dirk Pitt. I head up the project you've stumbled upon.'

'Thank God!' Plunkett boomed. 'At last, somebody who can speak.'

'And English at that,' added Salazar.

Pitt gestured at Giordino. 'Mr Albert Giordino, chief mover and doer around here. He'll be glad to conduct a grand tour, assign quarters, and help you with any needs in the way of clothing, toothbrushes, and whatever.'

Introductions and handshakes were traded across the table. Giordino ordered up a round of coffee, and the three visitors from *Old Gert* finally began to relax.

'I speak for all of us,' said Plunkett sincerely, 'when I say, thank you for saving our lives.'

'Al and I are only too happy we reached you in time.'

'Your accent tells me you're American,' said Stacy.

Pitt locked onto her eyes and gave her a devastating stare. 'Yes, we're all from the States.'

Stacy seemed to fear Pitt, as a deer fears a mountain lion, yet she was oddly attracted to him. 'You're the man I saw in the strange submersible before I passed out.'

'A DSMV,' Pitt corrected her. 'Stands for Deep Sea Mining Vehicle. Everyone calls it *Big John*. Its purpose is to excavate geological samples from the seabed.'

'This is an American mining venture?' asked Plunkett incredulously.

Pitt nodded. 'A highly classified suboceanic test mining and survey project, financed by the United States government. Eight years from the initial design through construction to start-up.'

'What do you call it?'

'There's a fancy code word, but we affectionately refer to the place as "Soggy Acres".'

'How can it be kept a secret?' asked Salazar. 'You must have a support fleet on the surface that can be easily detected by passing vessels or satellites.'

'Our little habitat is fully self-sustaining. A high-tech life-support system that draws oxygen from the sea and enables us to work under pressure equal to the air at sea level, a desalination unit for fresh drinking water, heat from hydrothermal vents on the seafloor, some food from mussels, clams, shrimp, and crabs that survive around the vents, and we bathe under ultraviolet light and antiseptic showers to prevent bacteria growth. What supplies or equipment replacement parts we can't provide on our own are dropped into the sea from the air and retrieved underwater. If it becomes necessary to transfer personnel, one of our submersibles rises to the surface where it is met by a jet-powered flying boat.'

Plunkett simply nodded. He was a man living a dream.

'You must have a unique method of communicating with the outside world,' said Salazar.

'A surface relay buoy tethered by cable. We transmit and receive via satellite. Nothing fancy but most efficient.'

'How long have you been down here?'

'We haven't seen the sun in a little over four months.'

Plunkett stared into his coffee cup in wonder. 'I had no idea your technology had developed to where you can tackle a research station this deep.'

'You might say we're a pioneer expedition,' said Pitt proudly. 'We have several projects going at the same time. Besides testing equipment, our engineers and scientists analyse the sea life, geology, and minerals on the seabed and file computerized reports of their findings. Actual dredging and mining operations come in future stages.'

'How many people in your crew?'

Pitt took a swallow of coffee before answering. 'Not many. Twelve men and two women.'

'I see your women have traditional duties,' Stacy said sourly, nodding at a pretty redheaded lady in her late twenties who was dicing vegetables in the galley.

'Sarah volunteered. She also oversees our computer records, working two jobs, as do most of us.'

'I suppose the other woman doubles as your maid and equipment mechanic.'

'You're close,' Pitt said, giving her a caustic smile. 'Jill really does help out as a marine equipment engineer. She's also our resident biologist. And if I were you, I wouldn't lecture her on female rights on the bottom of the sea. She took first in a Miss Colorado bodybuilding competition and can bench press two hundred pounds.'

Salazar pushed his chair from the table and stretched out his feet. 'I'll wager your military is involved with the project.'

'You won't find any uniformed rank down here,' Pitt sidestepped. 'We're all strictly scientific bureaucrats.'

74

'One thing I'd like you to explain,' said Plunkett, 'is how you knew we were in trouble and where to find us.'

'Al and I were retracing our tracks from an earlier sample-collection survey, searching for a gold-detection sensor that had somehow fallen off the *Big John*, when we came within range of your underwater phone.'

'We picked up your distress calls, faint as they were, and homed in to your position,' Giordino finished.

'Once we found your submersible,' Pitt continued, 'Al and I couldn't very well transport you from your vessel to our vehicle or you'd have been crushed into munchkins by the water pressure. Our only hope was to use the *Big John*'s manipulator arms to plug an oxygen line to your exterior emergency connector. Luckily, your adapter and ours mated perfectly.'

'Then we used both manipulator arms to lock onto your lift hooks,' Giordino came in, using his hands for effect, 'and carried your sub back to our equipment chamber, entering through our pressure airlock.'

'You saved *Old Gert*?' inquired Plunkett, quickly becoming cheerful.

'She's sitting in the chamber,' said Giordino.

'How soon can we be returned to our support ship?' Salazar demanded rather than asked.

'Not for some time, I'm afraid,' said Pitt.

'We've got to let our support crew know we're alive,' Stacy protested. 'Surely you can contact them?'

Pitt exchanged a taut look with Giordino. 'On our way to rescue you, we passed a badly damaged ship that had recently fallen to the bottom.'

'No, not the *Invincible*,' Stacy murmured, unbelieving.

'She was badly broken up, as though she suffered from a heavy explosion,' replied Giordino. 'I doubt there were any survivors.'

'Two other ships were nearby when we started our dive,' Plunkett pleaded. 'She must have been one of them.'

'I can't say,' Pitt admitted. 'Something happened up there. Some kind of immense turbulence. We've had no time to investigate and don't have any hard answers.'

'Surely you felt the same shock wave that damaged our submersible.'

'This facility sits in a protected valley off the fracture zone, thirty kilometres away from where we found you and the sunken ship. What was left of any shock wave passed over us. All we experienced was a mild rush of current and a sediment storm as the bottom was stirred into what is known on dry land as a blizzard condition.'

Stacy gave Pitt an angry look indeed. 'Do you intend to keep us prisoners?'

'Not exactly the word I had in mind. But since this *is* a highly classified project I must ask you to accept our hospitality a bit longer.'

'What do you call "a bit longer"?' Salazar asked warily.

Pitt gave the small Mexican a sardonic stare. 'We're not scheduled to return topside for another sixty days.'

There was silence. Plunkett looked from Salazar to Stacy to Pitt. 'Bloody hell!' he snapped bitterly. 'You can't hold us here two months.'

'My wife,' groaned Salazar. 'She'll think I'm dead.'

'I have a daughter,' said Stacy, quickly subdued.

'Bear with me,' Pitt said quietly. 'I realize I seem like a heartless tyrant, but your presence has put me in a difficult position. When we have a better grip on what happened on the surface, and I talk with my superiors, we might work something out.'

Pitt paused as he spotted Keith Harris, the project's seismologist, standing in the doorway nodding for Pitt to talk outside the room.

Pitt excused himself and approached Harris. He immediately saw the look of concern in Harris's eyes.

'Problem?' he asked tersely.

Harris spoke through a great grey beard that matched his

hair. 'That disturbance has triggered a growing number of shocks in the seabed. So far, most all are small and shallow. We can't actually feel them yet. But their intensity and strength are growing.'

'How do you read it?'

'We're sitting on a fault that's unstable as hell,' Harris went on. 'It's also volcanic. Crustal strain energy is being released at a rate I've never experienced. I'm afraid we could be looking at a major earthquake of a six-point-five magnitude.'

'We'd never survive,' Pitt said stonily. 'One crack in one of our domes, and the water pressure will flatten the entire base like peas under a sledgehammer.'

'I get the same picture,' said Harris dismally.

'How long have we got?'

'No way to predict these things with any certainty. I realize it's not much comfort, and I'm only guessing, but judging from the rate of build I'd guess maybe twelve hours.'

'Time enough to evacuate.'

'I could be wrong,' Harris came back hesitantly. 'If we actually experience initial shock waves, the big quake might be only minutes behind. On the other hand, the shocks could taper off and stop just as easily.'

He'd no sooner got the words out when they both felt a slight tremor beneath their feet and the coffee cups on the dining table began to clatter in their saucers.

Pitt stared at Harris, and his lips pulled into a tense grin. 'It seems that time is not on our side.'

9

The tremors increased with terrifying swiftness. A distant rumbling seemed to move closer. Then came sharp thumping sounds as small rocks tumbled down the canyon slopes and struck against the suboceanic buildings. Everyone kept glancing up at the great arched roof of the equipment chamber, fearful of an avalanche breaching the walls. One tiny opening, and the water would burst inside with the shattering power of a thousand cannons.

All was calm, no panic. Except for the clothes they wore, nothing was carried but the computer records of the project. Eight minutes was all it took for the crew to assemble and ready the deep-sea vehicles for boarding.

Pitt had known instantly that a few must die. The two manned submersibles were each designed to carry a maximum of six people. Seven might be crammed on board for a total of fourteen – the exact number of the project team – but certainly no more. Now they were burdened with the unplanned presence of the crewmen from *Old Gert*.

The shocks were coming stronger and closer together now. Pitt saw no chance of a sub reaching the surface, unloading survivors and returning in time to rescue those left behind. The round trip took no less than four hours. The suboceanic structures were slowly weakening under the increasing shocks, and it was only a question of minutes before they would give way and be crushed by the onslaught of the sea.

Giordino read the dire signs in the fixed expression on Pitt's face. 'We'll have to make two trips. Better I wait for the next – '

'Sorry, old pal,' Pitt cut him off. 'You pilot the first sub.

I'll follow in the second. Get to the surface, unload your passengers into inflatable rafts, and dive like hell for those who must stay behind.'

'No way I can make it back in time,' Giordino said tautly.

'Think of a better way?'

Giordino shook his head in defeat. 'Who gets the short end of the stick?'

'The British survey team.'

Giordino stiffened. 'No call for volunteers? Not like you to leave a woman.'

'I have to place our own people first,' Pitt answered coldly.

Giordino shrugged, disapproval in his face. 'We save them and then sign their death warrants.'

A long, shuddering vibration shook the seabed, chased by a deep, menacing rumble. Ten seconds. Pitt stared down at his wristwatch. The shock lasted ten seconds. Then all was silent and still again, deathly silent.

Giordino stared blankly for an instant into the eyes of his friend. Not the slightest fear showed. Pitt seemed incredibly indifferent. There was absolutely no doubt in his mind that Pitt was lying. There was never any intention to pilot the second sub. Pitt was set on being the last man out.

It was too late now, too late for arguments, no time for drawn-out goodbyes. Pitt grabbed Giordino by the arm and half pushed, half heaved the tough little Italian through the hatch of the first submersible.

'You should be just in time to greet the admiral,' he said. 'Give him my best.'

Giordino didn't hear him. Pitt's voice was drowned out by falling rock that smashed against the dome and reverberated all around them. Then Pitt slammed the hatch shut and was gone.

The six big men stuffed inside seemed to fill every square centimetre of the interior. They said nothing, avoiding each other's stares. Then, as if all eyes were following a thrown football in the last seconds of a game, they watched expectantly as Giordino weaved like an eel through their packed bodies into the pilot's seat.

He swiftly switched on the electric motors that ran the submersible over rails into the air lock. He rushed through the checklist and had just programmed the computer when the massive interior door closed and water began surging through special restriction valves from the ice-cold sea outside. The instant the lock was filled and equalized with the immense water pressure, the computer automatically opened the exterior door. Then Giordino took over manual control, engaged the thrusters to maximum power, and drove the sub toward the waves far above.

While Giordino and his passengers were in the lock, Pitt quickly turned his attention to the boarding of the second submersible. He ordered the NUMA team women to enter first. Then he silently nodded for Stacy to follow.

She hesitated at the hatch opening, shot him a strained, questioning look. She was standing quite still as though stunned by what was happening around her.

'Are you going to die because I took your place?' she asked softly.

Pitt flashed a madcap smile. 'Keep a date open for rum collins at sunset on the lanai of the Halekalani Hotel in Honolulu.'

She tried to form the words for a reply, but before they came out the next man in line pushed her none too gently into the sub.

Pitt stepped over to Dave Lowden, chief vehicle engineer on the project. About as perturbed as a clam, Lowden pulled up the zipper on his leather bomber jacket with one hand while pushing his rimless glasses up the bridge of his nose with the other.

'You want me to act as co-pilot?' Lowden asked in a low voice.

'No, you take her up alone,' said Pitt. 'I'll wait for Giordino to come back.'

Lowden could not control the saddened expression that crossed his face. 'Better I should stay than you.'

'You have a pretty wife and three kids. I'm single. Get your ass in that sub, and be quick about it.' Pitt turned his back on Lowden and walked over to where Plunkett and Salazar were standing.

Plunkett also showed no shred of fear. The big ocean engineer looked as content as a sheepherder casually eyeing his flock during a spring shower.

'Do you have a family, Doc?' Pitt asked.

Plunkett gave a slight shake of his head. 'Me? Not bloody likely. I'm an old confirmed bachelor.'

'I thought as much.'

Salazar was nervously rubbing his hands together, a frightened light in his eyes. He was achingly aware of his helplessness and a certainty that he was about to die.

'I believe you said you had a wife?' Pitt asked, directing his question to Salazar.

'And a son,' he muttered. 'They're in Veracruz.'

'There's room for one more. Hurry and jump in.'

'I'll make eight,' Salazar said dumbly. 'I thought your submersibles only held seven.'

'I put the biggest men in the first sub and crammed the smallest and three ladies in the second. There should be enough space left over to squeeze in a little guy like you.'

Without a thank you, Salazar scrambled into the submersible as Pitt swung the hatch cover closed against his heels. Then Lowden dogged it tight from the inside.

As the submersible rolled into the air lock and the door closed with a sickening finality, Plunkett slapped Pitt's back with a great bear paw of a hand.

'You're a brave one, Mr Pitt. No man could have played God better.'

'Sorry I couldn't find an extra seat for you.'

'No matter. I consider it an honour to die in good company.'

Pitt stared at Plunkett, mild surprise in his eyes. 'Who said anything about dying?'

'Come now, man. I know the sea. It doesn't take a seismographic genius to know your project is about to collapse around our ears.'

'Doc,' Pitt said conversationally through a heavy tremor, 'trust me.'

Plunkett gave Pitt a very sceptical look. 'You know something I don't?'

'Let's just say, we're catching the last freight out of Soggy Acres.'

Twelve minutes later, the shock waves came in an endless procession. Tons of rock cascaded down from the canyon walls, striking the rounded structures with shattering force.

Finally the battered walls of the undersea habitat imploded and billions of litres of icy black water boiled down and swept away man's creation as completely as though it had never been built.

10

The first submersible burst through a trough between the swells, leaping like a whale before belly-flopping into the blue-green sea. The waters had calmed considerably, the sky was crystal clear, and the waves were rolling at less than one metre.

Giordino quickly reached up to the hatch cover, gripped the quadrant of the handwheel, and twisted. After two turns it began to spin more easily until it hit the stops and he could push the cover open. A thin stream of water spilled inside the sub, and the cramped passengers thankfully inhaled the pure, clean air. For some it was their first trip to the surface in months.

Giordino climbed through the hatch and into the small oval-shaped tower that protected the opening from the waves. He'd expected to find an empty ocean, but as he scanned the horizons his mouth gaped in horror and astonishment.

Less than fifty metres away a junk, the classic Foochow Chinese sailing ship, was bearing down on the floating submersible. Square projecting deck over the bow and high oval-like stern, it carried three masts with square matting sails stretched by bamboo strips and a modern type jib. The painted eyeballs on the bows seemed to rise up and peer down at Giordino.

For a brief instant, Giordino could not believe the incredibility of the encounter. Of all the vast expanse of the Pacific Ocean, he'd surfaced at precisely the right spot to be rammed by a ship. He leaned over the sub's tower and shouted inside.

'Everybody out! Hurry!'

Two of the junk's crew spotted the turquoise submersible as it rose on a swell, and they began yelling at their helmsman to steer hard to starboard. But the gap was almost closed. Pushed by a brisk breeze, the gleaming teak hull bore down on the people spilling out of the sub and leaping into the water.

Nearer it came, the spray flying from the bows, the massive rudder swinging hard against the current. The crew of the junk stood rooted at the railing, staring in amazement at the unexpected appearance of the submersible in their path, fearful of an impact that could shatter the junk's bow and send it to the bottom.

The surprise, the reaction time of the spotters before they shouted a warning, the delay of the helmsman before he understood and twisted a modern wheel that replaced the traditional tiller, all worked toward an inevitable collision. Too late the ungainly vessel went into an agonizingly slow turn.

The shadow of the great projecting bow fell over Giordino as he grasped the outstretched hand from the last man inside. He was in the act of heaving him out when the junk's bow raised on a swell and came down on the stern of the submersible. There was no loud tearing noise of a crash, there was hardly a noise at all, except a soft splash followed by gurgling as the sub rolled to port and the water poured in through the open hatch.

Then came shouting on the decks of the junk as the crew pulled on the sails, dropping them like venetian blinds. The ship's engine coughed to life and was thrown into full astern as life rings were thrown over the side.

Giordino was pitched away from the junk as it slipped past only an arm's length away, yanking the last passenger through the hatch, grating the skin from his knees, and falling backward, forced underwater by the body weight of the man he saved. He had the foresight to keep his mouth closed but took saltwater up his nose. He snorted clear and gazed around. Thankfully, he counted six heads bobbing on the swells, some floating easily, some swimming for the life rings.

But the submersible had quickly filled and lost its buoyancy. Giordino watched in rage and frustration as the deep-sea craft slid under a swell stern-first and headed for the bottom.

He looked up at the passing junk and read the name on her ornately painted stern. She was called *Shanghai Shelly*. He swore a storm at the incredible display of dirty luck. How was it possible, he cursed, to be rammed by the only ship within hundreds of kilometres? He felt guilty and devastated for failing his friend Pitt.

He only knew that he must commandeer the second sub, dive to the bottom, and rescue Pitt no matter how vain the attempt. They had been closer than brothers, he owed too much to the maverick adventurer to let him go without a fight. He could never forget the many times Pitt had come through for him, times when he thought all hope had vanished. But first things first.

He looked about. 'If you're injured, raise a hand,' he called out.

Only one hand went up from a young geologist. 'I think I have a sprained ankle.'

'If that's all you've got,' grunted Giordino, 'consider yourself blessed.'

The junk came about and slowed, coming to a stop ten metres to the windward of the sub's survivors. An older man with snow-white hair in a windblown mass and a long curling white moustache bent over the railing. He cupped his hands to his mouth and shouted, 'Is anyone hurt? Shall we lower a boat?'

'Drop your gangway,' Giordino directed. 'We'll climb aboard.' Then he added, 'Keep a sharp watch. We've another sub about to surface.'

'I hear you.'

Within five minutes of the exchange, all of the NUMA crew were standing on the deck of the junk, all except the geologist with the bad ankle who was being lifted by a net over the side. The man who had hailed them walked up and spread out his hands apologetically.

'God, I'm sorry you lost your vessel. We didn't see you until it was too late.'

'Not your fault,' said Giordino, stepping forward. 'We came up almost under your keel. Your lookouts were more alert than we had any right to expect.'

'Was anyone lost?'

'No, we're all accounted for.'

'Thank God for that. This has been one crazy day. We picked another man out of the water not twenty kilometres to the west. He's in a bad way. Says his name is Jimmy Knox. He one of your men?'

'No,' Giordino said. 'The rest of my people are following in another submersible.'

'I've ordered my crew to keep their eyes peeled.'

'You're most courteous,' Giordino said mechanically, his mind taking one step at a time.

The stranger who seemed to be in command glanced around the open sea, a puzzled look on his face. 'Where are you all coming from?'

'Explanations later. Can I borrow your radio?'

'Of course. By the way, my name is Owen Murphy.'

'Al Giordino.'

'Right through there, Mr Giordino,' said Murphy, wisely putting his curiosity on hold. He motioned toward a doorway in the large cabin on the quarterdeck. 'While you're occupied, I'll see your men get into some dry clothes.'

'Much obliged,' Giordino threw over his shoulder as he hurried aft.

More than once, after the narrow escape from the submersible, the picture of Pitt and Plunkett standing helpless as millions of tons of water thundered down on them flashed through Giordino's mind. He was coldly aware that he was probably already too late, the chances of their being alive were somewhere between zero and non-existent. But the thought of abandoning them, giving them up for dead, was never remotely considered. If anything, he was more determined than ever to return to the seabed, regardless of the nightmare he might find.

The NUMA submersible piloted by Dave Lowden surfaced half a kilometre off the junk's beam. Thanks to the skilled ship handling of Murphy's helmsman, *Shanghai Shelly* came to a smart stop less than two metres from the sub's hatch tower. This time, all the submersible's crew, except Lowden, stepped aboard dry.

Giordino rushed back on deck after alerting Admiral Sandecker of the situation and advising the pilot of the flying boat to land alongside the junk. He stared straight down at Lowden, who was standing half in and half out of the sub.

'Stand by,' hailed Giordino. 'I want to take her back down.'

Lowden waved negatively. 'No can do. We developed a leak in the battery casing. Four of them shorted. Not nearly enough power left for another dive.'

Lowden's voice trailed away in icy silence. In the blank numbness of total failure, Giordino struck his fist against the railing. The NUMA scientists and engineers, Stacy and Salazar, even the crew of the junk, stared mutely into the beaten expression that lined his face.

'Not fair,' he muttered in a sudden seething anger. 'Not fair.'

He stood there a long time, staring down into the unsympathetic sea as if penetrating its depths. He was still standing there when Admiral Sandecker's aircraft appeared from the clouded sky and circled the drifting junk.

Stacy and Salazar were shown to the cabin where Jimmy

Knox lay barely conscious. A man with balding grey hair and a warm twinkle in his eyes rose from a chair by the bed and nodded.

'Hello, I'm Harry Deerfield.'

'Is it all right to come in?' Stacy asked.

'Do you know Mr Knox?'

'We're friends from the same British survey ship,' answered Salazar. 'How is he?'

'Resting comfortably,' said Deerfield, but the expression in his face suggested anything but a fast recovery.

'Are you a doctor?'

'Paediatrics actually. I took a six-week hiatus to help Owen Murphy sail his boat from the builder to San Diego.' He turned to Knox. 'You up to some visitors, Jimmy?'

Knox, pale and still, lifted the fingers of one hand in the affirmative. His face was swollen and blistered, but his eyes looked strong, and they noticeably brightened when he recognized Stacy and Salazar. 'Bless the Lord you made it safely,' he rasped. 'I never thought I'd see the two of you again. Where's that mad Plunkett?'

'He'll be along soon,' said Stacy, giving Salazar a keep-quiet look. 'What happened, Jimmy? What happened to the *Invincible*?'

Knox weakly shook his head. 'I don't know. I think there was some kind of explosion. One minute I was talking to you over the underwater phone, the next the whole ship was ripped apart and burning. I remember trying to raise you, but there was no response. And then I was climbing over debris and dead bodies as the ship sank under me.'

'Gone?' Salazar muttered, refusing to accept what he heard. 'The ship sunk and our crew gone?'

Knox gave an imperceptible nod. 'I watched her go to the bottom. I shouted and kept a constant lookout for the others who might have survived. The sea was empty. I don't know how long I floated or how far before Mr Murphy and his crew spotted and picked me up. They searched the immediate area but found nothing. They said I must be the only survivor.'

'But what of the two ships that were nearby when we began our dive?' asked Stacy.

'I saw no sign of them. They had vanished too.'

Knox's voice died to a whisper, and it was obvious he was losing a battle to keep from slipping into unconsciousness. The will was there but the body was exhausted. His eyes closed and his head rolled slightly to one side.

Dr Deerfield motioned Stacy and Salazar toward the door. 'You can talk again later, after he's rested.'

'He *will* recover?' asked Stacy softly.

'I can't say,' Deerfield hedged in good medical tradition.

'What exactly is wrong with him?'

'Two or more cracked ribs as far as I can tell without an X-ray. Swollen ankle, either a sprain or a fracture. Contusions, first degree burns. Those are injuries I can cope with. The rest of his symptoms are not what I'd expect from a man who survived a shipwreck.'

'What are you talking about?' Salazar asked.

'Fever, arterial hypotension, a fancy name for low blood pressure, severe erythema, stomach cramps, strange blistering.'

'And the cause?'

'Not exactly my field,' Deerfield said heavily. 'I've only read a couple of articles in medical journals. But I believe I'm safe in saying Jimmy's most serious condition was caused by exposure to a supralethal dose of radiation.'

Stacy was silent a moment, then, 'Nuclear radiation?'

Deerfield nodded. 'I wish I was wrong, but the facts bear me out.'

'Surely you can do something to save him?'

Deerfield gestured around the cabin. 'Look around you,' he said sourly. 'Does this look like a hospital? I came on this cruise as a deckhand. My medical kit contains only pills and bandages for emergency treatment. He can't be airlifted by helicopter until we're closer to land. And even then I doubt whether he can be saved with the therapeutic treatments currently available.'

'Hang them!' Knox cried, startling everyone. His eyes blinked open suddenly, gazing through the people in the cabin at some unknown image beyond the bulkhead. 'Hang the murdering bastards!'

They stared at him in astonishment. Salazar stood shaken. Stacy and Deerfield rushed toward the bed to calm Knox as he feebly tried to lift himself in an upright position.

'Hang the bastards!' Knox repeated with a vengeance. It was as though he was uttering a curse. 'They'll murder again. Hang them!'

But before Deerfield could inject him with a sedative, Knox stiffened, his eyes glistened for an instant, and then a misty film coated them and he fell back, gave a great heaving sigh, and went limp.

Deerfield swiftly applied cardiopulmonary resuscitation, fearful that Knox was too devastated by acute radiation sickness to bring back. He continued until he was panting from fatigue and sweating streams in the humid atmosphere. Finally he acknowledged sadly that he had done everything within his limited power. No man or miracle could bring Jimmy Knox back.

'I'm sorry,' he murmured between breaths.

As if under a hypnotic spell, Stacy and Salazar slowly walked from the cabin. Salazar remained quiet while Stacy began to softly cry. After a few moments, she wiped away the tears with her hand and straightened.

'He saw something,' she murmured.

Salazar looked at her. 'Saw what?'

'He knew, in some incredible way he knew.' She turned and looked through the open doorway to the silent figure on the bunk. 'Just before the end, Jimmy could see who was responsible for the horrible mass death and destruction.'

11

You could tell from his body, slim almost to the state of emaciation, that he was a fitness and nutrition fanatic. He was short, chin and chest thrust out like a bantam rooster, and nattily dressed in a light blue golf shirt with matching pants and a Panama straw hat pulled tight over closely cropped red hair to keep it from blowing away. He had an exactingly trimmed red Vandyke beard that came to a point so sharp you'd swear he could stab flesh with it if he lunged suddenly.

He stormed up the gangway of the junk, a huge cigar poked in his mouth throwing sparks from the breeze, as regally as if he was holding court. If style awards were handed out for dramatic entrances, Admiral James Sandecker, Director of the National Underwater and Marine Agency, would have won hands down.

His face looked strained from the grievous news he'd received from Giordino while in flight. As soon as his feet hit *Shanghai Shelly*'s deck, he raised his hand at the pilot of the flying boat, who gave an acknowledging wave. The aircraft turned into the wind and bounced forward over the crests of the waves until it was airborne and soaring in a graceful bank southeast toward the Hawaiian Islands.

Giordino and Murphy stepped forward. Sandecker focused his gaze on the junk's owner.

'Hello, Owen. I never expected to meet you out here.'

Murphy smiled and shook hands. 'Likewise, Jim. Welcome aboard. It's good to see you.' He paused and pointed to the grim-faced NUMA team who were crowded around them on the open deck. 'Now maybe someone will tell me what that big light and thunder show was on the horizon yesterday, and why all these people are popping up in the middle of the ocean.'

Sandecker did not reply directly. He looked about the deck and up at the draped sails. 'What have you got yourself here?'

'Had it custom built in Shanghai. My crew and I were sailing her to Honolulu and then on to San Diego, where I plan to dock her.'

'You know each other?' Giordino asked finally.

Sandecker nodded. 'This old pirate and I went to Annapolis together. Only Owen was smarter. He resigned from the Navy and launched an electronics company. Now he's got more money than the US Treasury.'

Murphy smiled. 'Don't I wish.'

Sandecker suddenly turned serious. 'What news of the base since you briefed me over the radio?' he asked Giordino.

'We're afraid it's gone,' Giordino replied quietly. 'Underwater phone communications from our remaining sub have gone unanswered. Keith Harris thinks the major shock wave must have struck shortly after we evacuated. As I reported, there wasn't enough space to evacuate everybody in two subs. Pitt and a British marine scientist volunteered to stay below.'

'What's being done to save them?' Sandecker demanded.

Giordino looked visibly cast down, as though all emotion had been drained away. 'We've run out of options.'

Sandecker went cold in the face. 'You fell down on the job, mister. You led me to believe you were returning in the backup submersible.'

'That was before Lowden surfaced with shorted batteries!' Giordino snapped back resentfully. 'With the first sub sunk and the second inoperable, we were stone-walled.'

Sandecker's expression softened, the coldness was gone, his eyes saddened. He realized Giordino had been dogged by ill luck. To even suggest the little Italian had not tried his best was wrong, and he regretted it. But he was shaken by Pitt's apparent loss too.

To him, Pitt was the son he never had. He'd have ordered out an entire army of specially trained men and secret equipment the American public had no idea existed if fate granted him another thirty-six hours. Admiral Sandecker had that kind of power in the nation's capital. He didn't arrive where he was because he'd answered a help wanted ad in the *Washington Post*.

He said, 'Any chance the batteries can be repaired?'

Giordino nodded over the side at the submersible rolling in the swells twenty metres away, tethered on a stern line to *Shanghai Shelly*. 'Lowden is working like a madman trying for a quick fix, but he's not optimistic.'

'If anyone is to blame, it's me,' Murphy said solemnly.

'Pitt could still be alive,' said Giordino, ignoring Murphy. 'He's not a man who dies easily.'

'Yes.' Sandecker paused, then went on almost absently. 'He's proven that many times in the past.'

Giordino stared at the admiral, a spark glowing in his eyes. 'If we can get another submersible out here . . .'

'The *Deep Quest* can dive to ten thousand metres,' Sandecker said, coming back on keel. 'She's sitting on our dock in Los Angeles Harbor. I can have her loaded aboard an Air Force C-five and on her way here by sundown.'

'I didn't know a C-five could land on water,' Murphy interrupted.

'They can't,' Sandecker said definitely. 'The *Deep Quest*, all twelve metric tons of her, will be air-dropped out the cargo doors.' He glanced at his watch. 'I'd guess about eight hours from now.'

'You're going to drop a twelve-ton submersible out of an aeroplane by parachute?'

'Why the hell not? It'd take a week to get here by boat.'

Giordino stared at the deck thoughtfully. 'We could

eliminate a mass of problems if we worked off a support ship with launch and retrieval capacity.'

'The *Sounder* is the closest ocean survey ship to our area that fits the picture. She's sonar-mapping the seafloor south of the Aleutians. I'll order her captain to cut his mission and head toward our position as fast as he can push her.'

'How can I be of help?' asked Murphy. 'After sinking your sub, the least I can do is offer the services of my ship and crew.'

Giordino smiled inwardly as Sandecker lifted his arms and gripped Murphy's shoulders. Laying on the hands, Pitt used to call it. Sandecker didn't just ask an unsuspecting subject for a favour, he made his victims feel as if they were being baptized.

'Owen,' the admiral said in his most reverent tone, 'NUMA will be in your debt if we can use your junk as a fleet command ship.'

Owen Murphy was no slouch when it came to recognizing a con job. 'What fleet?' he asked with feigned innocence.

'Why, half the United States Navy is converging on us,' answered Sandecker, as if his secret briefing by Raymond Jordan was common knowledge. 'I wouldn't be surprised if one of their nuclear submarines was cruising under our hull this minute.'

It was, Murphy mused, the craziest tale he'd ever heard in his life. But no one on board *Shanghai Shelly*, excepting the admiral himself, had the slightest notion of how prophetic his words were. Nor were they aware that the rescue attempt was the opening act for the main event.

Twenty kilometres away, the attack submarine *Tucson* was running at a depth of 400 metres and closing on the junk's position. She was early. Her skipper, Commander Beau Morton, had driven her hard after receiving orders at Pearl Harbor to reach the explosion area at full speed. On arrival, his mission was to run tests on underwater radiological contamination and salvage any floating debris that could be safely brought aboard.

Morton casually leaned against a bulkhead with an empty coffee cup dangling in one hand, watching Lieutenant Commander Sam Hauser of the Naval Radiological Defense Laboratory. The Navy scientist was indifferent to Morton's presence. He was intent on monitoring his radiochemical instruments and computing beta and gamma intensities received from probes trailing behind the submarine.

'Are we glowing in the dark yet?' asked Morton sarcastically.

'Radioactivity is pretty unevenly distributed,' replied Hauser. 'But well below maximum permissible exposure. Heaviest concentration is above.'

'A surface detonation?'

'A ship, yes, not a submarine. Most of the contamination was airborne.'

'Any danger to that Chinese junk north of us?'

Hauser shook his head. 'They should have been too far upwind to receive anything but a trace dosage.'

'And now that they're drifting through the detonation area?' Morton persisted.

'Due to the high winds and turbulent seas during and immediately after the explosion,' Hauser explained patiently, 'the worst of the radiation was carried into the atmosphere and far to the east. They should be within safe limits where they are.'

The compartment phone gave off a soft high-tech chime. Hauser picked it up. 'Yes?'

'Is the captain there, sir?'

'Hold on.' He handed the receiver to Morton.

'This is the captain.'

'Sir, Sonarman Kaiser. I have a contact. I think you should listen to it.'

'Be right there.' Morton hung up the phone, wondering

abstractedly why Kaiser didn't routinely call over the intercom.

The commander found Sonarman First Class Richard Kaiser leaning over his console listening through his earphones, a bewildered expression furrowing his brow. Morton's executive officer, Lieutenant Commander Ken Fazio, was pressing a spare set of phones against his ears. He looked downright dumbstruck.

'You have a contact?' asked Morton.

Kaiser didn't answer immediately but went on listening for a few more moments. At last he pulled up the phone over his left ear and muttered, 'This is crazy.'

'Crazy?'

'I'm getting a signal that shouldn't be.'

Fazio shook his head as if agreeing. 'Beats me.'

'Care to let me in on your secret?' Morton asked impatiently.

'I'll put it on the speaker,' said Kaiser.

Morton and several officers and men who had received the news of a strange contact by osmosis gathered around the sonar enclosure, staring up at the speaker expectantly. The sounds were not perfect but they were clear enough to be understood. No high-pitched squeak of whales, no whirring crick of propeller cavitation, but rather voices singing.

> 'And every night when the starfish came out,
> I'd hug and kiss her so.
> Oh, what a time I had with Minnie the Mermaid
> Down in her seamy bungalow.'

Morton fixed Kaiser with a cold stare. 'What's the gag?'

'No gag, sir.'

'It must be coming from that Chinese junk.'

'No, sir, not the junk or any other surface vessel.'

96

'Another submarine?' Morton inquired sceptically. 'A Russian maybe?'

'Not unless they're building them ten times tougher than ours,' said Fazio.

'What range and bearing?' Morton demanded.

Kaiser was hesitant. He had the look of a little boy who was in trouble and afraid to tell the truth.

'No horizontal compass bearing, sir. The singing is coming from the bottom of the sea, five thousand metres straight down.'

12

Yellowish ooze, made up of microscopic skeletons from a marine plant called the diatom, slowly drifted away in serpentine clouds, shrouded by the total blackness of the abyssal deep.

The bottom of the gorge where the NUMA mining station once stood had been filled by silt and rock slides into a broken, irregular plain littered with half-buried boulders and scattered wreckage. There should have been a deathly silence after the final rumblings of the earthquake died away, but a warped chorus of 'Minnie the Mermaid' rose from under the desolated wasteland and rippled out into the liquid void.

If one could have walked over the debris field to the sound source, they'd have found a single antenna shaft, bent and twisted, poking up through the mud. A greyish-pink ratfish briefly inspected the antenna but, finding it unsavoury, flicked its pointed tail and lazily swam into the dark.

Almost before the ratfish disappeared, the silt a few metres from the antenna began to stir, swirling in an ever-widening vortex that was weirdly illuminated from below. Suddenly a shaft of light burst through the ooze, joined by a mechanical hand shaped like a scoop and articulated at the wrist. The steel apparition paused and straightened like a prairie dog standing on its haunches and sniffing the horizon for a coyote.

Then the scoop arched downward, gouging through the seabed, excavating a deep trench that began to ascend at one end like a ramp. When it struck a boulder too large to fit in the scoop, a great metal claw appeared magically alongside. The claw's talon-like pincers bit around the boulder, yanked it free from the sediment, and dropped it clear of the trench in a billowing mud cloud. The claw then swung clear, and the scoop continued digging.

'Nice work, Mr Pitt,' said Plunkett, grinning with relief. 'You'll have us out and driving through the countryside by teatime.'

Pitt lay back in a reclining seat, staring up at a TV monitor with the same attentive concern he usually reserved for a football game. 'We're not on the road yet.'

'Boarding one of your Deep Sea Mining Vehicles and running it into the air pressure lock before the major quake hit was a stroke of genius.'

'I wouldn't go that far,' Pitt muttered while programming the vehicle's computer to slightly alter the angle of the scoop. 'Call it theft of Mr Spock's logic.'

'The air-lock walls held,' Plunkett argued. 'But for fickle providence, we'd have been crushed like bugs.'

'The chamber was built to withstand four times the pressure of the other project structures,' Pitt said with a quiet unarguable assertion. 'Fickle providence, as you call it, gave us time to pressurize the lock, open the outer door, and move forward enough for the scoop and claw to operate before the avalanche struck. Otherwise we'd be trapped for longer than I care to think about.'

'Oh, bloody hell.' Plunkett laughed. There was little that fazed him. 'What does it matter so long as we cheat the grave.'

'I wish you wouldn't use the word "grave".'

'Sorry.' Plunkett sat in a seat beside and slightly to the rear of Pitt. He stared around the interior of the DSMV. 'A damned fine machine. What's its power source?'

'A small nuclear reactor.'

'Nuclear, heh? You Yanks never cease to amaze me. I'll wager we can drive this monster right across the bottom and onto Waikiki Beach.'

'You'd win your bet,' said Pitt with a faint grin. '*Big*

John's reactor and life-support systems could get us there. The only problem being a flat-out speed of five kilometres per hour. We'd die of starvation a good week before we arrived.'

'You didn't pack a lunch?' Plunkett asked humorously.

'Not even an apple.'

Plunkett gave Pitt a dry look. 'Even death would be a treat if I didn't have to hear that blasted tune again.'

'You don't care for "Minnie"?' Pitt asked in mock surprise.

'After hearing the chorus for the twentieth time, no.'

'With the telephone housing smashed, our only contact with the surface is the acoustic radio transmitter. Not nearly enough range for conversation, but it's all we've got. I can offer you Strauss waltzes or the big band sounds of the forties, but they wouldn't be appropriate.'

'I don't think much of your musical inventory,' Plunkett grunted. Then he looked at Pitt. 'What's wrong with Strauss?'

'Instrumental,' Pitt answered. 'Distorted violin music can sound like whales or several other aquatic mammals through water. Minnie is a vocal. If anyone on the surface is listening, they'll know someone down here is still sucking air. No matter how garbled, there's no mistaking good old human babble.'

'For all the good that will do,' said Plunkett. 'If a rescue mission is launched, there's no way we can transfer from this vehicle to a submersible without a pressure lock. A commodity totally lacking on your otherwise remarkable tractor. If I may speak realistically, I fail to see anything in the near future but our inevitable demise.'

'I wish you wouldn't use the word "demise".'

Plunkett reached into a pocket of his big woollen sweater and produced a flask. 'Only about four swigs left, but it ought to keep our spirits up for a while.'

Pitt took the offered flask as a muffled rumble shook the

big tracked vehicle. The scoop had screeched into a mass of stone and attempted to lift it clear. Far beyond its load safety level, it struggled and groaned to hoist the debris. Like an Olympic weight lifter straining for the gold, the scoop heaved its massive burden above the seafloor and dumped it in a growing mound along the trench.

The outside lights failed to penetrate the mud clouds, and the monitors inside the control cabin showed only constantly merging colours of yellow and grey. But the computer monitor gave a three-dimensional sonar image that displayed the extent of the excavation.

Fully five hours had elapsed since Pitt began the digging operation. At last he could see an enhanced display showing a narrow but reasonably clear corridor slanting toward the surface of the seabed.

'We'll scrape some paint off the fenders, but I think we can squeeze through,' Pitt said confidently.

Plunkett's face lit up. 'Kick her in the butt, Mr Pitt. I'm sick to death of staring at this filthy muck.'

Pitt's head tilted slightly and he gave a wink of one green eye. 'As you wish, Mr Plunkett.' He took over manual control from the computer and rubbed his hands like a pianist about to play. 'Cross your fingers the tracks get a firm grip on the sediment or we'll have to take up permanent residence.'

He gently eased the throttle control forward. The wide track crawlers on the sides of *Big John* slowly began to move, churning through the soft ooze, turning faster as Pitt increased the power. Gradually they inched forward. Then one track caught and gripped on a layer of small stones, slewing the giant mining machine into the opposite side of the trench. Pitt fought to correct, but the wall gave way and the mudflow spread over one side of the vehicle.

He rammed the throttle against its stop, then pulled back as he shifted into reverse, then full forward again as he rocked *Big John* back and forth. The compact nuclear reactor had the power, but the tracks could not find the traction. Rock and silt flew from the pivoted cleats as they ripped through the slimy gumbo.

Still the DSMV remained stuck in its narrow prison.

'Maybe we should call a halt and scoop the mud off,' said Plunkett, dead serious. 'Or better yet, sit back and review the situation.'

Pitt spared a few moments to give the big Britisher a hard, icy stare. Plunkett swore Pitt's eyes burned out a goodly number of his brain cells.

'A lot of my people and I worked hard and long to build the first deep-water community,' he said in a voice that bordered on satanic. 'And someone, somewhere, is responsible for its destruction. They're also the cause behind the loss of your submersible, your support ship, and its crew. *That's* the situation. Now, speaking for myself, I'm going to bust through this crap if I have to tear the guts out of this thing, get to the surface in one piece, find the scum behind the disaster, and punch their teeth down their lungs.'

Then he turned and sent the tracks thrashing through the encasement of silt and rock. With an awkward wobble, the great machine dug in and lurched a metre forward, then two metres.

Plunkett sat like a tree, thoroughly intimidated yet quite convinced. By God, he thought, I think the man might damn well do it!

13

Eight thousand kilometres distant, deep in a shaft carved out of volcanic rock, a crew of diggers stepped aside as two men moved forward and peered through an excavated break in a concrete wall. A sickening stench drifted from the opening, filling the twenty-man mining crew with a dread of the unknown.

The floodlights illuminating the narrow shaft cast eerie distorted shadows in what appeared to be a large tunnel beyond the one-metre-thick concrete. Inside, an old rusty truck could be distinguished, surrounded by what looked to be a vast bed of grey-brown scrubwood.

Despite the cool damp air deep under the battle-scarred slopes of Corregidor Island at the entrance to Manila Bay, the two men who peered through the hole were sweating heavily. After years of research, they knew they were on the brink of discovering part of the huge World War II cache of war loot known as 'Yamashita's Gold', named after General Yamashita Tomoyuki, commander of Japanese forces in the Philippines after October of 1944.

The immense hoard that was seized by the Japanese during the war – from China, the Southeast Asian countries, the Dutch East Indies, and the Philippines – consisted of thousands of metric tons of exotic gems and jewellery, silver and gold bullion, and Buddhas and Catholic altarpieces encrusted with priceless gems and cast in solid gold.

Manila had been the collection point for future transshipment to Japan, but because of heavy shipping losses in the later stages of the war from American submarines, less than twenty percent of the loot actually arrived in Tokyo. With nowhere to go and faced with certain invasion by the avenging Americans, the Japanese guardians of the treasure were in a dilemma. They weren't about to give it back to the nations and people they had pillaged. Their only option was to hide the immense hoard in over a hundred different sites on and around the island of Luzon, hoping to return after the war and smuggle it home.

Conservative estimates of the stolen treasure on the current money markets were put at between 450 and 500 billion dollars.

The digging in this particular location on Corregidor, a few hundred metres west and a good kilometre deeper than the lateral tunnel that served as General Douglas MacArthur's headquarters before he was evacuated to Australia, had gone on for four months. Using copies of old OSS maps recently found buried in CIA archives at Langley, American and Philippine intelligence agents worked as a team directing the excavation. It was exhausting and very slow going.

The map instructions were deciphered from an ancient Japanese dialect unused for a thousand years. The shaft to the treasure location had to be approached from a side angle because the original access tunnel was booby-trapped with several one- and two-thousand-pound bombs and designed to collapse from a direct entry. The penetration through the twenty-mile labyrinth burrowed by the Japanese during their occupation of Luzon had to be precisely calculated or the miners might have wasted months by excavating on the wrong level and missing the treasure tunnel by centimetres.

The taller of the two men, Frank Mancuso, gestured for a large flashlight. One was passed, and he thrust it through the breach in the wall. His face turned pale in the yellow half-light. With numbed horror he realized what the scrubwood really was.

Rico Acosta, a mining engineer attached to the Philippine security forces, moved in closer to Mancuso. 'What do you see, Frank?'

'Bones,' Mancuso said, his voice just above a whisper. 'Skeletons. God, there must be hundreds of them in there.' He stepped back and nodded at Acosta.

The short little man motioned the diggers toward the opening. 'Widen it up,' he ordered.

It took less than an hour for the crew of Philippine miners to smash a hole with sledgehammers large enough for a man to pass through. The cement forming the tunnel walls was of poor quality, crusty and crumbling, and easy to break away. It was looked upon as a piece of luck, since none of them wished to run the risk of a cave-in by using explosives.

Mancuso sat off to one side and lit a stubby curved pipe while he waited. At forty-two, he still kept the long-limbed, thin body of a basketball player. His lengthy brown hair draped around the nape of his neck in oily strands badly in need of washing, and his soft, round Germanic face seemed better suited to an accountant than a get-dirty engineer. His blue eyes had a dreamy quality that never seemed to focus, and yet they took everything in view and then some.

A graduate of the Colorado School of Mines, he'd spent his early years wandering the world prospecting and working mines in search of precious gems. Opals in Australia, emeralds in Colombia, and rubies in Tanzania, with varying degrees of success. There was also a fruitless three-year hunt on Japan's northern island of Hokkaido for the rarest of the rare, red painite.

Shortly before he reached thirty, he was courted and recruited by an obscure intelligence agency in Washington and appointed a special agent under contract. His first assignment was to search for Yamashita's gold as part of a Philippine security force team.

The excavation was carried out in the strictest secrecy. None of the gold or gems were to be turned over to their former owners. All treasure found was to be kept by the Philippine government to decrease the debt burden and pump up the sagging economy devastated by the incalculable financial rape of the Marcos regime.

His counterpart, Acosta, had also served as a mining engineer before joining the security forces. He was tall for a Filipino, and his eyes indicated more than a trace of Chinese ancestry.

'So the stories are true,' said Acosta.

Mancuso looked up. 'Sorry?'

'The Nips forcing Allied prisoners to dig these tunnels, and then burying them alive so they could never reveal the location.'

'It looks that way. We'll know better when we get inside.'

Acosta lifted his hard hat and wiped one sleeve across his forehead. 'My grandfather was in the Fifty-seventh Philippine Scouts. He was taken prisoner and thrown in the Spanish dungeon at Fort Santiago. He never came out. Over two thousand POWs died either from suffocation or starvation. The count was never known.'

Mancuso nodded heavily. 'Later generations can't imagine the ungodly barbarism that stained the Pacific theatre of the war.' He drew from the pipe and exhaled a puff of blue smoke before continuing. 'The terrible statistic is that fifty-seven percent of the Allied soldiers in Japanese prison camps died, versus only one percent of those held by the Germans.'

'Strange the Japanese didn't come back and make an all-out effort to snatch the treasure,' said Acosta.

'Groups posing as construction companies *did* try to obtain contracts for postwar rebuilding so they could covertly excavate for the gold, but once Ferdinand Marcos learned of the treasure, he slammed the door and searched for it himself.'

'And he found some,' added Acosta. 'Maybe thirty billion US dollars' worth, which he smuggled out of the country before he was thrown out of office.'

'Plus what he stole from your own people.'

Acosta spat on the shaft floor disgustedly. 'He and his wife were sick with greed. It will take us a hundred years to recover from their rule.'

The foreman of the diggers waved a hand, beckoning them. 'You should be able to squeeze through now,' he said.

'Go ahead.' Acosta nodded to Mancuso. 'You first.'

The odour was rotten and nauseating. Mancuso tied a bandanna around his lower face and wriggled through the narrow breach in the tunnel wall. He heard a soft snap followed by a splashing sound as his boots met a small puddle. Standing clear, he waited a moment, hearing water dripping from cracks in the arched ceiling. Then he switched his flashlight on, aiming its naked beam downward.

He had stepped on and broken an outstretched bony arm that was attached to a skeleton dressed in the mouldering remains of a uniform and covered with slime. A pair of encrusted dog tags lay off to one side of the skull, the tiny chain still strung around the neck.

Mancuso knelt and held one of the tags under the light. He rubbed off the grime with one index finger and thumb until he could make out a name: *William A. Miller*.

There was an Army serial number, but Mancuso let the tag drop. Once he notified his superior of what he found, a graves registration team would be sent to Corregidor, and William A. Miller and his long-dead comrades would be returned to their homes for honoured burial fifty years late.

Mancuso turned and swung the flashlight in a full circle. As far as the beam could reach, the tunnel was carpeted with skeletons, some scattered, some heaped in piles. He'd studied several more ID tags before Acosta entered with a small floodlight on a cord.

'Holy mother of Jesus,' he gasped as he viewed the grisly remains. 'An army of the dead.'

'An Allied army,' said Mancuso. 'American, Philippine, even a few British and Australian. Looks like the Japs brought prisoners to Manila from other sectors of the war for slave labour.'

'Only God knows the hell they suffered,' Acosta muttered, his face reddening with anger, the bile rising in his throat. He fingered a cross hanging around his neck. 'How were they murdered?'

'No sign of bullet injuries. They must have suffocated after being sealed in.'

'Those who gave the orders for this mass execution must pay.'

'They're probably dead, killed in the slaughter around Manila by MacArthur's army. And if they're still breathing, their trail is cold. The Allies in the Pacific were too forgiving. No prolonged manhunt was launched after those responsible for atrocities, like the Jews did with the Nazis. If they haven't been found and hanged by now, they never will.'

'They must still pay,' Acosta repeated, his anger turned to frustrated hatred.

'Don't waste thoughts on revenge,' said Mancuso. 'Our job is to locate the gold.'

He walked toward the first truck in a long column that stood parked amid the dead. The tyres were flattened and the canvas top over the bed had rotted under the constant drip of the water. He jerked down the rusty tailgate and shone his light inside. Except for a litter of wood from broken crates it was empty.

A foreboding began to squeeze Mancuso's stomach. He rushed to the next truck, carefully stepping around and over the dead, his boots splashing in the slime-covered water. His sweat from the dampness had turned cold. He needed a strong effort of will to go on, a growing fear now of what he might not find.

The second truck was empty, as were the next six. Two hundred metres into the tunnel, he came to a blockage from a cave-in his miner's eye recognized as caused by explosives. But the shocker was the sight of a small auto house trailer whose modern aluminium construction did not fit in the time frame of the 1940s. There were no signs on the sides, but Mancuso noted the manufacturer's markings on the tyres.

He climbed a metal stand of steps and stopped in the doorway, playing the beam of his flashlight around the interior. It was furnished as an office, the kind often seen on construction sites.

Acosta came up, followed by four of his men who unreeled the cable to his floodlight. He stood back and lit the entire trailer in a bright halo.

'Where in hell did this come from?' Acosta said in astonishment.

'Bring your light inside,' said Mancuso, his worst fear realized.

With the added brightness they could see the trailer was clean. The desks were uncluttered, the wastebaskets emptied, and no ashtrays were to be seen anywhere. The only sign of previous occupancy was a construction worker's hard hat perched on a hook and a large blackboard hung on one wall. Mancuso studied the lined columns. The numerals were in Arabic, while the headings were written in katakana symbols.

'A schedule?' asked Acosta.

'An inventory of the treasure.'

Acosta sank into a chair behind a desk. 'Gone, all of it smuggled away.'

'About twenty-five years ago, according to a date on the board.'

'Marcos?' asked Acosta. 'He must have gotten here first.'

'No, not Marcos,' Mancuso answered as though he'd always known the truth. 'The Japanese. They returned, took the gold, and left us with the bones.'

14

Curtis Meeker parked his wife's Mercury Cougar and casually strode the three blocks to Ford's Theatre between E and F streets on Tenth. He buttoned his overcoat against the brisk fall air and fell in step with a group of senior citizens who were on a late Saturday evening walking tour of the capital city.

Their guide stopped them in front of the theatre where John Wilkes Booth had shot Abraham Lincoln and gave a brief lecture before taking them across the street to the Peterson House where the President had died. Unobtrusively, Meeker slipped away, flipped his federal shield at the doorman, and passed into the lobby of the theatre. He conversed briefly with the manager and then sat down on a sofa, where he appeared to be calmly reading a programme.

To any late first-nighters who quickly passed by Meeker to their seats, he looked like an indifferent theatregoer who was bored with the restaging of the late-nineteenth-century play based on the Spanish American War and preferred to sit it out in the lobby.

Meeker was definitely not a tourist or a theatregoer. His title was Deputy Director of Advanced Technical Operations, and he seldom went anywhere at night except to his office, where he studied satellite intelligence photos.

He was basically a shy man who rarely spoke more than one or two sentences at a time, but he was highly respected by intelligence circles as the best satellite photo analyst in the business. He was what women refer to as a nice-looking man, black hair speckled with grey, kind face, easy smile, and eyes that reflected friendliness.

While his attention seemed locked on the programme,

one hand slipped into a pocket and pressed a button on a transmitter.

Inside the theatre Raymond Jordan was fighting to stay awake. Under his wife's sideways glare he yawned as a defence against the hundred-year-old dialogue. Mercifully, to the audience sitting in the old-style hard seats, the plays and acts at Ford's Theatre were short. Jordan twisted to a more comfortable position in the hard wooden seat and allowed his mind to drift from the play to a fishing trip he'd planned for the following day.

Suddenly his reverie was broken by three soft beeps on a digital watch on his wrist. It was what was called a Delta watch because of the code it received, and was labelled as a Raytech so it looked ordinary and wouldn't stand out. He cupped one hand over the crystal display that lit up on the dial. The Delta code alerted him to the severity of the situation and indicated someone would fetch or meet him.

He whispered an excuse to his wife and made his way to the aisle and then to the lobby. When Jordan recognized Meeker, his face clouded. Though he welcomed any interruption, he was not happy that it concerned some kind of crisis.

'What's the situation?' he asked without preamble.

'We know what ship carried the bomb,' answered Meeker, rising to his feet.

'We can't talk here.'

'I've arranged with the manager for the theatre's executive suite. I can brief you privately in there.'

Jordan knew the room. He led off with Meeker trailing and entered an anteroom furnished in 1860s decor. He closed the door and stared at Meeker. 'Are you certain? There is no mistake?'

Meeker shook his head solemnly. 'Photos from an earlier weather bird showed three ships in the area. We activated our old Sky King intelligence satellite as it passed over after the explosion and factored out two of the ships.'

'How?'

'With computer enhancement of the radar-sonar system that enables us to see through water as though it was transparent.'

'Have you briefed your people?'

'Yes.'

Jordan stared Meeker in the eye. 'Are you satisfied with your conclusions?'

'I haven't a doubt,' Meeker replied squarely.

'The proof is solid?'

'Yes.'

'You know you'll share the responsibility if you've screwed up.'

'As soon as I've made my report, I'm going home and sleep like a baby . . . Well almost.'

Jordan relaxed and settled into a chair beside a table. He looked up at Meeker expectantly. 'Okay, what have you got?'

Meeker pulled a leather-bound file folder from a deep pocket inside his overcoat and laid it on the table.

Jordan smiled. 'You don't believe in briefcases, I see.'

'I like my hands free,' Meeker said with a shrug. He opened the file and spread out five photographs. The first three showed the ships on the surface with incredible detail. 'Here you see the Norwegian passenger-cargo liner circling the drifting Japanese auto carrier. Twelve kilometres away, the British survey ship is in the act of lowering a submersible into the sea.'

'The *before* shot,' said Jordan.

Meeker nodded. 'The next two are from the Sky King taken after the explosion, revealing two shattered hulks on the bottom. The third was disintegrated. Except for a few scattered pieces of her engines on the seabed, there is virtually nothing left of her.'

'Which one was she?' Jordan asked slowly, as if anticipating the answer.

'We made positive IDs on the two that sank intact.' Meeker paused to turn from the photographs and look into Jordan's eyes as if to underscore his answer. 'The ship that was transporting the bomb was the Japanese auto carrier.'

Jordan sighed and leaned back in the chair. 'It doesn't come as a great shock that Japan has the bomb. They've had the technology for years.'

'The giveaway came when they built a liquid-metal fast-breeder reactor. Fissioning with fast neutrons, the breeder creates more plutonium fuel than it burns. The first step in producing nuclear weaponry.'

'You've done your homework,' said Jordan.

'I have to know what to look for.'

'Like an elusive, yet-to-be-discovered factory for nuclear weapons production,' Jordan said acidly.

Meeker looked at him unwaveringly, then smiled. 'Your ground intelligence hasn't got a clue where they're making them either.'

'True,' Jordan admitted. 'The Japs have accomplished an incredible cover-up. I've a hunch their government leaders are in the dark as well.'

'If their production facility is above ground, our new satellite detection array would have nailed it.'

'Odd there are no areas of unusual radioactivity.'

'We've detected nothing outside their electrical power reactors and a nuclear waste dump near a coastal town called Rokota.'

'I've seen the reports,' said Jordan. 'They sank a four-thousand-metre shaft to throw their waste. Could it be we've overlooked something?'

Meeker gave a negative shake of his head. 'We've yet to detect indications of extensive construction or the right type of traffic in or out of the area.'

'Damn!' Jordan snapped. 'Japan freely sails the oceans with nuclear bombs destined for United States ports while we sit on our thumbs without knowing the site where they're manufactured, their final destinations, or the plan behind the whole operation.'

'You did say "bombs", plural?' asked Meeker.

'The readings from the seismographic centre in Colorado show there was a second detonation a millisecond after the first.'

'Too bad you couldn't have launched a major operation to find the answer ten years ago.'

'With what funding?' Jordan grunted. 'The last administration gutted intelligence-gathering budgets. All that politicians are interested in are Russia and the Middle East. The last people the State Department will allow us to probe are our good buddies in Japan. Two retired agents we've had to keep under contract are all we're allowed there. Israel is another nation that's off limits. You wouldn't believe the times we were ordered to look the other way while the Mossad pulled off deceptions the Arabs took the blame for.'

'The President will *have* to give you full discretionary power when you show him the seriousness of the situation.'

'I'll know first thing in the morning after I brief him.' Jordan's smooth, polished mask was showing a tiny crack, and his voice turned ice cold. 'No matter how we attack this thing, we'll be playing catch up. What scares me, really puts the fear of God in me, is that we're already too late to cut off the plot in midstream.'

The sounds of voices came through the lobby. The play was over and the audience was flowing into the lobby.

Jordan came to his feet. 'I'll have to break off and make an appearance or my wife will play iceberg on the ride home. Thanks for alerting me to your bird's discovery.'

'There is one more thing,' said Meeker. He slipped another photograph out of the file folder and held it up to the light.

Jordan peered at an object in the centre of the photo. 'Looks like some kind of big farm tractor. What's the significance?'

'What you see is an unknown deep-sea vehicle driving over the sea bottom five thousand metres below the surface, not more than twenty kilometres from the explosion area. You know who owns it or what it's doing there?'

'Yes . . .' Jordan said slowly. 'I didn't, but I do now. Thank you, Curtis.'

Jordan turned from a totally mystified Meeker, opened the door, and melted into the throng leaving the theatre.

15

True to his word, Pitt drove the mauled DSMV free of its buried prison. The metal tracks shrieked as they ground their way through the lava rock, a centimetre at a time. With tortured sluggishness the great vehicle clawed its way to the surface of the sea bottom, shook off the stone and ooze that trailed in a huge cloudy river from its rear end, and rolled onto the barren terrain.

'We're clear,' Plunkett cried in delight. 'Jolly well done.'

'Jolly well done,' Pitt mimicked. He switched on computer control and called up a series of geographical displays on the monitor. 'A miracle we broke out with no pressure leaks or mechanical damage.'

'My dear fellow, my faith in you is as deep as the sea . . . ah, we're under. I didn't doubt your fortitude for a minute.'

Pitt spared him a curious stare. 'If you're taken in that easily, I have a bridge in New York I'd like to sell you.'

'What was that about a bridge?'

'Do you play?'

'Yes, I'm quite good. Won more than a few tournaments. And you?'

'I deal a mean hand of Old Maid.'

The exchange was slightly less than bizarre considering their predicament, but they were men absorbed in their element and well aware of the danger of being trapped in the abyssal depths. If either Pitt or Plunkett felt any fear, he didn't show it.

'Now that we've escaped the landslide, what's the plan?' asked Plunkett as calmly as if he was requesting another cup of tea.

'The plan is to go up,' Pitt answered pointing toward the roof.

'Since this magnificent old crawler has no buoyancy and we've a good five kilometres of ocean above us, how do you expect to accomplish the impossible?'

Pitt grinned.

'Just sit back and enjoy the seascape. We're going to take a little ride through the mountains.'

'Welcome aboard, Admiral.' Commander Morton gave a razor-edge salute and extended his hand, but the greeting was purely official. He was not happy and made no attempt at hypocrisy. 'A rare occasion when we're ordered to surface at sea during a cruise to take on visitors. I have to tell you I don't like it.'

Sandecker smothered a smile as he stepped from the *Shanghai Shelly*'s launch onto the bridge of the partially surfaced sail tower of the *Tucson*. He shook Morton's hand with a casual unconcern and a dominating posture that, if anything, made his presence seem like an everyday affair.

'I didn't pull strings to have you deviate from operational procedure so I could drop in for cocktails, Commander. I'm here on presidential order. If it's an inconvenience, I'll be happy to return to the junk.'

A pained expression crossed Morton's face. 'No offence, Admiral, but Soviet satellites — '

'Will photograph us in vivid colour for the entertainment of their intelligence analysts. Yes, yes, but we don't really care what they see or think.' Sandecker turned as Giordino climbed aboard. 'My assistant project director, Al Giordino.'

Unconsciously almost, Morton acknowledged Giordino with a half salute and showed them through a hatch down to the control centre of the sub. They followed the commander into a small compartment with a transparent plotting table with a recessed interior that provided a three-dimensional sonar view of the seabed.

117

Lieutenant David DeLuca, the *Tucson*'s navigation officer, was leaning over the table. He straightened as Morton made the introductions and smiled warmly. 'Admiral Sandecker, this is an honour. I never missed your lectures at the academy.'

Sandecker beamed. 'I hope I didn't put you to sleep.'

'Not at all. Your accounts of NUMA projects were fascinating.'

Morton flicked a glance at DeLuca and nodded down at the table. 'The admiral is most interested in your discovery.'

'What can you show me, son?' Sandecker said, placing a hand on DeLuca's shoulder. 'The message was you've picked up unusual sounds on the seabed.'

DeLuca faltered for a moment. 'We've been receiving strange music – '

' "Minnie the Mermaid"?' Giordino blurted.

DeLuca nodded. 'At first, but now it sounds like John Philip Sousa marches.'

Morton's eyes narrowed. 'How could you possibly know?'

'Dirk,' Giordino said definitely. 'He's still alive.'

'Let's hope so,' Sandecker said with mounting joy. He stared at DeLuca. 'Can you still hear the music?'

'Yes, sir. Once we obtained a fix, we were able to track the source.'

'It's moving?'

'About five kilometres per hour across the bottom.'

'He and Plunkett must have survived the earthquake and escaped in *Big John*,' Giordino concluded.

'Have you attempted contact?' asked Sandecker of Morton.

'We've tried, but our systems are not designed to transmit in water deeper than a thousand metres.'

'We can contact them with the underwater phone in the submersible,' said Giordino.

'Unless . . .' Sandecker hesitated. He glanced at Morton.

'Could you hear them if they were trying to contact a surface vessel, Commander?'

'If we can hear their music, we could hear their voice transmissions. Might be garbled and distorted, but I think our computers could piece together a coherent message.'

'Any such sounds received?'

'None,' replied Morton.

'Their phone system must be damaged,' Sandecker speculated.

'Then why are they able to transmit music?'

'An emergency amplifying system located in case the vehicle had a breakdown,' answered Giordino. 'A rescue vehicle could home in on the sound. But it wasn't built for voice transmission or reception.'

Morton stirred in slow anger. He did not like losing control of a situation on board his own command. 'May I ask who these people are in *Big John*, as you call it, and how they came to be traipsing over the bottom of the Pacific Ocean?'

Sandecker gave a negligent wave of his hand. 'Sorry, Commander, a classified project.' He turned his attention back to DeLuca. 'You say they're on the move.'

'Yes, sir.' DeLuca pressed a series of buttons and the display recessed in the table revealed a section of the sea bottom in a three-dimensional holograph. To the men crowded around the table, it felt as though they were looking down into a submerged Grand Canyon from the top of an aquarium. The detail was enhanced by advanced computer and sonar digital mapping that showed the images in muted colour heavy on blues and greens.

The Mendocino fracture zone dwarfed the famous tourist sight of northern Arizona, its steep escarpments averaging 3,000 metres high. The uneven rims along the great crack in the earth's submarine surface were serrated with hundreds of ridges, giving it the appearance of a huge gash through a series of sand ripples. 'The latest underwater visual technology,' Morton offered proudly. 'The *Tucson* was the first sub to have it installed.'

'Code-named The Great Karnak,' Sandecker said loftily. 'Knows all, sees all. Our NUMA engineers helped develop it.'

Morton's face, now curiously red and sullen, looked abjectly defeated in the game of one-upmanship. But he took control and made a brave comeback. 'Lieutenant, show the admiral his toy in action.'

DeLuca took a short wandlike probe and traced a light beam across the floor of the display. 'Your underwater vehicle emerged at this point in a small canyon just off the main fracture zone and is now travelling in a zigzag pattern up the slopes toward the top of the fracture zone's edge.'

Giordino stared sombrely at the flattened area where the mining project once stood. 'Not much left of Soggy Acres,' he said sadly.

'It wasn't built to last forever,' Sandecker consoled him. 'The results more than paid for the loss.'

Without being asked, DeLuca enlarged the display until the fuzzy image of the DSMV could just be seen struggling up the side of a steep slope. 'This is as sharp as I can bring her in.'

'That's just fine,' Sandecker complimented him.

Looking at the tiny speck against the infinite desolation, it was impossible for any of them to believe there were two living, breathing men inside it. The moving projection seemed so real, they had to fight to keep from reaching out and touching it.

Their thoughts varied to the extreme. DeLuca imagined he was an astronaut peering down at life on an alien planet, while Morton was reminded of watching a truck on a highway from an aircraft flying at thirty thousand feet. Sandecker and Giordino both visualized their friend struggling against a hostile atmosphere to stay alive.

'Can't you rescue them with your submersible?' queried Morton.

Giordino clutched the rail around the display table until his knuckles went ivory. 'We can rendezvous, but neither craft has an air lock to transfer them from one to the other under tons of water pressure. If they attempted to leave *Big John* at that depth, they'd be squashed to a third their size.'

'What about hoisting them to the surface with a cable?'

'I don't know of a ship equipped to carry six kilometres of cable thick enough to support its own weight and that of the DSMV.'

'The *Glomar Explorer* could do it,' said Sandecker. 'But she's on an oil drilling job off Argentina. Impossible for her to cut off operations, re-equip, and get here inside of four weeks.'

Morton began to understand the urgency and the frustration. 'I'm sorry there is nothing my crew and I can do.'

'Thank you, Commander.' Sandecker sighed heavily. 'I appreciate that.'

They all stood silent for the next full minute, their eyes focused on the image of the miniature vehicle as it crept across the display like a bug climbing the side of a culvert.

'I wonder where he's headed,' murmured DeLuca.

'What was that?' asked Sandecker as if he had suddenly awakened.

'Since I've been tracking him, he's been travelling in a set direction. He'll go into a series of switchbacks when the slope steepens, but after it flattens out again he always returns to his original course.'

Sandecker, staring at DeLuca, suddenly knew. 'Dirk's heading for high ground. Lord, I almost wrote him off without considering his intentions.'

'Plot an approximate course destination,' Morton ordered DeLuca.

DeLuca programmed his navigational computer with the data, then eyed the monitor, waiting for the compass projection. The numbers flashed almost instantly.

'Your man, Admiral, is on a course bearing three-three-four.'

'Three-three-four,' Morton repeated firmly. 'Nothing ahead but dead ground.'

Giordino looked at DeLuca. 'Please enlarge the sector ahead of the DSMV.'

DeLuca nodded and broadened the display area in the direction Giordino requested. 'Looks pretty much the same except for a few seamounts.'

'Dirk is making for Conrow Guyot,' Giordino said flatly.

'Guyot?' asked DeLuca.

'A seamount with a smooth summit,' Sandecker explained. 'A submarine volcanic mountain whose top was levelled by wave action as it slowly sank beneath the surface.'

'What's the depth of the summit?' Giordino questioned DeLuca.

The young navigation officer pulled a chart from a cabinet under the table and spread it across the transparent top. 'Conrow Guyot,' he read aloud. 'Depth three hundred and ten metres.'

'How far from the DSMV?' This from Morton.

DeLuca checked the distance with a pair of dividers against a scale at the bottom of the chart. 'Approximately ninety-six kilometres.'

'At eight kilometres per hour,' Giordino calculated, 'then doubling the distance to allow for uneven terrain and detours around ravines, with luck they should reach the top of Conrow around this time tomorrow.'

Morton's eyes turned sceptical. 'Climbing the guyot may bring them closer to the surface, but they'll still be three hundred metres or nearly a thousand feet short. How does this guy – '

'His name is Dirk Pitt,' Giordino helped him.

'Okay, Pitt. How does he expect to make it topside – swim?'

'Not from that depth,' said Sandecker promptly. '*Big John* is pressurized to one atmosphere, the same as we're standing in at sea level. The outside water pressure down there is thirty-three times heavier. Even if we could supply them with high-tech dive gear and a helium-oxygen gas mixture for deep-water breathing, their chances are nil.'

'If the sudden increase in pressure as they left *Big John* didn't kill them,' Giordino added, 'decompression sickness on the way to the surface would.'

'So what does Pitt have up his sleeve?' Morton persisted.

Giordino's eyes seemed to peer at something beyond the bulkhead. 'I don't have the answer, but I suspect we'd better think of one damn quick.'

16

The sterile grey expanse gave way to a forest of oddly sculptured vents protruding from the seafloor. They rose like distorted chimneys and spouted hot – 365° Celsius – clouds of black steam that were quickly smothered by the cold ocean.

'Black smokers,' announced Plunkett, identifying them under the probing lights of *Big John*.

'They'll be surrounded by communities of sea creatures,' Pitt said without removing his eyes from the navigational display on his control monitor. 'We charted over a dozen of them during our mining surveys.'

'You'd better swing clear. I'd hate to see this brute run over them.'

Pitt smiled and took manual control, turning the DSMV to avoid the strange colony of exotic sea life that thrived without sunlight. It was like a lush oasis in the desert, covering nearly a square kilometre of seafloor. The wide tracks of the intruding monster skirted the spewing vents and the entwining thickets of giant tube worms that gently leaned with the current as though they were marsh reeds swaying under a breeze.

Plunkett gazed in awe at the hollow stalks as the worms inside poked their delicate pink and burgundy plumes into the black water. 'Some of them must be a good three metres in length!' he exclaimed.

Also scattered around the vents and the tube worms were huge white mussels and clams of varieties Plunkett had never seen before. Lemon-coloured creatures that looked like puff balls and were related to jellyfish mingled with spiny white crabs and bluish shrimp. None of them required photosynthesis to survive. They were nourished by bacteria that converted the hydrogen sulphide and oxygen overflow from the vents into organic nutrients. If the sun was suddenly snuffed out, these creatures in their pitch-black environment would continue to exist while all other life forms above them became extinct.

He tried to etch the image of the different vent inhabitants in his brain as they disappeared into the silt cloud trailing behind, but he couldn't concentrate. Sealed tight in the lonely cabin of the mining vehicle, Plunkett experienced a tremendous wave of emotion as he stared into the alien world. No stranger to the abyssal deep, he suddenly felt as isolated as an astronaut lost beyond the galaxy.

Pitt took only a few glimpses of the incredible scene outside. He had no time for distractions. His eyes and reflexes depended on his reaction to the dangers shown on the monitor. Twice he almost lost *Big John* in gaping fissures, stopping at the brink of one with less than a metre to spare. The rugged terrain often proved as impassable as a Hawaiian lava bed, and he had to rapidly program the computer to chart the least treacherous detour.

He had to be especially careful of landslide zones and canyon rims that could not support the vehicle. Once he was forced to circle a small but active volcano whose molten lava poured through a long crack and down the slope before turning solid under the frigid water. He steered around scarred pits and tall cones and across wide craters, every type of texture and contour one would expect to find on Mars.

Driving by the sonar and radar probes of the computer instead of relying on his limited vision under the DSMV's lights did not make for a joy ride. The strain was beginning to arrive in aching muscles and sore eyes, and he decided to turn temporary control over to Plunkett, who had quickly picked up the intricacies of operating *Big John*.

'We've just passed the two-thousand-metre mark,' Pitt reported.

'Looking good,' replied Plunkett cheerfully. 'We're better than halfway.'

'Don't write the cheque just yet. The grade has steepened. If it increases another five degrees, our tracks won't be able to keep their grip.'

Plunkett forced out all thoughts of failure. He had complete confidence in Pitt, a particular that irritated the man from NUMA no end. 'The slope's surface has smoothed out. We should have a direct path to the summit.'

'The lava rocks hereabouts may have lost their sharp edges and become rounded,' Pitt muttered wearily, his words coming slow with the edge of an exhausted man, 'but under no circumstance can they be called smooth.'

'Not to worry. We're out of the abyssal zone and into midwater.' Plunkett paused and pointed through the viewing window at a flash of blue-green bioluminescence. 'Porichthys myriaster, a fish that lights up for two minutes.'

'You have to feel sorry for him,' Pitt said tongue-in-cheek.

'Why?' Plunkett challenged. 'The porichthys has adapted very well. His luminescence is used to frighten predators, act as bait to attract food, as means to identify his own species and, of course, attract the opposite sex in the total blackness.'

'Swimming in a cold black void all their lives. I'd call that a real drag.'

Plunkett realized he was being had. 'Very clever observation, Mr Pitt. A pity we can't offer midwater fish some sort of entertainment.'

'I think we can give them a few laughs.'

'Oh, really. What have you got in mind?'

'They can watch you drive for a while.' He gestured to the control console. 'She's all yours. Mind you keep a tight eye on the monitor's geological display and not on jellyfish with neon advertising.'

Pitt slouched in his seat, blinked his eyes closed, and looked to be asleep in a moment.

Pitt came awake two hours later at the sound of a loud crack that came like a gunshot. He immediately sensed trouble. He came erect and scanned the console, spying a flashing red light.

'A malfunction?'

'We've sprung a leak,' Plunkett informed him promptly. 'The warning light came on in unison with the bang.'

'What does the computer say about damage and location?'

'Sorry, you didn't teach me the code to activate the program.'

Pitt quickly punched the proper code on the keyboard. The readout instantly swept across the display monitor.

'We're lucky,' said Pitt. 'The life-support and electronic equipment chambers are tight. So is the shielded reactor compartment. The leak is below, somewhere around the engine and generator compartment.'

'You call that lucky?'

'There's room to move around in that section, and the walls are accessible for plugging the entry hole. The battering this poor old bus has taken must have opened a microscopic casting flaw in the lower hull casing.'

'The force of the outer water pressure through a hole the size of a pin can fill the interior volume of this cabin in two hours,' Plunkett said uneasily. He stirred uncomfortably. The optimism had gone out of his eyes as he stared bleakly at the monitor. 'And if the hole widens and the hull collapses . . .' His voice dropped off.

'These walls won't collapse,' Pitt said emphatically. 'They were built to resist six times the pressure of this depth.'

'That still leaves a tiny shaft of water coming in with the power of a laser beam. Its force can slice an electric cable or a man's arm in the wink of an eye.'

'Then I'll have to be careful, won't I?' Pitt said as he slipped out of his chair and crawled toward the aft end of the control cabin. He had to maintain a constant handhold to keep from being thrown about by the swaying and pitching of the vehicle as it lurched over the broken terrain. Just before reaching the exit door, he leaned down and lifted a small trapdoor and switched on the lights, illuminating the small confines of the engine compartment.

He could hear a sharp hiss above the hum of the steam turbine but couldn't see where it was coming from. Already there was a quarter metre of water covering the steel walk matting. He paused and listened, trying to locate the sound. It wouldn't do to rush blindly into the razor-slashing stream.

'See it?' Plunkett shouted at him.

'No!' Pitt snapped nervously.

'Should I stop?'

'Not for anything. Keep moving toward the summit.'

He leaned through the floor opening. There was a threatening terror, a foreboding about the deadly hissing noise, more menacing than the hostile world outside. Had the spurting leak already damaged vital equipment? Was it too strong to be stopped? There was no time to lose, no time to contemplate, no time to weigh the odds. And he who hesitated was supposed to be lost. It made no difference now if he died by drowning, cut to ribbons, or crushed by the relentless pressure of the deep sea.

He dropped through the trapdoor and crouched inside for a few moments, happy to still be in one piece. The hissing was close, almost within an arm's length, and he could feel the sting from the spray as its stream struck something ahead. But the resulting mist that filled the compartment prevented him from spotting the entry hole.

Pitt edged closer through the mist. A thought struck him, and he pulled off a shoe. He held it up and swung it from side to side with the heel out as a blind man would sweep a cane.

Abruptly the shoe was nearly torn from his hand. A section of the heel was neatly carved off. He saw it then, a brief sparkle ahead and to his right.

The needlelike stream was jetting against the mounted base of the compact steam turbine that drove the DSMV's huge traction belts. The thick titanium mount withstood the concentrated power of the leak's spurt, but its tough surface had already been etched and pitted from the narrow onslaught.

Pitt had isolated the problem, but it was far from solved. No caulking, no sealant or tape could stop a spewing jet with power to cut through metal if given enough time. He stood and edged around the turbine to a tool and spare parts cabinet. He studied the interior for a brief instant and then pulled out a length of high-pressure replacement pipe for the steam generator. Next he retrieved a heavy sledge-type hammer.

The water had risen to half a metre by the time he was ready. His makeshift scheme just had to work. If not, then all hope was gone and there was nothing he and Plunkett could do but wait to either drown or be crushed by the incoming pressure.

Slowly, with infinite caution, he reached out with the pipe in one hand and the hammer in the other. He lay poised in the rapidly rising water, inhaled a deep breath, held it a moment, and then exhaled. Simultaneously he shoved one end of the pipe over the entry hole, careful to aim the opposite end away from him, and immediately jammed it against the angled slope of the thick bulkhead shield separating the turbine and reactor compartments. Furiously he hammered the lower end of the pipe up the angle until it was wedged tight and only a fine spray escaped from both top and bottom.

His jury-rigged stopgap may have been clever, but it wasn't perfect. The wedged pipe had slowed the incoming flood to a tiny spurt, enough to get them to the summit of the guyot, hopefully, but it was not a permanent solution. It was only a matter of hours before the entry hole enlarged itself or the pipe split under the laserlike force.

Pitt sat back, cold, wet, and too mentally drained to feel the water sloshing around his body. Funny, he thought after a long minute, how sitting in ice water he could still sweat.

Twenty-two gruelling hours after struggling from its grave, the faithful DSMV had climbed within sight of the sea-mount's summit. With Pitt back at the controls, the twin tracks dug, slipped, then dug their cleats into the silt-covered lava rock, struggling up the steep incline a metre at a time until finally the great tractor clawed over the rim onto level ground.

Only then did *Big John* come to a complete stop and become silent as the surrounding cloud of ooze slowly settled on the flattened top of Conrow Guyot.

'We did it, old man,' laughed Plunkett excitedly as he pounded Pitt on the back. 'We jolly well did it.'

'Yes,' Pitt agreed tiredly, 'but we've still one more obstacle to overcome.' He nodded at the digital depth reading. 'Three hundred and twenty-two metres to go.'

Plunkett's joy quickly vaporized. 'Any sign of your people?' he asked seriously.

Pitt punched up the sonar-radar probe. The display revealed the ten-kilometre-square summit as empty and barren as a sheet of cardboard. The expected rescue vehicle had failed to arrive.

'Nobody home,' he said quietly.

'Hard to believe no one on the surface heard our blasting music and homed in on our movement,' said Plunkett, more irritated than disappointed.

'They've had precious little time to mount a rescue operation.'

'Still, I'd have expected one of your submersibles to return and keep us company.'

130

Pitt gave a weary shrug. 'Equipment failure, adverse weather, they might have encountered any number of problems.'

'We didn't come all this way to expire in this hellish place now.' Plunkett looked up toward the surface. The pitch-black had become a twilight indigo-blue. 'Not this close.'

Pitt knew Giordino and Admiral Sandecker would have moved heaven and earth to save him and Plunkett. He refused to accept the possibility they hadn't smelled out this plan and acted accordingly. Silently he rose, went aft, and raised the door to the engine compartment. The leak had enlarged and the water level was above a metre. Another forty minutes to an hour and it would reach the turbine. When *it* drowned, the generator would die as well. Without functioning life-support systems, Pitt and Plunkett would quickly follow.

'They'll come,' Pitt said to himself with unwavering determination. 'They'll come.'

17

Ten minutes passed, twenty, as the dread of loneliness fell over them. The sense of being lost on the sea bottom, the unending darkness, the bizarre sea life that hovered around them – it was all like a ghastly nightmare.

Pitt had parked *Big John* in the centre of the seamount and then programmed the computer to monitor the leak in the engine compartment. He peered warily at the display screen as the numbers showed the water level creeping to within a few centimetres of the generator.

Though the climb to a shallower depth sharply relieved the outside water pressure, the entry flaw had enlarged, and Pitt's further efforts could not stem the growing flood. He evacuated air to offset the increased atmospheric compression caused by the rising flood.

Plunkett half turned and studied Pitt, whose strong craggy face was quite still, as firmly set as the eyelids that never seemed to flicker. The eyes seemed to reflect anger, not at any one person or object but anger simply directed at a situation he could not control. He sat frighteningly remote from Plunkett, almost as if the British oceanographer was a thousand kilometres away. Pitt's mind was armoured against all sensation or fear of death. His thoughts sifted through myriad escape plans, calculating every detail from every angle until one by one they were all discarded in the shredder inside his brain.

Only one possibility stood a remote chance of success, but it all depended on Giordino. If his friend didn't appear within the next hour, it would be too late.

Plunkett reached over and thumped Pitt's shoulder with

one big fist. 'A magnificent try, Mr Pitt. You took us from the deep abyss to almost within sight of the surface.'

'Not good enough,' Pitt murmured. 'We came up a dollar long and a penny short.'

'Mind telling me how you planned to do it without the convenience of a pressure lock to escape the vehicle and a personnel transfer capsule to carry us to the surface?'

'My original idea was to swim home.'

Plunkett raised an eyebrow. 'I hope you didn't expect us to hold our breath.'

'No.'

'Good,' Plunkett said, satisfied. 'Speaking for myself, I'd have expired before ascending thirty metres.' He hesitated and stared at Pitt curiously. 'Swim, you can't be serious?'

'A ridiculous hope bred of desperation,' Pitt replied philosophically. 'I know better than to believe our bodies could survive the onslaught of extreme pressure and decompression.'

'You say that was your original idea. Do you have another – like trying to float this monster off the bottom?'

'You're getting warm.'

'Lifting a fifteen-ton vehicle can only be accomplished in a vivid imagination.'

'Actually, it hinges on Al Giordino,' Pitt answered with forbearance. 'If he's read my mind, he'll meet us in a submersible equipped with –'

'But he let you down,' said Plunkett, sweeping an arm over the empty seascape.

'There has to be a damn good reason for it.'

'You know and I know, Mr Pitt, no one will come. Not within hours, days, or ever. You gambled on a miracle and lost. If they do come to search, it'll be over the wreckage of your mining community, not here.'

Pitt did not reply but gazed into the water. The lights of the DSMV had drawn a school of hatchetfish. Silver with deep bodies and flattened on the sides, slender tails wavered in the water as rows of light organs flashed along their lower stomachs. The eyes were disproportionately large and protruded from tubes that rose upward. He watched as they swirled gracefully in lazy spirals around the great nose of *Big John*.

Slowly he bent forward as if listening, then sank back again. 'Thought I heard something.'

'A mystery we can still hear over that blaring music,' Plunkett grunted. 'My eardrums have ceased to function.'

'Remind me to send you a condolence card at a later date,' said Pitt. 'Or would you rather we give up, flood the cabin, and end it?'

He froze into immobility, eyes focused on the hatchetfish. A great shadow crept over them, and as one they darted into the blackness and vanished.

'Something wrong?' asked Plunkett.

'We have company,' Pitt said with an I-told-you-so grin. He twisted in his seat, tilted his head, and looked through the upper viewing window.

One of the NUMA Soggy Acres submersibles hung suspended in the void slightly above and to the rear of the DSMV. Giordino wore a smile that was wide as a jack-o'-lantern's. Next to him, Admiral Sandecker threw a jaunty wave through the large round port.

It was the moment Pitt had wished for, indeed silently prayed for, and Plunkett's great bear hug showed how gladly he shared the moment.

'Dirk,' he said solemnly, 'I humbly apologize for my negative company. This goes beyond instinct. You are one crafty bastard.'

'I do what I can,' Pitt admitted with humorous modesty.

There were few times in his life Pitt had seen anything half as wonderful as Giordino's smiling face from inside the submersible. Where did the admiral come from? he wondered. How could he have arrived on the scene so quickly?

Giordino wasted little time. He motioned to a small door that shielded an exterior electrical receptacle. Pitt nodded and pressed a button. The door slipped open into a hidden slot, and in less than a minute one of the articulated robotic arms on the submersible connected a cable.

'Am I coming through?' Giordino's voice burst clearly over the speakers.

'You don't know how good it is to hear your voice, pal,' answered Pitt.

'Sorry we're late. The other submersible swamped and sank on the surface. This one shorted its batteries and we lost time in repairs.'

'All is forgiven. Good to see you, Admiral. I didn't expect your honoured presence down here.'

'Cut the apple-polishing,' Sandecker boomed. 'What's your status?'

'We have a leak that will close down our power source within forty or fifty minutes. Beyond that we're in good shape.'

'Then we'd better get busy.'

With no more wasted conversation, Giordino manoeuvred the submersible until its bow was on the same level and facing the lower broadside of the DSMV. Then he engaged the manipulator arms mounted on the front below the control sphere. They were much smaller than the arm system on *Big John* and more intricate.

The sub's modular arms were designed to accommodate several types of hand mechanisms and operate them hydraulically. The left hand was attached to the arm by a rotating wrist, which in turn was connected to three fingers with sensors in their tips that could identify any material from wood and steel to plastic, cotton, and silk. Under the operator's delicate touch, enhanced by a computer sensory system, the fingers could dexterously thread a small needle or tat lace or, if the occasion demanded, crush rock.

Smoothly the robotic arm unravelled a hose running from

135

a small tank to a large rod with a hole running through its centre core.

The right arm's wrist was fitted with a series of four circular metal-cutting discs. Each disc was serrated with a different edge and could be interchanged depending on the hardness of the material it was slicing.

Pitt peered at the left-hand assembly curiously. 'I knew the discs were stored on board the submersible, but where did you find the oxygen cutting equipment?'

'I borrowed it from a passing submarine,' Giordino answered without elaboration.

'Logical.' There was a tired acceptance in Pitt's voice, unsure whether his friend was stroking him.

'Beginning separation,' said Giordino.

'While you're cutting us free I'll pump up our air volume by a couple of atmospheres to compensate for the extra weight from the leakage flow.'

'Sound idea,' agreed Sandecker. 'You'll need all the buoyancy you can build. But mind your pressure safety limits or you'll run into decompression problems.'

'Decompression schedules will be monitored by our computer,' Pitt assured him. 'Neither Dr Plunkett nor I look forward to a case of the bends.'

As Pitt began pumping compressed air into the control and engine compartments, Giordino jockeyed the submersible so that both arm and hand manipulators could operate independently. The hand with the three articulated fingers positioned the fat welding rod against a bolt that ran through a mounting brace. The rod held a positive charge while the DSMV was negative. A bright arc suddenly flared when contact was made between the rod and bolt. As the metal glowed and melted, oxygen spurted through the hole in the rod, dispersing the buildup.

'Arc gouging,' Pitt explained to Plunkett. 'They're going to sever all mounts, drive shafts, and electrical connections until the control housing breaks free of the main frame and track mechanism.'

Plunkett nodded in understanding as Giordino extended the other arm until a spray of sparks signalled the cutting discs were attacking their target. 'So that's the ticket. We float to the surface as pretty as an emptied bottle of Veuve Cliquot-Ponsardin Gold Label champagne.'

'Or a drained bottle of Coors beer.'

'First pub we hit, Mr Pitt, the drinks are on me.'

'Thank you, Dr Plunkett. I accept, providing we have enough buoyancy to take us up.'

'Blow the guts out of her,' Plunkett demanded recklessly. 'I'd rather risk the bends than certain drowning.'

Pitt did not agree. The excruciating agony divers had suffered over the centuries from the bends went far beyond man-inflicted torture. Death was a relief, and survival often left a deformed body racked with pain that never faded. He kept a steady eye on the digital reading as the red numbers crept up to three atmospheres, the pressure at roughly twenty metres. At that depth their bodies could safely endure the increased pressure squeeze, he estimated, in the short time remaining before nitrogen gas began forming in their blood.

Twenty-five minutes later, he was about to rethink his estimate when a growing creaking noise reverberated inside the compartment. Then came a deep grinding that was magnified by the density of the water.

'Only one mount and a frame brace to go,' Giordino informed them. 'Be prepared to tear loose.'

'I read you,' replied Pitt. 'Standing by to close down all power and electrical systems.'

Sandecker found it insufferable that he could plainly see the faces of the men across the thin gap separating the two vehicles and know there was every likelihood they might die. 'How's your current air supply?' he asked anxiously.

Pitt checked the monitor. 'Enough to get us home if we don't stop for pizza.'

There came a screech that set teeth on edge as the control

compartment shuddered and tilted upward, nose first. Something gave then, and suddenly the structure acted as if it wanted to break free. Pitt quickly shut off the main generator power and switched over to the emergency batteries to keep the computer and speaker phone operating. But all movement abruptly stopped, and they hung frozen above the tractor's huge frame.

'Hold on,' came Giordino's reassuring voice. 'I missed some hydraulic lines.' Then he added, 'I'll try to stay close if I can, but should we spread too far apart, the phone cable will snap and we'll lose voice contact.'

'Make it quick. Water is gushing in through some of the severed lines and connections.'

'Acknowledged.'

'See to it you open your exit door and get the hell out fast when you hit the waves,' Sandecker ordered.

'Like geese with diarrhoea,' Pitt assured him.

Pitt and Plunkett relaxed for a few seconds, listening to the sound of the cutting discs chewing through the tubing. Then came a heavy lurch followed by a ripping noise, and they began slowly rising from the top of the seamount, leaving the tractor chassis with *Big John*'s torn cables and melted debris dangling behind them like mechanical entrails.

'On our way!' Plunkett roared.

Pitt's mouth tightened. 'Too slow. The incoming water has lowered our positive buoyancy.'

'You're in for a long haul,' said Giordino. 'I judge your rate of ascent at only ten metres a minute.'

'We're lugging the engine, reactor, and a ton of water with us. Our volume barely overcomes the excess weight.'

'You should rise a little faster as you near the surface.'

'No good. The water intake will offset the decrease in pressure.'

'No worry over losing the communication cable,' Giordino said happily. 'I can easily match your ascent rate.'

138

'Small consolation,' Pitt muttered under his breath.

'Twenty metres up,' said Plunkett.

'Twenty metres,' Pitt echoed.

Both pairs of eyes locked on the depth reading that flashed on the display screen. Neither man spoke as the minutes crawled past. The twilight world was left behind and the indigo-blue of deep water paled slightly from the approaching filtered light from above. The colour green made its first appearance, and then yellow. A small school of tuna greeted them before flashing away. At 150 metres Pitt could begin to make out the dial on his wristwatch.

'You're slowing,' Giordino warned them. 'Your rate of ascent has dropped to seven metres a minute.'

Pitt punched in the water leakage numbers. He didn't like what he read. 'Our flood level is redlined.'

'Can you increase your air volume?' asked Sandecker, concern obvious in his voice.

'Not without a fatal dose of the bends.'

'You'll make it,' Giordino said hopefully. 'You're past the eighty-metre mark.'

'When our ascent drops to four metres, grab on with your hand assembly and tow us.'

'Will do.'

Giordino moved ahead and angled his vessel until the stern was pointing toward the surface and he was looking down on Pitt and Plunkett. Then he set his autopilot to maintain a reverse speed to maintain the same ascent speed as *Big John*'s housing. But before he could extend the robotic arm, he saw that the DSMV was falling back and the gap was increasing. He quickly compensated and closed the distance.

'Two metres a minute,' Pitt said with icy calm. 'You'd better link up.'

'In the process,' Giordino anticipated him.

By the time the sub's articulated hand system had managed a vicelike grip on a protruding edge of wreckage, the compartment had come to a complete halt.

'We've achieved neutral buoyancy,' Pitt reported.

Giordino jettisoned the sub's remaining iron ballast weights and programmed full reverse speed. The thrusters bit into the water and the sub, with the DSMV housing in tow, began moving again with tormented slowness toward the beckoning surface.

Eighty metres, seventy, the fight to reach daylight seemed it would never end. Then at twenty-seven metres, or about ninety feet, their progress stopped for the final time. The rising water in the engine room was coming in through new openings from newly ruptured pipes and cracks with the force of a fire hose.

'I'm losing you,' Giordino said, shaken.

'Get out, evacuate!' cried Sandecker.

Pitt and Plunkett didn't need to be told. They had no wish for *Big John* to become their tomb. The manned housing began to descend, pulling the submersible with it. Their only salvation was the inside air pressure; it was nearly equalized with the outside water. But what fate gave them, fate snatched back. The flood couldn't have picked a worse time to short out the emergency battery system, cutting off the hydraulic power for the exit hatch.

Plunkett frantically undogged the hatch and fought to push it out, but the slightly higher water pressure was unyielding. Then Pitt was beside him, and they put their combined strength into it.

In the submersible, Giordino and Sandecker watched the struggle with mounting fear. Negative buoyancy was rapidly increasing and the compartment was beginning to drop into the depths at an alarming rate.

The hatch gave as though it was pushed through a sea of glue. As the water surged around the frame and into the compartment, Pitt shouted. 'Hyperventilate, and don't forget to exhale on the way up.'

Plunkett gave a brief nod, took a quick series of deep breaths to eliminate the carbon dioxide in his lungs, and

140

held the last one. Then he ducked his head into the water gushing through the hatch and was gone.

Pitt followed, overventilating his lungs to hold his breath longer. He flexed his knees on the threshold of the hatch and launched himself upward as Giordino released the robotic hand's grip, and the final remains of the DSMV fell away into the void.

Pitt couldn't have known, but he made his exit at forty-two metres, or 138 feet, from the surface. The sparkling surface seemed to be ten kilometres away. He'd have given a year's pay for a pair of swim fins. He also wished he was about fifteen years younger. More than once, when he was in his late teens and twenties, he'd free-dived to eighty feet while snorkeling the waters off Newport Beach in California. His body was still in good physical shape, but time and hard living had taken their toll.

He swam upward, using strong even strokes with hands and feet, exhaling in tiny spurts so the expanding gases in his lungs would not rupture the capillaries and force bubbles directly into his bloodstream, causing an air embolism.

The glare from the sun was dancing on the surface, sending shafts of light into the shallows. He discovered he was in the shadows of two vessels. Without a face mask, his blurred vision through the water could only discern vague outlines of their bottoms. One seemed like a large boat, while the other looked absolutely mammoth. He shifted his course so he'd surface between them and save a crack on the head. Below him, Giordino and Sandecker followed in the submersible, like a crew cheering on a channel swimmer.

He stroked alongside Plunkett, who was clearly in trouble. The older man looked as though all strength had drained from his muscles. It was obvious to Pitt that Plunkett was on the verge of blacking out. He grabbed him by the collar and pulled the Britisher behind him.

Pitt expelled the last of the air from his lungs. He thought the surface could never be breached. Blood was throbbing in his ears. Then suddenly, just as he was gathering all his physical resources for the final effort, Plunkett went limp. The Britisher had made a brave try before falling unconscious, but he was not a strong swimmer.

Darkness was circling Pitt's vision, and fireworks began to burst behind his eyes. Lack of oxygen was starving his brain, but the desire to reach the surface was overwhelming. The seawater was stinging his eyes and invading his nostrils. He was within seconds of drowning and he damn well wasn't going to give in to it.

He put his rapidly fading strength into one last thrust for the clouds. Pulling Plunkett's dead weight, he kicked furiously and stroked with his free hand like a madman. He could see the mirrorlike reflection of the swells. They looked tantalizingly near, and yet they seemed to keep moving away from him.

He heard a heavy thumping sound as if something was pounding the water. Then suddenly, four figures in black materialized in the water on both sides of him. Two snatched Plunkett and carried him away. One of the others pushed the mouthpiece of a breathing regulator into Pitt's mouth.

He sucked in one great gasping breath of air, one after another until the diver gently removed the mouthpiece for a few breaths of his own. It was plain old air, the usual mixture of nitrogen, oxygen, and a dozen other gases, but to Pitt it tasted like the sparkling dry air of the Colorado Rockies and a forest of pine after a rainfall.

Pitt's head broke water and he stared at the sun as if he'd never seen it before. The sky never looked bluer or the clouds whiter. The sea was calm, the swells no more than half a metre at their crests.

His rescuers tried to support him, but he shrugged them off. He rolled over and floated on his back and looked up at the huge sail tower of a nuclear submarine that towered above him. Then he spotted the junk. Where on earth did that come from? he wondered. The sub explained the Navy divers, but a Chinese junk?

There was a crowd of people lining the railings of the junk, most he recognized as his missing crew, cheering and waving like crazy people. He spotted Stacy Fox and waved back.

His concern swiftly returned to Plunkett, but he need not have worried. The big Britisher was already lying on the hull deck of the submarine, surrounded by US Navy crewmen. They quickly brought him around, and he began gagging and retching over the side.

The NUMA submersible broke the surface almost an arm's length away. Giordino popped from the hatch through the sail tower, looking for all the world like a man who had just won the jackpot of a lottery. He was so close he could talk to Pitt in a conversational tone.

'See the havoc you've caused?' He laughed. 'This is going to cost us.'

Happy and glad as he was to be among the living, Pitt's face was suddenly filled with wrath. Too much had been destroyed, and as yet unknown to him, too many had died. When he replied, it was in a tense, unnatural voice.

'Not me, not you. But whoever is responsible has run up against the wrong bill collector.'

PART TWO
The Kaiten Menace

18
October 6, 1993
Tokyo, Japan

The final farewell that kamikaze pilots shouted to each other before scrambling to their aircraft was 'See you at Yasukuni.'

Though they never expected to meet again in the flesh, they did intend to be reunited in spirit at Yasukuni, the revered memorial in honour of those who died fighting for the Emperor's cause since the revolutionary war of 1868. The compound of the shrine sits on a rise known as Kudan Hill in the middle of Tokyo. Also known as Shokonsha, or 'Spirit Invoking Shrine', the central ceremonial area was erected under the strict rules of Shinto architecture and is quite bare of furnishings.

A cultural religion based on ancient tradition, Shinto has evolved through the years into numerous rites of passage and sects cored around *kami*, or 'the way of divine power through various gods'. By World War II it had evolved into a state cult and ethic philosophy far removed from a strict religion. During the American occupation all government support of Shinto shrines was discontinued, but they were later designated as national treasures and honoured cultural sites.

The inner sanctuary of all Shinto shrines is off limits to everyone except for the chief priest. Inside the sanctuary, a sacred object representing the divine spirit's symbol is enshrined. At Yasukuni the sacred symbol is a mirror.

No foreigners are allowed to pass through the huge bronze gateway leading to the war heroes' shrine. Curiously overlooked is the fact that the spirits of two foreign captains of ships sunk while supplying Japanese forces during the Russo-Japanese war of 1904 are deified among the nearly 2,500,000 Nipponese war heroes. A number of villains are also enshrined at Yasukuni. Their spirits include early political assassins, underworld military figures, and the war criminals led by General Hideki Tojo who were responsible for atrocities that matched and often went beyond the savagery of Auschwitz and Dachau.

Since the Second World War, Yasukuni had become more than simply a military memorial. It was the rallying symbol of the right-wing conservatives and militants who still dreamt of an empire dominated by the superiority of Japanese culture. The annual visit by Prime Minister Ueda Junshiro and his party leaders to worship on the anniversary of Japan's defeat in 1945 was reported in depth by the nation's press and TV networks. A storm of impassioned protest usually followed from political opposition, leftists and pacifists, non-Shinto religious factions, and nearby countries who had suffered under Japanese wartime occupation.

To avoid open criticism and the spotlight of adverse opinion, the ultranationalists behind the resurrected drive for empire and the glorification of the Japanese race were forced to clandestinely worship at Yasukuni during the night. They came and went like phantoms, the incredibly wealthy, high government dignitaries, and the sinister manipulators who skirted the shadows, their talons firmly clutching a power structure that was untouchable even by the leaders of government.

And the most secretive and powerful of all was Hideki Suma.

A light drizzle fell as Suma passed through the gate and walked the gravel path toward the Shokonsha shrine. It was well after midnight, but he could see his way by the lights of Tokyo that reflected from the low clouds. He paused under a large tree and looked around the grounds inside the high walls. The only sign of life was a colony of pigeons nestled under the discs that crowned the curved roof.

Satisfied that he would not be studied by an observer, Hideki Suma went through the ritual of washing his hands in a stone basin and rinsing his mouth with a small ladle of water. Then he entered the outer shrine hall and met the chief priest, who was awaiting his arrival. Suma made an offering at the oratory and removed a sheaf of papers wrapped in a tissued scroll from the inside pocket of his raincoat. He gave them to the priest, who laid them on the altar.

A small bell was rung to summon Suma's specific deity or *kami*, and then they clasped their hands in prayer. After a short purification ceremony, Suma spoke quietly with the priest for a minute, retrieved the scroll, and left the shrine as inconspicuously as he'd arrived.

The stress of the past three days fell from him like glistening water over a garden fall. Suma felt rejuvenated by the mystical power and guidance of his *kami*. His sacred quest to purify Japanese culture from the poison of Western influences while protecting the gains of financial empire was guided by divine power.

Anyone catching a glimpse of Suma through the misty rain would have quickly ignored him. He looked quite ordinary in workman's overalls and a cheap raincoat. He wore no hat, and his hair was a great shock of brushed back white. The black mane common to almost all Japanese men and women had lightened at an early age, which gave Suma a look much older than his forty-nine years. By Western standards he was short, by Japanese ideals he was slightly on the tall side, standing at 170 centimetres.

It was only when you looked into his eyes that he seemed different from his native cousins. The irises were of a magnetic indigo blue, the legacy, possibly, of an early Dutch trader or English sailor. A frail youth, he'd taken up weight lifting when he was fifteen and laboured with cold determination until he had transformed his body into a muscled sculpture. His greatest satisfaction was not in his strength but the moulding of flesh and sinews into his own creation.

His bodyguard-chauffeur bowed and locked the heavy bronze gate after him. Moro Kamatori, Suma's oldest friend and his chief aide, and his secretary, Toshie Kudo, were sitting patiently in a backward-facing seat of a black custom-built Murmoto limousine powered by a twelve-cylinder 600-horsepower engine.

Toshie was much taller than her native sisters. Willowy, with long legs, jet-black hair falling to her waist, flawless skin enhanced by magical coffee-brown eyes, she looked as if she'd stepped out of a James Bond movie. But unlike the exotic beauties who hung on fiction's bon vivant master spy, Toshie possessed a high order of intellectual ability. Her IQ bordered on 165, and she operated at full capacity on both sides of the brain.

She did not look up as Suma entered the car, her mind was focused on a compact computer that sat in her shapely lap.

Kamatori was speaking over a telephone. His intellect may not have been on a level with Toshie's, but he was meticulous and deviously clever at managing Suma's secretive projects. He was especially gifted at behind-the-scenes finance, pulling the strings and fronting for Suma, who preferred to isolate himself from public view.

Kamatori had a stolid, resolute face flanked by oversized ears. Beneath heavy black brows, the dark lifeless eyes peered through a pair of thick-lensed rimless glasses. No smile ever crossed his tight lips. He was a man without emotions or convictions. Fanatically loyal to Suma, Kamatori's master talent was hunting human game. If someone, no matter how wealthy or high in government bureaucracy, presented an obstacle to Suma's plans, Kamatori would shrewdly despatch them so it seemed an accident or the blame could be fixed on an opposing party.

Kamatori kept a ledger of his killings with notes detailing

each event. Over the course of twenty-five years the tally came to 237.

He rang off and set the receiver in an armrest cradle and looked at Suma. 'Admiral Itakura at our embassy in Washington. His sources have confirmed the White House is aware the explosion was nuclear and originated with the *Divine Star*.'

Suma gave a stoic shrug. 'Has the President launched a formal protest with Prime Minister Junshiro?'

'The American government has remained strangely silent,' answered Kamatori. 'The Norwegians and British, however, are making noises about the loss of their ships.'

'But nothing from the Americans.'

'Only sketchy reports in their news media.'

Suma leaned forward and tapped Toshie's nyloned knee with his forefinger. 'A photo, please, of the explosion site.'

Toshie nodded respectfully and programmed the necessary code into the computer. In less than thirty seconds a coloured photo rolled out of a fax machine built into the divider wall separating the driver from the passenger compartment. She passed it to Suma, who turned up the interior car lights and took a magnifying glass from Kamatori.

'The enhanced infrared photo was taken an hour and a half ago during a pass by our Akagi spy satellite,' explained Toshie.

Suma peered through the glass without speaking for a few moments. Then he looked up questioningly. 'A nuclear hunter-killer submarine and an Asian junk? The Americans are not acting as I expected. Odd they didn't send half their Pacific fleet.'

'Several naval ships are steaming toward the explosion point,' said Kamatori, 'including a NUMA ocean survey vessel.'

'What about space surveillance?'

'American intelligence has already gathered extensive

151

data from their pyramider spy satellites and SR-Ninety aircraft.'

Suma tapped a small object in the photo with a finger. 'A submersible floating between the two vessels. Where did that come from?'

Kamatori peered over Suma's finger at the photograph. 'Certainly not the junk. It must have come from the submarine.'

'They won't find any sunken remains of the *Divine Star*,' Suma muttered. 'She must have been blown into atoms.' He tossed the photo back to Toshie. 'A readout, please, of auto carriers transporting our products, their current status and destinations.'

Toshie looked up at him over her monitor as if she'd read his mind. 'I have the data you requested, Mr Suma.'

'Yes?'

'The *Divine Moon* finished off-loading her auto cargo last night in Boston,' she reported, reading the Japanese characters on the display screen. 'The *Divine Water* . . . she docked eight hours ago in the Port of Los Angeles and is off-loading now.'

'Any others?'

'There are two ships in transport,' Toshie continued. 'The *Divine Sky* is scheduled to dock in New Orleans within eighteen hours, and the *Divine Lake* is five days out of Los Angeles.'

'Perhaps we should signal the ships at sea to divert to ports outside the United States,' said Kamatori. 'American customs agents may be alerted to search for signs of radiation.'

'Who is our undercover agent in Los Angeles?' asked Suma.

'George Furukawa directs your secret affairs in the South-western states.'

Suma leaned back, obviously relieved. 'Furukawa is a good man. He will be alert to any hardening of American customs procedure.' He turned to Kamatori, who was speaking into the phone. 'Divert the *Divine Sky* to Jamaica until we have more data, but allow the *Divine Lake* to proceed to Los Angeles.'

Kamatori bowed in acknowledgment and reached for his phone.

'Aren't you running the danger of detection?' asked Toshie.

Suma tightened his lips and shook his head. 'American intelligence agents will search the ships, but they'll never discover the bombs. Our technology will defeat them.'

'The explosion on board the *Divine Star* came at a bad time,' said Toshie. 'I wonder if we'll ever know what caused it.'

'I am not interested nor do I care,' Suma said coldly. 'The accident was unfortunate, but it won't delay completion of our Kaiten Project.' Suma paused, his face etched in a brutal expression. 'Enough pieces are set in place to destroy any nation which threatens our new empire.'

19

Vice President George Furukawa took the phone call from his wife in his plush office at the prestigious Samuel J. Vincent Laboratories. She reminded him of his dental appointment. He thanked her, said a few words of endearment, and hung up.

The woman on the other end of the line was not his wife but one of Suma's agents who could imitate Mrs Furukawa's voice. The dental appointment story was a code he'd received on five prior occasions. It meant a ship transporting Murmoto automobiles had arrived in port and was preparing to unload.

After informing his secretary that he would be having his teeth worked on the rest of the afternoon, Furukawa stepped into the elevator and punched the button for underground parking. Walking a few paces to his private stall, he unlocked the door to his mid-engined Murmoto sports car and sat behind the wheel.

Furukawa reached under the seat. The envelope was there, placed in his car after he came to work by one of Suma's people. He checked the contents for the proper documents to release three automobiles from the unloading dock area. The papers were complete and correct as usual. Satisfied, he turned over the potent 400-horsepower, 5.8-litre, 32-valve V-8. He drove up to the thick steel barrier that rose from the cement drive and slanted menacingly at the front end of the Murmoto.

A smiling guard came out of the gatehouse and leaned down. 'You checking out early, Mr Furukawa?'

'I have a dental appointment.'

'Your dentist must own a yacht that's been paid for by your teeth.'

'How about a villa in France,' Furukawa joked back.

The guard laughed and then asked the routine question. 'Taking any classified work home tonight?'

'Nothing. I left my attaché case in the office.'

The guard stepped on a switch to lower the barrier and gestured down the double drive leading to the street. 'Swish a shot of tequila around your mouth when you get home. That'll deaden the pain.'

'Not a bad idea,' said Furukawa, shifting the six-speed transmission into first. 'Thank you.'

Situated in a tall glass building hidden from the street by a grove of eucalyptus trees, Vincent Labs was a research and design centre owned by a consortium of space and aviation companies. The work was highly classified and the results carefully guarded, since much of the funding came from government contracts for military programmes. Futuristic advances in aerospace technology were conceived and studied, the projects with the highest potential going on to design and production, while the failures were put aside for future study.

Furukawa was what is known in intelligence circles as a sleeper. His parents were two of the many thousands of Japanese who immigrated to the United States shortly after the war. They quickly melted in with the Japanese-Americans who were picking up the pieces of their interrupted lives upon release from the internment camps. The Furukawas did not come across the Pacific because they'd lost their love of Japan. Far from it. They hated America and its multicultures.

They came as solid, hardworking citizens for the express purpose of raising their only son to become a leader of American business. No expense was spared to give their child the finest education the nation could offer, the money arriving mysteriously through Japanese banks into family

155

accounts. Incredible patience and long years of maintaining the façade paid off when son George received a PhD in aerodynamic physics and eventually achieved a position of power with Vincent Labs. Highly respected among aviation designers, Furukawa was now able to amass enormous quantities of information on America's finest aerospace technology, which he secretly passed to Suma Industries.

The classified data Furukawa had stolen for a country he had yet to visit saved Japan billions of dollars in research and development costs. Almost single-handedly, his traitorous activities had given Japan a five-year shortcut to becoming a world leader in the aerospace market.

Furukawa had also been recruited for the Kaiten Project during a meeting with Hideki Suma in Hawaii. He was honoured to be chosen by one of the most influential leaders of Japan for a sacred mission. His orders were to discreetly arrange for specially coloured cars to be collected at the dock and transported to undisclosed destinations. Furukawa did not ask questions. His ignorance of the operation failed to bother him. He could not be deeply involved for fear of compromising his own mission of stealing US technology.

The traffic had thinned between rush hours as he made his way onto Santa Monica Boulevard. Several kilometres later he swung south on the San Diego Freeway. With a bare touch of his shoe on the accelerator, the Murmoto wove through the slower stream of cars. His detector beeped, and Furukawa slowed to the speed limit three hundred metres before entering the range of a parked police radar unit. He cracked a rare smile as he speeded up again.

Furukawa worked into the right-hand lane and curled around the off-ramp down onto the Harbor Freeway. Ten minutes later he reached the shipping terminal area and cut into an alley, where he passed a huge truck and semitrailer parked behind an empty warehouse. The doors of the cab and the sides of the trailer were painted with the logo of a well-known moving and storage company. He hit his horn twice. The driver of the big rig tooted his air horn three times in reply and pulled behind Furukawa's sports car.

After dodging a heavy crowd of trucks backing in and out of the loading docks, Furukawa finally stopped at one of the gates to a holding yard for cars imported from foreign manufacturers. Other nearby yards were filled with Toyotas, Hondas, and Mazdas that had already come off ships before being loaded on two-deck auto transporters that would haul them to dealer showrooms.

While the guard checked the receiving documents from the envelope, Furukawa gazed at the sea of cars already driven off the *Divine Water*. Over one-third had been off-loaded and were sitting in the California sun. He idly counted the flow, as an army of drivers drove them through several gaping hatches and down ramps into the yard, and came up with a rate of eighteen a minute.

The guard handed him the envelope. 'Okay, sir, three SP-five hundred sport sedans. Please give your papers to the dispatcher down the road. He'll fix you up.'

Furukawa thanked him and motioned for the truck to follow him.

The ruddy cigar-smoking dispatcher recognized Furukawa. 'Back for more of those putrid brown cars?' he asked cheerfully.

Furukawa shrugged. 'I have a customer who buys them for his sales fleet. Believe it or not, that's his company's colour.'

'What does he sell, Kyoto lizard crap?'

'No, imported coffee.'

'Don't tell me the label. I don't want to know.'

Furukawa slipped the dispatcher a hundred-dollar bill. 'How soon before I can take delivery?'

The dispatcher grinned. 'Your cars are easy to find in the cargo holds. I'll have them for you in twenty minutes.'

An hour had passed before the three brown automobiles

157

were safely tied down inside the enclosed trailer and released from the holding yard. Not once did the driver and Furukawa exchange words. Even eye contact was avoided.

Outside the gate, Furukawa pulled his car to the side of the road and lit a cigarette. He watched in stony curiosity as the truck and semitrailer turned and headed for the Harbor Freeway. The licence on the trailer was California, but he knew it would be switched at some desert truck stop before crossing the state line.

Despite his practised detachment, Furukawa unconsciously found himself wondering what was so special about the brown cars. And why was their final destination so secret?

20

'First we'll body surf under the sunrise at Makapuu Point,' said Pitt, holding Stacy's hand. 'Later, it's snorkelling around Hanauma Bay before you rub suntan oil all over my body, and we spend a lazy afternoon dozing on a warm white sand beach. Then we'll soak up the sunset while sipping rum collins on the lanai of the Halekalani Hotel, and afterward it's off to this intimate little restaurant I know in the Manoa Valley.'

Stacy looked at him in amusement. 'Have you ever thought of forming an escort service?'

'I don't have it in me to charge a woman,' said Pitt amicably. 'That's why I'm always broke.'

He paused and looked out the window of the big twin-engine Air Force helicopter as it drummed through the night. In the early evening of Pitt and Plunkett's rescue, the big bird had appeared and plucked the entire Soggy Acres mining team and the crew of *Old Gert* off the deck of the Chinese junk. But not before everyone profusely thanked Owen Murphy and his crew for their hospitality. The final act was the removal of Jimmy Knox. Once his canvas-wrapped body was hoisted on board, the great craft rose above *Shanghai Shelly* and the *Tucson* and beat its way toward Hawaii.

The sea below shimmered under a bright three-quarter moon as the pilot flew almost directly over a cruise ship. Ahead to the southeast, Pitt caught sight of the lights on the island of Oahu. He should have been sound asleep like Sandecker, Giordino, and the others, but the exhilaration of escaping the bony character with the scythe kept his blood stirred up. That and the fact Stacy stayed awake to keep him company.

'See anything?' she asked between yawns.

'Oahu on the horizon. We should be passing over Honolulu in fifteen minutes.'

She looked at him teasingly. 'Tell me more about tomorrow, especially the after-dinner part.'

'I didn't come to that.'

'Well?'

'Okay, there are these two palm trees –'

'Palm trees?'

'Of course,' said Pitt, looking surprised that she asked. 'And between them is this carnal hammock built for two.'

The helicopter, its ultramodern Ferrari-like body lacking the familiar tail rotor, hovered momentarily above a small grass field on the outskirts of Hickam Field. Unseen in the darkness, the perimeter was patrolled by an Army special combat platoon. A lighted signal from the ground informed the pilot the area was secure. Only then did he lightly drop the huge craft onto the soft grass.

A small bus with KAWANUNAI TOURS painted on the sides immediately drove up and stopped just outside the radius of the rotor blades. It was followed by a black Ford sedan and an Army ambulance to carry Jimmy Knox's body to Tripler Army Hospital for autopsy. Four men in civilian clothes stepped from the car and stationed themselves at the helicopter's door.

As the weary NUMA people debarked, they were ushered into the bus. Pitt and Stacey were the last to exit. A uniformed guard held out his arm blocking their way and directed them to the car where Admiral Sandecker and Giordino were already standing.

Pitt pushed aside the guard's arm and walked over to the bus. 'Goodbye,' he said to Plunkett. 'Keep your feet dry.'

Plunkett fairly mashed Pitt's hand. 'Thank you for my life, Mr Pitt. When next we meet, the drinks are on me.'

'I'll remember. Champagne for you, beer for me.'

'God bless.'

When Pitt approached the black car, two men were holding up their gold shields to Sandecker's face, identifying themselves as agents of the federal government.

'I am operating under presidential order, Admiral. I'm to backstop and transport you, Mr Pitt, Mr Giordino, and Ms Fox to Washington immediately.'

'I don't understand,' said Sandecker irritably. 'What's the rush?'

'I can't say, sir.'

'What about my NUMA team? They've been working on an underwater project under extreme conditions for four months. They deserve time to rest and relax with their families.'

'The President has ordered a news blackout. Your NUMA people, along with Mr Plunkett and Salazar, will be escorted to a safe compound on the windward side of the island until the blackout is lifted. Then they're free to go at government expense wherever you direct.'

'How long will they be cooped up?' Sandecker demanded.

'Three or four days,' replied the agent.

'Shouldn't Ms Fox be going with the others?'

'No, sir. My orders are she travels with you.'

Pitt stared at Stacy shrewdly. 'You been holding out on us, lady?'

A strange little smile came to her lips. 'I'm going to miss our *tomorrow* in Hawaii.'

'Somehow I doubt that.'

Her eyes widened slightly. 'We'll have another time, perhaps in Washington.'

'I don't think so,' he said, his voice suddenly turning cold. 'You conned me, you conned me up and down the line, beginning with your phony plea for help in *Old Gert*.'

She looked up at him, a curious mixture of hurt and anger in her eyes. 'We'd have all died if you and Al hadn't shown up when you did.'

161

'And the mysterious explosion. Did you arrange that?'

'I have no idea who was responsible,' she said honestly. 'I haven't been briefed.'

'Briefed,' he repeated slowly. 'Hardly a term used by a freelance photographer. Just who do you work for?'

A sudden hardness came into her voice. 'You'll find out soon enough.' And then she turned her back on him and climbed in the car.

Pitt only managed three hours sleep on the flight to the nation's capital. He drifted off over the Rocky Mountains and woke as the dawn was breaking over West Virginia. He sat in the back of the Gulfstream government jet away from the others, preferring his thoughts to conversation. His eyes looked down at the *USA Today* paper on his lap without really seeing the words and pictures.

Pitt was mad, damned mad. He was irritated with Sandecker for remaining close-mouthed and sidestepping the burning questions Pitt had put to him about the explosion that caused the earthquake. He was angry with Stacy, certain now the British deep-water survey was a combined intelligence operation to spy on Soggy Acres. The coincidence of *Old Gert* diving in the same location defied all but the most astronomical odds. Stacy's job as a photographer was a cover. She was a covert operative, pure and simple. The only enigma left to solve was the initials of the agency she worked for.

While he was lost in his thoughts, Giordino walked to the rear of the aircraft and sat down next to him. 'You look beat, my friend.'

Pitt stretched. 'I'll be glad to get home.'

Giordino could read Pitt's mood and adroitly steered the talk to his friend's antique and classic car collection. 'What are you working on?'

'You mean car?'

Giordino nodded. 'The Packard or the Marmon?'

'Neither,' replied Pitt. 'Before we left for the Pacific, I rebuilt the engine for the Stutz but didn't install it.'

'That nineteen thirty-two green town car?'

'The same.'

'We're coming home two months early. Just under the wire for you to enter the classic car drag races at Richmond.'

'Two days away,' Pitt said thoughtfully. 'I don't think I can have the car ready in time.'

'Let me give you a hand,' Giordino offered. 'Together we'll put the old green bomb on the starting line.'

Pitt's expression turned sceptical. 'We may not get the chance. Something's going down, Al. When the admiral clams up, the cow chips are about to strike the windmill.'

Giordino's lips curled in a taut smile. 'I tried to pump him too.'

'And?'

'I've had more productive conversations with fence posts.'

'The only crumb he dropped,' said Pitt, 'was that after we land we go directly to the Federal Headquarters Building.'

Giordino looked puzzled. 'I've never heard of a Federal Headquarters Building in Washington.'

'Neither have I,' said Pitt, his green eyes sharp and challenging. 'Another reason why I think we're being had.'

21

If Pitt thought they were about to be danced around the maypole, he knew it after laying eyes on the Federal Headquarters Building.

The unmarked van with no side windows that picked them up at Andrews Air Force Base turned off Constitution Avenue past a secondhand dress store, went down a grimy alley, and stopped at the steps of a shabby six-storey brick building behind a parking lot. Pitt judged the foundation was laid in the 1930s.

The entire structure appeared in disrepair. Several windows were boarded shut behind broken glass, the black paint around the wrought-iron balconies was peeling away, the bricks were worn and deeply scarred, and for a finishing touch an unwashed tramp sprawled on the cracked concrete steps beside a cardboard box full of indescribably mangy artefacts.

The two federal agents who escorted them from Hawaii led the way up the steps into the lobby. They ignored the homeless derelict, while Sandecker and Giordino merely gave him a fleeting glance. Most women would have looked upon the poor man with either compassion or disgust, but Stacy nodded and offered him a faint smile.

Pitt, curious, stopped and said, 'Nice day for a tan.'

The derelict, a black man in his late thirties, looked up. 'You blind, man? What'd I do with a tan?'

Pitt recognized the sharp eyes of a professional observer, who dissected every square centimetre of Pitt's hands, clothes, body, and face, in that order. They were definitely not the vacant eyes of a down-and-out street dweller.

'Oh, I don't know,' Pitt answered in a neighbourly tone.

'It might come in handy when you take your pension and move to Bermuda.'

The tramp smiled, flashing unblemished white teeth. 'Have a safe stay, *my* man.'

'I'll try,' Pitt said, amused at the odd reply. He stepped past the disguised first ring of protection sentry and followed the others into the building's lobby.

The interior was as run down as the exterior. There was the unpleasant smell of disinfectant. The green tile floors were badly treadworn and the walls stark and smudged with years of overlaid handprints. The only object in the dingy lobby that seemed well maintained was an antique mail drop. The solid brass glinted under the dusty light fixtures hanging from the ceiling, and the American eagle above the words 'US Mail' was as shiny as the day it was buffed out of its casting. Pitt thought it a curious contrast.

An old elevator door slid open soundlessly. The men from NUMA were surprised to find a gleaming chrome interior and a US marine in dress blues who was the operator. Pitt noted that Stacy acted as though she's been through the drill before.

Pitt was the last one in, seeing his tired red eyes and the grizzly beginnings of a beard reflected in the polished chrome walls. The marine closed the doors, and the elevator moved with an eerie silence. Pitt could not feel any movement at all. No flashing lights over the door or on a display panel indicated the passing floors. Only his inner ear told him they were travelling very rapidly down a considerable distance.

At last the door opened onto a foyer and corridor that was so clean and orderly it would have done a spit-and-polish ship captain proud. The federal agents guided them to the second doorway from the elevator and stood aside. The group passed through a space between the outer and an inner door, which Pitt and Giordino immediately recognized as an air lock to make the room soundproof. As the second door was closed, air was pushed out with an audible pop.

Pitt found himself standing in a place with no secrets, an enormous conference room with a low ceiling, so dead to outside sounds the recessed fluorescent light tubes buzzed like wasps, and a whisper could be heard ten metres away. There were no shadows anywhere, and normal voice levels came almost like shouts. The centre of the room held a massive old library table once purchased by Eleanor Roosevelt for the White House. It fairly reeked of furniture polish. A bowl of Jonathan apples made up the centrepiece. Underneath the table lay a fine old blood-red Persian carpet.

Stacy walked to the opposite side of the table. A man rose and kissed her lightly on the cheek, greeting her in a voice laced with a Texas accent. He looked young, at least six or seven years younger than Pitt. Stacy made no effort to introduce him. She and Pitt had not spoken a word to each other since boarding the Gulfstream jet in Hawaii. She made an awkward display of pretending he was not present by keeping her back turned to him.

Two men with Asian features sat together next to Stacy's friend. They were conversing in low tones and didn't bother to look up as Pitt and Giordino stood surveying the room. A Harvard type, wearing a suit with a waistcoat adorned with a Phi Beta Kappa key on a watch chain, sat off by himself reading through a file of papers.

Sandecker set a course to a chair beside the head of the table, sat down, and lit one of his custom-rolled Havana cigars. He saw that Pitt seemed disturbed and restless, traits definitely out of character.

A thin older man with shoulder-length hair and holding a pipe walked over. 'Which one of you is Dirk Pitt?'

'I am,' Pitt acknowledged.

'Frank Mancuso,' the stranger said, extending his hand. 'I'm told we'll be working together.'

'You're one up on me,' Pitt said, returning a firm shake

and introducing Giordino. 'My friend here, Al Giordino, and I are in the dark.'

'We've been gathered to set up a MAIT.'

'A what?'

'MAIT, an acronym for Multi-Agency Investigative Team.'

'Oh, God,' Pitt moaned. 'I don't need this. I only want to go home, pour a tequila on the rocks, and fall into bed.'

Before he could expand on his grievances, Raymond Jordan entered the conference room accompanied by two men who wore faces with all the humour of patients just told by a doctor they had Borneo jungle fungus of the liver. Jordan made straight for Sandecker and greeted him warmly.

'Good to see you, Jim. I deeply appreciate your cooperation in this mess. I know it was a blow to lose your project.'

'NUMA will build another,' Sandecker stated in his usual cocksure way.

Jordan sat down at the head of the table. His deputies took chairs close by and laid out several document files on the table in front of him.

Jordan did not relax once he was seated. He sat stiffly, his spine not touching the backrest of the chair. His composed dark eyes moved swiftly from face to face as if trying to read everyone's thoughts. Then he addressed himself directly to Pitt, Giordino, and Mancuso, who were still standing.

'Gentlemen, would you care to get comfortable?'

There was silence for a few moments as Jordan spread the files before him in order. The atmosphere was reflective and heavy with the kind of tension and concern that brought about ulcers.

Pitt sat expressionless, his mind elsewhere. He was not mentally geared for heavy talk, and his body was tired from the strain of the last two days. What he desperately wanted was a hot shower and eight hours of sleep, but he forced himself to go along for the ride out of respect for the admiral, who was, after all, his boss.

'I apologize,' Jordan began, 'for any inconvenience that I may have caused, but I'm afraid we are dealing with a critical emergency that can affect the security of our nation.' He paused to peer down at the personnel files on the desk in front of him. 'A few of you know me and some of you have worked with me in the past. Mr Pitt and Mr Giordino, I have you at a disadvantage as I know something about you and you know very little about me.'

'Try zilch,' Giordino challenged him, avoiding Sandecker's angry stare.

'I'm sorry,' said Jordan graciously. 'My name is Ray Jordan, and I am empowered by direct presidential order to direct and manage all matters of national security, both foreign and domestic. The operation we're about to launch covers both sides. To explain the situation and your presence here, I will turn this discussion over to my Deputy Director of Operations, Mr Donald Kern.'

Kern was bony-thin, small, and lean. His intensely cool blue-green eyes seemed to reach into everyone's inner thoughts. All that is except Pitt's. It was as if two bullets had met in mid-air, neither passing through the other, both stopped dead.

'First off,' Kern opened in a surprisingly deep voice while still trying to read Pitt. 'We are all about to become part of a new federal organization consisting of investigators, specialists, support personnel, case review analysts, and field agents assembled for the purpose of defusing a serious threat to a great number of people here and around the world. In short, a MAIT team.' He pressed one of several buttons on a desk console and turned to one wall that was back-lit and displayed an organizational chart. There was a circle at the top and a larger one beneath. Four smaller circles extended from the bottom one like spider legs.

'The top circle represents the Command Centre here in Washington,' he lectured. 'The lower one is our Information Gathering and Collection Point on the Pacific island of

Koror in the Palau Republic chain. The Resident, who will act as our Director of Field Operations, is Mel Penner.' He stopped and glanced pointedly at Penner, who had entered the room with him and Jordan.

Penner nodded a red corduroy-wrinkled face and lazily raised a hand. He neither looked around the table at the others nor smiled.

'Mel's cover is acting as a UCLA sociologist studying native culture,' Kern added.

'Mel comes cheap.' Jordan smiled. 'His home and office furnishings include a sleeping cot, a phone, a document shredder, and a work desk that also serves as a dining table and a counter for his hotplate.'

Bully for Mel, Pitt thought to himself, fighting to stay awake while half wondering why they took so long to state a case.

'Our teams will carry code names,' Kern carried on. 'The code will be different makes of automobiles. For example, we at Central Command will be known as "Team Lincoln". Mel Penner is "Team Chrysler".' He paused to tap the appropriate circles on the chart before carrying on. 'Mr Marvin Showalter, who by the way is Assistant Director of Security for the US Department of State, will work out of our embassy in Tokyo and handle any diplomatic problems from the Japanese end. His team code is "Cadillac".'

Showalter stood, fingered his Phi Beta Kappa key, and bowed his head. 'A pleasure to work with you all,' he said politely.

'Marv, you'll inform your critical personnel that our MAIT operatives will be in the field should they spot what may appear to be unauthorized activity. I do not want our situation compromised through embassy cable traffic.'

'I'll see to it,' Showalter promised.

Kern turned to Stacy and the bearded man sitting next to her. 'Miss Stacy Fox and Dr Timothy Weatherhill, for those of you who haven't been introduced, will head the domestic

169

end of the investigation. Their cover will be as journalist and photographer for the *Denver Tribune*. They will be "Team Buick".' Next he motioned at the two men of Asian ancestry. ' "Team Honda" consists of Mr Roy Orita and Mr James Hanamura. They're in charge of the most critical phase of the investigation – Japan proper.'

'Before Don continues the briefing,' said Jordan, 'are there any questions?'

'How do we communicate?' asked Weatherhill.

'Reach out and touch someone,' answered Kern. 'Telephone behaviour is routine and does not arouse suspicion.' He touched another button on the console, and a series of digits appeared on the screen. 'Memorize this number. We'll give you a safe line that will be monitored twenty-four hours a day by an operator who is fully briefed and knows where to reach any of us at any given moment.'

'I might add,' said Jordan. 'You must check in every seventy-two hours. If you miss, somebody will be dispatched immediately to find you.'

Pitt, who was balancing his chair on the rear legs, held up a hand. 'I have a question.'

'Mr Pitt?'

'I'd be most grateful if someone will please tell me just what in hell is going on around here.'

There was a moment's frozen and incredulous silence. Predictably, everyone around the table with the exception of Giordino stared at Pitt in narrow-eyed disapproval.

Jordan turned to Sandecker, who shook his head and said testily, 'As you requested, Dirk and Al were not informed of the situation.'

Jordan nodded. 'I've been remiss by not having you gentlemen briefed. The fault is mine. Forgive me, gentlemen. You have been treated most shabbily after all you've been through.'

Pitt gave Jordan a penetrating gaze. 'Were you behind the operation to spy on NUMA's mining colony?'

Jordan hesitated, then said, 'We don't spy, Mr Pitt, we observe, and yes, I gave the order. A British ocean survey team happened to be working in the Northern Pacific, and they cooperated by moving their operation into your area.'

'And the surface explosion that blew away the British ship and crew and triggered the earthquake that levelled eight years of intense research and effort, was that your idea too?'

'No, that was an unforeseen tragedy.'

'Maybe I missed something,' Pitt said harshly. 'But I had this crazy idea that we were on the same side.'

'We are, Mr Pitt, I assure you,' Jordan answered quietly. He nodded at Admiral Sandecker. 'Your facility, Soggy Acres as you called it, was built under such tight secrecy that none of our intelligence agencies were aware that it was authorized.'

Pitt cut him short. 'So when you got wind of the project, your nose was bent out of joint and you had to investigate.'

Jordan was not used to being on the defensive, yet he did not meet Pitt's stare. 'What's done is done. I regret the tragic loss of so many people, but we cannot entirely be blamed for putting our operatives in an unfortunate position at the wrong time. We had no advance warning of a Japanese auto transport that was smuggling nuclear bombs across the ocean, nor could we predict those bombs would accidentally explode almost on top of two innocent ships and your mining colony.'

For a moment Pitt was stunned by the revelation, then his surprise was gone as quickly as it came. Pieces of the puzzle were falling into place. He stared at Sandecker and sensed hurt as he spoke. 'You knew, Admiral, you knew before you left Washington and said nothing. The *Tucson* wasn't on station to rescue Plunkett and me. It was there to record radioactivity and search for debris.'

It was one of the few times Pitt and Giordino ever witnessed Sandecker redden with chagrin. 'The President asked that I be sworn to secrecy,' he said slowly. 'I've never lied to you, Dirk, but I had no choice but to remain mute.'

Pitt felt sorry for the admiral, he knew it must have been difficult to be evasive with two close friends. But he made no effort to disguise his resentment of Jordan. 'Why are *we* here?' he demanded.

'The President has personally approved of the selection of each individual to the team,' replied Jordan. 'You all have a background and expertise that is indispensable for the success of this operation. The admiral and Mr Giordino will put together a project to search the ocean floor and salvage any evidence from the ship that blew up. For the record, their code is "Mercedes".'

Pitt's tired eyes squinted at Jordan steadily. 'You only half answered the question.'

Jordan obliged him by saying, 'I'm coming to it. You and Mr Mancuso, who I believe you met, will act as a support team.'

'Support for what?'

'For the phase of the operation that requires an underground or underwater search.'

'When and where?'

'Yet to be determined.'

'And our code name?'

Jordan stared at Kern, who shuffled through a file of papers and then shook his head. 'They haven't been assigned one yet.'

'May the condemned create their own code?' asked Pitt.

Jordan exchanged looks with Kern, and then shrugged. 'I don't see why not.'

Pitt smiled at Mancuso. 'You have a preference?'

Mancuso lowered the pipe from his lips. 'I leave it to you,' he said affably.

'Then we'll be "Team Stutz".'

Jordan cocked his head. 'I beg your pardon.'

'I never heard of it,' growled Kern.

'Stutz,' Pitt pronounced distinctly. 'One of America's

finest classic automobiles, built from nineteen eleven until nineteen thirty-five in Indianapolis, Indiana.'

'I like it.' Mancuso nodded agreeably.

Kern squinted at Pitt, and his eyes took on a ferrety look. 'You don't strike me as taking this operation seriously.'

Jordan made an acquiescent shrug. 'Whatever makes them happy.'

'Okay,' Pitt said steadily, 'now that vital item of the agenda is settled, I'm going to get up and walk out of here.' He paused to read the orange dial on his old Doxa divewatch. 'I was dragged here against my will. I've slept three hours out of the last forty-eight, and only eaten one meal in that time. I have to go to the bathroom. And I still don't know what's going down. Your plain-clothes security guards and your detachment of marines can stop me, of course, but then I might get hurt and can't play on the team. Oh, yes, there is one other point that no one has thought to bring up.'

'What point is that?' asked Kern, his anger rising.

'I don't recall that Al and I were officially requested to volunteer.'

Kern acted as if he'd swallowed a jalapeño pepper. 'What are you talking about, volunteer?'

'You know, one who offers himself for a service of his own free will,' Pitt defined stonily. He turned to Giordino. 'Were you formally invited to the party, Al?'

'Not unless my invitation was lost in the mail.'

Pitt stared defiantly into Jordan's eyes as he spoke. 'That's the old ball game.' Then he turned to Sandecker. 'Sorry, Admiral.'

'Shall we go?' said Giordino.

'Yes, let's.'

'You can't walk out,' Kern said with deadly seriousness. 'You're under contract to the government.'

'I'm not under contract to play secret agent.' Pitt's voice was calm, quite unperturbed. 'And unless there's been a revolution since we've returned from the bottom of the sea, this is still a free country.'

'One moment, please,' said Jordan, wisely accepting Pitt's viewpoint.

Jordan held an incredible range of power, and he was used to holding the whip hand. But he was also very astute and knew when to drift with the current, even if it flowed upstream. He stared at Pitt with curious interest. He saw no hatred, no arrogance, only a weary man who had been pushed too far. He had studied the file on NUMA's Special Projects Director. Pitt's background read like an adventure tale. His accomplishments were celebrated and honoured. Jordan was smart enough not to antagonize a man he was damned lucky to have on the team.

'Mr Pitt, if you will be patient a few more minutes I will tell you what you need to know. Some details will remain classified. I don't think it wise you and certain people present at this table should have full knowledge of the situation. I don't care a damn myself, but it is for your protection. Do you understand?'

Pitt nodded. 'I'm listening.'

'Japan has the bomb,' the chief of the National Security Service revealed. 'How long they've had it or how many they've built is unknown. Given their advanced nuclear technology, Japan has had the capability to build warheads for over a decade. And despite their highly touted adherence to the non-proliferation treaty, someone or some group within their power structure decided they needed a deterrent force for its blackmail value. What little we know comes after the fact. A Japanese ship carrying Murmoto automobiles and two or more nuclear devices detonated in the middle of the Pacific, taking a Norwegian passenger-cargo liner and the British survey ship and their crews with her. Why were nuclear bombs on a Jap ship? They were smuggling them into American ports. For what purpose? Probably nuclear extortion. Japan may have the bomb, but she doesn't have a missile force of the long-range bombers to deliver it. So what would we do in their shoes to protect a financial power structure that reaches into every pocket of every country of the world? We smuggle nuclear weapons into any nation or combination of nations such as Europe that pose a threat to our economic empire and hide them in strategic locations. Then, if a particular country, say the US, gets mad after our Japanese leaders attempt to dictate policy to the White House and Congress and the business community, the Americans retaliate by refusing to pay back hundreds of billions of dollars loaned to their Treasury by our Japanese banks. They also threaten boycotts and trade barriers on all Japanese goods. Extreme measures that Senator Mike Diaz and Congresswoman Loren Smith are proposing over at the Capitol as we speak. And maybe, just maybe, if the President gets riled up enough, he orders his superior military forces to blockade the Japanese islands, cutting off all our oil and vital raw materials, shutting down all our production. Follow me so far?'

Pitt nodded. 'I'm with you.'

'This backlash scenario is not farfetched, especially when the American people will someday realize they work one month out of the year to pay off debts owed to foreign, for the most part Japanese, creditors. Are the Japs worried? Not when they have the power to push buttons and blow up any city in the world in time for the six o'clock news. Why are we here? To stop them by finding where the bombs are hidden. And stop them before they discover we're onto them. That's where Team Buick comes in. Stacy is an operative with the National Security Agency. Timothy is a nuclear scientist who specializes in radioactivity detection. Team Honda, led by James and Roy, who are top CIA field agents, will concentrate on discovering the source of the bombs and the command centre that controls the detonations. Is this a frightening nightmare? Absolutely. The lives of five hundred million people in nations that compete with Japan depend on what we around this table can accomplish in the next few weeks. In a wisdom bred more of ignorance, our State Department does not allow us covert observation of friendly nations. As the front line of this nation's early warning system, we are forced to run in the shadows and die in obscurity. The alarm bells are about to be rung, and believe it or not, Mr Pitt, this MAIT team is the last resort before a full-scale disaster. Do you get the picture?'

'Yes . . .' Pitt said slowly. 'Thank you, Mr Jordan. I get the picture.'

'Now will you officially join the team?'

Pitt rose, and to the astonishment of everyone present except Giordino and Sandecker, he said, 'I'll think it over.'

And then he left the room.

As he walked down the steps into the alley beside the squalid old building, Pitt turned and gazed up at the dingy walls and boarded windows. He shook his head in wonderment, then looked down at the security guard in the ragged clothes sprawled on the steps and muttered to himself, 'So that's the eyes and ears of the great republic.'

Jordan and Sandecker remained in the conference room after the others had filed out.

The crusty little admiral looked at Jordan and smiled faintly. 'Do you mind my cigar?'

Jordan made a look of distaste. 'A little late in asking, aren't you, Jim?'

'Nasty habit.' Sandecker nodded. 'But I don't mind blowing smoke on someone, especially when they hard-ass my people. And that's exactly what you were doing, Ray, hard-assing Pitt and Giordino.'

'You know damn well we're in a state of crisis,' said Jordan seriously. 'We don't have time to cater to prima donnas.'

Sandecker's face clouded. He pointed to Pitt's packet that was on the top of the stack before Jordan. 'You didn't do your homework, or you'd know that Dirk Pitt is a bigger patriot than you and I put together. Few men have accomplished more for their country. There are few of his breed left. He still whistles "Yankee Doodle" in the shower and believes a handshake is a contract and man's word is his bond. He can also be devious as the devil if he thinks he's helping preserve the Stars and Stripes, the American family, and baseball.'

'If he knows the urgency of the situation,' said Jordan puzzled, 'why did he stall and cut out?'

Sandecker looked at him, then looked at the organizational chart on the backlit screen where Kern had written in 'Team Stutz'.

'You badly underestimated Dirk,' he said almost sadly. 'You don't know, you couldn't know, he's probably brewing up a scheme to reinforce your operation this minute.'

22

Pitt did not go directly to the old aircraft hangar on the edge of Washington's International Airport that he called home. He gave Giordino a set of instructions and sent him off in a cab.

He walked up Constitution Avenue until he came to a Japanese restaurant. He asked for a quiet booth in the corner, sat down, and ordered. Between the clear clam soup and a medley of sashimi raw fish, he left the table and walked to a pay phone outside the rest rooms.

He took a small address book from his wallet and flipped through the phone numbers until he found the one he was looking for: Dr Percival Nash (Payload Percy), Chevy Chase, Maryland. Nash was Pitt's uncle on his mother's side. The family character, Nash often bragged how he used to spike Dirk's baby formula with sherry. Pitt inserted the change and dialled the number under the name.

He waited patiently through six rings, hoping Nash was in. He was, answering half a second before Pitt was about to hang up.

'Dr Nash here,' came a youthful resonant voice (he was crowding eighty-two).

'Uncle Percy, this is Dirk.'

'Oh, my goodness, Dirk. About time I heard your voice. You haven't called your old uncle in five months.'

'Four,' Pitt corrected him. 'I've been on an overseas project.'

'How's my beautiful sister and that dirty old politician she married? They never call me either.'

'I haven't been over to the house yet, but judging from their letters, Mom and the senator are as testy as ever.'

'What about you, nephew? Are you in good health?'

'Fit and ready to race you around Marinda Park.'

'You remember that, do you? You couldn't have been much older than six at the time.'

'How could I forget? Every time I'd try and pass, you'd throw me in the bushes.'

Nash laughed like the jolly man that he was. 'Never try to better your elders. We like to think we're smarter than you kids.'

'That's why I need your help, and was wondering if you could meet me at the NUMA Building. I need to pick your brain.'

'On what subject?'

'Nuclear reactors for race cars.'

Nash knew instantly Pitt was dodging the real issue over the telephone. 'When?' he asked without hesitation.

'As soon as convenient.'

'An hour okay?'

'An hour will be fine,' said Pitt.

'Where are you now?'

'Eating Japanese sashimi.'

Nash groaned. 'Ghastly stuff. God only knows what pollutants and chemicals fish swim through.'

'Tastes good, though.'

'I'm going to speak to your mother. She didn't raise you right.'

'See you in an hour, Percy.'

Pitt hung up and went back to his table. Hungry as he was, he barely touched the sashimi. He idly wondered if one of the smuggled bombs might be buried under the floor of the restaurant.

Pitt took a cab to the ten-storey NUMA Building. He paid the driver and gazed briefly up at the emerald-green solar glass that covered the walls and ended in a curving pyramidal spire at the top. No lover of the classical look of

179

the capital's government buildings, Admiral Sandecker wanted a sleek contemporary look, and he got it. The lobby was an atrium surrounded by waterfalls and aquariums filled with exotic sea life. A huge globe rose from off the centre of the sea-green marble floor, contoured with the geological furrows and ridges of every sea, large lake, and primary river on the earth.

Pitt entered an empty elevator and pressed the button marked 10. He skipped his fourth-floor office and rode up to the communications and information network on the top level. Here was the brain centre of NUMA, a storehouse of every scrap of information ever recorded on the oceans – scientific, historical, fiction, or non-fiction. It was in this vast room of computers and memory cores where Sandecker spent a goodly percentage of NUMA's budget, a constant source of criticism from a small company of his enemies in Congress. Yet this great electronic library had saved enormous sums of money on hundreds of projects, led the way to numerous important discoveries, and helped avert several national disasters that were never reported in the news media.

The man behind this formidable data supermarket was Hiram Yaeger.

'Brilliant' was the compliment most often paid to Yaeger's mind, while 'rumpled' distinguished his appearance. With his greying blond hair tied in a long ponytail, a braided beard, granny spectacles, and frayed, patched Levi's, Yaeger exuded the aura of a hippie relic. Strangely, he had never been one. He was a decorated, three-tour Vietnam veteran who served as a Navy SEAL. If he had remained in computer design in California and launched his own company, he might have eventually headed a booming corporation and become a very wealthy man. But Yaeger cared nothing for being an entrepreneur. He was a class-act paradox, and one of Pitt's favourite people.

When Admiral Sandecker offered him the job of

command over NUMA's vast computer data complex with nearly unlimited funding, Yaeger took it, moved his family to a small farm in Sharpsburg, Maryland, and set up shop all within eight days. He put in long hours, running the data systems twenty-four hours a day, using three shifts of technicians to accumulate and disperse ocean data to and from ongoing American and foreign expeditions around the earth.

Pitt found Yaeger at his desk, which sat on a raised stage and revolved in the centre of the vast room. Yaeger had it specially constructed so he could keep an all-seeing eye on his billion-dollar domain. He was eating a pizza and drinking a non-alcoholic beer when he spied Pitt and jerked to his feet with a broad smile.

'Dirk, you're back.'

Pitt climbed the stairs to Yaeger's altar, as his staff called it behind his back, and they shook hands warmly. 'Hello, Hiram.'

'Sorry to hear about Soggy Acres,' Yaeger said seriously, 'but I'm real happy to see you're still among the living. God, you look like a felon just out of solitary. Sit down and rest yourself.'

Pitt gazed longingly at the pizza. 'You couldn't spare a slice, could you?'

'You bet. Help yourself. I'll send out for another. Like a fake beer to wash it down? Sorry I can't give you the real stuff, but you know the rules.'

Pitt sat and put away a large pizza plus two slices from Yaeger's, and three beers without alcohol the computer genius kept in a small refrigerator built into his desk. Between bites, Pitt filled Yaeger in on the events leading up to his rescue, stopping short of his flight to Hawaii.

Yaeger listened with interest and then smiled like a sceptical judge on a divorce trail. 'Made a quick trip home, I see.'

'Something's come up.'

Yaeger laughed. 'Here we go. You didn't rush back to eat my pizza. What's swirling in that evil mind of yours?'

'I'm expecting a relative of mine, Dr Percy Nash, to arrive in a few minutes. Percy was one of the scientists on the Manhattan Project which built the first atomic bomb. A former director on the Atomic Energy Commission, now retired. Together with your supercomputer intelligence and Percy's knowledge of nuclear weaponry, I want to create a scenario.'

'A conceptualization.'

'A rose, et cetera.'

'Involving what?'

'A smuggling operation.'

'What are we smuggling?'

'I'd rather spell it out after Percy gets here.'

'A tangible, a solid object, maybe like a nuclear warhead?' Yaeger asked smugly.

Pitt looked at him. 'That's one possibility.'

Yaeger lazily rose to his feet and started down the stairs. 'While we're waiting for your uncle, I'll warm up my CAD/CAM.'

He was gone and away on the computer floor before Pitt thought to ask what he was talking about.

23

A great white beard flowed down Payload Percy's face and covered half his paisley necktie. He had a knuckle for a nose and the set brows and squinting eyes of a wagon master intent on getting the settlers through Indian country. He beamed at the world from a face that belonged to a TV beer commercial, and seemed far younger than his eighty-two years.

He dressed natty for Washington. No regimented grey pinstripe or blue suit with red tie for Percy. He entered NUMA's computer complex in a lavender sports coat with matching pocket kerchief and tie, grey slacks, and lizard-skin cowboy boots. Sought and intimately entertained by half the attractive widows within a hundred miles, Percy had somehow managed to remain a bachelor. A wit who was in demand as a party guest and speaker, he was a gourmand who owned a wine cellar that was the envy of every society party thrower in town.

The serious side of his character was his tremendous knowledge of the deadly art of nuclear weaponry. Percy was in on the beginning at Los Alamos and stayed in harness at the Atomic Energy Commission and its succeeding agency for almost fifty years. Many a third-world leader would have given his entire treasury for Percy's talents. He was one of a very small band of experts who could assemble a working nuclear bomb in his garage for the price of a power lawn mower.

'Dirk my boy!' he boomed. 'How good to see you.'

'You look fit,' Pitt said as they hugged.

Percy shrugged sadly. 'Damned Motor Vehicle Department took away my motorcycle licence, but I can still drive my old Jaguar XK-One-twenty.'

'I appreciate you taking the time to help me.'

'Not at all. Always prime for a challenge.'

Pitt introduced Percy to Hiram Yaeger. The old man gave Yaeger a shoe to headband examination. His expression was one of benign amusement.

'Can you buy faded and prewashed clothes like that off the rack?' he asked conversationally.

'Actually my wife soaks them in a solution of camel urine, liverwort, and pineapple juice,' Yaeger came right back with a straight face. 'Softens and gives them that special air of savoir-faire.'

Percy laughed. 'Yes, the aroma made me wonder about the secret ingredients. A pleasure to meet you, Hiram.'

'The same.' Hiram nodded. 'I think.'

'Shall we begin?' said Pitt.

Yaeger pulled up two extra chairs beside a computer screen that was three times the size of most desk models. He waited until Pitt and Percy were seated and then held out both hands as if beholding a vision.

'The latest state-of-the-art,' he instructed. 'Goes by the name CAD/CAM, an acronym for Computer-Aided Design/Computer-Aided Manufacturing. Basically a computer graphics system, but also a supersophisticated visual machine that enables draftsmen and engineers to make beautifully detailed drawings of every mechanical object imaginable. No dividers, compasses, or T-squares. You can program the tolerances and then simply sketch a rough outline with an electronic pen on the screen. Then the computer will render them in precise and elaborate solid forms, or in three dimensions.'

'Quite astounding,' Percy murmured. 'Can you separate different sections of your drawings and enlarge details?'

'Yes, and I can also apply colours, alter shapes, simulate stress conditions, and edit the changes, then store the results in its memory to be recalled like a word processor. The applications from design to finished manufactured product are mind staggering.'

Pitt straddled his chair and rested his chin on the backrest. 'Let's see if it can lead us to the jackpot.'

Yaeger peered at him over his granny glasses. 'We in the trade refer to it as conceptualization.'

'If it'll make you happy.'

'So what are we looking for?' asked Percy.

'A nuclear bomb,' Pitt answered.

'Where?'

'In an automobile.'

'Expecting one to be smuggled across the border?' inquired Percy intuitively.

'Something like that.'

'By land or by sea?'

'Sea.'

'This have anything to do with the explosion in the Pacific a couple of days ago?'

'I can't say.'

'My boy, I'm unbeatable at Trivial Pursuit. I also keep up on nuclear affairs. And you know, of course, that, except for the President, I've carried the highest security clearance they've got.'

'You're trying to tell me something, uncle?'

'Would you believe I was the first one Ray Jordan consulted after the Pacific detonation?'

Pitt smiled in defeat. 'Then you know more than I do.'

'That Japan is hiding nuclear weapons around the country in automobiles, yes, I know that much. But Jordan didn't see fit to enlist an old man for his operation, so he merely picked my brains and sent me packing.'

'Consider yourself hired. You've just become a dues-paying member of Team Stutz. You too, Hiram.'

'You'll catch hell when Jordan finds out you've taken on reinforcements.'

'If we're successful, he'll get over it.'

'What's this about Japanese bombs in cars?' asked an incredulous Yaeger.

Percy put a hand on his shoulder. 'What we're about to attempt here, Hiram, must be held in strict security.'

'Hiram carries a Beta-Q clearance,' said Pitt.

'Then we're ready to begin the hunt.'

'I'd appreciate a little background,' said Yaeger, looking at Percy steadily.

The old atomic expert met his eyes. 'In the nineteen-thirties, Japan went to war to build a self-reliant economic empire. Now, fifty years later, they're willing to fight again, only this time to protect it. With utmost secrecy they built their nuclear weapons arsenal long before anyone thought of verifying its existence. The weapons-grade plutonium and uranium were spirited from civilian nuclear facilities. The fact they had the bomb was also overlooked because they didn't have a delivery system such as long-range missiles, cruise systems, bombers, or missile-carrying submarines.'

'I thought the Japanese were committed to nuclear non-proliferation,' said Yaeger.

'True, the government and the majority of the people are totally against atomic weapons. But forces deep beneath the mainstream of their bureaucracy clandestinely constructed a nuclear force. The arsenal was built more for defence against economic threat than as a military deterrent. Their concept was the bombs could be used as extortion in the event of an all-out trade war and a ban on their export goods into the United States and Europe. Or if worse came to worse, a naval blockade on the home islands.'

Yaeger was disturbed; Pitt could see it.

'You're telling me we may be sitting on a nuclear bomb?'

'Probably within a few blocks of one,' said Pitt.

'It's unthinkable,' Yaeger muttered angrily. 'How many have they smuggled into the country?'

'We don't know yet,' Pitt replied. 'It could be as many as a hundred. Also, we're not the only country. They're spread all over the world.'

'It gets worse,' said Percy. 'If the bombs have indeed been smuggled into major international cities, the Japanese possess total assured destruction. It's an efficient set-up. Once the bombs are in place, the chance of accidental or unauthorized launch of a missile is voided. There is no defence against them, no time to react, no star wars system to stop incoming warheads, no alert, no second strike. When they push the button, the strike is instantaneous.'

'Good God, what can we do?'

'Find them,' said Pitt. 'The idea is the bombs are brought in by auto ship carriers. I'm guessing hidden inside the imported cars. With your computer smarts, we're going to try and figure out how.'

'If they're coming in by ship,' Yaeger said decisively, 'customs inspectors searching for drugs would pick them out.'

Pitt shook his head. 'This is a sophisticated operation, run by high-tech professionals. They know their business. They'll design the bomb to be an integral part of the car to throw off an elaborate search. Customs inspectors are wary of tyres, gas tanks, upholstery, any place where there's an air space. So it has to be secreted in such a way that even the wiliest inspector would miss it.'

'Totally foolproof to known discovery techniques,' Yaeger agreed.

Percy thoughtfully stared at the floor. 'All right, now let's talk about size.'

'That's *your* department.' Pitt smiled.

'Give me a break, nephew. I at least have to know the model of the car, and I'm not a follower of Japanese machinery.'

'If it's a Murmoto, it's probably a sport sedan.'

The jovial look on Percy's face went dead serious. 'To

sum up, we're looking at a compact nuclear device in the neighbourhood of ten kilograms that's undetectable inside a medium-sized sedan.'

'That can be primed and detonated from a great distance,' Pitt added.

'Unless the driver is suicidal, that goes without saying.'

'What size bomb are we thinking about?' asked Yaeger innocently.

'They can vary in shape and size from an oil barrel to a baseball,' answered Percy.

'A baseball,' Yaeger murmured incredulously. 'But can one that small cause substantial destruction?'

Percy stared up at the ceiling as if seeing the devastation. 'If the warhead was high yield, say around three kilotons, it could probably level the heart of Denver, Colorado, with huge conflagrations ignited by the explosion spreading far out into the suburbs.'

'The ultimate in car bombings,' said Yaeger. 'Not a pretty thought.'

'A sickening possibility, but one that has to be faced as more third-world nations possess atomic weapons.' Percy gestured toward the empty display screen. 'What do we use as a model to dissect?'

'My family's eighty-nine Ford Taurus,' replied Yaeger. 'As an experiment I inserted its entire parts manual into the computer's intelligence. I can give you blown-up images of specific parts or the completed solid form.'

'A Taurus will make a good match-up,' Pitt agreed.

Yaeger's fingers flew over the keyboard for several seconds, and then he sat back with his arms folded. An image appeared on the screen, a three-D rendering in vivid colour. Another command by Yaeger and a metallic burgundy red Ford Taurus four-door sedan revolved on different angles as if on a turntable that went from horizontal to vertical.

'Can you take us inside?' asked Pitt.

'Entering,' Yaeger acknowledged. A touch of a button and they seemed to flow through solid metal into sectioned views of the interior chassis and body. Like ghosts floating through walls, they clearly viewed every welded seam, every nut and bolt. Yaeger took them inside the differential and up the driveshaft through the gears of the transmission into the heart of the engine.

'Astonishing,' Percy muttered admiringly. 'Like flying through a generating plant. If only we'd had this contrivance back in forty-two. We could have ended both the European and Pacific theatres of war two years early.'

'Lucky for the Germans you didn't have the bomb by nineteen forty-four,' Yaeger goaded Percy.

Percy gave him a stern stare for a moment and then turned his attention back to the image on the screen.

'See anything interesting?' Pitt put to him.

Percy tugged at his beard. 'The transmission casing would make a good container.'

'No good. Can't be in the engine or drivetrain. The car must be capable of being driven normally.'

'That eliminates a gutted battery or radiator,' said Yaeger. 'Maybe the shock absorbers.'

Percy gave a brief shake of his head. 'Okay for a plastic explosive pipe bomb but too narrow a diameter for a nuclear device.'

They studied the cutaway image silently for the next few minutes as Yaeger's keyboard skills took them on a journey through an automobile few people ever experience. Axle and bearing assemblies, brake system, starter motor, and alternator, all were probed and rejected.

'We're down to the optional accessories,' said Yaeger.

Pitt yawned and stretched. Despite his concentration, he could hardly keep his eyes open. 'Any chance of it being in the heating unit?'

'Configuration isn't right,' replied Percy. 'The windshield washer bottle?'

Yaeger shook his head. 'Too obvious.'

Suddenly Pitt stiffened. 'The air conditioner!' he burst out. 'The compressor in the air conditioner.'

Yaeger quickly programmed the computer to illustrate an interior view. 'The car can be driven, and no customs inspector would waste two hours dismantling the compressor to see why it didn't put out cold air.'

'Remove the guts and you've got an ideal casing to hold a bomb,' Pitt said, examining the computer image. 'What do you think, Percy?'

'The condenser coils could be altered to include a receiving unit to prime and detonate,' Percy confirmed. 'A neat package, a *very* neat package. More than enough volume to house a device capable of blasting a large area. Nice work, gentlemen, I think we've solved the mystery.'

Pitt walked over to an unoccupied desk and picked up the phone. He dialled the safe-line number given out by Kern at the MAIT team briefing. When a voice answered on the other end, he said, 'This is Mr Stutz. Please tell Mr Lincoln, the problem lies in his car's air conditioner. Goodbye.'

Percy gave Pitt a humorous look. 'You really know how to stick it to people, don't you?'

'I do what I can.'

Yaeger sat gazing at the interior of the compressor he'd enlarged on the display screen. 'There's a fly in the soup,' he said quietly.

'What?' asked Percy. 'What is that?'

'So we piss Japan off and they punch out our lights. They can't eliminate all of our defences, especially our nuclear submarines. Our retaliation force would disintegrate their entire island chain. If you want my opinion, I think this thing is unfeasible and suicidal. It's one big bluff.'

'There's one small problem with your theory,' Percy said, smiling patiently at Yaeger. 'The Japanese have out-foxed the best intelligence brains in the business and caught the world powers in their Achilles' heel. From their viewpoint

190

the consequences are not all that catastrophic. We contracted with the Japanese to help research the strategic defence system for the destruction of incoming missile warheads. While our leaders wrote it off as too costly and unworkable, they went ahead with their usual high-tech proficiency and perfected a working system.'

'Are you saying they're invulnerable?' asked Yaeger in a shocked voice.

Percy shook his head. 'Not yet. But give them another two years and they'll have a working in-place "Star Wars" system, and we won't.'

24

Behind closed doors in the Capitol building a select
subcommittee was meeting to investigate and evaluate
Japanese cultural and economic impact upon the United
States. The fancy words were a nice way of saying that
certain members of Congress were mad as hornets over
what they perceived as a United States held hostage by the
ever tightening screws of Japanese capital.

Ichiro Tsuboi, chief director of Kanoya Securities, the
largest security company in the world, sat at a table below
the long, curved counterlike desk in front of the congressional committee. He was flanked by four of his chief
advisers, who irritated the committee members with their
jabbering consultations before Tsuboi answered each
question.

Tsuboi did not appear as a financial giant who led a
securities company that had enough capital to swallow
Paine Webber, Charles Schwab, Merrill Lynch, and the rest
of Wall Street's honoured brokerage houses without so
much as a burp. He had, in fact, already purchased heavy
interest in several of them. His body was short and slender,
and he had a face that some likened to that of a jolly
proprietor of a geisha house.

Tsuboi's looks were deceiving. He could easily hold his
own against a protectionist Congress with fire in their eyes.
His competitors in Japan and abroad hated and feared him
with reasons bred from experience. Tsuboi was as ruthless
as he was shrewd. His canny financial manipulations had
elevated him to the level of a cult figure whose contempt for
America and the European nations was hardly a well-
guarded secret. Wall Street's cleverest investment brokers

and corporate raiders were pigeons next to the guru of the Tokyo Stock Exchange. Almost single-handedly he possessed the power to knock the props from under the American economy.

He sat and politely fielded the questions of the select committee, smiling with maddening courtesy throughout the questioning, speaking as comfortably as if he was conversing with guests over a dinner table.

'For the esteemed members of Congress to pass legislation forcing Japanese companies to sell our majority rights in our United States businesses to your companies at a fraction of their value is nothing less than nationalization. American business credibility will be shattered around the world. There will be chaos. Banking systems will collapse along with international currencies. Industrial nations will be bankrupted. And for what purpose? In my humble opinion, Japanese investors are the best thing that ever happened to the American people.'

'There is no such legislation in the works,' snapped Senator Mike Diaz. 'What I said was "Those of your companies operating and showing a profit on American soil should be subject to the same regulations and tax standards as ours." Your capital markets remain closed to us. Americans are restricted from buying real estate and ownership in your businesses, while Japanese interests are getting away with financial murder in this country, Mr Tsuboi, and you damn well know it.'

The one man who was not intimidated by Tsuboi was New Mexico Democrat Michael Diaz, chairman of the committee, the driving force behind a movement to not only limit but roll back foreign investment in American government, business, and real estate, and if he had his way, raise trade embargoes on all imported Japanese products.

A widower in his late forties, Diaz was the only senator who lived full time in his office. He kept a small private bath and a side room with a bed, refrigerator, stove, and sink.

Over the twenty-five years he had been called the hardest-working politician on the hill, his work patterns had remained unchanged. His wife had died of diabetes shortly after he was elected to his first term. They were childless, and since her death he never gave a thought to remarrying.

His hair was pure black and swept back in a high pompadour, the face round and brown with dark umber eyes and a mouth that easily flashed white perfect teeth. As an Army helicopter pilot in Vietnam he had been shot down and wounded in the knee. Captured and carried to Hanoi, he spent two years as a POW. His jailers had never properly attended to his leg, and he limped, walking with the aid of a cane.

A hard-liner against foreign influence and involvement in American affairs, Diaz had fought for trade restrictions and high tariffs, and against what he saw as unfair trade and investment practices by the Japanese government. He saw the fight with Japan as more than an economic battle but as a financial war, with the United States already the loser.

'Mr Chairman?'

Diaz nodded at an attractive female member of the committee. 'Yes, Congresswoman Smith, go right ahead.'

'Mr Tsuboi,' she began, 'you previously stated that the dollar should be replaced with the yen. Don't you think that's a bit extreme?'

'Not when you consider Japanese investors finance fifty-five percent of your budget deficit,' replied Tsuboi with an airy wave of one hand. 'Conversion of your currency to ours is only a matter of time.'

Congresswoman Loren Smith of Colorado couldn't believe she was hearing such talk. Tall, striking, with cinnamon hair cut long to frame her prominent cheekbones and violet eyes, she represented a district west of the continental divide. Tight-packed with energy, she was as elegant as a lynx and daring as a tomboy. Respected for her political cunning, she carried a great degree of clout in the House.

Many powerful men in Washington had tried to win her favours on and off the House floor, but she was a private person and dated only men who had nothing to do with business and politics. She carried on a loose secret affair with a man she deeply admired, and was comfortable with the thought that they could never live together as intimate friends or as husband and wife. They both went their separate ways, meeting only when it was convenient.

'How can we become closer than we are now?' asked Loren. 'The assets of Japanese branch banks in the United States far outnumber the combined assets of American banks. Over a million Americans already work for Japanese employers in this country. Your lobbyists have for all practical purposes bought our government. You own forty billion dollars' worth of prime US real estate. What you mean, Mr Tsuboi, is that our two nations become even closer so yours can dictate our economy and foreign policy. Am I correct? Please answer.'

Tsuboi was not used to being talked down to by a woman. The feminist movement is almost non-existent in Japan. Women are dealt out of the business reward system. No Japanese man will take orders from a woman. His composure began to crack, and his advisers sat open-mouthed.

'The President and Congress can begin with assurances that you will never close your markets to our products or investments,' Tsuboi answered evasively. 'Also, you should allow us to enter your country without the inconvenience of a visa.'

'And if we don't entertain such suggestions?'

Tsuboi shrugged and smiled venomously. 'We are a creditor nation. You are a debtor, the largest in the world. If threatened, we will have no option but to use our leverage in favour of our interests.'

'In other words, America has become subservient to Japan.'

'Since the United States is in a state of decline and my nation is rising at an incredible rate, perhaps you should consider accepting our methods over yours. Your citizens should study our culture in depth. They might learn something.'

'Is that one reason why your vast operations outside of Japan are staffed by your own people and not by workers in the guest country?'

'We hire local personnel,' Tsuboi replied as if hurt.

'But not for top positions. You hire low-end managers, secretaries, and janitors. I also might add, very few women and minorities. And you've been very successful at excluding unions.'

Congresswoman Smith had to wait for an answer while Tsuboi conversed in Japanese with his people. They were either unknowing or uncaring that their hushed voices were being recorded and translated. A constant stream of transcriptions was laid in front of Senator Diaz within minutes.

'You must understand,' Tsuboi finally answered. 'We are not prejudiced. We simply do not consider it good business practice to permit Westerners who are not versed in our methods, and who have no loyalty toward our native customs, to hold high-level positions in our foreign facilities.'

'Not a wise course, Mr Tsuboi,' said Loren tersely. 'I think I speak for most Americans when I say we don't care to be treated with contempt by foreign nationals in our own backyard.'

'That is unfortunate, Congresswoman Smith. Speaking for *my* people, I do not condone such interference as you imply. We merely wish to turn a profit without stepping on toes.'

'Yes, we're well aware of Japanese business's blatant self-interest. The selling of strategic military and computer technology to the Soviet Bloc. To corporate executives like yourself, the Soviet Union, East Germany, Cuba, Iran, and Libya are merely customers.'

'International ideological and moral issues do not concern us. To put them ahead of practical matters concerning economic trade makes little sense to our way of thinking.'

'One more question,' said Loren. 'Is it true you have proposed that your government buy the entire State of Hawaii so they can balance United States trade deficits with Japan?'

Tsuboi did not consult with his aides but fired right back. 'Yes, I proposed that measure. Japanese people make up the majority of the population of Hawaii, and our business interests now own sixty-two percent of the real estate. I've also suggested that California be turned into a combined economic community shared by Japan and America. We have a vast labour pool we can export, and our capital can build hundreds of manufacturing facilities.'

'I find your concepts most distasteful,' said Loren, fighting back a rising anger. 'The rape of California by the Japanese business community will never happen. Unfortunately, I'm told many of Hawaii's residential neighbourhoods are already for Japanese only, and a number of resort and golf clubs are off limits to American citizens.' Loren paused to stare Tsuboi in the eye, before continuing through tight lips. 'I for one am going to fight further encroachment with every means of my office.'

A murmur of approval ran through the room. A few hands clapped as Diaz smiled and lightly tapped his gavel for quiet.

'Who is to say what lies in the future.' Tsuboi smiled patronizingly. 'We do not have a secret plan to take over your government. You have lost the economic game by forfeit.'

'If we have lost, it is to corporate body snatchers backed by Kanoya Securities,' snapped Loren.

'You Americans must learn to accept the facts. If we buy America, it's because you're selling it.'

197

The few spectators allowed in the session and the numerous congressional aides shuddered at the veiled threat, hostility growing in their eyes. Tsuboi's strange mixture of arrogance and humility, politeness and strength, gave a disturbing and frightening atmosphere to the room.

Diaz's eyes were hard as he leaned over the desk counter toward Tsuboi. 'At least there are two benefits for our side in this unhappy situation.'

For the first time Tsuboi's expression turned puzzled. 'What benefits are you speaking of, Senator?'

'One, step too far and your investments, which are mostly words on paper and computer monitors, will be erased. Two, the ugly American is no more,' Diaz said, his voice cold as an Arctic wind. 'He's been replaced by the ugly Japanese.'

25

After he left Pitt at the Federal Headquarters Building, Giordino took a cab to the Department of Commerce on Constitution Avenue. Leaning on a friend, who was Assistant Secretary of Domestic and International Business, he borrowed a file on Murmoto auto import inventories. Then he taxied to Alexandria, Virginia. He stopped once to check an address in a phone book. The building he was looking for housed the distributing network of the Murmoto Motor Corporation for a five-state district. He called the number and asked the operator for directions.

It was late afternoon, and already a chilly breeze of early fall swept through the trees and began tearing away the leaves. The cab stopped at the kerb in front of a modern red-brick building with large bronze glass windows. A sign with copper letters on the lawn identified it as the Murmoto Motor Distribution Corp.

Giordino paid off the cabbie and stood for a moment studying the parking lot. It was filled entirely with Murmoto cars. Not one American or European make was in sight. He walked through the double front doors and stopped before a very pretty Japanese receptionist.

'May I help you?' she asked sweetly.

'Albert Giordino, Commerce Department,' he answered. 'I'd like to talk to someone regarding new car shipments.'

She thought for a moment, and then checked a book of personnel. 'That would be Mr Dennis Suhaka, our director of transportation. I'll tell him you wish to see him, Mr Giordano.'

'Giordino, Albert Giordino.'

'I'm sorry, thank you.'

Less than a minute later a tall, attractive secretary of Asian parentage but with a surgical job to remove the eye folds came out to the lobby and escorted Giordino to Suhaka's office. As he walked down a long, richly carpeted hallway, Giordino was amused at the titles on the doors. No manager, no superintendents, no vice presidents, everyone was a director of something or other.

Suhaka was round and jolly. He wore a grand smile as he came from behind his desk and shook Giordino's hand. 'Dennis Suhaka, Mr Giordino. What can I do for the Commerce Department?'

To Giordino's relief, Suhaka didn't question his unshaven appearance or ask him for identification. 'No big deal. Typical bureaucratic paper shuffling for statistical records. My supervisor asked me to stop by on my way home and check the number of cars imported and shipped to your dealers against the figures given by your headquarters in Tokyo.'

'For what period of time? We bring in an enormous number of cars.'

'The past ninety days.'

'No problem,' said Suhaka, going out of his way to be accommodating. 'Our shipment lists are all computerized, and I can have them for you in ten minutes. They should tally. Tokyo almost never makes mistakes. Would you care for a cup of coffee while you wait?'

'Yes,' said a weary Giordino. 'I could use one.'

Suhaka ushered him into a small empty office, the pretty secretary brought the coffee, and while he was sipping it, she returned with a neat stack of inventory sheets.

Giordino found what Pitt had sent him to find in less than half an hour. He sat back then and dozed, killing time to make it appear he was simply a drone in the great bureaucracy doing his job.

Precisely at five o'clock Suhaka entered the room. 'The staff is going home, but I'll be working late. Is there anything I can help you with?'

'No,' Giordino replied, closing the files. 'I'd like to get home too. I've put in my seven hours. Now I'm on my time. Thank you for being so helpful. Your import unit figures will be programmed into that great government computer in the sky. For what purpose? Only some little clerk in a basement office knows for sure.' He picked up the file from the Commerce Department and was halfway through the door when he turned as if something had occurred to him, in perfect Peter Falk–Columbo fashion. 'There is one thing.'

'Yes?'

'A small inconsistency hardly worth mentioning.'

'Yes?'

'I happened to run across six cars that are shown on your incoming inventory list as having been off-loaded in Baltimore from two different ships, but they're not accounted for on the export list from your Tokyo headquarters.'

Suhaka genuinely looked to be at a loss. 'It was never called to my attention. May I compare it against your figures?'

Giordino spread out the accounting sheets he'd borrowed from his friend at the Department of Commerce and placed them next to the ones given him by Suhaka's secretary. He underlined the cars itemized on his list but missing on the one from Tokyo. All six were SP-500 sport sedans.

'Speaking officially, we're not concerned with the discrepancy,' said Giordino indifferently. 'As long as you accounted for them upon entry into the country, your company is clean with the government. I'm sure it's only an error in your Tokyo accounting department that's since been cleared up.'

'An unforgivable oversight on my part,' Suhaka said, as though he'd dropped the crown jewels down a sewer. 'I put too much faith in the home office. Someone on my staff should have caught it.'

'Just out of curiosity, what dealers received those particular cars?'

201

'One moment.' Suhaka led Giordino to his office, where he sat down at his desk and poked at the keys on his desk computer. Then he sat back and waited. As the data flashed across the screen, his smile abruptly vanished and a paleness showed in his face.

'All six cars were hauled to different dealers. It would take several hours to track each down. If you'd care to check with me tomorrow, I'll be glad to give you their names.'

Giordino turned up his palms in a lukewarm gesture. 'Forget it. We both have more pressing business to worry about. Me, I've got to fight the rush hour traffic, get cleaned up, and take my wife out to dinner. It's our anniversary.'

'Congratulations,' said Suhaka, relief obvious in his eyes.

'Thank you. And thanks also for your cooperation.'

Suhaka's grand smile was back. 'Always glad to help. Goodbye.'

Giordino walked four blocks to a gas station and dialled from a pay phone. A male voice answered with a simple hello.

'This is your friendly Mercedes salesman. I have a model I think you'd be interested in.'

'You're out of your district, sir. You should be selling closer to the waterfront or, better yet, out in the Pacific Ocean.'

'Big deal,' grunted Giordino. 'If you can't afford a good German car, try a Murmoto. I have a lead on six SP-Five Hundred sport sedans that are specially discounted.'

'One moment.'

A voice came over the line that Giordino immediately recognized as Donald Kern's. 'Despite the fact you've stepped out of your territory, I'm always in the market to save money. Tell me where I can see your special discounts.'

'You have to get that information out of the Murmoto distributorship in Alexandria. Their computer records show six cars that came into the country but didn't leave the factory. I suggest you hurry before word gets out and someone else beats you to them. Half the cars were off-loaded at the customs dock in Baltimore on August fourth. The other three came in on September tenth.'

Kern quickly translated Giordino's meaning. 'Hold on,' he ordered. He turned to his deputy, who was listening on the speaker. 'Get on it. Gain access to Murmoto's computer system and dig out their shipping records for the where-abouts of those six cars before they get wise and erase the data.' He returned to Giordino. 'Nice work. All is forgiven. By the way, how did you happen to stumble onto the bargains?'

'The idea came from Stutz. Have you heard from him?'

'Yes, he called half an hour ago,' replied Kern. 'He discovered the source of the problem.'

'I sort of thought if anyone could troubleshoot a riddle, he could,' said Giordino, referring to Pitt's canny talent for discovering the unknown. 'It takes a devious mind to know one.'

26

It was dark when Yaeger dropped Pitt off at the old hangar on the far corner of Washington's International Airport. The structure was built in 1936 and once covered the planes of an old air carrier long since purchased by American Airlines. Except for the headlights of Yaeger's Taurus, the only other illumination came from the glow of the city across the Potomac River and a solitary road lamp two hundred metres to the north.

'For someone who hasn't been home for four months, you sure travel light.' Yaeger laughed.

'My luggage lies with the fishes,' Pitt mumbled through half-closed eyes.

'I'd love to see your car collection again, but I have to get home.'

'It's bed for me. Thanks for the lift. And thank you for this afternoon. A fine job as always.'

'Love doing it. Finding the key to your brain twisters beats solving the mysteries of the universe any day.' Yaeger waved, rolled up his window against the cold night air, and drove off into the darkness.

Pitt took a spare transmitter from his trouser pocket that he kept in his NUMA office and punched in a series of codes that shut down the hangar's security system and turned on the interior lights.

He unlocked the old, badly weathered side door and entered. The polished concrete floor of the hangar looked like a transport museum. An old Ford trimotor aeroplane was parked in one corner next to a turn-of-the-century railroad Pullman car. Over fifty automobiles covered the remaining 10,000 square metres. European exotica such as a Hispano-Suiza, a Mercedes-Benz 540K, and a beautiful blue Talbot-Lago were sitting across from magnificent American classics like a Cord L-29, a Pierce-Arrow, and a stunning turquoise-green Stutz town car. The only piece that seemed oddly out of place was an old cast-iron bathtub with an outboard motor attached to the backrest.

He tiredly walked up a circular iron stairway to his apartment overlooking the collection. What had once been an office, he had redecorated into a comfortable one-bedroom apartment with a large combination living room—study whose shelves were filled with books and glass-encased models of ships Pitt had discovered and surveyed.

An appetizing aroma drifted from the kitchen. He found a note hanging on a bird of paradise rising from a vase on the dining table. A smile crossed his face as he read it.

Heard you had sneaked back into town. Cleaned out the alien slime that invaded your refrigerator a month after you were gone. Thought you might be hungry. A salad is on ice and the bouillabaisse is warming in a pot on the stove. Sorry I couldn't be there to greet you, but must attend a dinner at the White House.

Love,
L

He stood for a moment trying to urge his sleep-fogged mind to come to a decision. Should he eat and then take a shower? Or jump in the shower first. He decided a hot shower would knock him out and he'd never make it back to the table. He undressed and slipped on a short robe. He ate the salad, a Waldorf, and almost the entire pot of bouillabaisse along with two glasses of Smothers Brothers 1983 Cabernet Sauvignon from a bottle that came from a closet wine rack.

He finished and was rinsing the dishes in the sink when the phone rang.

'Hello?'

'Mr Pitt?'

'Yes, Mr Jordan,' Pitt answered, recognizing the voice. 'What can I do for you?'

'I hope I didn't interrupt your sleep.'

'My head is still ten minutes away from the pillow.'

'I wanted to call and learn if you heard from Al.'

'Yes, he called right after he talked to you.'

'Despite your unauthorized project, the information was quite useful.'

'I know I shouldn't have stepped out of bounds, but I wanted to play out a hunch.'

'You're not much of a team player, are you, Dirk?' said Jordan, using Pitt's given name for the first time. 'You'd rather play your own game.'

' "Wisdom denotes the pursuing of the best ends by the best means." '

'Your words?'

'No, they belong to Francis Hutcheson, a Scot philosopher.'

'I give you credit for quoting in the exact form,' said Jordan. 'Most of official Washington would have plagiarized the original and quoted "The end justifies the means." '

'What do you want?' asked Pitt, desperately eyeing his bed.

'I thought you'd also like to know that we found the bomb carriers.'

'All six cars?' Pitt asked, astonished.

'Yes, they're hidden in a Japanese bank building in downtown Washington. Sealed in an underground basement until the day they're dusted off and driven to their scheduled targets and detonated.'

'That was fast work.'

'You have your methods, we have ours.'

'Have you placed them under surveillance?'

'Yes, but we have to tread softly. We don't dare tip our hand yet, not before we terminate those responsible for this horror and destroy their command centre,' said Jordan. 'As it was, Giordino came within a hair of blowing the operation this afternoon. Somebody at Murmoto Distributors was scared. We got in and out of their accounting system only minutes before they erased their imported shipping data.'

'The data led you to the cars?'

'We were able to track and penetrate a known Japanese-owned freight company whose trucks picked them up. They programmed no mention of destination in their records, of course, but we did manage to "borrow" a copy of the driver's delivery log. It revealed the number of kilometres the truck travelled after leaving the dockyard. The rest involved solid investigation and fancy footwork.'

'Like breaking and entering.'

'We never break when we enter,' said Jordan.

'Should it leak out that our good citizens are sitting on nuclear bombs belonging to a foreign power, the country will be torn apart by panic.'

'Not a healthy situation, I agree. The public uproar and the demand for revenge might scare the Japs into moving the cars to strategic positions and pressing the "fire" button before we can find and neutralize them.'

'An across-the-board search could take twenty years to find them all.'

'I don't think so,' said Jordan calmly. 'We know how they do it, and thanks to you and Giordino, we know what to look for. The Japanese are not half the pros we are in the intelligence business. I'll bet we'll find every Murmoto and its bomb within thirty days.'

'I applaud optimism,' said Pitt. 'But what about our allies and the Russians? The Japanese may have hidden bombs under them too. Is the President going to warn their leaders of the possibility?'

'Not yet. The NATO nations can't be trusted not to leak a secret this critical. On the other hand, the President may feel that letting the Kremlin in on it might tighten relations. Think about it. We're both in the same boat now, both threatened suddenly by another superpower.'

'There is one other frightening threat.'

'There are so many, what have I missed?'

'Suppose Japan set off a few of the bombs in either the US or Russia? We'd each think one attacked the other, go to war, and leave the crumbs for the wily Japs to pick over.'

'I don't want to go to bed with that in my head,' said Jordan uneasily. 'Let's just take things as they come. If our operation is successful, then it's in the hands of the politicians again.'

'Your last thought,' said Pitt, feigning apprehension, 'would keep anyone awake nights.'

He was just dozing off when the security chime alerted him to the presence of someone trying to enter the hangar. Forcing himself from his comfortable bed, he walked into the study and turned on a small TV monitoring system.

Stacy Fox was standing at the side entrance door staring up and smiling into what Pitt thought was his well-camouflaged hidden security camera.

He pressed a switch, and the door opened. Then he walked out and stood on the stairway balcony.

She stepped into the hangar looking sexy yet demure in a blue collarless jacket, a matching slim skirt, and a jewel-neck white blouse. She moved slowly amid the array of grand machinery in reverent amazement. She stopped at a beautiful 1948 metallic-blue Talbot-Lago Grand Sport coupe with special coachwork by a French body maker known as Saoutchik and lightly ran her fingers over one fender.

She was not the first. Almost every woman who ever visited Pitt's unusual living quarters was drawn to the

Talbot. He saw it as a masterpiece of mechanical art, but women felt a sensual attraction when they gazed upon it. Once they saw the sleek, almost feline, flow of the body, sensed the fierce power of the engine, and smelled the elegant leather of the interior, the car became an erotic symbol.

'How did you find me?' he asked, his voice echoing around the vast interior.

She looked up. 'I studied your packet for two days before I flew out to the Pacific and boarded the *Invincible*.'

'Find anything interesting?' he asked, annoyed that his life was laid bare for anyone with the authority to break his privacy.

'You're quite a guy.'

'Flattery indeed.'

'Your car collection is breathtaking.'

'There are many larger collections with more expensive models and makes.'

She turned back to the Talbot-Lago. 'I love this one.'

'I prefer the green town car next to it.'

Stacy turned and peered at the Stutz as if she was studying a manikin modelling a dress at a fashion show. Then she shook her head. 'Handsome but massive, too masculine for a woman's taste.'

Then she stared up at him again. 'Can we talk?'

'If I can stay awake. Come on up.'

She climbed the circular stairs, and he gave her a brief tour of the apartment. 'Can I get you a drink?' Pitt asked.

'No thanks.' She stared at him, and compassion came to her eyes. 'I shouldn't have come. You look like you're about to collapse.'

'I'll bounce back after a good night's sleep,' he said ruefully.

'What you need is a good back rub,' she said unexpectedly.

'I thought you came to talk.'

'I can talk while I rub. Swedish or shiatsu? What method of massage do you prefer?'

'What the hell, do both.'

She laughed. 'All right.' She took him by the hand and led him into the bedroom and pushed him face down on the bed. 'Take off your robe.'

'Can't I keep my modesty with a sheet?'

'You have something I haven't seen before?' she said, pulling the sleeves of the robe from his arms.

He laughed. 'Don't ask me to turn over.'

'I want to apologize before Tim and I leave for the West Coast,' she said seriously.

'Tim?'

'Dr Weatherhill.'

'You've worked together before, I assume.'

'Yes.'

'Will I see you again sometimes?' he asked.

'I don't know. Our missions may take us in different directions.' She hesitated a moment. 'I want you to know I feel badly about the trouble I've caused. You saved my life, and because I took up extra space in the last submersible, you almost lost yours.'

'A good massage and we'll call it even,' Pitt said, flashing a tired smile.

She looked down on his outstretched body. 'For living underwater for four months, you have a good tan.'

'My gypsy blood,' he slurred in a sleepy voice.

Using finger pressure of the basic shiatsu technique, Stacy pressed her fingers and thumbs into the sensitive areas of Pitt's bare feet.

'That feels great,' he murmured. 'Did Jordan brief you on what we learned about the warheads?'

'Yes, you threw him a curve. He thought you had walked out on him. Now that Tim and I know exactly where to target our investigation, we should make good progress at pinpointing the bomb cars.'

'And you're going to probe the West Coast ports.'

'Seattle, San Francisco, and Los Angeles are the ports where the Murmoto auto carriers dock.'

Pitt went silent as Stacy worked up his legs, combining shiatsu with Swedish kneading methods. She massaged his arms, back, and neck. Then she lightly slapped him on the buttocks and ordered him to turn over, but there was no response.

Pitt was dead asleep.

Sometime during the early morning hours he came awake, feeling her body wildly entangled with his. The movements, the sensations, the soft cries of Stacy's voice, came through the mist of exhaustion like a dream. He felt as though he was soaring through a thunder and lightning storm before it all faded and he plunged into the black void of deep sleep again.

'Surprise, sleepyhead,' said Congresswoman Loren Smith, trailing a finger down Pitt's back.

Pitt's mind brushed away the cobwebs as he rolled onto his side and looked up at her. She was sitting cross-legged in bare feet on the empty side of the bed wearing a flowered cotton knit top with a crew neckline and sage-green sailcloth pants with pleats. Her hair was tied back with a large scarf.

Then suddenly he remembered and shot an apprehensive look at the opposite side of the bed. To his lasting relief, it was empty.

'Aren't you supposed to be doing wondrous deeds in Congress?' he asked, secretly pleased Stacy had left before Loren arrived.

'We're in recess.' She held a cup of coffee out of his reach, tempting him.

'What do I have to do for the coffee?'

'Cost you a kiss.'

'That's pretty expensive, but I'm desperate.'

'And an explanation.'

Here it comes, he thought, quickly focusing his thoughts. 'Concerning what?'

'Not what but who. You know, the woman you spent the night with.'

'What woman was that?' he asked with practised innocence.

'The one who slept in this bed last night.'

'You see another woman around here?'

'I don't have to see her,' said Loren, taking great delight in teasing him. 'I can smell her.'

'Would you believe it was my masseuse?'

She leaned down and gave him a long kiss. When she finally pulled back, she handed him the coffee and said, 'Not bad. I'll give you an A for creativity.'

'I was conned,' he said, hoping to change the flow of the conversation. 'This cup is only half full.'

'You didn't want me to spill it all over your blankets, did you?' She laughed as if actually enjoying Pitt's indiscretion. 'Drag your great hairy bod out of bed and wash off that perfume. Not a bad odour, I admit. Rather expensive. I'll start breakfast.'

Loren was standing at the counter slicing the grapefruit as Pitt came out of the shower for the second time in eight hours. He wrapped a towel around his hips, stepped up behind her, and circled his arms around her waist. He nuzzled her neck.

'Long time, no see. How did you ever get along without me for so long?'

'I buried myself in legislation and forgot all about you.'

'You didn't find time to play?'

'I was a good girl. Not that I'd have been bad if given half the chance, especially if I knew you weren't wasting any time since coming home.'

Loren bore up quite well, Pitt thought. There was only a slight flush of jealous anger. But she knew better than to

212

crowd the issue. Pitt was not the only man in her life. Neither dictated to the other or displayed undue jealousy, situations that made their affair all the more desirable.

As he nibbled her earlobe, she turned and put her arms around his neck. 'Jim Sandecker told me about the destruction of your project, and how you barely escaped.'

'That's supposed to be secret,' he said as they brushed noses.

'Congresswomen *do* have privileges.'

'You can have privileges with me any time.'

Her eyes turned dark. 'Seriously, I'm sorry the facility was lost.'

'We'll build another.' He smiled down at her. 'The results of all our tests were saved. That's what counts.'

'Jim said you came within seconds of dying.'

Pitt grinned. 'Water under the bridge, as they say.' He released her and sat down at the table. It seemed just another Sunday morning domestic scene between a comfortably married man and wife, yet neither Loren nor Dirk had ever been married.

He picked up a newspaper she'd brought along with the groceries and scanned the stories. His eyes stopped at one article, and after scanning its contents he looked up.

'I see you made the *Post* again,' he said, grinning. 'Getting nasty with our friends in the Orient, are we?'

Loren expertly flipped an omelette onto a dish. 'Ownership of a third of our businesses has been transferred to Tokyo. And with it went our prosperity and independence as a nation. America no longer belongs to Americans. We've become a financial colony of Japan.'

'That bad?'

'The public has no idea how bad,' said Loren, setting the omelette and a plate of toast in front of Pitt. 'Our huge deficits have created an open door for our economy to flow out and Japanese money to rush in.'

'We have only ourselves to blame,' he said, waving a fork.

'They underconsume, we overconsume, burying ourselves deeper in debt. We gave away or sold out our lead in whatever technology that wasn't stolen. And we stand in line with open pocketbooks and tongues hanging in greedy anticipation to sell them our corporations and real estate to make a fast buck. Face the facts, Loren, none of this could have happened if the public, the business community, you people in Congress, and the economic cretins in the White House had realized this country was engaged in a no-quarter financial war against an enemy who looks upon us as inferior. As it stands, we've thrown away any chance of winning.'

Loren sat down with a cup of coffee and passed Pitt a glass of orange juice. 'That's the longest speech I've ever heard you give. You thought of running for the Senate?'

'I'd rather have my toenails torn out. Besides, one Pitt on Capitol Hill is enough,' he said, referring to his father, Senator George Pitt of California.

'Have you seen the senator?'

'Not yet,' Pitt said, taking a bit of egg. 'I haven't had a chance.'

'What are your plans?' Loren asked, staring wistfully into Pitt's opaline green eyes.

'I'm going to putter on the cars and take it easy for the next couple of days. Maybe if I can tune up the Stutz in time, I'll enter it in the classic car races.'

'I can think of something more fun than getting greasy,' she said, her voice throaty.

She came around the table, reached down and took a surprisingly strong grip of his arm. He could feel desire flowing from her like nectar, and suddenly he wanted her more than he ever had before. He only hoped he was up to a second round. Then as if drawn by a magnet, he allowed himself to be pulled to the couch.

'Not in the bed,' she said huskily. 'Not until you change the sheets.'

27

Hideki Suma stepped out of his private Murmoto tilt-rotor executive jet followed by Moro Kamatori. The aircraft had landed at a heliport beside a huge solar plastic dome that rose fifty metres into the sky. Centred in a densely land-scaped park, the dome covered a vast atrium that comprised the inner core of a subterranean project called 'Edo' after the city renamed Tokyo during the Meiji Restoration of 1868.

The first unit of Japan's new underground frontier, Edo City was designed and built by Suma as a scientific research and think-tank community that supported 60,000 people. Shaped like a great cylinder around the atrium, the twenty-storey circular complex contained living quarters for the scientific community, offices, public baths, convention halls, restaurants, a shopping mall, library, and its own thousand-man security force.

Smaller underground cylinders connected by tunnels to the main core held the communications equipment, heating and cooling systems, temperature and humidity controls, electrical power plants, and waste processing machinery. The elaborate structures were constructed of ceramic concrete and reached 150 metres deep in the volcanic rock.

Suma funded the project himself without any government involvement. Any laws or restrictions that hindered con-struction were quickly resolved by the enormous power wielded by Suma's corporate and underworld tentacles.

He and Kamatori boarded a concealed elevator that took them to a suite of his corporate offices covering the entire fourth floor of the outer cylinder. His secretary, Toshie Kudo, stood waiting as the doors opened to his heavily guarded private office and apartment. The spacious three-tiered rooms were decorated with delicately painted screens and murals and showcases of beautiful ceramics and sixteenth-century robes of ornately woven brocades, satins, and crepe. Paintings of land- and seascapes covered most of the walls, some depicting dragons, leopards, tigers, and hawks that represented the martial prowess of the warrior class.

'Mr Ashikaga Enshu is waiting,' announced Toshie.

'I don't recall the name.'

'Mr Enshu is an investigator who specializes in hunting down rare art and negotiating its sale for his clients,' explained Toshie. 'He called and said he'd discovered a painting that fits your collection. I took the liberty of setting an appointment for him to display it for your approval.'

'I have little time,' said Suma, glancing at his watch.

Kamatori shrugged. 'Won't hurt to see what he's brought you, Hideki. Maybe he's found the painting you've been looking for.'

He nodded at Toshie. 'All right, please send him in.'

Suma bowed as the art dealer stepped into the room. 'You have a new acquisition for my collection, Mr Enshu?'

'Yes, I hope so, one that I believe you will be most happy I was able to find for you.' Ashikaga smiled warmly beneath a perfect mane of silver hair, heavy eyebrows, and full moustache.

'Please set it on the stand in the light,' said Suma, pointing at an easel in front of a large window.

'May I draw the blinds open a little more?'

'Please do so.'

Enshu pulled the draw lines to the slatted blinds. Then he set the painting on the easel but kept it covered by a silk cloth. 'From the sixteenth-century Kano school, a Masaki Shimzu.'

'The revered seascape artist,' said Kamatori, displaying a rare hint of excitement. 'One of your favourites, Hideki.'

'You know I am a devotee of Shimzu?' Suma asked Enshu.

'A well-known fact in art circles that you collect his work, especially the paintings he made of our surrounding islands.'

Suma turned to Toshie. 'How many of his pieces do I have in my collection?'

'You presently own eleven out of the thirteen island seascapes and four of his landscape paintings of the Hida Mountains.'

'And this new one would make twelve in the island set.'

'Yes.'

'What Shimzu island painting have you brought me?' Suma asked Enshu expectantly. 'Ajima?'

'No, Kechi.'

Suma looked visibly disappointed. 'I had hoped it might be Ajima.'

'I'm sorry.' Enshu held out his hands in a defeatist gesture. 'The Ajima was sadly lost during the fall of Germany. It was last seen hanging in the office of the ambassador in our Berlin embassy in May of nineteen forty-five.'

'I will gladly pay you to keep up the search.'

'Thank you,' said Enshu, bowing. 'I already have investigators in Europe and the United States trying to locate it.'

'Good, now let's have the unveiling of Kechi Island.'

With a practised flourish, Enshu undraped a lavish painting of a bird's-eye view of an island in monochrome ink with an abundant use of brilliant colours and gold leaf.

'Breathtaking,' murmured Toshie in awe.

Enshu nodded in agreement. 'The finest example of Shimzu's work I've ever seen.'

'What do you think, Hideki?' asked Kamatori.

'A masterwork,' answered Suma, moved by the genius of the artist. 'Incredible that he could paint an overhead view with such vivid detail in the early sixteen-hundreds. It's almost as if he did it from a tethered balloon.'

'Legend says he painted from a kite,' said Toshie.

'*Sketched* from a kite is more probable,' corrected Enshu. 'And painted the scene on the ground.'

'And why not?' Suma's eyes never left the painting. 'Our people were building and flying kites over a thousand years ago.' He turned finally and faced Enshu. 'You have done well, Mr Enshu. Where did you find it?'

'In a banker's home in Hong Kong,' Enshu replied. 'He was selling his assets and moving his operations to Malaysia before the Chinese take over. It took me nearly a year, but I finally persuaded him to sell over the telephone. I wasted no time and flew to Hong Kong to settle the transaction and return here with the painting. I came directly to your office from the airport.'

'How much?'

'A hundred and forty-five million yen.'

Suma rubbed his hands in satisfaction. 'A very good price. Consider it sold.'

'Thank you, Mr Suma. You are most gracious. I shall keep looking for the Ajima painting.'

They exchanged bows, and then Toshie escorted Enshu from the office.

Suma's eyes returned to the painting. The shores were littered with black rock, and there was a small village with fishing boats at one end. The perspective was as precise as an aerial photo.

'How strange,' he said quietly. 'The only painting of the island collection I don't possess is the one I desire the most.'

'If it still exists, Enshu will find it,' Kamatori consoled him. 'He strikes me as being tenacious.'

'I'll pay him ten times the Kechi price for the Ajima.'

Kamatori sat in a chair and stretched out his legs. 'Little did Shimzu know when he painted Ajima what the island would come to represent.'

Toshie returned and reminded Suma, 'You have a meeting with Mr Yoshishu in ten minutes.'

'The grand old thief and leader of the Gold Dragons.' Kamatori smiled mockingly. 'Come to audit his share of your financial empire.'

Suma pointed through the huge curved windows overlooking the atrium. 'None of this would have been possible without the organization Korori Yoshishu and my father built during and after the war.'

'The Gold Dragons and the other secret societies have no place in the future Nippon,' said Kamatori, using the traditional word, meaning 'source of the sun'.

'They may seem quaint alongside our moden technology,' Suma admitted, 'but they still share an important niche in our culture. My association with them through the years has proven most valuable to me.'

'Your power goes beyond the need for fanatical factions or personality cults or underworld syndicates,' Kamatori said earnestly. 'You have the power to pull the strings of a government run by your personal puppets, and yet you are chained to corrupt underworld figures. If it ever leaked out that you are the number-two dragon it will cost you dearly.'

'I am not chained to anyone,' said Suma in a patient explaining tone. 'What the laws call criminal activity has been a tradition in my family for two centuries. I've honoured the code by following in my ancestors' footsteps and building an organization on their foundation that's stronger than many nations of the world. I'm not ashamed of underworld friends.'

'I'd be happier if you showed respect for the Emperor and followed the old moral ways.'

'I'm sorry, Moro. Though I pray at Yasukuni Shrine for the spirit of my father, I feel no urge to venerate the myth of a God-like Emperor. Nor do I take part in tea ceremonies, meet with geishas, attend Kabuki plays, watch sumo wrestling, or believe in the superiority of our native culture. Nor do I subscribe to the new theory that we are superior in our customs, intelligence, emotions, language, and particularly the design of our brains to people in the West. I refuse to underestimate my competitors and indulge in national conformity and group thinking. I am my own god, and my faith is in money and power. Does that anger you?'

Kamatori looked down at his hands that lay open in his lap. He sat silent, a growing look of sadness in his eyes. Finally he said, 'No, it saddens me. I bow to the Emperor and our traditional culture. I believe in his divine descent and that we and our islands are also of divine origin. And I believe in the blood purity and spiritual unity of our race. But I follow you too, Hideki, because we are old friends, and despite your sinister operations you have greatly contributed to Nippon's new claim as the most powerful nation on earth.'

'Your loyalty is deeply appreciated, Moro,' said Suma honestly. 'I'd expect no less from one who takes pride in his samurai ancestry and his prowess with the *katana*.'

'The *katana*, more than a sword, but the living soul of the samurai,' Kamatori said with reverence. 'To be expert in its use is divine. To wield it in defence of the Emperor is to ensure my soul's rest in Yasukuni.'

'Yet you've drawn your blade for me when I've asked you.'

Kamatori stared at him. 'I gladly kill in your name to honour the good you do for our people.'

Suma looked into the lifeless eyes of his hired killer, a living throwback to the times when samurai warriors murdered for whatever feudal lord offered them security and advancement. He was also aware that a samurai's absolute loyalty could be reversed overnight. When he spoke, his voice was pleasantly firm.

'Some men hunt wild game with a bow and arrow, most use a firearm. You are the only one I know, Moro, who hunts human game with a sword.'

'You're looking well, old friend,' said Suma as Korori Yoshishu was ushered into his office by Toshie. Yoshishu was accompanied by Ichiro Tsuboi, who had just arrived

220

from the United States after his debate with the congressional select subcommittee.

The old man, a devout realist, smiled at Suma. 'Not well but older. A few more passings of the moon and I'll sleep with my esteemed ancestors.'

'You'll see a hundred new moons.'

'The prospect of leaving all these age-inflicted aches and pains behind makes my exit an event I look forward to.'

Toshie closed the door and left as Suma bowed to Tsuboi. 'Good to see you, Ichiro. Welcome home from Washington. I'm told you gave the American politicians another Pearl Harbor.'

'Nothing so dramatic,' said Tsuboi. 'But I do believe I put a few cracks in their Capitol building.'

Unknown but to a select few, Tsuboi became a member of the Gold Dragons when he was only fourteen. Yoshishu took an interest in the young boy and saw to his advancement in the secret society and taught him the art of financial manipulation on a grand scale. Now as head of Kanoya Securities, Tsuboi personally guarded Yoshishu and Suma's financial empires and guided their secret transactions.

'You both know my trusted friend and adviser, Moro Kamatori.'

'A swordsman almost as good as me in my youth,' said Yoshishu.

Kamatori bowed to his waist. 'I'm sure your *katana* is still swifter than mine.'

'I knew your father when he was fencing master at the university,' said Tsuboi. 'I was his worst pupil. He suggested I buy a cannon and take up elephant shooting.'

Suma took Yoshishu by the arm and led him to a chair. Japan's once most feared man walked slow and stiffly, but his face wore a granite smile and his eyes missed nothing.

He settled into a straight-backed chair and looked up at Suma and came straight to the point of his visit. 'What is the state of the Kaiten Project?'

'We have eighteen bomb vehicles on the high seas. They are the last. Four are destined for the United States. Five for the Soviet Union, and the rest divided up among Europe and the Pacific nations.'

'The time until they're concealed near targets?'

'No later than three weeks. By then our command centre will come on-line with its defence-detection and detonation systems.'

Yoshishu looked at Suma in surprise. 'The untimely explosion on board the *Divine Star* did not set back the project?'

'Fortunately I planned for a possible ship loss due to storm, collision, or other maritime accident. I held six warheads in reserve. The three that were lost in the explosion I replaced. After installation in the autos, they were shipped to Veracruz, Mexico. From there they will be driven across the Texas border into the US to their target areas.'

'The remainder are safely deposited, I hope.'

'On a surplus tanker anchored fifty miles off a desolate shore of Hokkaido.'

'Do we know what caused the detonation on board the *Divine Star*?'

'We're at a loss to explain the premature explosion,' explained Suma. 'Every conceivable safeguard was in place. One of the autos must have become thrown about in rough seas and damaged the warhead container. Radiation then leaked and spread throughout the cargo decks. The crew panicked and abandoned ship. A Norwegian ship discovered the derelict and sent over a boarding party. Shortly after, the *Divine Star* mysteriously blew up.'

'And the escaped crew?'

'No trace. They vanished during the storm.'

'What is the total number of cars in the system?' asked Yoshishu.

Suma stepped to his desk and pushed a button on a small

hand-held control box. The far wall rose into the ceiling revealing a large transparent screen. He pressed another command into the box and a holographic image of the global earth appeared in pulsating neon-like colours. Then he programmed the detonation sites that burst into tiny points of gold light at strategic locations around nearly twenty countries. Only then did Suma answer Yoshishu's question.

'One hundred and thirty in fifteen countries.'

Yoshishu sat silent, staring at the little beams as they flashed around the room with the rotation of the globe like reflections on a mirrored ball above a dance floor.

The Soviet Union had more light clusters than any other nation, suggesting a greater threat to Japan than her trade rivals in Europe and the United States. Strangely, no military installations or major cities were targeted. All of the lights appeared to emanate from barren or lightly populated areas, making the Kaiten menace all the more mysterious as an extortion tool.

'Your father's spirit is proud of you,' Yoshishu said in quiet awe. 'Thanks to your genius we can take our rightful place as a world power of the first magnitude. The twenty-first century belongs to Nippon. America and Russia are finished.'

Suma was pleased. 'The Kaiten Project could not have been created and built without your support, my dear old friend, and certainly not without the financial wizardry of Ichiro Tsuboi.'

'You are most kind,' said Tsuboi with a bow. 'The Machiavellian intrigue of arranging secret funding to build a clandestine nuclear weapons plant came as a great challenge.'

'Soviet and Western intelligence know we have the capacity,' Kamatori said, bringing a realistic bent into the conversation.

'If they didn't know before the explosion,' added Suma, 'they do now.'

'The Americans have suspected us for several years,' said Suma. 'But they have been unable to penetrate our security rings and confirm the exact location of our facility.'

'Lucky for us the fools keep searching horizontal instead of vertical.' Yoshishu's voice was ironic. 'But we must face the very real possibility that sooner or later the CIA or KGB will track the site.'

'Probably sooner,' said Kamatori. 'One of our under-cover agents has informed me that a few days after the *Divine Star* explosion, the Americans launched an all-out covert operation to investigate our involvement. They've already been sniffing around one of Murmoto's automotive distributors.'

A worried crease appeared on Yoshishu's face. 'They are good, the American intelligence people. I fear the Kaiten Project is in jeopardy.'

'We'll know before tomorrow just how much they've learned,' said Kamatori. 'I meet with our agent, who has just returned from Washington. He claims to have updated information.'

The worry in Yoshishu's mind deepened. 'We cannot allow the project to be endangered before the command centre is fully operational. The consequences could spell the end of our new empire.'

'I agree,' said Tsuboi grimly. 'For the next three weeks we are vulnerable while the warheads sit useless. One leak and the Western nations would band together and strike us from all sides, economic as well as militarily.'

'Not to worry,' said Suma. 'Their agents may stumble onto our nuclear weapons manufacturing plant, but they will never discover the whereabouts of the Kaiten Project's brain centre. Not in a hundred years, much less three weeks.'

'And even if fortune smiled on them,' said Kamatori, 'they

can never neutralize it in time. There is only one way in, and that's fortified by massive steel barriers and guarded by a heavily armed security force. The installation can take a direct hit by a nuclear bomb and still function.'

A tight smile cut Suma's lips. 'Everything is working to our advantage. The slightest hint of an attempted penetration or an attack by enemy special forces, and we could threaten to detonate one or more of the auto warheads.'

Tsuboi wasn't convinced. 'What good is an empty threat?'

'Hideki makes a good point,' said Kamatori. 'No one outside this room or the engineers in the command centre knows our system is three weeks away from completion. Western leaders can easily be bluffed into thinking the system is fully operational.'

Yoshishu gave a satisfied nod of his head. 'Then we have nothing to fear.'

'A guaranteed conclusion,' Suma stated without hesitation. 'We're making too much out of a nightmare that will never happen.'

Silence then in the richly decorated office, the four men sitting, each one with his own thoughts. After a minute, Suma's desk interoffice phone buzzed. He picked up the receiver and listened a moment without speaking. Then he set it down.

'My secretary informs me that my chef has dinner prepared in the private dining room. I would be most happy if my honoured guests will dine with me.'

Yoshishu came slowly to his feet. 'I happily accept. Knowing the superb culinary qualities of your chef, I was hoping you'd ask.'

'Before we break off,' said Tsuboi, 'there is one other problem.'

Suma nodded. 'You have the floor, Ichiro.'

'Obviously we can't go around exploding nuclear bombs every time an unfriendly government rattles a sabre over trade restrictions or increased import tariffs. We must have alternatives that are not so catastrophic.'

Suma and Kamatori exchanged looks. 'We've given that very situation considerable thought,' said Suma, 'and we think the best solution is abduction of our enemies.'

'Terrorism is not the way of our culture,' objected Tsuboi.

'What do you call the Blood Sun Brotherhood, my son?' asked Yoshishu calmly.

'Crazy fanatical butchers. They cut down innocent women and children in the name of some vague revolutionary dogma that makes no sense to anyone.'

'Yes, but they're Japanese.'

'A few, but most are East Germans, trained by the KGB.'

'They can be used,' Suma said flatly.

Tsuboi was not sold. 'I do not advise the slightest association with them. Any suspected connection, and outside probes will be launched into areas we dare not have opened.'

'Hideki is not advocating assassination,' elaborated Kamatori. 'What he is suggesting is that abduction of unharmed hostages be blamed on the Blood Sun Brotherhood.'

'Now that makes more sense.' Yoshishu smiled. 'I think I understand. You're advocating the silken prison.'

Tsuboi shook his head. 'I've never heard of it.'

'From the old days,' explained Yoshishu. 'When a shogun did not want an enemy assassinated, he had him abducted and placed secretly in a prison of luxury as a sign of respect. Then he set the blame for the disappearance on his prisoner's jealous rivals.'

'Exactly.' Suma nodded. 'I have built such a facility on Ajima Island. A small but modern estate.'

'Isn't that a bit risky?' inquired Tsuboi.

'The obvious is never suspected.'

Kamatori looked at Tsuboi. 'If you have candidates for oblivion, you need only give me their names.'

Tsuboi's eyes turned down, unseeing. Then he looked up. 'There are two people in the United States who are causing us much grief. But you must be most careful. They are members of Congress, and their abduction will certainly cause a storm of outrage.'

'A Blood Sun Brotherhood kidnapping and ransom situation should make a good cover for their sudden disappearance,' said Suma as if he was describing the weather.

'Who precisely do you have in mind?' asked Kamatori.

'Congresswoman Loren Smith and Senator Michael Diaz.'

Yoshishu nodded. 'Ah, yes, the pair who are promoting a total trade barrier against us.'

'Despite our lobbying efforts, they're gathering enough votes to force their legislation through both houses. Eliminate them and the drive would fall apart.'

'There will be great outrage in their government,' Suma warned. 'It may backlash.'

'Our lobby interests have acquired a powerful influence on Congress and will direct the outrage toward a terrorist conspiracy.' Tsuboi's anger at his treatment by the select subcommittee had not cooled. 'We have lost enough face at the hands of American politicians. Let them learn their power no longer protects them from harm.'

Yoshishu stared out the window unseeing for a few moments. Then he shook his head. 'A great pity.'

Suma looked at him. 'What is a great pity, old friend?'

'The United States of America,' Yoshishu spoke softly. 'She's like a beautiful woman who is dying of cancer.'

28

Marvin Showalter sat on a train travelling through Tokyo's clean and efficient subway. He made no attempt to act as if he was reading a newspaper or a book. He calmly stared at his fellow passengers, 'making', as they say in the trade, the two Japanese secret service agents who were keeping him under surveillance from the next car.

Showalter had walked from the US embassy shortly after a boring meeting with junketing congressmen over Japan's refusal to allow American construction equipment to be used on a new building ready to go up for an American oil company. It was simply another case of throwing up protectionist barriers while the Japanese could freely enter the United States and raise buildings with their architects, foremen, materials, and equipment without major problems over government restrictions.

'Fair is fair' did not apply to two-way trade with Japan.

He appeared to be on his way to the small condominium his wife and two young children called home during his assignment in Japan. The building was owned by the American government and housed most of the embassy workers and their families. The construction cost of the entire ten-storey building was less than a third the price of the land it stood on.

His shadows had fallen into his travel routine, which never varied except when he put in an hour or two overtime. He smiled to himself as his stop came up and the two agents rose in anticipation of his getting off. He stepped to the door with the rest of the crowd, waiting for it to open onto the platform. It was the oldest trick in the world, one shown in the movie *The French Connection*.

As the door opened, Showalter flowed with the crowd to the platform and began counting. He hesitated and casually glanced at the two Japanese agents. They had stepped from the middle door in the next car and were walking slowly in his direction, shielded by a group of departing passengers.

When he hit twenty-five, he swiftly turned around and stepped back inside the car. Two seconds later the door closed and the train began moving. Too late, the Japanese secret service agents realized they'd been had. Frantically they attempted to pry the doors apart and reboard the train. But it was useless. They leaped back on the platform as the train picked up speed and disappeared into the tunnel.

Showalter wasn't overly pleased with the simple dodge. Next time his tails would be wary and make his evasive moves more intricate. He transferred to a connecting line at the next stop and rode to Asakusa, an atmospheric area northeast of Tokyo in a section known as Shitamachi. Asakusa was part of the old city of Tokyo that had preserved much of its past.

Showalter sat and studied the people around him as he had done so many times. Some of his fellow passengers studied him in return. They called anyone who did not share their thick black straight hair, dark eyes, and skin colouring a *gaijin*, literally translated as an 'outside person'. He theorized that the close similarity in their physical looks was perhaps the basis for their unity and conformity. That and the isolation of their island home.

Their society evolved around the family and expanded to include everyone who worked around them. Lives were lived in a complicated quilt of obligations, contentedness, duty, and accomplishment. They accepted a regimented lifestyle as if all others were a waste to be pitied.

The uncohesive melting pot of the United States could not be conceived, nor would it be tolerated in Japan, a country with the toughest immigration laws to be found in the world.

The train stopped at the Tawaramachi subway station,

and he stepped off and joined the crowd that rose to the busy street of Kappabashi. He hailed a cab and rode past the restaurant wholesale supply stores that sold the plastic food replicas seen in eatery windows. He directed the driver to a several-square-block section crowded with craftsmen's shops, ancient temples, and old houses.

He got out and paid the driver at an intersection, and then walked down a narrow flower-lined lane until he came to a Japanese inn known as a *ryokan*.

Although rustic and worn on the outside, the *ryokan* was quite neat and attractive inside. Showalter was met at the door by one of the staff, who bowed and said, 'Welcome to the Ritz.'

'I thought this was the Asakusa Dude Ranch,' Showalter replied.

Without another word, the muscular doorman with arms and legs like railroad ties showed him over the smooth flattened river stones of the entry. They stepped onto the polished oak floor of the reception area, where Showalter was politely asked to remove his shoes and put on a pair of plastic slippers.

Unlike most slippers that are too small for large Anglo feet, Showalter's fit like they were custom-ordered, which indeed they were, since the *ryokan* was secretly owned and operated by an American intelligence agency that specialized in covert and safe retreats.

Showalter's room had a sliding shoji paper door that opened onto a small veranda overlooking a formal garden with water trickling restfully onto rocks through bamboo tubes. The floor was covered by the traditional tatami straw matting. He had to take off the slippers and walk in his socks while on the fragile mats.

There were no chairs or furniture, only cushions on the floor, and a bed made up of many pillows and heavy cushions the Japanese called 'futons'. A small fire pit sat in the centre of the guest room with warm glowing coals.

Showalter undressed and donned a light cotton *yukata*, a short robe. Then a maid in a kimono led him to the inn's communal bathing facilities. He left the *yukata* and his wristwatch in a wicker basket, and shielded by only a washcloth-size towel, he entered the steamy bath area. He stepped around the low stools and wooden pails and stood under a simple faucet. He lathered up and rinsed off. Only then was he ready to sink slowly into the hot water of a huge wooden pool-like tub.

A shadowy figure was already sitting chest deep in the water. Showalter greeted him.

'The Honda Team, I presume.'

'Only half of it,' answered Roy Orita. 'Jim Hanamura should be along any time. Like a saki?'

'Against orders to drink during an operation,' said Showalter, easing into the steaming water. 'But what the hell. I'm colder than ice cream. Pour me a double.'

Orita filled a small ceramic cup out of a bottle sitting on the edge of the pool. 'How's life at the embassy?'

'The usual dung one would expect from the State Department.' Showalter took a long sip of the saki and let it settle into his stomach. 'How goes the investigation? Any information on the leads we received from Team Lincoln?'

'I checked out the company management of Murmoto. I can't uncover a direct link between the corporate executive officers and the warheads. My own opinion is they're clean. They haven't the slightest idea of what is going on beneath their noses.'

'Some of them must know.'

Orita grinned. 'Only two assembly line workers have to be in on it.'

'Why only two?'

'All that are required. The assembly line worker who oversees the installation of the air conditioners. He's in a position to select specific cars to get the warheads. And the inspector who checks out the units to make sure they work before the cars are shipped to the dealers. He okays the phony units that don't operate.'

'There has to be a third man,' disagreed Showalter. 'An agent in the factory's computerized shipping department who erases all trace of the bomb cars, except on the bill of lading which is required to satisfy foreign customs officials.'

'Have you followed the thread from factory to air conditioner supplier to nuke plant?'

'To the supplier, yes. Then the trail vanishes. I hope to pick up a scent and follow it to the source in the next few days.'

Orita's voice became silent as a man came from the dressing room and walked toward the heated pool. He was short with silver hair and moustache and held the small wash towel in front of his groin.

'Who the hell are you?' demanded Showalter, alarmed that a stranger had broken the security of the *ryokan*.

'My name is Ashikaga Enshu.'

'Who?'

The man stood there without answering for several seconds. Showalter began frantically looking around, wondering why no security sentries were present.

Then Orita began laughing. 'Great disguise, Jim. You fooled hell out of both of us.'

James Hanamura removed the silver-haired wig and pulled off the eyebrows and moustache. 'Not bad if I do say so. I faked out Hideki Suma and his secretary as well.'

Showalter exhaled a great breath and sank in the water up to his chin. 'Jesus, you gave me a scare. For all I knew you had penetrated the security rings and were about to despatch Orita and me.'

'That saki looks good. Any left?'

Orita poured him a cup. 'There's a whole case of it in the kitchen.' Then suddenly a surprised expression swept his face. 'What was that you just said?'

'Beg your pardon?'

'Hideki Suma.'

'My half of the operation. I traced ownership of the Murmoto Automotive and Aircraft Corporation and the Sushimo Steamship Company through a string of phony business fronts to Hideki Suma, the recluse tycoon. Murmoto and Sushimo are only a drop in the bucket. This guy has more assets than the entire State of California, with Nevada and Arizona thrown in.'

'Didn't the ship that blew up, the *Divine Star*, belong to Sushimo Steamship?' asked Showalter.

'Yes indeed. A neat package, wouldn't you say? It looks to me like Hideki Suma is up to his ears in this mess.'

'Suma is a very powerful man,' said Showalter. 'He prospers in strange and devious ways. They say that if he commands Prime Minister Junshiro and his cabinet ministers to flap their arms and fly, they'd fight over who jumps out the window first.'

'You actually got in to see Suma?' Orita asked in amazement.

'Nothing to it. You should see his office and secretary. Both very choice.'

'Why the disguise?'

'Team Lincoln's idea. Suma collects paintings by a sixteenth-century Japanese artist named Masaki Shimzu. Jordan hired an expert forger to paint what is called in art circles an undiscovered Shimzu, one it was known Suma didn't have in his collection. Then, as the reputable finder of lost art, Ashikaga Enshu, I sold it to him.'

Showalter nodded. 'Clever, clever. You must have studied your Japanese art.'

'A crash course.' Hanamura laughed. 'Suma elaborated on how Shimzu painted islands from a balloon. He'd have ordered me drawn and quartered if he knew he was laying out a hundred and forty-five million yen for a fake painted from a satellite photo.'

'For what purpose?' asked Orita, his face oddly taut.

'To plant bugs in his office, naturally.'

'How come I wasn't in on this?'

'I thought it best you two didn't know what the other was doing,' Showalter answered Orita, 'so you couldn't reveal anything of importance if either of you were compromised.'

'Where did you set the bugs?' Orita asked Hanamura.

'Two in the frame of the painting. One in an easel he's got standing in front of a window, and another inside the draw handle for the blinds. The latter two are in perfect alignment with a relay transmitter I placed in a tree outside the atrium dome of the city.'

'What if Suma has hidden sweep equipment?'

'I "borrowed" the electrical blueprints to his floor of the building. His detection equipment is first rate, but it won't pick up our bugs. And when I say bugs, I'm talking in the literal sense.'

Orita missed Hanamura's implication. 'You lost me.'

'Our miniature receiving and sending units are not designed with the look of tiny electronic objects. They're moulded to look like ants. If discovered, they'll either be ignored or simply mashed without suspicion.'

Showalter nodded. 'That's pretty slick.'

'Even our Japanese brothers have to take a back seat to our home-grown eavesdropping technology.' Hanamura smiled widely. 'The relay transmitter, which is about the size of a golf ball, sends all conversations, including telephone or intercom calls from the office bugs, to one of our satellites, and then beams it down to Mel Penner and his Team Chrysler on Palau.'

Orita stared into the water. 'Do we know for certain if they're picking up Suma's conversations?'

'The system is fully operational,' Showalter assured him. 'I contacted Penner before I left for our meeting. He's receiving the signals loud and clear. And so are we. A member of my team at the embassy is also tuned in on Jim's listening gear.'

'You'll alert us, I hope, if any information comes through we can use in the investigation.'

'Absolutely.' Showalter poured himself another saki. 'As a matter of interest, there was an intriguing conversation going on between Suma and Korori Yoshishu when I left the embassy. Too bad I only caught the first couple of minutes of it.'

'Yoshishu,' muttered Hanamura. 'Good lord, is that old crook still alive?'

'Ninety-one and rotten as ever,' answered Showalter.

Hanamura shook his head. 'The master criminal of the age, personally responsible for more than a million deaths. If Yoshishu is behind Suma and a worldwide organization of hidden nuclear warheads, we're all in deep, deep trouble.'

An hour before dawn a Murmoto limousine pulled to a stop and a figure stepped from the shadows and quickly ducked through the opened door. Then the car crawled slowly through the narrow back streets of Asakusa.

'Mr Suma's office is bugged,' said Orita. 'One of our agents posing as an art dealer hid sophisticated listening devices in the frame of a painting, an easel, and the draw pull of the window blinds.'

'Are you certain?' demanded a stunned Kamatori. 'The dealer produced an original Shimzu.'

'A fake painted from a satellite photo.'

Kamatori hissed. 'You should have informed me sooner.'

'I only learned of it a few hours ago.'

Kamatori said nothing but stared at Orita's face in the semi-darkness of the limousine as if reinforcing his trust.

Like George Furukawa, Roy Orita was an intelligence sleeper, born in the United States of Japanese parents and groomed for employment in the CIA.

Finally Kamatori said, 'Much was said this afternoon that could prove damaging to Mr Suma. There can be no mistake about this?'

'Did the dealer say his name was Ashikaga Enshu?'

Kamatori felt shock mingled with shame. His job was to protect Suma's organization from penetration. He had failed miserably and lost much face.

'Yes, Enshu.'

'His real name is James Hanamura. The other half of my team whose job is to investigate the source of the nuclear car bombs.'

'Who fathomed the tie between the cars and the warheads?'

'An amateur by the name of Dirk Pitt. He was borrowed from the National Underwater and Marine Agency.'

'Is he dangerous to us?'

'He might cause trouble. I can't say for sure. He's not assigned to the investigative operations. But he does have an awesome reputation for successfully carrying through impossible projects.'

Kamatori sat back and idly stared out the window at the darkened buildings. At last he turned to Orita.

'Can you give me a list of names of the agents you're working with and provide updates on their activities?'

Orita nodded. 'The list of names, yes. The activities, no way. We all work separately. Like a magical act, no one knows what the other hand is doing.'

'Keep me informed as best you can.'

'What do you intend to do about Pitt?'

Kamatori looked at Orita with venom in his cold eyes. 'If a safe opportunity arises, kill him.'

29

Guided by Loren Smith on one side and Al Giordino on the other, Pitt backed the Stutz town car down the ramps of a trailer and parked it between a red 1926 Hispano-Suiza, a big cabriolet manufactured in France, and a beautiful 1931 Marmon V-16 town car. He cocked an ear and listened to the engine a minute, revving the rpm's, satisfying himself it was turning over smoothly without a miss. Then he switched off the ignition.

It was an Indian summer day. The sky was clear and warm for early fall. Pitt wore corduroy slacks and a suede sports coat, while Loren looked radiant in a dusty rose jumpsuit.

While Giordino moved the pickup truck and trailer to a parking lot, Loren stood on the running board of the Stutz and gazed at the field of over a hundred classic cars arranged around the infield of the Virginia Memorial racetrack. The concours d'elegance, a show where the cars were judged on appearance, was combined with one-lap races around the track between classic vehicles designed and built as road and tour cars.

'They're all so gorgeous,' Loren said wonderingly. 'I've never seen so many exotic cars in one place.'

'Stiff competition,' Pitt said as he raised the hood and wiped down the engine. 'I'll be lucky to take a third in my class.'

'When is the judging?'

'Any time.'

'And the races?'

'After the concours, winners are announced and the awards passed out.'

'What car will you race against?'

'According to the programme, the red Hispano next to us.'

Loren eyed the attractive Paris-built drop-head cabriolet. 'Think you can beat it?'

'I don't know. The Stutz is six years newer, but the Hispano has a larger engine and a lighter body.'

Giordino approached and announced, 'I'm hungry. When do we eat?'

Loren laughed, gave Giordino a light kiss on the cheek, and produced a picnic basket from the back seat of the Stutz. They sat on the grass and ate mortadella and brie with sourdough bread, accompanied with a paté and fruit and washed down by a bottle of Valley of the Moon zinfandel.

The judges came and began examining Pitt's car for the concours. He was entered in Class D, American classic 1930 to 1941 closed top. After fifteen minutes of intense study, they shook his hand and moved off to the next car in his class, a 1933 Lincoln V-12 Berline.

By the time Pitt and his friends had polished off the zinfandel, the winners were announced over the public announcement system. The Stutz came in third behind a 1938 Packard sport coupe and a 1934 Lincoln limousine.

Pitt had lost one and a half points out of a perfect hundred because the Stutz cigarette lighter didn't work and the exhaust system did not strictly adhere to the original design.

'Better than I expected,' said Pitt proudly. 'I didn't think we'd place.'

'Congratulations,' said Frank Mancuso.

Pitt stared blankly at the mining engineer who had seemingly appeared out of nowhere. 'Where did you pop from?'

'I heard through the grapevine you'd be here,' said Mancuso warmly, 'so I thought I'd drop by, see the cars, and talk a little shop with you and Al.'

'Time for us to go to work?'

'Not yet.'

Pitt turned and introduced Mancuso to Loren. Giordino simply nodded and passed the newcomer a glass of wine from a newly opened bottle. Mancuso's eyes widened when he was introduced to Loren.

He looked at Pitt with an approving expression, then nodded at Loren and the Stutz. 'Two classic beauties. You have excellent taste.'

Pitt smiled slyly. 'I do what I can.'

'That's quite a car,' Mancuso said, eyeing the lines of the Stutz. 'LeBaron coachwork, isn't it?'

'Very good. You into old automobiles?'

'My brother is a car nut. I soaked up what little I know about them from him.' He motioned up the aisle separating the line of cars. 'Would you care to give me a guided lecture on all this fine machinery?'

They excused themselves to Loren, who struck up a conversation with the wife of the owner of the Hispano-Suiza. After they strolled past a few cars, Giordino grew impatient.

'What's going on?' he demanded.

Mancuso stared at him. 'You'll probably hear about it from Admiral Sandecker. But Team Mercedes has been put on hold. Your project to salvage any remains of the ship that carried the bomb cars has been scrubbed.'

'Any particular reason?'

'The President decided it would be best if we kept hands off for now. Too many problems. Soviet propaganda is already trying to lay the blast on our doorstep. Congress is talking about launching investigations, and the President is in no mind to explain an undercover salvage operation. He can't afford discovery of your Soggy Acres venture. That went against international laws governing mining of the seafloor.'

'We only took samples,' said Pitt defensively. 'It was purely an experimental programme.'

239

'Maybe so, but you got the jump on the rest of the world. Third-world nations especially would howl their heads off at the UN if they thought they were being cut out of an undersea bonanza.'

Pitt stopped and studied a huge open car. 'I'd love to own this one.'

'A Cadillac touring?'

'A Cadillac V-16 phaeton,' Pitt corrected. 'They're bringing close to a million dollars at the auctions.'

Giordino nodded. 'Right up there with the Duesenbergs.'

Pitt turned and looked at Mancuso steadily. 'How many cars with warheads have they found?'

'Only your six so far. Stacy and Weatherhill haven't sent word of their progress on the West Coast yet.'

'The Japanese must have a fleet of those things scattered around the country,' said Pitt. 'Jordan will need an army to nail them down.'

'There's no lack of manpower, but the trick is to do it without pushing the Japs into a corner. If they think their nuclear bomb project is threatened, they might overreact and set one off manually.'

'Nice if Team Honda can penetrate the source and snatch a map of the locations,' Giordino said quietly.

'They're working on it,' Mancuso stated firmly.

Pitt leaned over and peered at a Lalique crystal head of a rooster that adorned the radiator of a Pierce-Arrow roadster. 'In the meantime we all sit around with our fingers in our ears.'

'Don't feel left out. You accomplished more in the first four hours than the entire team in forty-eight. We'll be called when we're needed.'

'I don't like waiting in the dark for something to happen.'

Giordino switched his attention from the cars to a girl walking past in a tight leather skirt and said vaguely, 'What could possibly happen at a concours?'

*

They seemed an unlikely group, but there they were, seriously observant in their dark suits and attaché cases amid the casually dressed classic car owners and spectators. The four Japanese men gazed studiously at the cars, scribbling in notebooks and acting as though they were advance men for a Tokyo consortium of collector car buyers.

It was a good front. People noticed them, were bemused by their antics, and turned away, never suspecting they were a highly trained team of undercover operatives and their attaché cases were arsenals of gas grenades and assault weapons.

The Japanese team had not come to admire the automobiles, they came to abduct Loren Smith.

They combed the area around the concours, noting the exits and placement of armed security guards. Their leader, his dark face glistening in the midday sun, noted that Pitt's Stutz was parked in the centre of the field of classic automobiles, making it next to impossible to spirit Loren away without causing an outcry.

He ordered his three men to return to their stretch limousine that was parked by the track while he hung around keeping an eye on Loren's movements. He also followed Pitt, Giordino, and Mancuso for a short distance, examining their clothing for any telltale bulge of a handgun. He saw nothing suspicious and assumed all three were unarmed.

Then he wandered about patiently, knowing the right moment would eventually arrive.

A race steward informed Pitt that he and the Stutz were due on the starting line. With his friends going along for the ride, he drove along the grass aisle between the rows of cars and through a gate onto the asphalt one-mile oval track.

Giordino raised the hood and gave a final check of the engine while Mancuso observed. Loren gave Pitt a long good-luck kiss and then jogged to the side of the track, where she sat on a low wall.

When the Hispano-Suiza pulled alongside, Pitt walked over and introduced himself as the driver stepped from behind the wheel to recheck his hood latches.

'I guess we'll be competing against each other. My name is Dirk Pitt.'

The driver of the Hispano, a big man with greying hair, a white beard, and blue-green eyes, stuck out a hand. 'Clive Cussler.'

Pitt looked at him strangely. 'Do we know each other?'

'It's possible,' replied Cussler, smiling. 'Your name is familiar, but I can't place your face.'

'Perhaps we met at a party or a car club meet.'

'Perhaps.'

'Good luck,' Pitt wished him graciously.

Cussler beamed back. 'The same to you.'

As he settled behind the steering wheel, Pitt's eyes scanned the instruments on the dashboard and then locked on the official starter, who was slowly unfurling the green flag. He failed to notice a long white Lincoln Limousine pull to a stop in the pit area along the concrete safety wall just in front of Loren. Nor did he see a man exit the car, walk over to her, and say a few words.

Giordino's attention was focused on the Stutz. Only Mancuso, who was standing several feet away, saw her nod to the man, a Japanese, and accompany him to the limousine.

Giordino lowered the hood and shouted over the windscreen, 'No oil or water leaks. Don't push her too hard. We may have rebuilt the engine, but she's over sixty years old. And you can't buy spare Stutz parts at Pep Boys.'

'I'll keep the rpm's below the red,' Pitt promised him. Only then did he miss Loren and glance around. 'What happened to Loren?'

Mancuso leaned over the door and pointed at the white

stretch Lincoln. 'A Japanese businessman over there in the limo wanted to talk to her. Probably some lobbyist.'

'Not like her to miss the race.'

'I'll keep an eye on her,' said Mancuso.

Giordino reached in and gripped Pitt's shoulder. 'Don't miss a shift.'

Then he and Mancuso stepped away to the side of the track as the starter positioned himself between the two cars and raised the green flag over his head.

Pitt eased down on the accelerator until the tachometer read 1,000 rpm's. His timing was on the edge of perfect. He second-guessed the starter official and popped the clutch the same instant the flag began its descent. The turquoise Stutz got the jump and leaped a car length ahead of the red Hispano-Suiza.

The Stutz eight-cylinder engine featured twin overhead camshafts with four valves per cylinder. And though the horsepower was comparable, the Hispano's six-cylinder displacement was eight litres against five for the Stutz. In chassis and body weight, the big town car gave away a 200-kilogram handicap to the cabriolet.

Both drivers had removed the cutout that allowed the exhaust to bypass their mufflers and thunder into the air just behind the manifolds. The resulting roar from the elderly engines as the cars accelerated from the starting line excited the crowd in the stands, and they shouted and applauded, urging on the beautiful but monstrous masterworks of mechanical art to higher speeds.

Pitt still led as they surged into the first turn in a haze of exhaust and a fury of sound. He shifted through the gears as smoothly as the old transmission let him. First gear was worn and gave off a banshee howl, with second coming much quieter. Given enough time and distance, both cars might have reached a speed of 160 kilometres (100 mph), but their accelerating velocity did not exactly snap necks.

Pitt kept a wary eye on the tach as he made his final shift

with the Warner four-speed. Coming onto the back stretch, the Stutz was pushing a hundred kilometres, with the Hispano pressing hard and gaining in the turn.

Onto the straightaway, the Hispano moved up on the Stutz. Cussler was going all out. He pushed the big French car to the limit, the noisy valve train nearly drowning out the roar of the exhaust. The flying storm ornament that was mounted on the radiator crept even with the Stutz's rear door handle.

There was nothing Pitt could do but keep the front wheels aimed straight, the accelerator pedal mashed to the floorboard, and hurtle down the track at full bore. The tach needle was quivering a millimetre below the red line. He dared not push the engine beyond its limits, not just yet. He backed off slightly as the Hispano drew alongside.

For a few moments they raced wheel to wheel. Then the superior torque of the Hispano began to tell, and it edged ahead. The exhaust from the big eight-litre engine sounded like a vulcan cannon in Pitt's ears, and he could see the trainlike taillight that wagged back and forth when the driver stepped on the brakes. But Cussler wasn't about to brake. He was pushing the flying Hispano to the wall.

When they sped into the final turn, Pitt slipped in behind the big red car, drafting for a few hundred metres before veering high in the curve. Then, as they came onto the home stretch, he used the few horses the Stutz had left to give and slingshotted down to the inside of the track.

With the extra power and momentum, he burst into the lead and held off the charging Hispano just long enough to cross the finish line with the Stutz sun-goddess radiator ornament less than half a metre in front of the Hispano stork.

It was a masterful touch, the kind of finish that excited the crowd. He threw back his head and laughed as he waved to them. He was supposed to continue and take a victory lap, but Giordino and Mancuso leaped from the pit area waving their hands for him to stop. He veered to the edge of the track and slowed.

Mancuso was frantically gesturing toward the white limousine that was speeding toward an exit. 'The limousine,' he yelled on the run.

Pitt's reaction time was fast, almost inhumanly so, and it only took him an instant to transfer his mind from the race to what Mancuso was trying to tell him.

'Loren?' he shouted back.

Giordino leaped onto the running board of the still-moving car. 'I think those Japs in the limousine snatched her,' he blurted.

Mancuso rushed up then, breathing heavily. 'They drove away before I realized she was still in the car.'

'You armed?' Pitt asked him.

'A twenty-five Colt auto in an ankle holster.'

'Get in!' Pitt ordered. Then he turned to Giordino. 'Al, grab a guard with a radio and alert the police. Frank and I'll give chase.'

Giordino nodded without a reply and ran toward a security guard patrolling the pits as Pitt gunned the Stutz and barrelled past the gate leading from the track to the parking lot behind the crowd stands.

He knew the Stutz was hopelessly outclassed by the big, newer limousine, but he'd always held the unshakable belief that insurmountable odds were surmountable.

He settled in the seat and gripped the wheel, his prominent chin thrust forward, and took up the pursuit.

30

Pitt got away fast. The race official at the gate saw him coming and hustled people out of the way. The Stutz hit the parking lot at eighty kilometres an hour, twenty seconds behind the white Lincoln.

They tore between the aisles of parked cars, Pitt holding the horn button down in the centre of the steering wheel. Thankfully, the lot was empty of people. All the spectators and concours entrants were in the stands watching the races, many of whom now turned and stared at the turquoise Stutz as it swept toward the street, twin chrome horns blasting the air.

Pitt was inflamed with madness. The chances of stopping the limousine and rescuing Loren were next to impossible. It was a chase bred of desperation. There was little hope a sixty-year-old machine could run down a modern limousine pulled by a big V-8 engine giving out almost twice the horsepower. This was more than a criminal kidnapping, he knew. He feared the abductors meant for Loren to die.

Pitt cramped the wheel as they hit the highway outside the racetrack, careening sideways in a protesting screech of rubber, fishtailing down the highway in chase of the Lincoln.

'They've got a heavy lead,' Mancuso said sharply.

'We can cut it,' Pitt said in determination. He snapped the wheel to one side and then back again to dodge a car entering the two-lane highway from a side road. 'Until they're certain they're being chased, they won't drive over the speed limit and risk being stopped by a cop. The best we can do is keep them in sight until the state police can intercept.'

Pitt's theory was on the money. The charging Stutz began to gain on the limousine.

Mancuso nodded through the windscreen. 'They're turning onto Highway Five along the James River.'

Pitt drove with a loose and confident fury. The Stutz was in its element on a straight road with gradual turns. He loved the old car, its complex machinery, the magnificent styling, and fabulous engine.

Pitt pushed the old car hard, driving like a demon. The pace was too much for the Stutz, but Pitt talked to it, ignoring the strange look on Mancuso's face, urging and begging it to run beyond its limits.

And the Stutz answered.

To Mancuso it was incredible. It seemed to him that Pitt was physically lifting the car to higher speeds. He stared at the speedometer and saw the needle touching ninety-eight mph. The dynamic old machine had never been driven that fast when it was new. Mancuso held on to the door as Pitt shot around cars and trucks, passing several at one time, so fast Mancuso was amazed they didn't spin off the road on a tight bend.

Mancuso heard another sound above the exhaust of the Stutz and looked up from the open chauffeur's compartment into the sky. 'We have a helicopter riding herd,' he announced.

'Police?'

'No markings. It looks commercial.'

'Too bad we don't have a radio.'

They had drawn up within two hundred metres of the limousine when the Stutz was discovered, and the Lincoln carrying Loren immediately began to pick up speed and slip away.

Then to add to the growing setback, a good ole farm boy driving a big Dodge pickup truck with two rifles slung across the rear window spotted the antique auto climbing up his truck bed and decided to do a little funnin' to keep the Stutz from passing.

Every time Pitt pulled over the centre line to overtake the Dodge, the wiry oily-haired driver, who grinned with half a mouth of vacant teeth, just cackled and veered to the opposite side of the road, cutting the Stutz off.

Mancuso pulled his little automatic from its ankle holster. 'I'll put one through the clown's windscreen.'

'Give me a chance to bulldog him,' said Pitt.

Bulldogging was an old-time race driver's trick. Pitt eased up on the right side of the Dodge, then backed off and came at the other. He repeated the process, not trying to force his way past, but taking control of the situation.

The skinny truck driver swerved side to side to block what he thought were Pitt's attempts to pass. Holding the Stutz at bay after numerous assaults, his head began to swivel to see where the old classic car was coming from next.

And then he made the mistake Pitt was hoping for.

He lost his concentration on a curve and slipped onto the gravel shoulder. His next mistake was to oversteer. The Dodge whipped wildly back and forth and then hurtled off the road, rolling over in a clump of low trees and bushes before coming to rest on its top and crushing a hornet's nest.

The farm boy was only bruised in the crash, but the hornets almost killed him before he escaped the upside-down truck and leaped into a nearby pond.

'Slick work,' said Mancuso, staring back.

Pitt allowed a quick grin. 'It's called methodical reckless-ness.'

The grin vanished as he swerved around a truck and saw a flatbed trailer on the blind side of a curve. The truck had lost part of its cargo, three oil barrels that had fallen off the trailer. One had burst and spread a wide greasy slick on the pavement. The white limousine had missed striking the truck but lost traction in the oil and made two complete 360-degree circles before its driver incredibly straightened it out and darted ahead.

The Stutz went into a sideways four-wheel drift, tyres

smoking, the sun flashing on its polished wheel covers. Mancuso braced himself for the impact against the rear of the truck he was sure would come.

Pitt fought the skid for a horrifying hundred metres before the black tyre marks were finally behind him. Then he was into the oil. He didn't touch his brakes or fight the car but shoved in the clutch and let the car roll free and straight over the slippery pool. Then he eased the car along the grass shoulder beside the road until the tyres were rid of the oil, then resumed the chase only a few seconds now behind the Lincoln.

After the near miss, Mancuso was amazed to see Pitt blithely carry on as if he was on a Sunday drive.

'The helicopter?' Pitt asked conversationally.

Mancuso bent his head back. 'Still with us. Flying above and to the right of the limo.'

'I have a gut feeling they're working together.'

'Does seem strange there are no markings on the bird,' agreed Mancuso.

'If they're armed, we could be in for a bad time.'

Mancuso nodded. 'That's a fact. My pea shooter won't do much against automatic assault weapons from the air.'

'Still, they could have opened up and shut off our water miles back.'

'Speaking of water,' said Mancuso, pointing at the radiator.

The strain on the old car was beginning to tell. Steam was beginning to hiss from the filler cap under the sun goddess, and oil was streaking from the louvres of the hood. And as Pitt braked before a tight turn, he might just as well have raised a sail. The brake lining was overheated and badly faded. The only event that occurred when Pitt pushed the pedal was the flash of the taillights.

Pitt had visions of Loren tied and gagged in the plush rear seat of the limousine. Fear and anxiety swept through him like a gust of icy wind. Whoever abducted her might have already murdered her. He pushed the terrible thought from his mind and told himself the kidnappers could not afford to lose her as a hostage. But if they harmed her, they would die, he vowed ruthlessly.

Driving as if possessed, he was consumed with determination to rescue Loren. Using every scrap of his stubborn spirit, he pursued the Lincoln relentlessly.

'We're holding on to them,' Mancuso observed.

'They're toying with us,' Pitt replied, eyeing the road between the sun goddess hood ornament and the rear bumper of the white limousine racing only fifty metres ahead. 'They should have enough power to leave us in their fumes.'

'Could be an engine problem.'

'I don't think so. The driver is a professional. He's maintained an exact distance between us since the oil spill.'

Mancuso looked at his watch as the sun's rays flashed through the trees branching over the road. 'Where in hell are the state police?'

'Chasing all over the countryside. Giordino has no way of knowing which direction we took.'

'You can't keep up this pace much longer.'

'Al will smell out our trail,' Pitt said with complete confidence in his longtime friend.

Mancuso tilted his head as his ears picked up a new sound. He rose up on his knees and looked back and upward through the overhanging trees. He began waving madly.

'What is it?' Pitt asked, decelerating around a sharp turn and over a short bridge that spanned a narrow stream, his foot pushing the near useless brake pedal to the floor.

'I think the cavalry has arrived,' Mancuso shouted excitedly.

'Another helicopter,' Pitt acknowledged. 'Can you see markings?'

The speeding cars raced out of the trees and into open farmland. The approaching helicopter banked to one side, and Mancuso could read the wording on the cowling under the engine and rotor blades.

'Henrico County Sheriff's Department!' he yelled above the heavy thump of the rotor blades. Then he recognized Giordino waving from an open doorway. The little Italian had arrived, and not a minute too soon. The Stutz was on its last breath.

The pilot in the strange copter flying above the limousine saw the new arrival too. He suddenly veered off, dropped low, and headed northeast at full throttle, quickly disappearing behind a row of trees bordering a cornfield.

The Lincoln appeared to slowly drift to one side of the road. Pitt and Mancuso watched in helpless horror as the long white limo angled onto the shoulder, soared over a small ditch, and surged into the cornfield as if chasing the fleeing helicopter.

Pitt took in the rapid change of scene in one swift, sweeping glance. Reacting instantly, he twisted the wheel, sending the Stutz after the Lincoln. Mancuso's mouth hung in shock as the dry and brittle cornstalks, left standing after husking, whipped the windscreen. Instinctively he ducked down in the seat with his arms over his head.

The Stutz plunged after the limousine, bouncing wildly on its ancient springs and shock absorbers. The dust clouds flew so thick Pitt could hardly see past the sun goddess, yet his foot remained jammed flat on the accelerator.

They burst through a wire fence. A piece of it clipped Mancuso on the side of the head, and then they were out of the cornfield almost on top of the limousine. It had shot into the open at an incredible rate of speed in a direct line toward a concrete silo with the Stutz right behind.

'Oh God,' Mancuso murmured, seeing the grim reaper.

Despite the shock of witnessing an approaching crash that he was helpless to prevent, Pitt jerked the steering wheel violently to his right, throwing the Stutz in a spin around the other side of the silo and missed piling into the Lincoln by an arm's length.

He heard rather than saw the convulsive crush of metal tearing apart followed by the crackled splash of shattered glass against concrete. A great cloud of dust burst from the base of the silo and shrouded the devastated limousine.

Pitt was out of the Stutz before it stopped and running toward the crash site. Fear and dread spread through his body as he came around the silo and viewed the shattered, twisted car. No one could have lived after such a terrible impact. The engine had pushed through the firewall and was shoved against the front seat. The steering wheel was thrust up against the roof. Pitt could not see any sign of the chauffeur and assumed his body must have been thrown to the other side of the car.

The passenger compartment had accordioned, raising the roof in a strange peak and bending the doors inward, jamming them shut so tightly nothing less than an industrial metal saw could cut them away. Pitt desperately kicked out the few glass shards remaining in a broken door window and thrust his head inside.

The crumpled interior was empty.

In numbed slow motion Pitt walked around the car, searching under it for signs of bodies. He found nothing, not even a trace of blood or torn clothing. Then he looked at the caved-in dashboard and found the reason for the vacant ghost car. He tore a small instrument from its electrical connectors and studied it, his face reddening in anger.

He was still standing by the wreckage as the chopper landed and Giordino ran up, trailed by Mancuso, who was holding a bloodied handkerchief to one ear.

'Loren?' Giordino asked with grim concern.

Pitt shook his head and tossed the strange instrument to Giordino. 'We were hoodwinked. This car was a decoy, operated by an electronic robot unit and driven by someone in the helicopter.'

Mancuso stared wildly about the limo. 'I saw her get in,' he said dazedly.

'So did I,' Giordino backed him up.

'Not this car.' Pitt spoke quietly.

'But it was never out of your sight.'

'But it was. Think about it. The twenty-second head start when it left the track and drove under the stands to the parking lot. The switch must have been made then.'

Mancuso removed the handkerchief, revealing a neat slice just above his ear lobe. 'It fits. This one was never out of our sight once we hit the highway.'

Mancuso broke off suddenly and looked miserably at the demolished limo. No one moved or said anything for several moments.

'We lost her,' Giordino said as if in pain, his face pale. 'God help us, we lost her.'

Pitt stared at the car unseeing, his big hands clenched in anger and despair. 'We'll find Loren,' he said, his voice empty and cold as Arctic stone. 'And make those pay who took her.'

PART THREE
Ajima Island

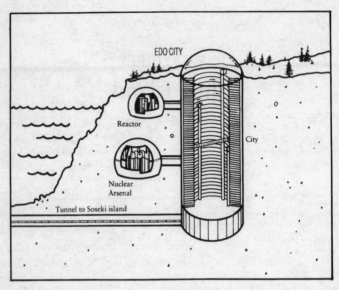

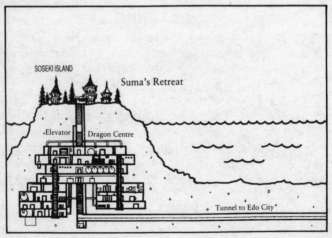

31
October 12, 1993
Bielefeld, West Germany

The fall morning was crisp with a biting wind from the north when August Clausen stepped out of his half-timbered house and gazed across his fields toward the slopes of the Teutoburg Forest near Bielefeld in North Rhine-Westphalia. His farm lay in the valley, bordered by a winding stream that he had recently dammed up. He buttoned up his heavy wool coat, took a few deep breaths, and then walked the path to his barn.

A big hardy man just past seventy-four, Clausen still put in a full day's work from sunup to sundown. The farm had been in his family for five generations. He and his wife raised two daughters, who married and left home, preferring city living in Bielefeld to farming. Except for hired hands during harvesting, Clausen and his wife ran the farm alone.

Clausen pushed open the barn doors and mounted a large tractor. The tough old gas engine turned over and fired on the first revolution. He slipped the transmission into top gear and moved into the yard, turning on a dirt road and heading toward the fields that had been harvested and cultivated for the next spring planting.

Today he planned to fill in a small depression that appeared in the southwest corner of a lettuce field. It was one of the few outdoor chores he wanted to get out of the way before the winter months set in. The evening before, he had set the tractor up with a front-end scoop to move dirt from a mound near an old concrete bunker left from the war.

One section of Clausen's land was once an airfield for a Luftwaffe fighter squadron. When he returned home after serving in a Panzer brigade that fought Patton's Third Army through France and half of Germany, he found a junkyard of burned and destroyed aircraft and motor vehicles piled and scattered over most of his fallow fields. He kept what little that was salvageable and sold the rest to scrap dealers.

The tractor moved at a good speed over the road. There had been little rain the past two weeks and the tracks were dry. The poplar and birch trees wore bright dabs of yellow against the fading green. Clausen swung through an opening in the fence and stopped beside the depression. He climbed down and studied the sinking ground close-up. Curiously, it seemed wider and deeper than the day before. He wondered at first if it might be caused by underground seepage from the stream he had dammed. And yet the earth in the depression's centre looked quite dry.

He remounted the tractor, drove to the dirt pile beside the old bunker that was now half hidden by bushes and vines, and lowered the scoop. When he'd scraped up a full load, he backed off and approached the depression until his front wheels were on the edge. He raised the scoop slightly with the intention of tilting it to drop the dirt load, but the front of the tractor began to tip. The front wheels were sinking into the ground.

Clausen gaped in astonishment as the depression opened up and the tractor dived into a suddenly expanding pit. He froze in horror as man and machine fell into the darkness below. He was mute with terror, but he instinctively braced his feet against the metal floor and clutched the steering wheel in a tight grip. The tractor hurtled a good twelve metres before it splashed into a deep underground stream. Huge clods of soil struck the water, churning it into a maelstrom that was soon blanketed by clouds of falling dust. The noise echoed into unseen reaches as the tractor sank into water up to the top treads of its high rear tyres before coming to rest.

The impact drove the breath from Clausen's body. An agonizing pain shot through his back, and he knew it meant an injured vertebra. Two of his ribs, and perhaps more, cracked after his chest impacted against the steering wheel. He went into shock, his heart pounding, his breath coming in painful gasps. Bewildered, he hardly felt the water swirling around his chest.

Clausen blessed the tractor for landing right side up. If it had tumbled on one of its sides or top, in all probability he'd have been crushed to death or pinned and drowned. He sat there trying to comprehend what had happened to him. He looked up at the blue sky to get a grasp of his predicament. Then he peered around through the gloom and the drifting layers of dust.

The tractor had fallen into the pool of a limestone cave. One end was flooded but the other rose above the pool and opened into a vast cavern. He saw no signs of stalactites, stalagmites, or other natural decorations. Both the small entry cave and the larger chamber appeared to have low six-metre-high flat ceilings that were carved by excavation equipment.

Painfully he twisted out of the tractor seat and half crawled, half swam up the ramplike floor leading into the dry cavern. Knees sliding, hands slipping on the slimy coating covering the cave's floor, he struggled forward on all fours until he felt dry ground. Wearily he hauled himself up into a sitting position, shifted around, and stared into dim recesses of the cavern.

It was filled with aircraft, literally dozens of them. All parked in even rows as if waiting for a squadron of phantom pilots. Clausen recognized them as the Luftwaffe's first turbojet aircraft, Messerschmitt-262 Schwalben (Swallows). They sat like ghosts in their mottled grey-green colours, and despite almost fifty years of neglect, they appeared in prime condition. Only mild corrosion on the aluminium surfaces and flattened tyres suggested long abandonment. The hidden air base must have been evacuated and all entrances sealed before the Allied armies arrived. And now it rested completely forgotten.

His injuries were temporarily forgotten as Clausen reverently walked between the planes and into the flight quarters and maintenance repair areas. As his eyes became adjusted to the darkness, he became amazed at the neat orderliness. There was no sign of a hurried departure. He felt the pilots and their mechanics were standing at inspection in the field above and expected back at any time.

He entered a state of rapture when it struck him that all the wartime artefacts were on his property, or under it, and belonged to him. The worth of the aircraft to collectors and museums must have ranged in the millions of Deutschmarks.

Clausen made his way back to the edge of the underground pool. The tractor looked a sorry sight with only the steering wheel and upper tyres rising out of the water. Once more he gazed up at the hole to the sky. There was no hope of climbing out on his own. The opening was too high and the walls too steep.

He wasn't a tiny bit worried. Eventually his wife would come looking for him and summon neighbours when she found him standing happily in their newly discovered subterranean bonanza.

There had to be a generator somewhere for electrical power. He decided to search out its location. Perhaps, he thought, he might be able to fire it up and light the cavern. He squinted at his watch and figured another four hours would pass before his wife became curious over his prolonged absence.

He hesitated, thoughtfully staring into the far end of the cave that sloped into the forbidding pool, wondering if maybe another cavern waited in the darkness beyond the flooded depths.

32

'If the public only knew what goes on behind their backs, they'd burn Washington,' said Sandecker as the Virginia countryside flashed past the heavily tinted and armoured windows of the customized mobile command centre disguised as a nationally known bus line.

'We're in a war right up to our damned teeth,' the MAIT team's Deputy Director, Donald Kern, grumbled. 'And nobody knows but us.'

'You're right about the war,' said Pitt, contemplating a glass of soda water he held in one hand. 'I can't believe these people had the guts to abduct Loren and Senator Diaz on the same day.'

Kern shrugged. 'The senator stepped from his fishing lodge at six o'clock this morning, rowed out into a lake not much bigger than a pond, and vanished.'

'How do you know it wasn't an accidental drowning or suicide?'

'There was no body.'

'You dragged and searched the entire lake since this morning?' Pitt asked sceptically.

'Nothing so primitive. We diverted our newest spy satellite over the area. There was no body floating on or below the water.'

'You have the technology to see an object as small as a body underwater from space?'

'Forget you heard it,' Kern said with a slight grin. 'Just take my word for the fact that another Japanese team of professional operatives snatched Diaz in broad daylight along with his boat and outboard motor, and they managed it within sight of at least five other fishermen who swear they witnessed nothing.'

Pitt looked at Kern. 'But Loren's abduction *was* witnessed.'

'By Al and Frank, who guessed what was going down, sure. But the spectators in the stands were concentrating on the race. If any of them happened to glance in Loren's direction during the excitement, all they saw was a woman entering the limo under her own free will.'

'What screwed up the abductors' well-laid plan,' said Sandecker, 'was that you men *knew* she was being seized and gave chase. Your alert action also confirmed the Japanese connection behind Senator Diaz's kidnapping.'

'Whoever masterminded the separate plots was good,' Kern admitted. 'Too good for the Blood Sun Brotherhood.'

'The terrorist organization,' said Pitt. 'They were behind it?'

'That's what they want us to think. The FBI received a phone call by someone who said he was a member and claiming responsibility. Strictly a red herring. We saw through the façade in less than a minute.'

'What about the helicopter that controlled the limousine?' Pitt asked. 'Did you track it?'

'As far as Hampton Roads. There it blew up in midair and fell in the water. A Navy salvage team should be diving on it now.'

'A bottle of scotch they won't find bodies.'

Kern gave Pitt a canny look. 'A bet you'd probably win.'

'Any trace of the limousine that got away?'

Kern shook his head. 'Not yet. It was probably hidden and abandoned after they transferred Congresswoman Smith to another vehicle.'

'Who's in charge of the hunt?'

'The FBI. Their best field agents are already forming investigative teams and assembling all known data.'

'You think this is tied to our search into the bomb cars?'

asked Giordino, who along with Pitt and Mancuso had been picked up by Kern and Sandecker a few miles from the accident site.

'It's possible they could be warning us to lay off,' answered Kern. 'But our consensus is they wanted to shut down the Senate investigating committee and eliminate the legislators who were ramrodding a bill to cut off Japanese investment in the US.'

Sandecker lit one of his expensive cigars after clipping the end. 'The President is in a hell of a bind. As long as there's a chance Smith and Diaz are alive, he can't allow the abductions to leak to the news media. God knows what hell would erupt if Congress and the public found out.'

'They have us over the proverbial barrel,' Kern said grimly.

'If it isn't the Blood Sun Brotherhood, then who?' Giordino asked as he lit a cigar he'd stolen from Admiral Sandecker's supply in Washington.

'Only the Japanese government has the resources for an intricate abduction operation,' Pitt speculated.

'As far as we can determine,' said Kern, 'Prime Minister Junshiro and his cabinet are not directly involved. Very possibly they have no idea of what's going on behind their backs. Not a rare occurrence in Japanese politics. We suspect a highly secretive organization made up of wealthy ultranationalist industrialists and underworld leaders, who are out to expand and protect Japan's growing economic empire as well as their own interests. Our best intelligence from Team Honda and other sources points to an extremely influential bastard by the name of Hideki Suma. Showalter is certain Suma is the kingpin behind the bomb cars.'

'A very nasty customer,' Sandecker added. 'Shrewd, earthy, a brilliant operator, he's pulled the strings behind Japanese politics for three decades.'

'And his father pulled them three decades before him,'

said Kern. He turned to Mancuso. 'Frank here is the expert on the Sumas. He's compiled an extensive file on the family.'

Mancuso was sitting in a large swivel chair drinking a root beer, since no alcoholic beverages were allowed on the National Security Agency's command bus. He looked up. 'Suma, the father or the son. What do you wish to know?'

'A brief history of their organization,' answered Kern.

Mancuso took a few sips from his glass and stared at the ceiling as if arranging his thoughts. Then he began speaking as if reciting a book report to an English class.

'During the Japanese conquest of World War Two, their armies confiscated an immense hoard of loot from religious orders, banks, business corporations, and the treasuries of fallen governments. What began as a trickle from Manchuria and Korea soon became a flood as China and all of Southeast Asia, Malaya, Singapore, the Dutch East Indies, and the Philippines fell before the onslaught from the empire of the rising sun. The total of the stolen gold, gems, and priceless artefacts can only be speculated, but estimates have put it as high as two hundred billion, repeat, billion, dollars at current values.'

Sandecker shook his head. 'Inconceivable.'

'The gold bullion alone was figured at over seven thousand tons.'

'It all went to Japan?' asked Giordino.

'Up until nineteen forty-three. After that, American warships, and especially our submarines, interrupted the flow. Records indicate more than half of the total hoard was sent to the Philippines for inventory and forwarding to Tokyo. But toward the end of the war it was buried in secret locations around the islands and became known as "Yamashita's Gold".'

'Where do the Sumas fit in?' Pitt inquired.

'I'm coming to them,' said Mancuso. 'Japanese underworld societies quickly moved in after the occupation troops and helped themselves to the deposits in banks, national treasuries, and the wealth of private citizens, all in the name of the Emperor. Two minor agents of a criminal organization known as the Black Sky, which dominated Japan's underworld after the turn of the century, deserted and launched their own society, naming it the 'Gold Dragons'. One was Korori Yoshishu. The other was Koda Suma.'

'Koda, being the father of Hideki,' Sandecker concluded.

Mancuso nodded. 'Yoshishu was the son of a temple carpenter in Kyoto. He was kicked out of the house by his father when he was ten. He fell in with the Black Sky and rose in its ranks. In nineteen twenty-seven, at the age of eighteen, his bosses arranged for him to join the Army, where he craftily advanced to the rank of captain by the time the Imperial Army seized Manchuria. He set up a heroin operation that brought the gang hundreds of millions of dollars that was divided with the Army.'

'Hold on,' said Giordino. 'You're saying the Japanese Army was in the drug business?'

'They ran an operation that would be the envy of the drug kings of Colombia,' Mancuso replied. 'In concert with Japanese gang lords, the military ran the opium and heroin trades, forced the occupied citizenry to participate in rigged lotteries and gambling houses, and controlled the sale of black market goods.'

The bus stopped at a red light, and Pitt looked into the face of a truck driver who was trying in vain to see through the darkened windows of the bus. Pitt may have been staring out the window, but his mind followed Mancuso's every word.

'Koda Suma was the same age as Yoshishu, the first son of an ordinary seaman in the Imperial Navy. His father forced him to enlist, but he deserted and was recruited by Black Sky mobsters. At about the same time they put Yoshishu in the Army, the gang leaders smoothed over Suma's desertion record and had him reinstated in the Navy, only this time as an officer. Dispensing favours and money into the right hands, he quickly rose to the rank of captain. Being agents for the same criminal outfit, it was only natural that they work together. Yoshishu coordinated the heroin operations, while Suma systemized the looting and arranged shipments on board Imperial naval vessels.'

'A monumental ripoff to end all ripoffs,' Giordino observed moodily.

'The full scope of the network can never be documented.'

'More expensive even than the plunder of Europe by the Nazis?' Pitt asked, opening another bottle of soda water.

'By far,' Mancuso replied, smiling. 'Then as now, the Japanese were more interested in the economic side – gold, precious gems, hard currency – while the Nazis concentrated on masterworks of art, sculpture, and rare artefacts.' His expression suddenly turned serious again. 'Following the Japanese forces into China and then the rest of Southeast Asia, Yoshishu and Suma proved themselves to be archcriminal plotters. Like characters out of Heller's book *Catch-22*, they worked beneficial deals with their enemies. They sold luxury goods and war materials to Chiang Kaishek, becoming quite chummy with the generalissimo, an arrangement that paid handsome dividends after the Communists swept over China and later when the Chinese government moved to Formosa, which became Taiwan. They bought, sold, pillaged, smuggled, extorted, and murdered on an unheard-of scale, bleeding every country dry that came under their heel. It goes without saying that Suma and Yoshishu played a "one for you, two for me" game when the loot was inventoried and divided with the Imperial forces.'

Pitt rose from his chair and stretched, easily touching the ceiling of the bus. 'How much of the total plunder actually reached Japan?'

'A small percentage made it into the Imperial War Treasury. The more easily transportable treasure hoard, the precious gems and platinum, Suma and Yoshishu safely smuggled into Tokyo on board submarines and hid them on a farm in the country. The great mass of the bullion stayed behind on the main island of Luzon. It was stored in hundreds of kilometres of tunnels dug by thousands of allied POWs used as slave labour, who were either worked to death or executed to secure the hidden locations for recovery after the war. I excavated one tunnel on Corregidor that contained the bones of three hundred prisoners who had been buried alive.'

'Why is it this was never brought to the public attention?' asked Pitt.

Mancuso shrugged. 'I can't say. Not until forty years later was there mention of the barbarism in a few books. But by then, the Bataan death march and the armies of American, British and Philippine soldiers who perished in POW camps were only dim memories.'

'The Germans are still haunted by the holocaust,' mused Pitt, 'but the Japanese have remained mostly unstained by their atrocities.'

Giordino's face was grim. 'Did the Japs recover any of the treasure after the war?'

'Some was dug up by Japanese construction companies, who claimed to be helping the Philippines rise from the ravages of the conflict by developing various industrial building projects. Naturally, they worked on top of the burial sites. Some was dug up by Ferdinand Marcos, who shipped several hundred tons of gold out of the country and discreetly converted it to currency on the world bullion markets. And a fair share was retrieved by Suma and Yoshishu twenty years later. Maybe as much as seventy percent of it is still hidden and may never be recovered.'

Pitt looked at Mancuso questioningly. 'What happened to Suma and Yoshishu after the war ended?'

'No fools, these guys. They read defeat in their tea leaves as early as nineteen forty-three and began laying plans to survive the end in grand style. Not about to die in battle during MacArthur's return to Luzon, or commit ritual suicide in the humiliation of defeat, Suma ordered up a submarine. Then with a generous helping of the Emperor's share, they sailed off to Valparaiso, Chile, where they lived for five years in lavish comfort. When MacArthur became occupied with the Korean war, the master thieves returned home and became master organizers. Suma devoted his genius to economic and political intrigue, while Yoshishu consolidated his hold over the underworld and the new generation of Asian wheeler-dealers. Within ten years they were the major power brokers of the Far East.'

'A real pair of sweethearts,' Giordino said caustically.

'Koda Suma died of cancer in nineteen seventy-three,' Mancuso continued. 'Like a couple of prohibition Chicago gangsters, Suma's son, Hideki, and Yoshishu agreed to divide up the massive organization into different areas of activity. Yoshishu directed the criminal end, while Hideki built a power base in government and industry. The old crook has pretty much retired, keeping his fingers in various pies, guiding the present crime leaders of the Gold Dragons, and occasionally cutting a joint venture with Suma.'

'According to Team Honda,' Kern informed them, 'Suma and Yoshishu joined forces to underwrite the weapons plant and the Kaiten Project.'

'The Kaiten Project?' Pitt repeated.

'Their code name for the bomb-car operation. Literally translated into English it means "a change of sky". But to the Japanese it has a broader meaning: "a new day is coming, a great shift in events". '

'But Japan claims to ban the introduction of nuclear weapons,' Pitt ventured. 'Seems damned odd that Suma and Yoshishu could build a nuclear weapons facility without some knowledge or backing from the government.'

'The politicians don't run Japan. The back-room movers and shakers behind the bureaucracy pull the reins. It was no secret when Japan built a Liquid Metal Fast Breeder Reactor. But it wasn't general knowledge that besides functioning as a power source it also produces plutonium and converted lithium into tritium, essential ingredients for thermonuclear weapons. My guess is Prime Minister Junshiro gave his secret blessing to a nuclear arsenal, however reluctantly because of the risk of public outcry, but he was purposely cut out of the Kaiten Project.'

'They certainly don't run a government like we do,' said Sandecker.

'Has Team Honda located the weapons plant?' Pitt asked Kern.

'They've narrowed it to a sixty-square-kilometre grid around the subterranean city of Edo.'

'And they still can't find it?'

'Jim Hanamura thinks the city has deep tunnels that connect to the facility. An ingenious cover. No aboveground buildings or roads as a giveaway. Supplies entering for the thousands of people who live and work in Edo, and their trash exiting. Most any nuclear equipment or material could be smuggled in and out.'

'Any leads to the detonation command?' asked Giordino.

'The Dragon Centre?'

'Is that what they call it?'

'They have a name for everything.' Kern smiled. 'Nothing solid. Hanamura's last report said he was onto a lead that had something to do with a painting.'

'That makes a hell of a lot of sense,' Giordino carped.

The door opened to a cramped communications compartment in the rear of the bus, and a man stepped out and handed three sheets of paper to Kern.

As his eyes flicked over the wording, his face became stricken. Finally, after coming to the end of the third page, he rapped his knuckles against the arm of his chair in shock. 'Oh, my God.'

Sandecker leaned toward him. 'What is it?'

'A status report from Mel Penner on Palau. He says Marvin Showalter was abducted on his way to the embassy. An American tourist couple reported seeing two Japanese men enter Showalter's car when he stopped for a stalled truck a block from the embassy. The husband and wife only happened to report it to embassy officials because of the US licence tags and the surprise shown by the driver as the intruders leaped into the car. They saw nothing more, as a tourist bus pulled alongside them and blocked their view. By the time they could see the street again, Showalter's car had disappeared in traffic.'

'Go on.'

'Jim Hanamura is late reporting in. In his last report to Penner, Jim said he had confirmed the location of the weapons plant one hundred and fifty metres underground. The main assembly area is connected to Edo City, four kilometres to the north, by an electric railway that also runs through a series of tunnels to arsenals, waste disposal caverns, and engineering offices.'

'Is there more?' Sandecker gently persisted.

'Hanamura went on to say he was following a strong lead to the Dragon Centre. That's all.'

'What word on Roy Orita?' Pitt asked.

'Only a brief mention.'

'He vanished too?'

'No, Penner doesn't say that. He only says Orita insists on sitting tight until we can sort things out.'

'I'd say the visitors have outscored the home team by three to one,' said Pitt philosophically. 'They've snatched two of our legislators, cut Teams Honda and Cadillac off at the knees, and last but easily the worst, they know what we're after and where we're coming from.'

'Suma is holding all the high cards,' Kern conceded. 'I'd better inform Mr Jordan at once so he can warn the President.'

Pitt leaned over the back of his chair and fixed Kern with a dry stare. 'Why bother?'

'What do you mean?'

'I see no need to panic.'

'The President must be alerted. We're not only looking at the threat of nuclear blackmail but political ransom for Diaz and Smith. Suma can drop the axe any moment.'

'No he won't. Not yet anyway.'

'How do you know?' Kern demanded.

'Something is holding Suma back. He's got a fleet of those bomb cars hidden away. All he needs is one driving the streets of Manhattan or Los Angeles to put the fear of God into the White House and the American public. He's literally got the government by the scrotum. But what does he do? He plays petty kidnapper. No, I'm sorry. Something's not going down the right chute. Suma isn't ready for prime time. I say he's stalling.'

'I think Dirk has a case,' said Mancuso. 'It's possible Suma's agents smuggled the bomb cars into position before they could bring the detonation command on line.'

'It fits,' Sandecker concurred. 'We might still have time to send in a new team to find and neutralize it.'

'At the moment everything hinges on Hanamura.' Kern hesitated apprehensively. 'We can only hope he's unearthed the Dragon Centre. But we also have to consider the very real possibility he's either dead or captured by Suma's security force.'

They went quiet as the Virginia countryside rolled past the windows of the bus. The leaves on the trees gleamed gold under the fall sun. Few people walking beside the road paid any attention to the passing bus. If any had seen the charter sign above the driver's windscreen, they'd have simply thought it was a group of vacationers touring Civil War battlefields.

At last Sandecker spoke the thought that was on all their minds: 'If only we knew what thread Jim Hanamura was unravelling.'

33

At that moment, halfway across the world, Jim Hanamura would have given his new Corvette and his Redondo Beach bachelor pad's state-of-the-art sound system to trade places with any man on that bus in Virginia.

The cold night rain soaked his clothes and skin as he lay covered by mud and rotting leaves in a drainage ditch. The police and the uniformed security force that were hunting him had canvassed the area and moved on ten minutes earlier, but he lay there in the slime trying to rest and formulate a plan of action. He painfully rolled over on his good elbow and peered up and across the road. The only sign of movement was a man in the garage of a small house who was bent under the open hood of a small delivery truck.

He dropped back in the ditch and passed out for the third time since being shot during his escape from Edo City. When Hanamura regained consciousness, he wondered how long he was out. He held up his right wrist, but the watch had stopped, broken when he wrecked his car. It couldn't have been very long, however, because the driver of the delivery truck was still tinkering with its engine.

The three slugs from the security guards' automatic rifles had caught him in the left arm and shoulder. It was one of those flukes, a thousand-to-one unforeseen incident that catches a professional operative from a blind side.

His plans had been precise and exactingly executed. He'd forged the security clearance pass of one of Suma's chief structural engineers by the name of Jiro Miyaza, who closely resembled Hanamura in face and body.

Entering Edo City and walking through the checkpoints leading to the design and construction department had been a piece of cake. None of the guards saw anything suspicious about a man who returned to his office after hours and worked on past midnight. All Japanese men put in long hours, seldom working a normal eight-hour day.

The inspection was loose, yet tighter than what it takes to walk into the Pentagon Building in Washington. The guards nodded to Hanamura and watched as he slipped his pass card into the electronic identity computer. The correct buzz sounded, a video camera's light flashed green, and the guards waved him through, satisfied that Hanamura was cleared to enter that section of the building. With so many people passing in and out all hours of the day and night, they failed to recall that the man Hanamura was impersonating had only left for home a few minutes previously.

Hanamura tossed three offices in an hour and a half before he struck pay dirt. In the rear of a drawer of a draughtsman's table he found a rolled cylinder of rough sketches of a secret installation. The sketches should have been destroyed. He could only assume the draughtsman had neglected to drop them in a nearby shredder. He took his time, ran the drawings through a copy machine, inserted them in an envelope, and put the originals back in the drawer exactly as he found them. The envelope he curled and taped to the calf of one leg.

Once he passed the guards on the way out, Hanamura thought he was home free. He walked out into the vast atrium and waited his turn to take an elevator that opened on a pedestrian tunnel leading to the parking level where he'd left his Murmoto four-wheel-drive pickup truck. There were twenty people packed in the enclosure, and Hanamura had the misfortune of having to stand in the front row. When the doors opened on his parking level, fate dealt him a bad hand.

Pushed ahead by the crowd behind him, Hanamura stepped right into Jiro Miyaza.

The engineer, whose identity Hanamura borrowed, had

exited the adjacent elevator with his wife and two children. They were headed for the same parking level for an evening drive above ground. Inexplicably, Miyaza's eyes were drawn to the clearance pass clipped to Hanamura's pocket.

For a moment he simply stared, then his eyes widened and he looked into Hanamura's face with disbelieving eyes.

'What are you doing with my pass?' he demanded indignantly.

'Internal security,' Hanamura answered calmly with an air of authority. 'We're examining security areas to see if the guards are alert and pick us out. I happened to be issued your name and ID number.'

'My brother is assistant head of security. He never mentioned such an inspection to me.'

'We don't advertise,' Hanamura said, glaring at Miyaza, who refused to back down.

Hanamura tried to edge his way past Miyaza, but the engineer grabbed his arm.

'Wait! I want to verify this.'

Hanamura's lightning move was almost undetectable. He rammed his palm into Miyaza's chest, breaking the sternum. The engineer gasped for air, clutched his chest, and sank to his knees. Hanamura pushed him aside and calmly walked toward his vehicle, which he had backed into its stall. He quickly threw open the unlocked door of the Murmoto V-6 four-wheel-drive, slipped behind the wheel, and turned the ignition key. The engine started on the second turn, and he shoved the shift lever into drive and headed for the exit ramp and the gate only one level above.

He might have made it if Miyaza's wife and children hadn't screamed their heads off and pointed frantically toward Hanamura. A nearby security guard rushed over and questioned them. He barely made any sense of their hysterical jabbering, but he was smart enough to use his portable radio to alert the guards manning the main entry gate.

Nothing went Hanamura's way. He was a fraction of a second too late. A guard stepped from the gatehouse and raised his hand for Hanamura to stop. Two of his comrades posted on opposite sides of the exit tunnel lifted their weapons at the ready position. And then there was the heavy steel barrier shaft across the drive.

Hanamura took in the scene with one trained glance. There was no stopping in an attempt to bluff his way past. He braced himself for the impact, slammed his foot against the gas pedal, and crouched down in the seat as far as he could go. He struck the shaft partly on the raised bumper of the truck and partly across the headlights, smashing them back into the fenders and pushing the grillwork against the radiator.

The shock was not as bad as Hanamura expected, just a crunch of metal and glass and a twisting screech as the momentum of the truck snapped the steel barrier off where it hinged into a concrete piling. Then the windows vanished in a spray of slivers as the guards opened up with their automatic rifles. It was the only small bit of luck that came his way. The guards aimed high instead of blasting the engine compartment and gas tank or blowing out the tyres.

The firing abruptly ceased as he broke clear of the tunnel and raced through a stream of cars entering the under-ground city from the other, incoming road. Hanamura paid as much attention to the view in his rearview mirror as he did to the road and traffic ahead. He didn't doubt for a second that Suma's security people were alerting the police to set up roadblocks. Throwing the Murmoto into four-wheel-drive, he cut off the pavement and shot down a dirt road muddied by a pouring rainstorm. Only after bumping through a forested area for ten kilometres did he become aware of a burning pain in his shoulder and a sticky flow of fluid down his left side. He pulled to a stop under a large pine tree and examined his left shoulder and arm.

He'd been struck three times. One bullet through the

biceps, one that cut a groove in his collarbone, and another through the fleshy part of his shoulder. They were not killing injuries, but if not cared for they could become extremely serious. It was the heavy loss of blood that worried Hanamura. Already he felt the early stages of lightheadedness. He tore off his shirt and made a couple of crude bandages, stemming the blood flow as best he could.

The shock and the pain were slowly replaced with numbness and the haze that was seeping into his mind. The embassy was a hundred and sixty kilometres away in the heart of Tokyo. He'd never make it through the multitude of busy streets without being stopped by a policeman, curious about the bullet-riddled truck, or by Suma's network of armed forces, who would block every major road leading into the city. Briefly he considered making for the safety of the MAIT team's inn, but Asakusa was on the northeast of Tokyo, opposite Edo City on the west.

He looked up through the shattered windscreen at the rainy sky. The low clouds would hinder an air hunt by helicopter. That was a help. Relying on the rugged Murmoto's four-wheel traction, Hanamura decided to drive cross-country and travel the back roads before abandoning the pickup and hopefully stealing a car.

Hanamura drove on through the rain, detouring around streams and rice paddies, always headed toward the lights of the city, glowing dimly against the overcast sky. The closer he came to the metropolitan mainstream, the more densely populated it became. The open country ended almost immediately, and the small back roads soon widened into busy highways and expressways.

The Murmoto was faltering too. The radiator was damaged from the collision with the barrier, and steam hissed from under the hood in growing wisps of white. He glanced at the instrument panel. The heat gauge needle was quivering into the red. It was time to find another car.

Then he blacked out from the loss of blood and slumped across the wheel.

The Murmoto drifted off the road and sideswiped several parked cars before crashing through the thin wooden wall of a house. The jolt brought him back to consciousness, and he stared dazedly around a small courtyard the Murmoto had demolished. He was thankful the inhabitants of the house were away and he'd missed any furnished rooms.

The one headlight still threw a beam, illuminating a gate at the back of the courtyard. Hanamura stumbled through it into an alley behind the house as the shouting of startled neighbours erupted behind him. Ten minutes later, after staggering across a small park, he stopped in exhaustion and hid in a muddy ditch.

He lay there listening to the sirens screaming toward his wrecked pickup truck. Once, after he felt strong enough, he began to move deeper into one of Tokyo's secluded neighbourhoods, but a security vehicle drove slowly up and down the road beaming searchlights into the park and surrounding narrow streets. It was then he lost consciousness again.

When the wet cold woke him, he fully realized he was too weak to steal a car and go on. Slowly, stiffly, and clenching his teeth against the pain that returned in agonizing waves, he swayed across the road and approached the man working on the engine of his truck.

'Can you please help me?' Hanamura begged feebly.

The man turned around and stared dumbly at the injured stranger weaving before him. 'You're hurt,' he said. 'You're bleeding.'

'I was in an accident up the street and need help.'

The man put his arm around Hanamura's waist. 'Let me get you in the house, my wife can aid you while I call an ambulance.'

Hanamura shook him off. 'Never mind that, I'll be all right.'

'Then you should go directly to a hospital,' the man said sincerely. 'I will drive you.'

'No, please,' Hanamura evaded. 'But I'd be most grateful if you will deliver a packet for me to the American embassy. It's quite urgent. I'm a courier and was on my way from Edo City when my car skidded and ran off the road.'

The owner of the delivery truck stood uncomprehending as Hanamura scribbled something in English on the back flap of the envelope and handed it to him. 'You want me to take this to the American embassy instead of taking you to the hospital?'

'Yes, I must return to the scene of my accident. The police will see to an ambulance.'

None of it made any sense to the delivery truck driver, but he accepted the request without argument. 'Who do I ask for at the embassy?'

'A Mr Showalter.' Hanamura reached in his pocket and pulled out his wallet and handed the driver a large wad of yen notes. 'For any inconvenience. Do you know where to go?'

The driver's face lit up at his unexpected windfall. 'Yes, the embassy is near the junction of number three and four expressways.'

'How soon can you leave?'

'I have just finished rebuilding the truck's distributor. I can leave in a few minutes.'

'Good.' Hanamura bowed. 'Thank you very much. Tell Mr Showalter that he is to double what I paid you upon receiving the envelope.' Then Hanamura turned and walked shakily into the rain and the black of the night.

He could have ridden with the truck driver to the embassy, but he dared not risk passing out or even dying. In either event the driver might have panicked and driven to the nearest hospital or hailed a policeman. Then the precious drawings would have probably been confiscated and returned to Suma's headquarters. Better that he trust in

278

luck and the delivery truck driver's honour while he led the manhunt in another direction.

Hanamura, on little more than guts and willpower, hiked nearly a kilometre before an armoured vehicle rolled out of the darkness inside the park, swung onto the street, and sped after him. Too exhausted to run, he sank to his knees beside a parked car and groped in his coat for a despatch pill. His fingers had just closed around the poison capsule when the armoured car with military markings and red lights flashing stopped with its headlights painting Hanamura's shadow on the wall of a warehouse a few metres beyond.

A silhouetted figure stepped from the car and approached. Incongruously, he was wearing an odd-looking leather overcoat cut like a kimono and carrying a samurai *katana* sword whose polished blade glinted under lights. When he stepped around so his face was visible from the headlight beams, he looked down at Hanamura and spoke in a smug voice.

'Well, well, the famous art sleuth, Ashikaga Enshu. I hardly recognized you without your wig and false beard.'

Hanamura looked up into the rattlesnake face of Moro Kamatori. 'Well, well,' he echoed. 'If it isn't Hideki Suma's water boy.'

'Water boy?'

'Stooge, you know, ass kisser, brown nose.'

Kamatori's face went livid and his gleaming teeth bared in anger. 'What did you find in Edo?' he demanded.

Hanamura didn't give Kamatori the benefit of an answer. He was breathing quickly, his lips in a hard grin. Suddenly he popped the despatch pill in his mouth and bit down on it with his molars to eject the fluid. The poison was instantly absorbed in the gum line through the tissue. In thirty seconds his heart would freeze and he'd be dead.

'Goodbye, sucker,' he muttered.

Kamatori had only a moment to act, but he raised the sword, gripping the long hilt with both hands, and cut a wide arc with every ounce of his strength. The shock of disbelief flashed in Hanamura's eyes a brief instant before it was replaced with the glaze of death.

Kamatori had the final satisfaction of seeing his sword win the race with the poison as the blade sliced Hanamura's head from his shoulders as cleanly as a guillotine.

34

The fertilizer-brown Murmotos were parked in a loose line behind the ramp leading up to the cavernlike interior of the big semi-trailer. George Furukawa was greatly relieved these four cars were the last shipment. The release documents he'd found as usual under the front seat of his sports car included a short memo notifying him that his part of the project was finished.

He also received new instructions to examine the cars for homing devices. No explanation was given, but he concluded that Hideki Suma had become belatedly worried his last shipment might be followed by some unspecified group. The thought that they might be federal investigators made Furukawa extremely uneasy. He walked quickly around each car while studying the digital readout of an electronic unit that detected transmitted radio signals.

Satisfied the sport sedans with their ugly brown paint schemes were clean, he gestured to the truck driver and his helper. They bowed slightly without an acknowledging word and took turns driving the cars up the ramps into the trailer.

Furukawa turned and walked toward his car, happy to be rid of an assignment he felt was beneath his position as vice president of Samuel J. Vincent Laboratories. The handsome fee Suma had already paid him for his effort and loyalty would be wisely invested in Japanese corporations that were opening offices in California.

He drove to the gate and handed the guard copies of the release documents. Then he aimed the sloped nose of his Murmoto sports car into the busy truck traffic around the dock terminal and drove toward his office. There was no curiosity this time, no looking back. His interest in the auto transport's secret destination had died.

Stacy zipped up her windbreaker, snapping it tight across her throat. The side door of the helicopter had been removed, and the cool air from the ocean whistled inside the control cabin. Her long blonde hair whipped in front of her face, and she tied it back with a short leather band. A video camera sat in her lap, and she lifted it and set the controls. Then she turned sideways as far as her seat belt would allow and focused the telephoto lens on the tail of the Murmoto sports car exiting the dock area.

'You get the licence number?' asked the blond-haired pilot as he held the copter on a level course.

'Yes, a good sharp shot. Thank you.'

'I can come in a little closer if you like.'

'Stay well clear,' ordered Stacy, speaking into her headset microphone while peering through the eyepiece. She released the trigger and laid the compact camera in her lap again. 'They must be alerted to the fact somebody's onto them, or they wouldn't have swept the cars for homing devices.'

'Lucky for old Weatherhill he wasn't transmitting.'

Bill McCurry made Stacy cold just looking at him. He only wore cutoff denim shorts, a T-shirt advertising a Mexican beer, and sandals on his feet. When they were introduced earlier that same morning, Stacy saw him more as a lifeguard than as one of the National Security Agency's top investigators.

Long sun-bleached hair, skin dark-tanned by the Southern California sun, and the light blue eyes wide open behind red plastic-rimmed sunglasses, McCurry's mind was half on tailing the auto transport truck and half on a volleyball game he'd promised to play later that evening on the beach at Marina del Ray.

'The truck is turning onto the Harbor Freeway,' said

Stacy. 'Drop back out of the driver's sight and we'll follow on Timothy's beam.'

'We should have better backup,' McCurry said seriously. 'With no team following in vehicles on the ground, and no copter to replace us in case we have engine problems, we could lose the chase and endanger Weatherhill.'

Stacy shook her head. 'Timothy knows the score. You don't. Take my word for it, we can't risk using ground vehicles or a flight of helicopters milling about. Those guys in the truck have been alerted and are watching for a surveillance operation.'

Suddenly Weatherhill's Texas drawl came through their earphones. 'You up there, Buick Team?'

'We read you, Tim,' answered McCurry.

'Safe to transmit?'

'The bad guys did a bug sweep,' replied Stacy, 'but you're okay to send.'

'Do you have visual contact?'

'Temporarily, but we're dropping a few kilometres back so we won't be spotted from the driver's cab.'

'Understood.'

'Don't forget to keep transmitting on the fixed frequency.'

'Yes, mamma,' said Weatherhill jovially. 'I'm leaving this sweat box now and going to work.'

'Keep in touch.'

'Will do. I wouldn't think of running out on you.'

Removing the false panel from behind and below the rear seat and unravelling his body from its contorted position, Weatherhill crawled into the enclosed luggage area of the third Murmoto loaded in the trailer. He sprung the lock from the inside and swung the rear hatch up and open. Then he climbed out, stood up, and stretched his aching joints.

Weatherhill had suffered in his cramped position for nearly four hours after a special team of customs agents helped conceal him in the car before Furukawa and the truck arrived. The sun beating on the roof and the lack of ventilation – the windows could not even be cracked for fear of arousing suspicion by the truck drivers – soon had him drenched in sweat. He never thought he would find himself sick of a new car smell.

The interior of the trailer was dark. He took a flashlight from a pouch he carried on the belt of a nondescript auto mechanic's uniform and beamed it around the cars tied down inside the trailer. Two were on ramps above the two on the floor below.

Since the truck was travelling over a level California freeway and the ride in the trailer was smooth, Weatherhill decided to examine the Murmotos on the upper ramp first. He climbed up and quietly opened the hood of the one nearest the driver's cab. Then he removed a small radiation analyser from the pouch and studied the readout as he circled it around the auto's air-conditioning compressor unit.

He wrote the readings on the back of his hand. Next he laid out a set of compact tools on the fender. He paused and spoke into the radio.

'Hello, Team Buick.'

'Come in,' Stacy answered.

'Beginning exploratory operation.'

'Don't slip and cut an artery.'

'Never fear.'

'Standing by.'

Within fifteen minutes, Weatherhill had disassembled the compressor case and neutralized the bomb. He was mildly disappointed. The design was not as advanced as he predicted. Clever, yes, but he could have devised and built a more efficient and destructive unit by himself.

He froze as he heard the sound of the air brakes and felt the truck slow. But it was only taking an off-ramp to another freeway and soon speeded up again. He re-assembled the compressor and moved on to the next car.

'Still with me?' he asked briefly.

'Still here,' answered Stacy.

'Where am I?'

'Passing through West Covina. Heading east toward San Bernardino.'

'One down. Three to go.'

'Good luck.'

An hour later Weatherhill closed the hood of the fourth and final car. He sagged with relief. All the bombs were neutralized. None would detonate under any signal sent from Japan. Sweat was pouring down his face, and he deduced the truck was moving into the desert east of San Bernardino.

'I've withdrawn the account and have no more business at the bank,' he radioed. 'What stop should I depart the bus?'

'One moment while I check the schedule,' Stacy acknowledged. After a few moments she came back. 'There's a weight station this side of Indio. It's mandatory. The drivers will have to stop for inspection. If for some reason they turn off, we'll plan on having them pulled over by a sheriff's car. Otherwise you should arrive at the weight station in another forty-five or fifty minutes.'

'See you there,' said Weatherhill.

'Enjoy your trip.'

Like most undercover agents, whose adrenaline pumps during the critical stages of an operation, now that the difficult part was behind him, Weatherhill quickly relaxed and became bored with nothing to do. All that remained now was for him to climb through the fume ventilators on the roof and drop down behind the trailer out of view of the drivers' side mirrors.

He opened the glove box and pulled out the packet containing the car's warranty papers and owner's manual. Switching on the interior lights, Weatherhill idly began thumbing through the manual. Though his prime expertise was nuclear physics, he was always fascinated by electronics. He turned to the page displaying the Murmoto's electrical diagram with the intention of tracing out the wiring.

But the page in the manual was no electrical wiring diagram. It was a map with instructions for placing the cars in their designated positions for detonation.

Suma's strategy became so boldly obvious to Weatherhill that he had to force himself to believe it. The car bombs were not simply part of a threat to protect Japan's economic expansionist plans. The fear and the horror were real.

They were meant to be used.

35

At least ten years had passed since Raymond Jordan forced an entry, certainly not since he worked up through the ranks as a field agent. On a whim he decided to see if he still had the touch.

He inserted a tiny computer probe into the wires on the security alarm system of Pitt's hangar. He pressed a button and backwashed the combination into the probe. The alarm box recognized the code and gave it to him on an LED display. Then with a deceptive ease and nonchalance, he punched the appropriate combination that turned off the alarm, picked the lock to the door, and stepped soundlessly inside.

He spied Pitt kneeling in front of the turquoise Stutz, back toward him, at the far end of the hangar. Pitt seemed intent on repairing a headlight.

Jordan stood unobserved and gazed over the collection. He was astonished it was so extensive. He'd heard Sandecker speak of it, but verbal description failed to do it justice. Softly he walked behind the first row of cars, circled around, and approached Pitt from under the apartment side of the hangar. It was a test. He was curious as to Pitt's reaction to an intruder who suddenly appeared within arm's reach.

Jordan paused before he closed the final three metres and studied Pitt and the car for a moment. The Stutz was badly scratched in many areas and would require a new paint job. The windscreen was cracked and the left front headlight seemed to be dangling by a wire.

Pitt was dressed casually, wearing a pair of corduroy trousers and a knitted sweater. His black hair was wavy and carelessly brushed. There was a decisive look about him, the green eyes were set under heavy black eyebrows and had a piercing quality that seemed to transfix whatever they were aimed at. He looked to be screwing the headlight lens into a chrome rim.

Jordan was in midstep when Pitt suddenly spoke without turning. 'Good evening, Mr Jordan. Good of you to drop in.'

Jordan froze, but Pitt went on with his work with the indifferent air of a bus driver expecting the correct change from a fare.

'I should have knocked.'

'No need. I knew you were on the premises.'

'Are you hyperperceptive or do you have eyes in the back of your head?' asked Jordan, moving slowly into Pitt's peripheral vision.

Pitt looked up and grinned. He lifted and tilted the old headlight's reflector that revealed Jordan's image on its silver surface. 'I observed your tour of the hangar. Your entry was most professional. I'd judge it didn't take you more than twenty seconds.'

'Missed spotting a back-up camera, I must be getting senile.'

'Across the road. The small box on top of the telephone pole. Most visitors expect to spot one hanging on the building. Infrared. It activates an alert chime when a body moves near the door.'

'You have an incredible collection,' Jordan complimented Pitt. 'How long did it take you to build it?'

'I began with the maroon forty-seven Ford club coupe over there in the corner about twenty years ago, and collecting became a disease. Some I acquired during projects with NUMA, some I bought from private parties or at auctions. Antique and classic cars are investments you can flaunt. Far more fun than a painting.' Pitt finished screwing the headlight rim around its lens and rose to his feet. 'Can I offer you a drink.'

'A glass of milk for an overstressed stomach sounds good.'

'Please come up.' Pitt gestured toward the stairs leading to his apartment. 'I'm honoured the head man came to see me instead of sending his deputy director.'

As Jordan reached the first step, he hesitated and said, 'I thought I should be the one to tell you. Congresswoman Smith and Senator Diaz have been smuggled out of the country.'

There was a pause as Pitt slowly turned and glared at him through eyes suddenly filled with relief. 'Loren is unharmed.' The words came more as a demand than a question.

'We're not dealing with brain-sick terrorists,' Jordan answered. 'The kidnap operation was too sophisticated for injury or death. We have every reason to believe she and Diaz are being treated with respect.'

'How did they slip through the cracks?'

'Our intelligence determined she and Diaz were flown out of the Newport News, Virginia, airport in a private jet belonging to one of Suma's American corporations. By the time we were able to sift through every flight, scheduled or unscheduled, from airports within a thousand-square-kilometre area, trace every plane's registration until we nailed one to Suma, and track its path by satellite, it was heading over the Bering Sea for Japan.'

'Too late to force down on one of our military bases by a military aircraft?'

'Way too late. It was met and escorted by a squadron of FSX fighter jets from Japan's Air Self-Defence Force. Aircraft that were built in partnership between General Dynamics and Mitsubishi, I might add.'

'And then?'

Jordan turned and gazed at the gleaming cars. 'We lost them,' he said tonelessly.

'After they landed?'

'Yes, at Tokyo International. Little need to go into details why they weren't intercepted or at least followed, but for reasons known only to the cretin mentality at the State Department, we have no operatives in Japan who could have stopped them. That's all we have at the moment.'

'The best intelligence minds on the face of the earth, and that's all you have.' Pitt sounded very tired. He went into his kitchen, opened the refrigerator and poured a milk, then handed the glass to Jordan. 'What about all your big speciality teams in Japan? Where were they when the plane touched down?'

'With Marvin Showalter and Jim Hanamura murdered –'

'Both men murdered?' Pitt interrupted.

'Tokyo police found Hanamura's body in a ditch, decapitated. Showalter's head, minus the body, was discovered a few hours ago, impaled on our embassy's fence. To add to the mess, we suspect Roy Orita is a sleeper. He sold us out from the beginning. God only knows how much information he's passed to Suma. We may never be able to assess the damage.'

Pitt's anger softened when he read the sadness along with the frustration in Jordan's face. 'Sorry, Ray, I had no idea things had gone so badly.'

'I've never had a MAIT team take a battering like this.'

'What put you onto Orita?'

'A couple of broad hints. Showalter was too clever to be snatched without inside help. He never followed a routine or travelled the same routes twice. He was betrayed by someone who had his confidence and knew his exact movements. And there was Jim Hanamura; he expressed bad vibes on Orita but nothing solid to go on. To add to the suspicion, Orita has dropped out and gone undercover. He hasn't reported to Mel Penner since Showalter vanished. Kern thinks he's hiding under Suma's skirts in Edo City.'

'What of his background?'

'Third-generation American. His father won the Silver Star in the Italian campaign. We can't figure what bait Suma used to recruit him.'

'Who handled the execution of Hanamura and Showalter?'

'The evidence isn't in yet. It appears a ritual killing. A police pathologist thought their heads were taken off by a samurai sword. Suma's chief assassin is known to be a lover of ancient martial arts, but we can't prove he did it.'

Pitt sank slowly into a chair. 'A waste, a damned waste.'

'Jim Hanamura didn't go out a loser,' Jordan said with sudden doggedness. 'He gave us our one and only lead to the detonation control centre.'

Pitt looked up expectantly. 'You have a location?'

'Nothing to celebrate yet, but we're half a step closer.'

'What information did Hanamura turn up?'

'Jim penetrated the offices of Suma's construction designers and found what looks to be rough drawings of an electronic control centre that fits the layout we're looking for. Indications suggest it's an underground installation reached by a tunnel.'

'Anything on the whereabouts?'

'The brief message he wrote on the back of an envelope that was delivered to the embassy by the driver of an auto parts delivery truck is too enigmatic to decipher with any accuracy.'

'The message?'

'He wrote, "Look on the island of Ajima." '

Pitt made a slight shrug. 'So what's the problem?'

'There *is* no Ajima Island,' Jordan answered defeatedly. He held up the glass and examined it. 'This is skim milk.'

'It's better for you than whole milk.'

'Like drinking water,' Jordan muttered as he studied a glass case of trophies. Most were awards for outstanding automobiles at concours shows, a few were old high school and Air Force Academy football trophies, and two were for fencing. 'You a fencer?'

291

'Not exactly Olympic material, but I still work out when I get the time.'

'Epée, foil, or sabre?'

'Sabre.'

'You struck me as a slasher. I'm into foil myself.'

'You prefer a deft touch.'

'A pity we can't have a match,' said Jordan.

'We could compromise and use the épée.'

Jordan smiled. 'I'd still have the advantage, since touches by the foil and épée are made with the points, while the sabre is scored by hits on the edges.'

'Hanamura must have had a good reason for suggesting Ajima as the control centre site,' said Pitt, returning to business.

'He was an art nut. His operation to plant bugs in Suma's office was designed around his knowledge of early Japanese art. We knew Suma collected paintings, especially works by a sixteenth-century Japanese artist who produced a series on small islands surrounding the main isle of Honshu, so I had one forged. Then Hanamura, posing as an art expert, sold it to Suma. The one island painting Suma does not own is Ajima. That's the only link I can think of.'

'Then Ajima must exist.'

'I'm sure it does, but the name can't be traced to any known island. Nothing on ancient or modern charts shows it. I can only assume it was a pet name given by the artist, Masaki Shimzu, and listed as such in art catalogues of his work.'

'Did Hanamura's bugs record any interesting talk?'

'A most informative conversation between Suma, his butcher Kamatori, old Korori Yoshishu, and a heavy hitter named Ichiro Tsuboi.'

'The financial genius behind Kanoya Securities. I've heard of him.'

'Yes, he was in a heated debate with the senator and congresswoman during the select subcommittee hearing on Capitol Hill a few days before they were seized.'

'And you say he's tied to Suma?'

'Tighter than a banjo string,' answered Jordan. 'Thanks to Jim's bugs in Suma's office, we learned Tsuboi juggled the funding for the construction of the nuclear arsenal behind the backs of Japan's political leaders, and most certainly their people. We also heard the code name Kaiten Project for the first time.'

Pitt poured a cup of old, cold coffee and stuck it in the microwave. He stared through the glass window at the cup as it revolved, his eyes narrowed in thought.

Jordan broke the spell. 'I know what you're thinking, but I haven't been given the manpower to rescue Diaz and Smith and break up the Kaiten Project in one operation.'

'I can't believe the President is turning his back on them.'

'He's not about to go public and threaten a war over the abductions when he's at a distinct disadvantage. Our first priority is to dismantle the Kaiten Project. Once we've accomplished that matter, only then will the President give us his blessing to use whatever force it takes to free Smith and Diaz.'

'So we're back to mystical Ajima Island,' Pitt said harshly. 'You say it's the only painting of the series Suma doesn't own?'

'Yes,' Jordan replied. 'Hanamura said he acted almost desperate to get his hands on it.'

'Any clue to where it might be?'

'The Ajima painting was last seen in the Japanese embassy in Berlin just before Germany fell. Old OSS records claim it was included with art the Nazis plundered from Italy, and transported by train to northwestern Germany ahead of the advancing Russian Army in the last weeks of the war. Then it disappeared from history.'

'No record at all of it having been recovered?'

'None.'

'And we have no idea as to the island's general location or its appearance?'

'Not a scrap.'

'Unfortunate,' Pitt commented. 'Find the painting, match the shape of the shoreline portrayed by the artist, and you have the location of Hideki Suma's extortion hideaway, or so it says in a bedtime story.'

Jordan's eyes narrowed. 'It happens to be the best lead we've got going for us.'

Pitt wasn't convinced. 'Your spy planes and satellites should easily detect the installation.'

'The four main islands of Japan – Honshu, Kyushu, Hokkaido, and Shikoku – are surrounded by nearly a thousand smaller islands. Finding the right one can hardly be called *easy*.'

'Then why not isolate only those that can be connected by a tunnel to any of the four main islands?'

'Give us some credit for brains,' Jordan said irritably. 'We've already eliminated any island farther than ten miles offshore and concentrated on the rest. First of all, no suspicious activities or structures appear above their surfaces. Not unusual when we assume the entire installation must be deep underground. And lastly, almost all the islands' geology is made up of volcanic rock our sensors can't penetrate. Have I answered your question?'

Pitt dug in. 'No one can excavate a tunnel without hauling away dirt and rock.'

'Apparently the Japanese have. Analysis of our satellite photos shows no signs of a coastal tunnel excavation or roads leading into an entrance.'

Pitt shrugged his shoulders and waved the white flag. 'So we're back to a painting somewhere in the great beyond.'

Jordan suddenly leaned forward in his chair and stared hard at Pitt. 'This is where you earn your pay.'

Pitt could see it coming, but not quite. 'You're going to send me to Japan to dive around islands, is that the pitch?'

'Wrong,' said Jordan with a patronizing smile Pitt didn't

like one bit. 'You're going to Germany and dive in a Luftwaffe bunker.'

36

'They simply dived in and vanished.'

Pitt crouched on one knee and stared past the half-submerged tractor into the black ominous water. He was tired from jet lag, and he'd barely slept a couple of hours on the plane from Washington. How rotten not to have time to enjoy a good breakfast at a local inn and sleep past noon, he wallowed in self-pity.

'Their safety lines were sliced apart.' The young officer who led the German naval dive team held up a nylon line whose end appeared razor-severed. 'By what? We can't begin to guess.'

'Communication line too?' Pitt slowly sipped at a cup of coffee. He picked up a small stone with his free hand and idly tossed it in the water, observing the ripples that spread from the splash.

'The phone line connected to the lead diver was also cut,' admitted the German. He stood tall and well muscled. His English carried only a slight trace of an accent. 'Soon after the two-man team dropped into the pond, they discovered an underwater tunnel leading to the west. They swam a distance of ninety metres before reporting the tunnel ended at a small chamber with a steel door. A few minutes later the phone and safety lines went slack. I sent another team in to investigate. They disappeared like the others.'

Pitt turned his head and looked at the men of the German Navy dive team who stood helpless and saddened at the loss of their friends. They were clustered around the folding tables and chairs of a portable command post manned by a group of police underwater rescue divers. A trio of men in civilian clothes, who Pitt assumed were government officials, questioned the divers in low voices.

'When did the last man go in?' Pitt asked.

'Four hours before you arrived,' said the young dive officer, who had introduced himself as Lieutenant Helmut Reinhardt. 'I had a devil of a time keeping the rest of my men from following. But I'm not about to risk another life until I know what's going on in there.' He paused and tipped his head toward the police divers, who were attired in bright orange dry suits. 'Those idiot police, however, think they're invincible. They're planning to send one of their teams inside.'

'Some people are born for suicide,' said Giordino with a yawn. 'Take me for example. I wouldn't go in there without a nuclear submarine. No daredevil ventures by Mrs Giordino's boy. I intend to die in bed entwined with an erotic beauty from the Far East.'

'Don't pay any attention to him,' said Pitt. 'Put him in a dark place and he hallucinates.'

'I see,' murmured Reinhardt, but obviously he didn't.

Finally Pitt rose and nodded in Frank Mancuso's direction. 'Booby-trapped,' he said simply.

Mancuso nodded. 'I agree. The entrances to the treasure tunnels in the Philippines were packed with bombs rigged to go off if struck by digging equipment. The difference is the Japs planned to return and retrieve the treasure, while the Nazis intended for their booby traps to destroy the loot along with the searchers.'

'Whatever *trapped* my men in there,' said Reinhardt bitterly, unable to say the word 'killed', 'were not bombs.'

One of the official-looking men walked over from the comand post and addressed Pitt. 'Who are you, and who do you represent?' he demanded in German.

Pitt turned to Reinhardt, who translated the question. Then he refaced his interrogator. 'Tell him the three of us were invited.'

'You are American?' the stranger blurted in broken English, his face blank in astonishment. 'Who gave you authorization to be here?'

'Who's this mook?' Giordino inquired in blissful ignorance.

Reinhardt couldn't suppress a slight grin. 'Herr Gert Halder, Minister of Historic Works. Sir, Herr Dirk Pitt and his staff from the American National Underwater and Marine Agency in Washington. They are here at the personal invitation of Chancellor Lange.'

Halder looked like he'd been punched in the stomach. He quickly recovered, straightened to his full height, half a head short of tall, and attempted to intimidate Pitt with a superior Teutonic demeanour. 'Your purpose?'

'We've come for the same reason as you,' replied Pitt, studying his fingernails. 'If old interrogation records of Nazi officials in your Berlin archives and our Library of Congress are correct, eighteen thousand works of art were hidden in excavated tunnels under a secret airfield. This could very well prove to be *that* secret airfield with its art depository chamber extending somewhere beyond the water barrier.'

Halder wisely realized he couldn't bluster the tough, purposeful-looking men dressed in loose blue-green Viking dry suits. 'You know, of course, any art that is found belongs to the German Republic until it can be traced and returned to the original owners.'

'We're fully aware of that,' said Pitt. 'We're only interested in one particular piece.'

'Which one?'

'Sorry, I'm not allowed to say.'

Halder played his last card. 'I must insist the police dive team be the first to enter the chamber.'

'Fine by us.' Giordino bowed and gestured toward the dark water. 'Maybe if one of your deputies is lucky enough to make it in and back, we'll find out what's eating people in that hell hole down there.'

'I've lost four of my men.' Reinhardt spoke solemnly.

'They may be dead. You cannot allow more men to die through ignorance of the unknown.'

'They are professional divers,' Halder retorted.

'So are the men I sent in there. The finest divers in the Navy, in superior condition and more extensively trained than the police rescue team.'

'May I suggest a compromise,' said Pitt.

Halder nodded. 'I'm willing to listen.'

'We put together a seven-man probe team. The three of us because Mancuso here is a mining engineer, an expert on tunnel construction and excavation, while Al and I are experienced in underwater salvage. Two of Lieutenant Reinhardt's Navy men, since they're trained in defusing any demolitions we might encounter. And two of the police divers as rescue and medical backup.'

Halder stared into Pitt's eyes and saw only grim tenacity. It was a solid proposal fortified with logic. He forced a smile. 'Who goes in first?'

'I do,' Pitt said without hesitation.

His two short words seemed to echo in the cavern for long seconds, and then the tension suddenly evaporated and Halder stuck out his hand.

'As you wish.' He shook Pitt's hand and puffed out his chest to regain an image of authoritative dignity. 'But I hold you responsible, Herr Pitt, if you trip any explosive devices and destroy the artworks.'

Pitt gave Halder a contemptuous grin. 'In that case, Herr Halder, you may have my head – literally.'

Pitt set the time on the microelectronic computer attached by a line to his air tank and made a final check of his regulator and buoyancy compensator. For the fiftieth time since dropping down the ladder from farmer Clausen's field he stared into the beckoning black pool.

'Your gears are turning,' observed Giordino as he adjusted the straps to his tank pack.

Pitt rubbed his chin thoughtfully without replying.

'What do you think is going on in there?' asked Mancuso.

'I think I've solved half the puzzle,' answered Pitt. 'But the cutting of the lines? Now that's downright puzzling.'

'How's your acoustic speaker?' asked Mancuso.

Pitt inserted the regulator's mouthpiece and spoke into it. 'Mary had a little lamb . . .' The words came out muffled but understandable.

'I guess it's time, fearless leader,' grunted Giordino.

Pitt nodded at Reinhardt, who was accompanied by one of his men. 'Ready, gentlemen? Please try to stay within two metres of the man in front of you. Visibility appears to be four metres, so you should have no trouble keeping the distance. My team will communicate with you through our acoustic speakers.'

Reinhardt acknowledged with a wave and turned, relaying instructions in German to the police divers behind him. Then he threw a brief military salute to Pitt. 'After you, sir.'

There was no delaying it any longer. Pitt held out both hands at arm's length, index fingers pointing outward. 'I'll take the centre point. Frank, two metres behind and to my left. Al, you take the right. Keep a sharp watch on any unusual mechanisms sticking out of the walls.'

With nothing more to be said, Pitt switched on his dive light, gave a tug on his safety line to make sure it was clipped, and launched himself facedown into the water. He floated for a moment, and then very slowly ducked his head and dived toward the bottom, his dive light held ahead of him.

The water was cold. He glanced at the digital readout of the computer. The water temperature stood at 14 degrees Celsius or 57 degrees Fahrenheit. The concrete bottom was covered with green slime and a thin layer of silt. He was careful not to drag his fins or kick them into the sediment, raising clouds that would block the vision of the men behind.

Pitt actually enjoyed it. Once again he was a man totally at home in his own element. He aimed the dive light upward and stared at the ceiling of the bunker. It had sloped downward, becoming fully submerged and narrowing into a tunnel as expected. The water along the bottom was murky, and the particles that floated past his mask dropped the visibility down to three metres. He stopped and advised the men to close up a bit. Then he continued, swimming easily and smoothly as the ghostly outline of the floor gradually dropped until it levelled out and became swallowed by the dark.

After covering another twenty metres, he paused again and hung suspended for a minute while he twisted around and looked for Giordino and Mancuso. They were only shadowy figures behind the dull glow of their lights, but they faithfully held their instructed positions. He checked his computer. The pressure readout indicated a depth of only six metres.

A short distance later the underwater tunnel seemed to narrow, and the bottom began to rise. Pitt moved cautiously, his eyes straining into the gloom. He lifted his free hand above his head and felt it break the surface. He rolled over on his back and shone the light. The surface flashed and rolled like unleashed mercury from his movements a few centimetres in front of his face mask.

Like some unspeakable creature from the deep, his rubber-helmeted head with mask and regulator, eerily illuminated by the dive light, broke the cold water into the musty damp air of a small chamber. He lightly kicked his fins and softly bumped into a short flight of concrete stairs. He crept up and pulled himself onto a level floor.

The sight he feared did not materialize, at least not yet. Pitt found no bodies of the Germany Navy dive team. He could see where they had scraped their fins across the slime of the concrete floor, but that was the only sign of them.

He carefully examined the walls of the chamber, finding

no protrusion that appeared threatening. At the far end, the dive light lit up a large rust-coloured metal door. He stepped awkwardly up the steps in his fins and approached the door. He leaned against it with his shoulder. The hinges turned in their pins with incredible ease and silence, almost as if they were oiled sometime in the past week. The door swung inward, and then quickly returned as Pitt released the pressure, forced back by springs.

'Hello, what have we got here.' The words were audible, but Mancuso sounded like he was gargling through the acoustic speaker on his breathing regulator.

'Guess what's behind door number one, and you win a year's supply of Brillo pads,' said Giordino in a masterpiece of dry-rot humour.

Pitt pulled off his fins and knelt down and cracked the door a few more centimetres. He studied the threshold for a moment and gestured at the bottom edge of the rust-encrusted door. 'This explains the severed phone and safety lines.'

Giordino nodded. 'Cut by the sharp bottom edge of the door after the divers entered and the spring system slammed it closed.'

Mancuso looked at Pitt. 'You said you solved the other half of the puzzle.'

'Yeah,' muttered Giordino, 'the choice part, like what killed the German Navy's finest.'

'Gas,' Pitt answered curtly. 'Poison gas, triggered after they passed beyond this door.'

'A sound theory,' agreed Mancuso.

Pitt flashed his light on the water and saw the approaching air bubbles of Reinhardt and his teammate. 'Frank, you stay and keep the others from entering. Al and I will go it alone. And whatever happens, make damn sure everyone breathes only the air from their tanks. Under no circumstances are they to remove their regulators.'

Mancuso held up an acknowledging hand and turned to greet the next team.

Giordino leaned against a wall, crooked one leg, and removed a fin. 'No sense traipsing in there like a duck.'

Pitt removed his fins too. He scraped his rubber boots across the rough concrete floor to feel what little grip they had across the slick surface. The friction was nil. The slightest loss of balance and he'd go down.

One final check of his tank pressure on the computer. Enough breathing time at atmospheric pressure for another hour. Free of the cold water, the air temperature stood at a point where he was reasonably comfortable in his dry suit.

'Mind your step,' he said to Giordino. Then he pushed the door half open and stepped inside as lightly as though he was walking a tightrope. The atmosphere went abruptly dry, and the humidity dropped off to almost zero percent. He paused and swept the light beam on the concrete floor, carefully searching for trip-strings and cables leading to explosive detonators or poison gas containers. A thin broken fish line, grey in colour and nearly invisible in the dim light, lay snapped in two almost under his toes.

The light beam followed one end of the line to a canister marked PHOSGENE. Thank God, Pitt thought, deeply relieved. Phosgene is only fatal if inhaled. The Gemans invented nerve gas during World War II, but for some reason lost in the dim past, they failed to rig it here. A fortunate stroke for Pitt and Giordino and the men who followed them. The nerve-type agent could kill on contact with flesh, and they all had skin exposed on their hands and around their face masks.

'You were right about the gas,' said Giordino.

'Too late to help those poor seamen.'

He found four more poison gas booby traps, two of them activated. The phosgene had done its deadly work. Bodies of the Navy divers lay in contorted positions only a few metres apart. All had removed their air tanks and breathing regulators, unsuspecting of the gas until it was too late. Pitt did not bother trying for a pulse. Their blue facial colour and unseeing eyes gave evidence they were stone dead.

He played the light into a long gallery and froze.

Nearly eyeball to eyeball a woman stared back at him, her head tilted in a coquettish pose. She smiled at him from an adorable face with high cheekbones and smooth pink skin.

She was not alone. Several other female figures stood beside and behind her, their unblinking eyes seemingly locked on Pitt. They were naked, covered only by long tresses that fell almost to their knees.

'I've died and gone to Amazon heaven,' Giordino muttered in rapt awe.

'Don't get excited!!' Pitt warned him. 'They're painted sculptures.'

'I wish I could mould them like that.'

Pitt stepped around the life-size sculptures and held the dive light over his head. Gold gleamed in an ocean of gilded picture frames. As far as the light could reach and beyond, way beyond, the long gallery was filled with tier upon tier of racks containing an immense cache of fine paintings, sculpture, religious relics, tapestries, rare books, ancient furniture, and archaeological antiquities, all stored in orderly bins and open crates.

'I think,' Pitt murmured through his acoustic speaker, 'we've just made a lot of people very happy.'

37

The Germans were characteristically efficient. Within four hours, decontamination experts arrived and set up pumping equipment and laid hose into the treasure gallery. The poisoned atmosphere was quickly and safely drawn into a chemical tank truck parked on the surface. While the clean-up process was in operation, Reinhardt and his men deactivated the phosgene release mechanisms and turned the canisters over to the decontamination crew. Only then did the Navy divers carry their dead to waiting ambulances.

Next, a large aluminium pipe was fed through the opening in the ground like a giant straw and attached to a huge suction pump that soon began draining the water from the subterranean tunnel into a small nearby stream. An excavating crew appeared with their equipment and began digging into the original entry ramp leading down to the bunker that had been filled in at the end of the war.

Mancuso paced the bunker impatiently, stopping every few minutes and peering at the instruments that measured the decreasing levels of the poison gas. Then he'd move to the edge of the ramp and stare at the rapidly receding water. Back and forth, watching the progress, counting the minutes until he could safely enter the gallery containing the Nazis' plundered loot.

Giordino, true to form, slept the whole time. He found a musty old cot in a former Luftwaffe mechanic's quarters and promptly sacked out.

After Pitt made his report to Halder and Reinhardt, he killed time by accepting an invitation to a home-cooked meal prepared by Frau Clausen in her warm and comfortable farmhouse. Later he roamed the bunker examining the old aircraft. He stopped and circled one of the Messerschmitt 262s, admiring the slim cigar shape of the fuselage, the triangular vertical stabilizer, and the ungainly jet pods that hung from the razor knifelike wings. Except for the black crosses outlined in white on the wings and fuselage, and the swastika on the tail, the only other marking was a large numeral 9 painted just forward of the cockpit.

The world's first operational jet fighter, it was produced too late to save Germany, though it scared hell out of the British and American air forces for a few short months.

'It flew as though the angels were pushing.'

Pitt turned at the voice and found Gert Halder standing behind him. The German's blue eyes were wistfully gazing at the cockpit of the Messerschmitt.

'You look too young to have flown her,' said Pitt.

Halder shook his head. 'The words of one of our leading aces during the war, Adolf Galland.'

'Shouldn't take much work to get them airworthy.'

Halder gazed at the fleet of aircraft that sat in spectral silence in the vast bunker. 'The government rarely provides funding for such a project. I'll be lucky if I can keep five or six of them for museum display.'

'And the others?'

'They'll be sold or auctioned off to museums and collectors around the world.'

'I wish I could afford to place a bid,' Pitt said yearningly.

Halder looked at him, the arrogance was gone. A canny smile curved his lips. 'How many aircraft do you count?'

Pitt stood back and mentally totalled the number of jet craft in the bunker. 'I make it forty even.'

'Wrong. It's thirty-nine.'

Pitt re-counted and again came up with forty. 'I hate to disagree, but –'

Halder waved him off. 'If one can be removed when the entry ramp is cleared and transported across the border before I take the official inventory . . .'

Halder didn't need to finish his sentence. Pitt heard, but he wasn't sure he interpreted the meaning. An Me-262 had to be worth over a million dollars in good restorable condition.

'When do you expect to take inventory?' he asked, feeling his way.

'After I catalogue the contents of the plundered art.'

'That could take weeks.'

'Possibly longer.'

'Why?' Pitt put to Halder.

'Call it penitence. I was most rude to you earlier. And I feel obligated to reward your courageous effort in reaching the treasure, saving perhaps five lives and preventing me from making a blue-ribbon ass of myself and quite probably losing my job.'

'And you're offering to look the other way while I steal one.'

'There are so many, one won't be missed.'

'I'm grateful,' Pitt said sincerely.

Halder looked at him. 'I asked a friend on our intelligence service to run a file on you while you were busy in the tunnel. I think a Messerschmitt two-six-two will make a nice addition to your collection and complement your Ford trimotor.'

'Your friend was very thorough.'

'As a collector of fine mechanical relics, I think you will give it the proper respect.'

'It will be restored to original condition,' Pitt promised.

Halder lit a cigarette and leaned casually against a jet pod as he exhaled blue smoke. 'I suggest you see about renting a flatbed truck. By tonight the bunker entrance will have been widened enough to tow a plane to the surface. I'm certain Lieutenant Reinhardt and his surviving team will be happy to assist you in removing your latest acquisition.'

Before a stunned and thankful Pitt could say another word, Halder had turned and walked away.

Another eight hours passed before the massive pump

307

suctioned off most of the water and the air in the gallery of wartime loot was safe to breathe. Halder stood on a chair with a bullhorn, briefing his staff of art experts and historians and a gathering of German government officials and politicians who wanted to be in on the discovery. An army of TV and newspaper correspondents was building in Clausen's now ravaged lettuce field, demanding to enter the bunker. But Halder was under orders from his superior in Bonn. No entry by the news media until the hoard was surveyed.

Beginning at the steel door, the gallery stretched a good half a kilometre. The racks and bins were filled to the far wall and rose four metres high. Despite the water in the tunnel, the entry door had been sealed tightly and the concrete construction was of top quality, so no moisture had penetrated inside. Even the more delicate objects had survived in excellent condition.

The Germans immediately began setting up a photo and conservation laboratory, a workshop, and a records area. After the briefing, Halder moved into the art chamber and directed the activities from a prefabricated office hurriedly assembled and furnished complete with telephones and fax machine.

Unconsciously almost, Pitt shook his head and walked through the now dry tunnel with Mancuso, marvelling that so much had been accomplished in less than twenty-four hours.

'Where's Al?' asked Mancuso.

'Off scrounging a truck.'

Mancuso stared at him with an arched eyebrow. 'Not thinking of absconding with a load of masterpieces, are we? If so, I don't recommend it. The Krauts will shoot you down before you've cleared the farm.'

'Not when you have friends in high places,' Pitt smiled.

'I don't even want to know about it. Whatever your evil scheme, do it after I leave.'

They passed through the entry door into the gallery and stepped into Halder's closed office that was set off to one side. Halder waved them in and motioned to a pair of camp stools as he conversed in German over one of four telephones. He hung up as they sat down.

'I fully realize you have permission from Chancellor Lange to search for whatever it is you're after, but before you begin digging through the bins and crates, I'd like to know what it is.'

'We're only interested in art objects removed from the Japanese embassy in Berlin,' Pitt answered.

'You think they're here?'

'There was no time to transport them to Japan,' Mancuso explained. 'The Russians were encircling the city. The ambassador locked up the building and barely escaped with his staff into Switzerland. Historical records show the antique art that decorated the interior of the embassy was entrusted to the Nazis for safekeeping, and they hid it under an airfield.'

'And you think it may be included with the cache discovered here.'

'We do, yes.'

'Can I ask why the American government is so interested in lost works of Japanese art?'

'I'm sorry,' Pitt said honestly. 'We can't give out that information. But I can assure you our search poses no problems for the German government.'

'I'm thinking of the Japanese. They'll demand their property be returned.'

'Possession is not our intent,' Mancuso assured Halder. 'We only wish to photograph a few pieces.'

'All right, gentlemen.' Halder sighed. He gave Pitt a hard stare. 'I trust you, Herr Pitt. We have an agreement. Do what you say, and I'll guarantee to look the other way.'

As they left Halder's office, Mancuso whispered, 'What was he talking about? What agreement?'

'Recruitment.'

'Recruitment?' Mancuso repeated.

Pitt nodded. 'He talked me into joining the Luftwaffe.'

They found the rack containing the inventory from the Japanese embassy about fifty metres back of the sculptured figures that once graced the museums of Europe. The Germans had already installed a string of lamps that ran off a portable generator, throwing light on the great hoard that seemed to stretch into infinity.

The Japanese section was easy to identify, the packing boxes having been marked by *kana* characters and hand-crafted with far more finesse than the crude crates knocked together by the Nazi looters.

'Let's start with that one,' said Mancuso, pointing to a narrow container. 'That looks to be about the right size.'

'You spent time prospecting in Japan. What does it read?'

'"Container number four,"' Mancuso translated. '"Property of his Imperial Majesty, the Emperor of Japan."'

'That's a big help.' Pitt went to work and carefully lifted the lid with a hammer and pry bar. Inside was a small, delicate folding screen depicting birds flying around several mountain peaks. 'Definitely not an island.' He shrugged.

He opened two more, but the paintings he pulled into the dim light were of a later period than the sixteenth-century master Masaki Shimzu. Most of the smaller crates were carefully packed with porcelain. There was only one more crate in the rear of the rack that might conceivably hold a painting.

Mancuso showed signs of stress. Sweat was glistening on his forehead and he nervously fidgeted with his pipe. 'This better be it,' he muttered. 'Or we've wasted a lot of time.' Pitt said nothing but went about his work. This box seemed more heavily constructed than the others. He pried the lid and peered inside. 'I see water. I think we've got a seascape. Better yet, it's an island.'

'Thank God. Pull it out, man, let's see it.'

'Hold on.' There was no ornate outer frame, so Pitt gripped the painting under its rear support and painstakingly eased it out of the crate. Once free, he held it up under the light for inspection.

Mancuso hurriedly pulled a small catalogue showing colour plates of Masaki Shimzu art from his pocket and flipped through the pages, comparing the photos with the painting. 'I'm no expert, but that looks like Shimzu's style.'

Pitt turned the painting around and studied the other side. 'There's some writing. Can you make it out.'

Manuso squinted. ' "Ajima Island by Masuki Shimzu," ' he burst out triumphantly. 'We've got it, the site of Suma's command centre. Now all we have to do is match its shoreline with satellite photos.'

Mechanically, Pitt's eyes travelled over the picture Shimzu had painted four hundred and fifty years ago of an island then called Ajima. It would never make a tourist paradise. Steep volcanic rock cliffs towering above pounding surf, no sign of a beach, and almost total absence of vegetation. It looked barren and forbidding, grim and impregnable. There was no way to approach and make a landing from sea or air without detection. A natural fortress, Suma would have it heavily defended against assault.

'Getting inside that rock,' Pitt said thoughtfully, 'is going to be damn near impossible. Whoever tries it will surely die.'

The triumphant expression on Mancuso's face quickly vanished. 'Don't say that,' he murmured. 'Don't even think it.'

Pitt looked into the mining engineer's eyes. 'Why? Gaining entrance is not our problem.'

'But you're wrong.' He made a weary swipe at the sweat from his forehead. 'With teams Cadillac and Honda down the dumper, Jordan has no choice but to send in you and me and Giordino. Think about it.'

311

Pitt did, and Mancuso was right. It was all too clear now. Wily Jordan had been saving the three of them in reserve for a covert strike on Suma's nuclear bomb detonation centre.

38

The President stared down at the open file on his desk. His face had a bleak expression as he looked up. 'They really intend to set these things off? It's not a bluff?'

Jordan's face was impassive as he nodded. 'They're not bluffing.'

'It's unthinkable.'

Jordan did not answer, but let the President gather his own thoughts. The man never seemed to change. He looked exactly as he did the first day Jordan was introduced to the newly elected senator from Montana. The same lean build, bright blue eyes, the same warm, outgoing personality. The incredible power never fazed him. He was polite and cordial to the White House staff, and seldom missed remembering a birthday.

'It's not like we've ringed their islands with an invasion fleet, for God's sake.'

'They've become paranoid because global opinion has suddenly come down on them,' said Donald Kern. 'With China and Russia embracing democracy, the Eastern Bloc countries going independent, South Africa holding free elections, and the Middle East simmering on the back burner, world focus has fallen on the Japanese for going too far too fast.'

Kern nodded. 'Their economic aggressiveness hasn't exactly been tempered with subtlety. The more markets they conquer, the more hard-nosed they become.'

'But you can't blame them for creating an economic world the way they want it to be,' said Jordan. 'Their business ethics are not the same as ours. They see nothing immoral in exploiting commercial opportunities and taking advantage of trade weaknesses, regardless of the flak. The only crime in their eyes is any attempt to prevent their systematic progress. Frankly, we were no different in our overseas trade practices after World War Two.'

'I can't argue with you,' conceded the President. 'Few of our past and present business leaders will ever qualify for sainthood.'

'Congress and the European Market countries are on an anti-Japanese business kick. If they vote for trade embargoes and nationalization of Japanese corporations, Tokyo will attempt to negotiate, but Suma and his cronies are dead set on retaliation.'

'But to threaten nuclear death and destruction . . .'

'They're playing for time,' explained Jordan. 'Their worldwide commercial thrust is only part of a broader plan. The Japanese live under terrible conditions of high density. A hundred and twenty-five million people on a land mass the size of California, with most of it too mountainous to live on. Their unadvertised long-range goal is to export millions of their best-educated people into other countries and form colonies while maintaining loyalty and strong ties to Japan. Brazil is a case in point, and so is the United States when you consider their mass immigration into Hawaii and California. The Japanese are obsessed with survival, and unlike us, they plan decades into the future. Through economic trade they're building a vast economic global society with Japanese traditions and culture as the hub. What even they don't realize is that Suma intends to set himself up as executive director.'

The President glanced at the open file again. 'And he protects his criminal empire by strategically placing nuclear bombs in other nations.'

'We can't blame the Japanese government or the great mass of their people,' Jordan qualified. 'I'm firmly convinced Prime Minister Junshiro was misled and duped by Hideki Suma and his cartel of industrialists, financiers, and underworld leaders who secretly built a nuclear arsenal and expanded it into the Kaiten Project.'

The President opened his hands. 'Perhaps I should set a meeting with Junshiro and inform him of our intelligence revelations.'

Jordan shook his head. 'I don't recommend it just yet, sir. Not until we have a chance at cutting off the Kaiten Project at its head.'

'When last we met, you didn't have the location of the command centre.'

'New information has put us in the neighbourhood.'

The President looked at Jordan with renewed respect. He understood his chief intelligence gatherer, the dedication to his country, the many years of service beginning when he was still a few years shy of high school and already entered into training for the intelligence fieldwork. The President also saw the toll that years of incredible stress had taken. Jordan consumed a steady stream of Maalox tablets as if they were popcorn.

'Do you know yet where the car bombs are to be placed for detonation?'

Kern answered. 'Yes, sir, one of our teams discovered the plan while tracking a shipment of the cars. Suma's engineers have created a diabolic and well-contrived disaster.'

'I assume they'll be parked in densely populated areas to slaughter the largest number of American citizens possible.'

'Dead wrong, Mr President. They will be strategically located for a minimal loss of life.'

'You've lost me.'

'Throughout the United States and the industrialized world,' Kern briefed, 'the cars will be staged in systematic grids in deserted areas so their synchronized explosions will set off an electromagnetic pulse on the ground that rises into the atmosphere. This will create an umbrella-like chain reaction that shuts down uplinks to worldwide satellite communications systems.'

315

'All radio, television, and phone networks simply cease to exist,' added Jordan. 'Federal and local governments, military commands, police and sheriff departments, fire departments, ambulances, and all transportation will roll to a halt because they can't operate deaf.'

'A world without communication,' murmured the President. 'It's unimaginable.'

'The picture gets worse,' Kern continued ominously. 'Much worse. You know, of course, Mr President, what happens when you have a magnet near a computer disk or a cassette tape.'

'They're erased.'

Kern nodded slowly. 'The electromagnetic pulse from the nuclear explosions would do the same thing. For hundreds of miles around each explosion the memories of every computer would be totally erased. Silicon chips and transistors, the backbone of our modern computerized world, are defenceless against a pulse running through electrical and telephone circuits and aerials. Anything made of metal would carry the pulse from pipes to rails to microwave towers and steel supports inside of buildings.'

The President stared at Kern with unbelieving eyes. 'We're talking total chaos.'

'Yes, sir, a complete national breakdown with catastrophic results that are beyond recovery. Any and every record ever programmed into a computer by banks, insurance companies, giant corporations, small businesses, hospitals, supermarkets, department stores – the list is endless – would vanish, along with all stored scientific and engineering data.'

'Every disk, every tape?'

'In every home and office,' said Jordan.

Kern kept his eyes on the President to reinforce his dire commentary. 'Any computer electronics that runs on memory, and that includes ignition and carburation on modern autos, operation of diesel train engines, and controls on aircraft in flight, would stop functioning. The aircraft especially could suffer horrible consequences, since many would fall to the ground before their crews could take manual command.'

'And there are also the mundane everyday devices we take for granted,' said Jordan, 'that would also be affected, such as microwave ovens, video cassette recorders, and security systems. We've come to rely so heavily on computer chips that we've never considered how vulnerable they are.'

The President picked up a pen and tapped it nervously on the desk. His face was drawn, his expression distraught. 'I cannot allow that curse to paralyse the American people well into the next century,' he stated flatly. 'I have to seriously consider a strike, nuclear if necessary, on their warhead arsenal and detonation command centre.'

'I advise against it, Mr President,' said Jordan with quiet conviction, 'except as a last resort.'

The President looked at him. 'What's your angle, Ray?'

'Suma's installation won't be on-line for another week. Let us try to devise a penetration plan to destroy it from within. If successful, it will save you enormous fallout from a hailstorm of international condemnation for what will be looked upon as an unprovoked attack on a friendly nation.'

The President was silent, a thoughtful look on his face. Then he said slowly, 'You're right, I'd be forced into making excuses no one would believe.'

'Time is on our side as long as no one but our MAIT team and the three of us knows what's going down,' Jordan continued.

'Good thing,' Kern muttered. 'If the Russians knew their landscape was littered with foreign warheads, they wouldn't hesitate to threaten a full-scale invasion of Japan.'

'And we don't need that,' the President said quietly.

'Nor do the innocent Japanese, who have no idea of Suma's insane threat,' said Jordan, hammering in another nail.

317

The President came to his feet, ending the briefing. 'Four days, gentlemen. You have ninety-six hours.'

Jordan and Kern exchanged tight smiles.

The assault on Suma had been planned before they walked into the Oval Office. All it took was a phone call to set it in motion.

39

At four o'clock in the morning the small landing strip on a government reservation near Seneca, Maryland, looked to be deserted. There were no lights bordering the narrow band of asphalt. The only guide to a pilot making a night landing was a triangle of blue mercury vapour streetlights arched over an intersection of two dirt roads that pointed to the south end of the runway.

The early morning stillness was broken as the whine of throttled-back jet engines cut the still air. A pair of headlights flashed on, their beams falling across the centre of the landing strip. The Gulfstream jet transport with CIRCLEARTH AIRLINES painted across the top of the fuselage touched down and taxied to a stop beside a Jeep Grand Wagoneer station wagon.

Less than three minutes after the passenger door opened and two men and their luggage were on the ground, the plane rolled toward the end of the runway and was airborne again. As the roar faded in the black sky, Admiral Sandecker shook hands with Pitt and Giordino.

'Congratulations,' he said warmly, 'on a very successful operation.'

'We haven't heard the results,' said Pitt. 'Did the photos of the painting Mancuso transmitted match an existing island?'

'Right on the money,' replied Sandecker. 'Turns out the island was called Ajima by fishermen after one of them became stranded on it in the seventeen-hundreds. But it remained on the charts as Soseki Island. And like many geographical sites connected with local folklore, the name Ajima was eventually lost.'

'Where's the location?' asked Giordino.

'About sixty kilometres off the coast due east of Edo City.'

Pitt's face suddenly became etched with anxious concern. 'What word of Loren?'

Sandecker shook his head. 'Only that she and Diaz are alive and hidden in a secret location.'

'That's it?' Pitts said, irritated. 'No investigation, no operation to free them?'

'Until the bomb-car threat is eliminated, the President's hands are tied.'

'Bed,' mumbled Giordino, cagily changing the subject to cool Pitt down. 'Take me to my bed.'

Pitt dipped his head at the little Italian. 'Get him. His eyes haven't been open since we left Germany.'

'You made good time,' said Sandecker. 'Have a pleasant flight?'

'Slept most of it. And with the jet lag working in our favour flying west, I'm wide awake.'

'Frank Mancuso remained with the art objects?' Sandecker inquired.

Pitt nodded. 'Just before we took off, he received a message from Kern ordering him to pack up the Japanese embassy art and fly it to Tokyo.'

'A smokescreen to pacify the Germans.' Sandecker smiled. 'The art is actually going to a vault in San Francisco. When the time is ripe, the President will present it to the Japanese people as a goodwill gesture.' He gestured to the seats of the Jeep. 'Get in. Since you're so bright and bushytailed, I'll let you drive.'

'Fine by me,' Pitt said agreeably.

After they threw their bags in the luggage compartment, Pitt slid behind the steering wheel as the admiral and Giordino entered from the opposite side. Sandecker took the front passenger seat, Giordino the back. Pitt shifted the running engine into drive and wheeled the Jeep down a dark road to a gatehouse that stood hidden in a grove of trees. A uniformed security guard stepped out, peered inside the car a moment, then saluted Sandecker and waved them through to a back-country highway.

Three kilometres later, Pitt turned the Jeep onto the Capital Beltway and headed toward the lights of Washington. Traffic at that time of the morning was almost non-existent. He set the cruise control on 110 kilometres and sat back as the big four-wheel-drive rolled effortlessly over the pavement.

They drove in silence for several minutes. Sandecker stared absently through the windscreen. Pitt didn't need a strong imagination to know the admiral didn't leave a warm bed to meet them without a good reason. The huge Havana was strangely missing from his mouth, and his hands were clasped across his chest, sure signs of inner tension. His eyes were like ice cubes. He definitely had something heavy on his mind.

Pitt decided to give him an opening. 'Where do we go from here?' he asked.

'Say again,' Sandecker mumbled in mock distraction.

'What does the great eagle have in store for us next? A nice week's vacation, I hope.'

'Do you really want to know?'

'Probably not, but you're going to tell me, right?'

Sandecker yawned to prolong the agony. 'Well, I'm afraid you two are off on another aeroplane ride again.'

'Where?'

'The Pacific.'

'Where exactly in the Pacific?'

'Palau. The team, or what's left of it, is to assemble at the Information Gathering and Collection Point for new instructions from the Director of Field Operations.'

'Without the bureaucratic title crap, what you're saying is we're meeting with Mel Penner.'

Sandecker smiled, and his eyes softened considerably. 'You have a deft manner of slicing to the gut of the matter.'

321

Pitt was wary. He could see the axe was to about to fall. 'When?' he asked quickly.

'In precisely one hour and fifty minutes. You're taking a commercial airline out of Dulles.'

'A pity we didn't land there,' Pitt said sourly, 'and saved you the drive.'

'Security reasons. Kern thought it best if you arrive at the terminal by car, pick up the tickets, and board like any other tourists flying to the South Seas.'

'We could use a change of clothes.'

'Kern sent a man to pack clean things in suitcases. They've already been checked through.'

'Very thoughtful of him. I must remind myself to change my security alarms when I return –'

Pitt broke off and studied the reflection in his rearview mirror. The same pair of headlights had been on the Jeep's tail since they swung onto the beltway. For the last several kilometres they had maintained an exact distance. He punched off the cruise control and increased speed slightly. The lights dropped back and moved forward again.

'Something wrong?' asked Sandecker.

'We've picked up a tail.'

Giordino turned and peered through the big rear window. 'More than one. I make out three vans in convoy.'

Pitt stared thoughtfully into the mirror. The beginning of a grin drew across his face. 'Whoever is after us isn't taking any chances. They've sent a full platoon.'

Sandecker snatched a car phone and dialled the MAIT team safe line. 'This is Admiral Sandecker!' he snapped, ignoring any attempt at procedural codes. 'I'm on the Capital Beltway heading south near Morning Side. We are being followed –'

'Make that pursued,' Pitt interrupted him. 'They're closing fast.'

Suddenly a burst of gunfire tore through the roof of the

Jeep just above their heads. 'Correction,' Giordino said in utter calm. 'Change pursued to attacked.'

Sandecker slouched down on the floor and spoke rapidly into the car phone's mouthpiece, giving location and instructions. Pitt had already slammed his foot down on the accelerator. The high torque of the big 5.9-litre V-8 kicked in, and the Jeep swiftly leaped down the beltway at 150 kph.

'The agent on duty is sending out a call for the highway patrol,' announced Sandecker.

'Tell them to put on some speed,' Pitt urged, whipping the big Jeep back and forth across the three lanes of highway to throw off their pursuers' aim.

'They're not playing fair,' Giordino said contritely. He dropped down on the floor between the seats as another burst sprayed the rear window's glass over him, passed through the car, and took out half the windscreen. 'They've got guns, and we don't.'

'I think I can fix that.' Pitt spared him a quick glance down and back.

'How?'

'By getting off this damn highway, where we make a perfect target, and taking every bend in the next road I can find until we hit a town.'

'The turnoff for Phelps Point is coming up,' advised Sandecker, peeping over the dashboard.

Pitt stole a quick look in the rearview mirror. He could see now that the vans were painted in the colour scheme of ambulances. Even as he obseved them, their red and blue flashing lights blinked. Their sirens remained mute, however, as the drivers pulled abreast of each other, covering the entire southbound lanes of the beltway to increase their firepower.

Pitt could make out men clad in black aiming automatic weapons out the side windows. Whoever planned the assassination had covered every base. There must have been four men to a van. Twelve who were armed to the teeth against three who probably had only one Swiss Army knife between them.

Pitt had an idea for evening the odds a bit. The off-ramp to Phelps Point was still two hundred metres ahead. No time. The next barrage of massed fire would blow them off the road. Without touching the brakes and warning the pursuing killers of his intention by flashing red taillights, he abruptly threw the Jeep into a crabwise slide and shot across two lanes and down an embankment.

The timing was perfect. A hail of gunfire missed the big Grand Wagoneer as it swept over the landscaped grass and surfed through a shallow ditch filled with half a metre of water. Then all tyres bounced free of the ground as it soared over the other edge of the ditch, landing with a screeching of rubber on a frontage road that paralleled the beltway.

The pursuers lost time as they skidded to a stop in confusion. Pitt gained almost ten seconds before they regrouped and roared down the off-ramp onto the frontage road and resumed the chase.

For the second time in nearly as many days, Pitt was driving as if he was competing in a Grand Prix road race. Professional drivers, though, had an advantage. They wore helmets with visors against the wind resistance. The cold morning air washed over Pitt's face through the bullet-shattered windscreen, and he was forced to turn his head sideway and squint against the icy gust.

They tore onto a long avenue flanked by oak trees before bursting into a residential area. He threw the Jeep into a series of sharp turns, left on one block of houses, left again, and then to the right. The drivers of the vans were well versed in the routine. They split up and attempted to cut him off at the intersections, but he always managed to get there ahead and dash past with scant seconds to spare.

The killers held their fire amid the populated homes, relentlessly closing the net and cutting off avenues of escape. When Pitt was able to make a turn before they came in sight from the previous block, he turned out his lights and sped through the darkness. Unfortunately, the streetlights gave him away. He tried every trick he knew, gaining a few metres here, a few seconds there, but he could not entirely shake the stubborn killers.

Pitt circled back and threw the Jeep onto the main avenue into the town. A gas station, a theatre, and several small shops flicked past. 'Watch for a hardware store,' he shouted above the scream of the protesting tyres.

'A what?' asked Sandecker incredulously.

'A hardware store. There's got to be one in town.'

'Oscar Brown's Hardware Emporium,' announced Giordino. 'I saw it on a sign right after we sailed off the beltway.'

'Whatever you've got in mind,' said the admiral steadily, 'you better manage it quick. The red light on the gas gauge just flashed on.'

Pitt glanced at the dash instruments. The needle was pegged on 'empty'. 'They must have stitched the fuel tank.'

'Oscar's Emporium is coming up on the right side of the street,' said Giordino, motioning through the open windscreen.

'You have a flashlight?' Pitt snapped to Sandecker.

'There's one in the glove compartment.'

'Get it out.'

Pitt took one final look in the mirror. The first van was sliding around a corner two blocks back. He steered the Jeep into the gutter on the left side of the street, and then cramped the wheel to the right.

Sandecker stiffened in shock.

Giordino croaked, 'Oh, no!'

The Jeep spun sideways for an instant, then the four drive wheels dug in and it raced over the kerb, across the sidewalk, and crashed through a huge plate-glass window into the hardware store. The Jeep bashed through the front counters, sending cash registers spinning into the darkness.

An end display, a cluster of garden rakes on sale, burst up like toothpicks. The car careened down an aisle between shelves hurling plumbing fixtures and nuts, bolts, and screws in the air like grape and canister out of a cannon.

Insanely, it seemed to Giordino and Sandecker, Pitt didn't stop. He kept his foot pressed on the accelerator, travelling up and down the aisles as though he was searching for something, leaving total destruction in his wake. The tumult as the Jeep ran wild was enhanced by the sudden whoop of the security alarm.

At last Pitt shoved the front bumper into a display case, resulting in a great spray of jagged glass. The one remaining headlight flickered dimly on twenty or thirty handguns scattered about the shattered case and stacked rows of rifles and shotguns in a large cabinet against the wall.

'You sneaky bastard,' Sandecker uttered in awe.

40

'Choose your weapons,' Pitt shouted over the banshee cry of the alarm as he kicked open the door.

Sandecker needed no urging. He was out of the Jeep and ransacking the cabinet for ammunition while clutching the flashlight under his arm. 'What's your pleasure, gentlemen?' he yelled out.

Pitt snatched a pair of Colt Combat Commander automatic pistols, one with blue finish, the other in stainless steel. He ejected the clips. 'Forty-five automatic!'

Sandecker fumbled through the boxes in the cabinet for only a few seconds before he spotted the right calibre. He tossed two boxes to Pitt. 'Winchester Silver Tips.' Then he turned to Giordino. 'What do you need, Al?'

Giordino had pulled three Remington-1100 shotguns off the rack. 'Twelve gauge, double-aught load.'

'Sorry,' Sandecker snapped back. He handed Giordino several boxes of shotgun casings. 'Number-four magnum buckshot is the best I can do on short notice.' Then he crouched low and dashed over to the paint department.

'Hurry and douse your light,' Pitt warned him, smashing the remaining headlight with the butt of one Colt.

The vans had slammed to a stop up the block and out of sight of the men inside the store. The assassins flowed from the vehicles in their black *ninja* suits swiftly and smoothly. They did not rush toward the hardware store, but paused, taking their time.

Their rehearsed tactical operation to riddle the Jeep and its occupants to shreds had been fouled by Pitt's unexpected dive from the beltway into Phelps Point. Now they were forced to formulate a new tactical operation on the spot. Coolly, they sized up the situation.

Overconfidence clouded their judgement. Because they had experienced no return fire from the three men in the fleeing four-wheel-drive, and were certain their intended victims were unarmed, they were overanxious to rush through the storefront and finish the job.

Their team leader was wise enough to gesture for caution. He stood in a doorway across the street and peered into the darkness inside the wrecked hardware store. He could see nothing beyond the debris as evidenced by the glow from a solitary streetlight. The Jeep was lost in the shadows. Nor could he hear sounds from the interior over the annoying wail from the alarm.

His analysis of the situation was rushed as lights blinked on in apartments above several of the stores. He could not afford to attract a crowd of witnesses. Then there was the local law-enforcement agency. He could expect the sheriff and his deputies to charge on the scene within minutes.

Then he allowed a misjudgement to guide him into a fatal error. He wrongly assumed the men in the Jeep were badly injured in the crash or cowering in fear, and he failed to send a team of his men around to seal off the rear of the store.

He allowed three minutes to rush the Jeep, finish off his prey, and retreat in the vans. The kill should be quick and easy, he thought. As a precaution he shot out the streetlight, plunging the street into blackness and preventing his men from being outlined when they made the assault. He held a whistle to his lips and gave the signal to prepare weapons and ensure that the selector switches were off 'safe' on their 5.56-millimetre, 51-round Sawa automatic rifles. Then he blew three short chirps, and they began to move in.

They glided swiftly through the gloom, like water moccasins in a Georgia bayou, slipping through the shattered display window in pairs and quickly fading into the shadows. The first six men to enter froze in position, muzzles extended and sweeping back and forth, their eyes straining to pierce the blackness.

Then suddenly a five-gallon can of paint thinner with a burning cloth wick in its spout sailed between them and fell on the sidewalk, exploding in a maelstrom of blue and orange flame. In unison, Pitt and Giorgino opened up as Sandecker hurled another can of the volatile fluid.

Pitt worked the Colts in both hands, pointing but not taking careful aim. He laid down a barrage that dropped the three men who were crouched to the right of the window almost before they realized they'd been hit. One of them had time to let off a short burst that smashed into a row of paint cans, leaving coloured spurts of enamel gushing onto the shambles of merchandise broken and trashed on the floor.

Giordino blew the first man on the left back through the window and half into the street. The other two were only shadows in the darkness, but he blasted away at them until one Remington went empty. Then he dropped it and picked up another he'd preloaded and fired again and again until all return fire had ceased.

Pitt reloaded his cartridge clips by feel as he stared through the flame and smoke that swirled around the front of the store. The killers in the black ninja outfits had vanished completely, frantically seeking cover or lying in the gutter behind the thankful protection of a high kerb. But they hadn't run away. They were still out there, still as dangerous as ever. Pitt knew they were stunned but mad as hornets now.

They would regroup and come again, but more shrewdly, more cautiously. And next time they could see; the interior of the hardware store was brightly illuminated by the flames that had attacked the wooden storefront. The entire building and the men in it were only minutes away from becoming ashes.

'Admiral?' Pitt shouted.

'Over here,' answered Sandecker. 'In the paint department.'

'We've overstayed our visit. Can you find a back door while Al and I hold the fort?'

'On my way.'

'You okay, pal?'

Giordino waved a Remington. 'No new holes.'

'Time to go. We still have a plane to catch.'

'I hear you.'

Pitt took a final look at the huddled corpses of strangers he had killed. He reached down and pulled off the hood from one of the dead. Under the light of the flames he could see a face with Asian features. A rage began to seethe within him. The name Hideki Suma flooded his mind. A man he'd never met, had no idea of what he looked like. But the thought that Suma represented slime and evil was enough to prevent Pitt from feeling any remorse for the men he'd killed. There was a calculated determination in him that the man responsible for the death and chaos must also die.

'Through the lumber section,' Sandecker suddenly shouted. 'There's a door leading to the loading dock.'

Pitt grabbed Giordino by the arm and pushed his friend ahead of him. 'You first. I'll cover.'

Clutching one of the Remingtons, Giordino slipped between the shelves and was gone. Pitt turned and opened up one last time with the Colts, squeezing the triggers so hard and fast they fired off like machine guns. And then the automatics were empty, dead in his hands. He quickly decided to keep them and pay later. He stuffed them in his belt and ran for the door.

He almost made it.

The team leader of the assassins, more cautious than ever after losing six men, threw a pair of stun grenades in the now blazing store, followed by a sleet of gunfire that sent lead splattering all around Pitt.

Then the grenades went off in a crushing detonation that tore the ravaged heart out of what was left of Oscar Brown's Hardware Emporium. The shock waves brought down the roof in a shower of sparks as the thunderous roar rattled every window in Phelps Point before rumbling out into the countryside. All that remained was a fiery cauldron in the shell left by the still-standing brick walls.

The blast caught Pitt from behind and flung him through the rear door, over the loading dock, and into an alley behind the store. He landed on his back, knocking the wind out of his lungs. He was lying there gasping, trying to regain his breath, when Giordino and Sandecker hoisted him to his feet and helped him stagger through the backyard of an adjoining house into the temporary safety of a park bandstand across the next street.

The security alarm had gone dead when the electrical wires burned, and now they could hear sirens approaching as the sheriff and the volunteer fire department raced towards the flames.

Giordino had a talent for getting in the last word, and he rose to the occasion as the three of them lay there under the roof of the bandstand, exhausted, bruised, and just plain thankful to be alive.

'Do you suppose,' he wondered dryly, staring absently at the fire lighting the dawn sky, 'it was something we said?'

41

It was a Saturday night and the strip in Las Vegas was alive with cars crawling along the boulevard, their paint gleaming under the brilliant lighting effects. Like elegant old hookers blossoming after dark under expensive, sparkling jewellery, the ageing hotels along Las Vegas Boulevard hid their dull exteriors and brutally austere architecture behind an electrical aurora borealis of blazing light that advertised more flash for the cash.

Somewhere along the line the style and sophistication had been lost. The exotic glitter and brothel-copied decor inside the casinos seemed as dull and indifferent as the croupiers at the gambling tables. Even the customers, women and men who once dressed fashionably to attend dinner-show spec-taculars, now arrived in shorts, shirt-sleeves, and polyester pantsuits.

Stacy leaned her head back against the seat of the Avanti convertible and gazed up at the big marquees that promoted the hotel shows. Her blonde hair streamed in the breeze blowing off the desert, and her eyes glinted beneath the onslaught of flashing lights. She wished she could have relaxed and enjoyed the stay as a tourist, but it was strictly business as she and Weatherhill acted out their instructed role of affluent honeymooners.

'How much do we have for gambling?' she asked.

'Two thousand dollars of the taxpayers' money,' Weatherhill replied as he dodged the heavy traffic.

She laughed. 'That should keep me going on the slot machines for a few hours.'

'Women and the slots,' he mused. 'It must have something to do with grabbing a lever.'

'Then how do you explain men's fascination with *craps*?'

Stacy wondered how Pitt might have replied. Acidly and chauvinistic, she bet. But Weatherhill had no comeback. Wit was not one of his strong points. On the drive across the desert from Los Angeles he had bored her almost comatose with unending lectures on the possibilities of nuclear space flight.

After Weatherhill had escaped from the truck that hauled the bomb cars, he and Stacy were ordered by Jordan to return to Los Angeles. Another team of surveillance experts had taken over and followed the car transporter to Las Vegas and the Pacific Paradise Hotel, where they reported it had departed empty after depositing the cars in a secure vault in an underground parking area.

Jordan and Kern then created an operation for Stacy and Weatherhill to steal an air-conditioning compressor containing a bomb for study, a feat that was deemed too risky during the break-in on the road. They also needed time to construct a replica replacement from the dimensions recorded by Weatherhill.

'There's the hotel,' he finally said, nodding up the boulevard to a giant sign festooned with neon palm trees and flashing dolphins that soared around the borders. The main attraction featured on the marquee promoted the greatest water show on earth. Another sign stretched across the roof of the main building, blinking in glowing pink, blue, and green letters and identifying the huge complex as the Pacific Paradise.

The hotel was constructed of concrete painted light blue with round porthole windows on the rooms. The architect should have been flogged with his T-square for designing such a tacky edifice, Stacy thought.

Weatherhill turned in the main entrance and drove past a vast swimming pool landscaped like a tropical jungle with a multitude of slides and waterfalls that ran around the entire hotel and parking lot.

Stacy gazed at the monstrosity of a hotel. 'Is there anything Hideki Suma doesn't own?'

'The Pacific Paradise is only one of ten resort hotels around the world he's got his hands in.'

'I wonder what the Nevada Gaming Commission would say if they knew there were four nuclear bombs under the casino.'

'They'd probably care less,' said Weatherhill. 'So long as his dealers aren't mechanics.'

'Mechanics?'

'Cheats for the house.'

He pulled the Avanti to a stop at the main entrance and tipped the doorman, who removed their luggage from the trunk. An attendant parked the car, and they registered at the front desk, Stacy looking starry-eyed and smiling demurely in an attempt to seem like a new bride, an event she had trouble remembering in her own past.

In their room, Weatherhill tipped the bellman and closed the door. He immediately opened a suitcase and removed a set of blueprints of the hotel and spread them on the bed.

'They've sealed the cars inside a large vault in a third-level basement,' he said.

Stacy studied the sheet showing the plan of the entire lower basement and a report from one of the surveillance team. '"Double reinforced concrete with a steel overlay,"' she read aloud. '"One large steel door that raises into the ceiling. Security cameras and three guards with two Dobermans." We won't be breaking in from the front. Easy enough to beat the electronic systems, but the human factor and the dogs make it tough for just the two of us.'

Weatherhill tapped a section of the blueprint. 'We'll go in through the ventilator.'

'Lucky for us it has one.'

'A requirement in the construction code. Without ventilation to prevent expansion and contraction of the concrete, cracks could form and affect the foundation of the hotel.'

'Where does the vent originate?'

'The roof.'

'Too far for our gear.'

'We can make entry from a utility room on the second underground parking level.'

'Want me to go in?'

Weatherhill shook his head. 'You're smaller, but nuclear devices fall in my department. I'll make the entry while you handle the lines.'

She examined the dimensions on the ventilator duct. 'It's going to be a tight fit. I hope you're not claustrophobic.'

Carrying tote bags and rackets and dressed in white tennis togs, Weatherhill and Stacy passed unobtrusively as a couple going to play on the hotel courts. After waiting for an elevator free of people, they rode it down to the second-level parking garage, where Weatherhill slipped the lock on the door to the utility room in less than five seconds.

The small interior was laced with steam and water pipes and digital-dialled instruments that monitored temperatures and humidity. A row of cabinets held push brooms, cleaning supplies, and jumper cables for stalled cars in the parking area.

Stacy quickly unzipped their tote bags and laid out a variety of equipment as Weatherhill donned a nylon one-piece suit. He clipped on a Delta belt and body harness, attaching it around his waist.

Stacy then assembled a spring-powered piston tube with a wide-diameter barrel oddly called a 'beanbag gun'. Then she attached it to a 'hedgehog', a strange object that was covered by round ball bearing-like wheels with a pulley in its centre. Next she uncoiled three lengths of thin nylon line and connected them to the hedgehog and beanbag gun.

Weatherhill consulted the blueprint showing the ventilating system for the final time. A large vertical shaft falling from the roof joined smaller ducts that ran horizontally between the ceilings and floors of the parking areas. The duct running to the vault that held the bomb cars ran between the floor beneath their feet and the ceiling of the basement below.

He took a small battery-operated electric saw and began cutting a large hole in the thin sheet-metal wall. Three minutes later he set aside the cover, took out a tiny flashlight, and beamed it inside the duct.

'It drops about a metre before branching out toward the vault,' he said.

'Then how far?' Stacy asked.

'According to the blueprint, about ten metres.'

'Can you get through the elbow where the duct curves from vertical to horizontal?'

'Only if I hold my breath,' he replied with a slight grin.

'Radio check,' she said, setting a miniature microphone and receiver over her head.

He turned and whispered into a tiny transmitter on his wrist. 'Testing, testing. Am I coming through?'

'Clear as crystal, and me?'

'Good.'

Stacy gave him a reassuring hug and then leaned into the ventilator and pulled the trigger on the beanbag gun. The spring-loaded piston shot the hedgehog into the darkness, where its momentum and roller bearing wheels took it smoothly around the bend. They could hear it sailing through the duct for a few seconds, dragging the three nylon lines behind it, before there was an audible clink, signalling that it had stopped on impact with the filter screen set in the vault's wall. Then Stacy pulled another trigger, and twin rods shot out of the hedgehog against the sides of the duct and jammed it solidly in place.

'I hope you've been working out at the gym,' said Weatherhill as he slipped the rope through the clips in his harness. 'Because your little old muscles will be taxed tonight.'

She smiled and pointed to a pulley she'd already attached to one line and a water pipe. 'It's all in the leverage,' she said slyly.

Weatherhill clamped the small but powerful flashlight around one wrist. He bent down and took what looked like an exact replica of an air-conditioning compressor out of his tote bag. He had constructed it to replace the one he was about to steal. Then he nodded. 'Might as well get going.'

He leaned into the vertical shaft and slowly dropped down headfirst, extending the dummy compressor beyond his head as Stacy took up the strain on one line. There was plenty of room here, but when he came to the elbow into the horizontal duct, he had to contort his body like a snake and squeeze through. He entered on his back in order to bend his body around the narrow curve. And then he was in.

'Okay, Stacy, pull away,' he spoke into his wrist radio. 'How's the fit?'

'Let's just say I can hardly breathe.'

She pulled on a pair of gloves and began to heave on one of the nylon ropes that wound around the pulley on the hedgehog and attached to Weatherhill's harness, pulling him through the narrow confines of the ventilation duct.

He could do little to help her, except exhale when he felt her tug on the rope. He began to sweat inside the nylon suit. There was no air conditioning running through the ventilator, and the outside atmosphere that wafted down from the opening on the hotel roof was hot and stifling.

Stacy wasn't enjoying mild temperatures either. The steam pipes that ran through the utility room kept the heat and humidity close to that of a steam bath.

'I can see the hedgehog and ventilator screen,' he reported after eight minutes.

Another five metres and he was there. The blueprints had not shown any TV cameras in the vault, but he peered into the darkened interior for signs of them. He also removed a small sensor from a sleeve pocket and checked for laser or

337

heat-seeking scanners. His inspection thankfully came up dry.

He smiled to himself. The elaborate defence and alarm measures were all on the outside of the vault, a flaw that was common in many security systems.

He tied a small string to the screen and lowered it to the floor quietly. He slipped the lever that released the hedgehog anchor prongs and lowered it into the vault along with the bogus compressor. Then he slowly descended headfirst until he finally rolled onto the concrete floor.

'I'm inside,' he told Stacy.

'I read you.'

He shone the light around the vault. The bomb cars seemed doubly menacing, sitting ominously in musty blackness and surrounded by thick concrete walls. The awesome destruction in such a cloistered area was difficult to imagine.

Weatherhill came to his feet and detached his harness. He moved around the nearest bomb car and laid out a small packet of tools that had been tied around one leg and spread it on one fender. The replica compressor he set on the floor. Then without bothering to glance inside the car, he reached in and pulled the hood lever.

He stared at the actual bomb unit for a moment, sizing it up. It was designed to explode from a coded radio signal. That much he knew. Activating the detonation mechanism by a sudden movement was doubtful. Suma's nuclear scientists would have built a bomb that could absorb the shock from an automobile driven at high speeds over rough roads. But he wasn't about to take chances, especially since the cause behind the blast on the *Divine Star* was still unknown.

Weatherhill brushed all dire thoughts from his mind and set to work removing the pressure hoses from the compressor. As he suspected, the electrical leads to the evaporator coils that acted as an antenna were concealed inside one of the hoses. The electronics were exactly as he would have designed them himself. He delicately spliced off the leads and reconnected them to the fake compressor without breaking their circuits. He could now take his time to remove the bolts on the compressor's mounting brackets.

'Bomb safely out of the car,' he reported. 'Will now make the switch.'

Six more minutes and the fake compressor was in place and connected.

'Coming out.'

'Standing by to retrieve you,' Stacy answered.

Weatherhill stepped back to the ventilator opening and snapped on his harness. Suddenly he noticed something he'd missed in the darkness of the vault.

Something was sitting in the front seat of the car.

He flashed the light around the vault. He could now see that all four cars had some sort of mechanism seated behind the steering wheels. The vault was cool, but Weatherhill felt as if he was in a sweat-box. He was soaked inside the nylon suit. Still holding the flashlight in one hand, he wiped his face with a sleeve and crouched until his head was even with the window frame on the driver's side of the car he'd worked on.

It would be ridiculous to call the thing behind the wheel a mechanical man. It was stretching things to even consider it a robot, but that's what it was. The head was some sort of computerized visual system perched on a metal spine with a box full of electronics for a chest. Clawlike steel hands with three fingers gripped the steering wheel. The arms and legs were articulated at the proper joints like a human's, but any remote resemblance stopped there.

Weatherhill took several minutes and studied the robot driver, fixing the design in his memory.

'Please report,' Stacy ordered, becoming anxious at his late return.

'I found something interesting,' he replied. 'A new accessory.'

339

'You better get a move on.'

He was happy to leave. The robots that sat in dark silence waiting for a command to drive the car to their preprogrammed targets began to look to him like skeletons. He clipped the ropes to his harness and lay on the cold floor, raising his feet above his head, up the wall, back to the wall.

'Pull away.'

Stacy braced a leg against a pipe and began tugging on the rope that circled the pulley on the hedgehog. On the other end, Weatherhill's feet reached the ventilator and he went in as he'd come out, on his back, except this time he was holding the compressor containing a nuclear bomb in outstretched hands beyond his head.

As soon as he was completely in the shaft he spoke over his headset. 'Okay, stop while I replace the hedgehog and ventilator screen. Won't do to leave a clue to our visit.'

Hand over hand, working around the bomb compressor, he raised the hedgehog and sprung its rods against the ventilator walls. Then he pulled the screen up by the string and quickly screwed it back in place. Now he allowed himself to relax and go limp. He could only lie there and be dragged up the shaft, leaving all physical effort to Stacy, staring at the bomb and wondering about his life expectancy.

'I can see your feet,' Stacy said at last. Her arm muscles were losing all feeling, and her heart was pounding from the exertion.

As he came out of the narrow horizontal shaft, he helped her as much as he could, pushing out and up. There was room now to pass the bomb over his shoulder to where she could reach down and pull it safely into the utility room. As soon as she wrapped a soft cloth around the cylinder and laid it in the tote bag, she finished hauling Weatherhill through the opening in the ventilator shaft.

He quickly released the nylon lines and shrugged out of his harness as Stacy actuated a second trigger releasing the jamming prongs on the hedgehog. Then she reeled it up through the shaft, curled the nylon lines around it, and set it in a tote bag. Next, while Weatherhill changed back into his tennis sweater and shorts, she used duct tape to reseal the panel over the forced opening.

'No interruptions?' Weatherhill asked her.

She shook her head. 'A few persons walked by after parking their cars, but the hotel employees stayed clear.' She paused and pointed at the tote bag containing the compressor. 'Almost impossible to believe we have a nuclear bomb in there.'

He nodded. 'One with enough power to vaporize the entire hotel.'

'Any problems?' Stacy asked.

'None, but I did find that our friend Suma has come up with a new twist,' he said, stuffing his suit and harness in a bag. 'The cars have robotic drivers. They don't require humans to drive the bombs to their detonation points.'

'The bastard.' The tiredness and stress were gone, replaced with vehemence. 'No human emotions to contend with, no second thoughts by a defector who refuses to deploy the bomb, no one to question or betray the source if police should stop the car.'

'Suma didn't get where he is by being stupid. Using robots to do his dirty work is damned smart. Japan leads the world in robotics, and an investigation will undoubtedly prove his scientists and engineering facilities at Edo City are heavily into the design and manufacture.'

A shocked understanding came into Stacy's eyes. Her voice came in whispered foreboding. 'The detonation centre, what if it's manned and guarded by robots?'

Weatherhill gave a final zip of his tote bag. 'That's Jordan's problem. But my guess is we're going to find it next to impossible to penetrate.'

'Then we can't stop Suma from coming on-line and priming the bombs.'

'There may be no stopping him,' he said with grim apprehension in his tone. 'Our best resources fall far short of his.'

42

Toshie, wearing a very brief ungeisha-cut kimono loosely tied at the waist with an obi sash, discreetly bowed her head and held up a large soft towel for Suma as he stepped from a tiled steam room. He wrapped the towel about his body toga style and sat on a low pillowed stool. Toshie dropped to her knees and began massaging his feet.

Toshie was the daughter of a poor fisherman, the fourth of eight children, when Suma first saw her. She had been a skinny, unattractive child whom the boys ignored until, that is, she began to develop a body that was beautifully proportioned, with breasts far more ample than most Japanese girls. Bit by bit her facial features became defined with prominent cheekbones that were enhanced by eyes that were large and dark.

Suma, walking alone at sunset, had spied her standing in the surf casting a net into the rolling breakers. She stood serene and golden under the rays of the dying sun. A thin shift was all she wore, dampened into transparency by the waves, revealing all and hiding nothing.

He was captivated. Without speaking to her, he sought out her name, and by the time the stars began to appear had struck a deal with her father and bought Toshie for a sum that suddenly turned the struggling fisherman into the wealthiest man on the island and the owner of a new fishing boat loaded with the latest in state-of-the-art electronics.

At first Toshie was hysterical with shock and sorrow at having to leave her family, but gradually she became awed by Suma's wealth and power and soon became attracted to him. In her own way she enjoyed her subservient role as secretary and mistress. He had her tutored by the best teachers he could hire, trained in languages, business, and finance, taught the ins and outs of high fashion, and coached in the finer subtleties of lovemaking.

She knew he would never marry her. There were too many other women, and Hideki was incapable of loving only one. But he was kind to her, and when the time came for her to be replaced, she knew he would be generous.

Kamatori, wearing a yellow *yukata* lounging robe with indigo bird patterns, sat nearby at a low black lacquered table directly opposite Roy Orita and sipped tea. Out of respect to their superior, both men patiently waited for Suma to speak first.

Suma ignored them for several minutes as he enjoyed the pleasure of Toshie's foot manipulations. Kamatori avoided Suma's angry stare and kept his eyes lowered. He had lost face for the second time that week and was extremely humiliated.

'So your team of idiots failed,' Suma said at last.

'There was a mishap,' Kamatori replied, still looking down at the surface of the table.

'Mishap?' Suma snapped. 'Disaster would be closer to the truth.'

'Pitt, Admiral Sandecker, and the man called Giordino were very lucky.'

'There was no luck. Your assassins merely underestimated the Americans' canny ability to survive.'

'Professional operatives are predictable,' said Kamatori, making a lame excuse. 'Civilians do not adhere to the rules.'

Suma signalled Toshie to stop. 'How many men did you lose?'

'Seven, including the leader.'

'None were captured, I trust.'

'All bodies were recovered and the survivors escaped before the local authorities arrived. Nothing was left behind to leave a trail.'

'Raymond Jordan will know who was responsible,' said Roy Orita.

'A matter of no concern.' Kamatori's face took on an expression of scorn. 'He and his pathetic MAIT team are no longer an effective force. The Japanese end of his operation has been terminated.'

Suma ignored the tea and took a small cup of saki offered by Toshie. 'Jordan can still be dangerous if his operatives root out the location of our command centre.'

'Jordan and Kern were at a dead end when I broke off contact twenty-four hours ago,' Orita said with assurance. 'They had no clue to the site.'

'They're attempting to trace the bomb cars,' Suma argued. 'That much we know.'

Kamatori shrugged indifferently. 'Jordan is chasing shadows in a smoked mirror. The cars are securely hidden and guarded. Until an hour ago, none had been found and confiscated. And even if his operatives stumble on a few and neutralize their bombs, it will be a case of too little too late. We'll still have more than required to produce an electro-magnetic shield over half the earth.'

'Any news from the KGB or the European community intelligence agencies?' asked Suma.

'They're completely in the dark,' answered Orita. 'For reasons unknown to us, Jordan hasn't revealed his investigation to them.'

Kamatori sipped at his tea and stared over the cup at Suma.

'You have beaten him, Hideki. Our robotic technicians have nearly completed the weapon system electronics. Soon, very soon, you will be in a position to dictate terms to the decadent Western world.'

Suma's face was a stone mask carved in self-satisfying evil. Like so many men who were stained by money, Suma had advanced far beyond wealth to the highest form of addictive corruption – the overwhelming thirst for absolute power.

'I think it's time,' he said in a tone edged with sadistic

pleasure, 'to begin enlightening our guests of the purpose behind their presence here.'

'If I may suggest,' said Orita with a slight bow of the head.

Suma nodded without speaking.

'The *gaijins* are impressed with status and power. Their psychology is easily measured by their reverence of entertainers and wealthy celebrities. You are the most important financial expert in the world. Allow the congresswoman and the senator to simmer in suspense and confusion while you remain aloof and out of reach. Send others to torment their curiosity by feeding them small pieces of bait until their minds are ripe for your honoured appearance and divine orders.'

Suma considered Orita's advice. It was a childish game that played on his ego, but one that was also practical. He looked at Kamatori. 'Moro, I leave it to you to begin our guests' initiation.'

Loren was lost. She had never been so lost in her life. She had been drugged almost immediately after being seized at the classic car race and had clawed her way back to full consciousness only two hours ago.

When she finally cleared the drug-induced haze from her mind, she found herself in a beautifully furnished bedroom with a lavish bathroom complete with sunken marble tub and bidet. It was furnished in a sort of South Pacific island decor with bamboo furniture and a small forest of potted tropical plants. The floor was light polished cedar, and the walls seemed to be covered with woven palm fronds.

It reminded her of a village resort where she'd once vacationed in Tahiti – except for two unusual features. There was no inside handle to the door and no windows.

She opened an armoire that stood against one wall and peered inside. Several expensive silk kimonos hung there. She tried one on and was pleasantly surprised to discover it was almost a tailored fit. She pulled open the lower drawers.

They contained feminine underwear that was also in her exact size, as were the matching sandals on the floor of the armoire.

It beats hell out of being chained in a dungeon, Loren thought. Whoever captured her did not seem intent on torture or execution. The question of why she was abducted was pushed to the back of her mind. Making the most of an unwinnable situation, she relaxed in the tub and took a bubble bath. Then she dried and set her hair with the necessary dryer and styling odds and ends that were thoughtfully laid out on the bathroom counter along with a select array of expensive cosmetics and perfumes.

She was just slipping into a white and rose-flowered kimono when there was a soft knock on the door and Kamatori stepped quietly into the room.

He stood there in silence a moment, his arms and hands buried in the sleeves of his *yukata*, a haughty look of scorn on his face. His eyes rose slowly from Loren's bare feet, lingered on her breasts, and then lifted to her face.

Loren pulled the kimono tightly around her body and knotted the belt and turned her back to him. 'Do Japanese men always enter a lady's room without being invited?'

'My profound apologies,' said Kamatori with a noticeable hint of sarcasm. 'I did not mean to show disrespect to a renowned American legislator.'

'What do you want?'

'I was sent by Mr Hideki Suma to see that you are comfortable. My name is Moro Kamatori. I am Mr Suma's friend, bodyguard, and confidant.'

She replied decisively, 'I guessed he was responsible for my kidnapping.'

'The inconvenience is only temporary, I promise you.'

'Why am I held hostage? What does he expect to gain besides hatred and vengeance from the American government?'

'He wishes your cooperation in delivering a message to your President and Congress.'

'Tell Mr Suma to insert a sharp stick up his rectum and deliver the message himself.'

Brassiness born from vulnerability, Kamatori mused. He was pleased. He decided to pierce Loren's first line of defence. 'How coincidental. Almost the exact words of Senator Diaz, except his terms were much saltier.'

'Mike Diaz?' Loren's brave front suffered a widening crack. 'You kidnapped him too?'

'Yes, you were brought here together.'

'Where is *here*?'

'An island resort off the coast of Japan.'

'Suma is insane.'

'Hardly,' Kamatori said patiently. 'He is a very wise and perceptive man. And in a few days he will announce his rules for the Western economies to follow in the future.'

A tinge of red anger flushed Loren's face. 'He's even a bigger lunatic than I gave him credit for.'

'I think not. No man in history has accumulated as much wealth. He did not accomplish this out of ignorance. Soon you will come to believe that he can also wield absolute control over your government and its economy.' Kamatori paused, and his eyes turned down, gazing at the rounded flesh of Loren's breasts that were pressing against the upper folds of the kimono. 'In view of the coming transition, you might do well to consider a new turn of loyalty.'

Loren could not believe she was hearing such gibberish. 'If anything happens to Senator Diaz or me, you and Mr Suma will suffer. The President and Congress will not stand by and do nothing while we're held hostage.'

'Moslem terrorists have been taking American hostages for years and you do nothing.' Kamatori's eyes showed amusement. 'Your President was informed within an hour of your disappearance, and was told who was responsible. Trust what I say. He has ordered that no rescue attempt be made and no word be leaked to the news media. Your aides, relatives, and fellow congressmen – none are aware that you were flown secretly to Japan.'

348

'You're lying. My friends wouldn't keep quiet.'

'By friends, do you mean Dirk Pitt and Alfred Giordino?'

Loren's mind was in a ferment. She was teetering off balance. 'You know of them?'

'Yes, they meddled in affairs that were not their concern and had an accident.'

'Were they injured?' she stammered.

'I don't know, but it's safe to say they did not escape unscathed.'

Loren's lips trembled. She searched for something to say. 'Why me? Why Senator Diaz?'

'You and the senator are mere pawns in a strategic game of economic power,' Kamatori continued. 'So do not expect deliverance until Mr Suma permits it. An assault by your Special Forces would be a wasted effort, because your intelligence agencies haven't the slightest clue to your whereabouts. And if they did, there is no way for an army to penetrate our defences. In any case, you and the Senator will be free and on a flight to Washington the day after tomorrow.'

The bewilderment in Loren's eyes was what Kamatori hoped for. He removed his hands from the wide sleeves of his *yukata*, reached out suddenly, and pulled Loren's kimono down around her waist, pinning her arms to her sides.

Kamatori smiled sadistically. 'I'll do everything at my command to make your short stay enjoyable. Perhaps I might even give you a lesson on how women should defer to men.'

Then he turned and gave two heavy raps on the door. It opened from the outside by an unseen guard, and Kamatori was gone, leaving little doubt in Loren's mind of what was in store for her before she would be released.

43

'There she is,' said Mel Penner as he yanked the cover off a large table with the flourish of a magician, revealing a three-dimensional model of an island surrounded by a blue plaster-of-paris sea and inlaid with tiny trees and buildings. 'Soseki Island, known in the past as Ajima.'

'You did a marvellous job,' Stacy complimented Penner. 'It looks so real.'

'I'm an old model railroad buff,' said the Director of Field Operations proudly. 'My hobby is building dioramas.'

Weatherhill leaned over the table examining the steep realistic cliffs rising from the sea. 'What's its size?'

'Fourteen kilometres long by five at its widest point. About the same configuration as San Miguel, one of the channel islands off the coast of California.'

Penner pulled a blue bandanna from a hip pocket and dabbed at the sweat rolling down his temples. The air conditioner kept a comfortable temperature inside the small building, not much larger than a hut actually, that stood in the sand of a beach on Koror Island in Palau, but the 98 percent humidity could not be overcome.

Stacy, dressed in snug shorts and a halter top, walked around the table staring at Penner's exacting model. The rocky crags spanned by miniature Oriental bridges and the twisted pine trees gave the island a mystical quality. 'It must be . . .' She hesitated, groping for the right description. 'Heavenly,' she said finally.

'Hardly the word that leaps to mind,' Pitt muttered while swilling a glass half filled with tequila, lime, and ice from a bottle he'd carried from Washington. He wore swimming trunks and a NUMA T-shirt. His long tan legs were propped on the back of the chair in front of him, his feet in leather sandals. 'A garden spot on the outside, maybe, but with a monster lurking inside.'

'You think Suma's nuclear arsenal and detonation control centre is under the island?' asked Frank Mancuso, who was the last of the five team members to arrive at the South Pacific Information Gathering and Collection Point.

Penner nodded. 'We're sure of it.'

Stacy reached out and touched the sheer palisades climbing almost vertically from the sea. 'There's no place to dock ships. They must have brought in construction equipment by air.'

'How was it possible they built it without our spy satellites detecting the activity?' Weatherhill wondered aloud.

With a smug expression of pride on his face, Penner lifted off a section of the sea that ran from the island to the thick edge of the table. He pointed at a tiny tube running through the grey plaster. 'A tunnel,' he explained. 'Suma's engineers constructed a tunnel that begins under the deepest subterranean level of Edo City and travels ten kilometres to the coast, and then another fifty beneath the seafloor to Soseki.'

'Score one for Suma,' said Pitt. 'Our satellites didn't spot any unusual movement because the earth dug from the tunnel was removed along with that excavated during the building of the city.'

'A perfect cover,' said Giordino, bordering on a pun. He straddled a chair and stared pensively at the scaled model. He sat cool in cutoff jeans and nothing else.

'The longest bore in the world,' said Penner, 'exceeding the one the Japs built beneath the ocean from Honshu to Hokkaido.'

Weatherhill shook his head from side to side in amazement. 'An incredible undertaking. A pity the effort wasn't put to a more peaceful purpose.'

As a mining engineer, Mancuso could appreciate the

enormous problems involved in such a massive project. 'Working only from one end, it must have taken a good seven years,' he said, highly impressed.

Penner shook his head negatively. 'Working around the clock with newly designed boring equipment, Suma's engineers finished the job in four.'

'All the more fantastic knowing it was accomplished in total secrecy.' Stacy's eyes had never left the model since its unveiling.

Penner now lifted off a section of the island, revealing a miniature labyrinth of passageways and rooms, all spreading like spokes from one large spherical chamber.

'Here we have the interior layout of the facility. The scale may be slightly off, but I did what I could from the rough sketches Jim Hanamura got through to us.'

'I think you did a sensational job,' said Stacy, admiring Penner's handiwork. 'The detail is so precise.'

'A lot is pure guesswork, but Kern put a design and engineering team to work and they drafted the dimensions pretty close to what we expect from the original.' He paused to pass out a stack of folders to the four MAIT team members in the hut. 'Here are the plans of the Edo City end of the tunnel and the control centre as expanded and detailed by Kern's people.'

Everyone unfolded the drawings and studied the layout of the facility that represented the worst threat the free world had faced since the Cuban missile crisis. No one spoke as they traced the passageways, memorized the labels describing the rooms, and examined the dimensions.

'The centre must be a good three hundred metres below the island's surface,' observed Mancuso.

'There's no airstrip or dock on the island,' Stacy murmured in concentration. 'The only entry is by helicopter or from Edo City through the tunnel.'

Pitt drank the last of his tequila. 'No way in by sea unless the assaulting force were professional mountain climbers.

352

And at that, they'd be picked off by Suma's defence systems like ants crawling up a white wall.'

'What are those buildings on the surface?' asked Weatherhill.

'A luxury retreat for Suma's top management. They meet there for business conferences. It also makes an ideal location for secret meetings with politicians, government bureaucrats, and underworld leaders.'

'Shinzu's painting showed an island barren of plant life,' said Pitt. 'Half the island appears covered by trees.'

'Planted by Suma's landscape people over the past twenty years,' explained Penner.

Mancuso scratched his nose thoughtfully. 'What about an elevator between the retreat and the control centre?'

Penner shook his head. 'Nothing showed on the plans. We can't risk penetration down the shaft if we don't have a location.'

'An underground facility of this scope requires outside ventilation.'

'Our engineering team believes several of the houses within the resort area are dummy covers for air vents and exhaust ducts.'

'We might give that a try.' Weatherhill laughed. 'I'm good at ducts.'

Penner shrugged. 'Again, not enough information. It's possible air is pumped in from Edo, and the foul returned and vented along with the city's outflow.'

Pitt looked at Penner. 'What are the chances Loren and Diaz are held prisoners on the island?'

Penner gave an unknowing shrug. 'Fair to good. We haven't tracked them down yet. But resortlike accommodations on an impregnable island would certainly make an ideal safe house to hide hostages.'

'Hostages, yes,' said Stacy, 'but under what terms? No word of Congresswoman Smith and Senator Diaz has been heard since they were abducted.'

'No demands have been received,' explained Penner, 'forcing the President into a wait-and-see game. And until we can provide him with enough intelligence to make a judgement call on a rescue operation, he won't give the order.'

Giordino gazed at Penner with a small air of contemplation. 'There must be a plan to trash the joint, there's always a plan.'

'We have one,' replied Penner, committing himself. 'Don Kern has created an intricate but viable operation to penetrate and disable the centre's electronic systems.'

'What kind of defences are we talking about?' inquired Pitt. 'Suma wouldn't sink heavy effort and money into the eighth wonder of the modern world without protecting the hell out of it.'

'We can't say with any accuracy.' Penner's eyes swept over the island model with a look of concern. 'We do know what security and military technology is available to Suma, and must assume he's installed the best sensory gear his money can buy. Exotic radar equipment for land and sea detection, sonar sensors for underwater approach, laser and heat detection ringing the perimeter of the shore. Not the least of which is an army of armed robots.'

'And lest we forget, an arsenal of hidden surface-to-sea-and-air missiles.' This from Pitt.

'It won't be an easy nut to crack,' Weatherhill said in a classic understatement.

Giordino looked at Penner, amused, curious. 'Looks to me like an assault by at least five Special Forces assault teams, preceded by an attack of naval carrier aircraft and a bombardment by a strike fleet to soften up the defences, is the only way anybody's going to get inside that rock.'

'Either that,' Pitt tagged, 'or a damn big nuclear bomb.'

Penner smiled dryly. 'Since neither of your suggestions fits into the practical scheme of things, we'll have to use other means to do the job.'

'Let me guess.' Mancuso was acid. As he spoke he gestured to Stacy, Weatherhill, and himself. 'The three of us go in through the tunnel.'

'All five of you are going in,' Penner murmured quietly. 'Though not all by way of the tunnel.'

Stacy gasped in surprise. 'Frank, Timothy and I are highly trained professionals at forced entry. Dirk and Al are marine engineers. They have neither the skill nor the experience for a tricky penetration operation. Surely you don't intend to send them in too?'

'Yes I do,' Penner insisted quietly. 'They are not as helpless as you imply.'

'Do we get to wear black ninja suits and flit through the tunnel like bats?' There was no mistaking the cynicism in Pitt's voice.

'Not at all,' Penner said calmly. 'You and Al are going to drop in on the island and create a diversion to coincide with the entry of the others from Edo City.'

'Not by parachute,' Giordino groaned. 'God, I hate parachutes.'

'So!' Pitt said thoughtfully. 'The great Pitt and Giordino the magnificent fly into Hideki Suma's private resort fortress with bugles sounding, bells ringing, and drums beating. Then get executed Samurai style as trespassing spies. Kind of taking us for granted, aren't you, Penner?'

'There is some risk, I admit,' Penner said defensively. 'But I have no intention of sending you to your deaths.'

Giordino looked at Pitt. 'Do you get the feeling we're being used?'

'How about screwed?'

With his partisan eye Pitt knew the Director of Field Operations wasn't acting purely on his own authority. The plan had come from Kern with Jordan's approval and the President's blessing on top of that. He turned and stared at Stacy. She had 'Don't go' written all over her face.

'Once we get on the island, what then?' he queried.

'You avoid capture as long as possible to distract Suma's security forces, hiding out until we can mount a rescue mission to evacuate the entire team.'

'Against state-of-the-art security, we won't last ten minutes.'

'No one expects miracles.'

Pitt said, 'Well?'

'Well what?'

'We fall from the sky and play hide-and-seek with Suma's robots while the three pros sneak in through a sixty-kilometre tunnel?' Any hint of irritation, incredulity, and despair was contained with great force of will by Pitt. 'That's the plan? That's all there is?'

'Yes,' Penner said, self-consciously avoiding Pitt's blazing stare.

'Your pals in Washington must have drawn that brilliant piece of creativity out of a fortune cookie.'

In his mind, Pitt never doubted his decision. If there was the slightest chance Loren was held prisoner on the island, he would go.

'Why can't you simply cut off their power source on the mainland?' asked Giordino.

'Because the control centre is entirely self-sustaining,' replied Penner. 'It has its own generating station.'

Pitt looked at Giordino. 'What do you say, big Al?'

'That resort have geishas?'

'Suma has a reputation for hiring only beautiful women,' Penner answered with a faint smile.

Pitt asked, 'How do we fly in without being blown out of the sky?'

Penner smiled a smile that seemed to portend something good for a change. 'Now that part of the plan has an A-number-one gilt-edge rating for success.'

'It had better,' said Pitt with ice in his opaline eyes. 'Or somebody's going to get hurt real bad.'

44

As Penner had suggested, being shot down in flames was not a likely prospect. The ultralight power gliders that Pitt and Giordino were to fly off the landing pad of the US Navy detection and tracking ship *Ralph R. Bennett* looked like pint-sized stealth bombers. They were painted a dark grey and sported the same weird Buck Rogers shape that made them impossible to see on radar.

They sat like alien bugs under the shadow of the ship's giant box-shaped phased array radar. The six-storey-high system was composed of 18,000 antenna elements that collected a wide range of intelligence data on Soviet missile tests with an incredible degree of accuracy. The *Ralph R. Bennett* had been pulled away from its mission near the Kamchatka Peninsula by presidential order to launch the power gliders and monitor activity in and around Soseki Island.

Lieutenant Commander Raymond Simpson, a man on the young side of thirty with sun-bleached blond hair, stood next to the men from NUMA on the open deck. There was an air of capable toughness about him as he kept a tight eye on his maintenance crew, who swarmed around the tiny aircraft fuelling tanks and examining instruments and controls.

'Think we can manage without a check flight?' Pitt asked.

'A piece of cake for old Air Force pilots like yourselves,' answered Simpson lightly. 'Once you get the hang of flying while lying on your stomach, you'll wish you could take one home and keep it for your personal use.'

Pitt had never laid eyes on one of the odd ultralight craft until he and Giordino landed on the ship by an Osprey tilt-motor aircraft an hour before. Now after only forty minutes of class instruction, they were supposed to fly them over a hundred kilometres of open sea and make an injury-free landing on the dangerously rugged surface of Soseki Island.

'How long have these birds been around?' Giordino queried.

'The Ibis X-Twenty,' Simpson corrected him, 'is fresh off the drawing boards.'

'Oh, God,' groaned Giordino. 'They're still experimental.'

'Quite so. They haven't completed their testing programme. Sorry I couldn't have given you something more proven, but your people in Washington were in an awful rush, insisting we deliver them halfway across the world in eighteen hours and all.'

Pitt said consideringly, 'They do fly, naturally?'

'Oh, naturally,' Simpson said enthusiastically. 'I've got ten hours' flying time in them myself. Super aircraft. Designed for one-man reconnaissance flights. Powered by the very latest in compact turbine engines that provide a three-hundred-kilometre-per-hour cruising speed with a range of a hundred twenty kilometres. The Ibis is the most advanced power glider in the world.'

'Maybe when you get discharged you can open up a dealership,' Giordino said dryly.

'Don't I wish,' said Simpson without feeling the barb.

The skipper of the radar ship, Commander Wendell Harper, stepped onto the landing pad with a large photo gripped in one hand. Tall and beefy with a solid paunch, Harper's bowlegged gait gave him the appearance of a man who had just ridden across the Kansas plains for the Pony Express.

'Our meteorology officer promises you'll have a four-knot tail wind for the flight,' he said pleasantly. 'So fuel won't be a problem.'

Pitt nodded a greeting. 'I hope our reconnaissance satellite came up with a decent landing site.'

Harper spread an enlarged computer-enhanced satellite photo up against a bulkhead. 'Not exactly O'Hare Airport in Chicago, the only flat spot on the island is a grassy area measuring twenty by sixty metres.'

'Plenty of room for an upwind landing,' Simpson injected optimistically.

Pitt and Giordino moved in and stared at the amazingly detailed picture. The central feature was a landscaped garden clustered around a rectangular lawn that was only open from the east. The other three sides were thickly bordered by trees, shrubbery, and pagoda-roofed buildings with high curved bridges leading down from open balconies to an Oriental pond at one end.

Like condemned men who'd just been told they had a choice of being hanged on the gallows or shot against a wall, Pitt and Giordino looked into each other's eyes and exchanged tired cynical smiles.

'Hide out until rescued,' Giordino muttered unhappily. 'Why do I get the feeling my ballot box has been stuffed?'

'Nothing like arriving at the front door with a brass band,' Pitt agreed.

'Something wrong?' asked Harper innocently.

'Victims of high-pressure salesmanship,' Pitt replied. 'Someone in Washington took advantage of our gullible nature.'

Harper looked uneasy. 'Do you wish to scrub the operation?'

'No,' Pitt sighed. 'In for a dime, in for a dollar.'

'I don't mean to crowd you, but sunset is only an hour away. You'll need daylight to see your way in.'

At that moment, Simpson's crew chief came over and informed him the power gliders were serviced and ready for launch.

Pitt looked at the fragile little aircraft. Calling it a glider was a misnomer. Without the strong thrust of its turbine engine, it would drop like a brick. Unlike the high, wide wing of a true ultralight, with its maze of wires and cables, the airfoils on the Ibis were short and stubby and internally braced. It also lacked the ultralight's canard wing that resisted stalls and spins. He was reminded of the adage about the bumblebee as having all the wrong features for flight, and yet it flew as well as, if not better than, many other insects that Mother Nature had aerodynamically designed.

After finishing their preflight check, the flight crew stood off to the side of the landing pad. In Pitt's mind they all wore the look of spectators at an auto race anticipating a crash.

'Maybe we can land in time for cocktails,' he said, pulling on his helmet.

With routine calm Giordino merely yawned. 'If you get there first, order me a vodka martini straight up.'

Harper incredulously realized that glacial nonchalance was the highest state of emotional nervousness these men were capable of displaying.

'Good luck,' he said, offering both men a firm handshake. 'We'll monitor you all the way. Be sure to activate your signal unit after landing. We'd like to tell Washington you came down safely.'

Pitt gave him a wry smile. 'If I'm able.'

'Never a doubt,' Simpson said, as if cheering the home team. 'Mind you don't forget to set the self-destruct timer. Can't make the Japs a gift of our ultralight technology.'

'Goodbye, and thanks to you and your crews for looking out for us.'

Giordino touched Pitt on the shoulder, gave him an encouraging wink of one eye, and without another word walked toward his craft.

Pitt approached his power glider and eased in from the bottom through a narrow hatch in the fabric-covered fuselage and onto his stomach until his body fitted the contours of a body-length foam rubber pad. His head and shoulders were elevated only slightly higher than his legs, elbows swinging free a centimetre above the floor. He adjusted his safety harness and belts that strapped across his shoulder blades and buttocks. Then he inserted his outstretched feet into grips on the vertical stabilizer and brake pedals, and then gripped the stubby control stick in one hand while adjusting the throttle setting with the other.

He waved through the minuscule windscreen at the crew who were standing by to release tie-down cables, and he engaged the starter. The turbine, smaller than a beer keg, slowly increased its whine until it became a high-pitched shriek. He looked over at Giordino, just making out a set of spirited brown eyes. Pitt made a thumbs-up gesture that was returned accompanied with a grin.

One last sweep of the instruments to make sure the engine was functioning as stated in the flight manual, which he barely had time to scan, and a final glimpse at the ensign flapping on the stern under a stiff breeze that beat in from the port side.

Unlike from an aircraft carrier, a forward takeoff was blocked by the great radar housing and the superstructure, so Commander Harper had brought the *Bennett* around into a quartering wind.

Pitt held the brake on by pressing his toes outward. Then he ran up the throttle, feeling the Ibis try to surge forward. The lip of the landing pad looked uncomfortably close. The lifting force of the Ibis occurred at forty-five kph. The combined wind force and the speed of the *Bennett* gave him a twenty-five kph running start, but that still left twenty kph to achieve before the landing wheels rolled into air.

The moment of decision. He signalled the flight crew to release the tie-down cables. Then Pitt eased the throttle to the 'full' stop, and the Ibis shuddered under the force of the breeze and the thrust of the turbine. His eyes fixed on the end of the landing pad, Pitt released the brakes and the Ibis leaped ahead. Five metres, ten, and then gently but firmly he pulled the control stick back. The craft's little nose wheel lifted and Pitt could see clouds. With only three metres to spare, he drilled the Ibis into the sky and over the restless sea.

He banked and levelled off at forty metres and watched Giordino sweep into the air behind him. One circle around the ship, dipping his wings at the waving crew of the *Ralph R. Bennett*, and he set a course for Soseki Island toward the west. The waters of the Pacific rushed beneath the Ibis' undercarriage, dyed a sparkling iridescent gold by the setting sun.

Pitt slipped the throttle back to a cruise setting. He wished he could put the little craft through its paces, gain altitude, and try some acrobatics. But it was not to be. Any wild manoeuvres might show on a Japanese radar screen. In straight and level flight at a wave-top altitude the Ibis was invisible.

Pitt now began to wonder about a reception committee. He saw little hope of escaping from the retreat's compound. A nice set-up, he thought grimly. Crash-land in Suma's front yard from out of nowhere and create bedlam among the security forces as a distraction for the others.

The crew in the *Bennett*'s situation room had detected the incoming radar signals sent out by Suma's security defences, but Commander Harper decided not to jam the probes. He allowed the *Bennett* to be monitored, rightly assuming the island's defence command would relax once they saw the lone US ship was sailing leisurely away toward the east as if on a routine voyage.

Pitt concentrated on his navigation, keeping an eye on the compass. At their present air speed, he calculated, they should set down on the island in thirty-five minutes. A few degrees north or south, however, and they might miss it completely.

It was all seat-of-the-pants flying and navigation. The Ibis could not afford the extra weight of an on-board computer and an automatic pilot. He rechecked speed, wind direction and velocity, and his estimated course heading four times to make certain no errors slipped in.

The thought of running out of fuel and ditching in a rough sea in the dead of night was a hardship he could do without.

Pitt noted grimly that the radios had been removed. By Jordan's orders, no doubt, so neither he nor Giordino would be tempted to launch into idle conversation and give their presence away.

After twenty-seven minutes had passed, and only a small arc of the sun showed on the horizon line, Pitt peered forward through the windscreen.

There it was, a purple-shadowed blemish between sea and sky, more imagined than real. Almost imperceptibly it became a hard tangible island, its jagged cliffs rising vertically from the rolling swells that crashed into their base.

Pitt turned and glanced out his side window, Giordino hung just off his tail and less than ten metres behind and to his right. Pitt waggled his wings and pointed. Giordino pulled closer until Pitt could see him nod in reply and gesture with the edge of his hand toward the island.

One final check of his instruments and then he tilted the Ibis into a gentle bank until he came at the centre of the island from out of the darkening eastern sky. There would be no circling to study the layout of the ground, no second approach if he came in too low or high. Surprise was their only friend. They had one chance to set their little Ibises on the garden lawn before surface-to-air missiles burst in their laps.

He could clearly see the pagoda roofs and the opening in the trees round the open garden. He spotted a helicopter pad that wasn't on Penner's mock-up, but he dismissed it as a secondary landing site because it was too small and ringed with trees.

An easy twist of the wrist to the left, right, and then hold. He lowered the throttle setting a notch at a time. The sea was a blur, the towering cliff face rushing closer, swiftly filling the windscreen. He pulled the stick back slightly. And then suddenly, as if a rug was pulled out from under him, the sea was gone and his wheels were hurtling only a few metres above the hard lava rock of the island.

Straight in without a sideways glance, a gentle kick to the right rudder pedal to compensate for a crosswind. He soared over a row of bushes, the tyres of his landing gear grooving the tops. Throttle back on idle, the Ibis settled beyond the point of recovery. A tender tug on the stick and the power glider flared. He felt the landing wheels thump as they lightly touched down on the lawn no more than five metres from the edge of a flower bed.

Pitt flipped the kill switch and applied gentle but firm pressure on the brakes. Nothing happened. There was no slowing force pulling his body forward. The grass was wet and the tyres slide across the lawn as though coated with oil.

The urge to cram the throttle full forward and pull back on the stick was overpowering, especially since his face was only a few centimetres from the nose of the Ibis. Impact with a tree, a building, a rock wall? Directly ahead, a row of shrubs ablaze in autumn red and gold shielded any solid barrier beyond.

Pitt tensed, bent his head down and hung on.

The craft was still travelling at thirty kph when it tore through the shrubs, ripping the wings off and ploughing with a great shuddering splash into a small pond filled with huge carp.

For a moment there was a deathly silence, broken a few seconds later by splintering and tearing noise as Giordino's Ibis ripped through the bushes alongside Pitt's shattered craft and skidded to a stop in a sand garden, devastating intricate designs precisely raked in an artful composition.

Pitt struggled to release his safety harness, but was pinned by the legs, and his arms had no freedom of movement. His head was half submerged in the pond, and he had to tilt his face up to breathe. He could plainly see a school of giant white, black, and gold carp, their gaping mouths opening and closing, large round eyes staring blankly at the intruder in their private domain.

Giordino's fuselage was relatively undamaged, and he managed to extricate himself without a problem. He rushed over, leaped into the pond, and surged through the muck and lily pads like a maddened hippo. With strength built from long years of bodybuilding, he tore apart the crumpled structural braces that pinned Pitt's legs as if they were toothpicks. Then he unfastened the safety harness, pulled Pitt out of the mangled craft, and dragged him to the bank.

'You okay?' he asked.

'Bruised shins and a bent thumb,' Pitt replied. 'Thanks for the deliverance.'

'I'll send you a bill,' said Giordino, distastefully eyeing his muck-covered boots.

Pitt removed his crash helmet and threw it in the pond, causing the gawking carp to burst for the safety of the lily pads. He nodded at the wrecked power gliders. 'They'll be coming for us. You'd best switch on the signal units and set the destruct timers.'

While Giordino went about the business of alerting the *Bennett* of their arrival before setting the timers on small packets of plastic explosives carried inside the aircraft, Pitt raised stiffly to his feet and stared around the garden.

It appeared deserted. The army of human and robotic guards did not materialize. The porches and windows of the buildings were empty of life. He found it impossible to believe no one heard the cry of the turbine engines and the sounds of the twin impacts from within the thin walls of the Japanese-style constructions. Someone had to live in the neighbourhood. The gardeners must be about somewhere, the grounds were immaculate and displayed constant care.

Giordino returned. 'We've less than two minutes to make tracks before they blow,' he said quickly.

'I'm out of here,' Pitt spoke as he began jogging toward the forested area behind the resort compound.

And then he stiffened suddenly as a strange electronic voice called out, 'Remain where you stand!'

Pitt and Giordino both reacted by darting behind the cover of heavy brush and the safety of the trees, crouching and swiftly moving from one to another, trying to distance themselves from the unknown pursuer. They'd only covered fifty metres when they abruptly met a high fence that was bristling with electrified wire and insulators.

'The shortest escape in history,' Pitt muttered dolefully. At that instant the explosives in the Ibises went off within five seconds of each other. Pitt couldn't see, but he imagined the ugly indolent carp flying through the air.

He and Giordino turned to face the music, and although they'd been warned, they were not totally prepared for the three mechanical apparitions that emerged from the under-brush in a half circle, cutting off all avenues of escape. The trio of robots did not look like the semi-human figures out of television and motion pictures. These travelled on rubber tractor treads and showed no human qualities, except maybe speech.

The mobile automated vehicles were loaded with a jumbled assortment of articulated arms, video and thermal image cameras, speakers, computers, and a quad of auto-matic rifles pointed directly at Pitt and Giordino's navels.

'Please do not move or we will kill you.'

'They don't mince words, do they?' Giordino was frankly disbelieving.

Pitt studied the centre robot and observed that it appeared to be operated under a sophisticated telepresence system by a controller at a distant location.

'We are programmed to recognize different languages and respond accordingly,' said the middle robot in a hollow voice, sounding surprisingly articulate. 'You cannot escape without dying. Our guns are guided by your body heat.'

There was a brief uneasy silence as Pitt and Giordino briefly looked at each other with the looks of men committed to a job that was accomplished and they could do no more. Carefully, slowly, they raised their hands above their heads, aware that the gun muzzles pointing at them in the horizontal position never wavered.

'I do believe we've been cut off at the pass by a mechanical posse,' Pitt muttered softly.

'At least they don't chew tobacco,' Giordino grunted.

Twelve guns in the front, an electrified fence at their backs, there was no way out. Pitt could only hope the robots' controllers were wise enough to know he and Giordino presented no threat.

'Is this a good time to ask them to take us to their leader?' Giordino spoke through a grin that was cold as stone.

'I wouldn't if I were you,' Pitt answered mildly. 'They're liable to shoot us for using a bad cliché.'

45

No one gave Stacy, Mancuso, and Weatherhill a second look as they penetrated the depths of Edo city with relative ease and precision. The Hollywood make-up expert Jordan flew to Tokyo did a masterful job of applying false folds to their eyes, realigning and darkening the eyebrows, and designing wigs of luxuriant thick black hair. Mancuso, because he spoke flawless Japanese, was dressed in a business suit and acted as boss to Stacy and Weatherhill, who wore the yellow jumpsuits of Suma's engineering inspection teams.

Using data from Jim Hanamura's report on the security procedures, along with identification cards and pass codes provided by a British deep cover operative working in cooperation with Jordan, they smoothly passed through the checkpoints and finally reached the entrance to the tunnel. This was the tricky part of the operation. The human security guards and identity detection machines had not proven difficult to deceive; but according to Penner during their final briefing, the final barrier would be the toughest test.

A robotic sensory security system met them as they entered a totally featureless, glaringly lit white-painted room. The floor was empty of all furniture and the walls barren of signs or pictures. The door they entered from seemed to be the only entrance and exit.

'State your business,' the robot demanded in mechanical Japanese.

Mancuso hesitated. He was told to expect robot sentry machines, but not something that looked like a trash can on wheels that spouted orders. 'Fibre optic communications section to modify and inspect system,' he complied, trying to hide his awkwardness at interacting with artificial intelligence.

'Your job order and pass code.'

'Emergency order forty-six-R for communications inspection and test programme.' Then he brought his open hands together, touching the fingertips lightly and repeated the word '*sha*' three times.

Mancuso could only hope the British operative had supplied them with the correct pass sign and code word and had programmed their genetic codes into the memories of the robotic security memories.

'In sequence, press your right hands against my sensing screen,' ordered the roboguard.

All three dutifully took turns placing their hands on a small blinking blue screen recessed in the barrel-round chest. The robot stood mute for a few moments, processing the data from its computer and comparing facial features and body size against the names and description in its memory disks – a remarkable advance, thought Weatherhill. He'd never seen a computer that could put into memory the data fed to it by a television camera and process the images in real time.

They stood composed and businesslike, knowing from their briefing the robot was programmed to spot the slightest measure of nervousness. They also kept their eyes trained on him. Wandering, avoiding eyes would have invited suspicion. Weatherhill managed a bored yawn while their genetic codes and finger and hand prints were matched up.

'Clearance confirmed,' the roboguard said at last. Then the entire wall at the opposite end of the barren room swung inward and he rolled aside. 'You may enter. If you remain beyond twelve hours, you must notify security force number six.'

The British operative had come through. They had passed the obstacle with flying colours. They walked through the door into a carpeted passageway that led to the main tunnel. They exited onto a boarding platform as a buzzer sounded and red and white strobe lights flashed. A work train loaded with construction materials was pulling away from an expansive underground rail yard with the tracks converging at the main tunnel entrance that Mancuso judged was four metres in diameter.

After three eerie minutes of complete silence, an aluminium car with a glass bubble top that could seat ten people approached the platform on a single rail. The interior was empty, the controls unmanned. A door slid open with a slight hiss and they entered.

'A Maglev,' Weatherhill said quietly.

'A what?' Stacy asked.

'Maglev, for "magnetic levitation". It's the concept based on the repulsion and attraction between two magnets. The interaction between powerful magnets mounted under the train with others lining a single rail raised in the centre moves the cars on a field of electromagnetism. That's why it's usually referred to as a floating train.'

'The Japs have developed the most advanced system in the world,' Mancuso added. 'Once they mastered the cooling of the on-board electromagnetic superconductors, they had a vehicle that literally flies inches above its track at aircraft speeds.'

The doors closed and the little car paused as its computerized sensors waited for the all-clear-ahead. A green light blinked on above the track, and they glided into the main tube soundlessly, picking up speed until the sodium vapour lamps embedded in the roof of the tunnel merged into an eye-dazzling yellow blur.

'How fast are we going?' Stacy wondered.

'A wild guess would be three hundred and twenty kilometres an hour,' Weatherhill replied.

Mancuso nodded. 'At this rate the trip should only take about five minutes.'

It seemed the floating train had no sooner reached its cruising speed than it began to slow. With the smoothness of a skyscraper elevator, it slid to a quiet stop. They stepped out onto another deserted platform. Once they were clear, the car came about on a turntable, aligned itself on the opposite rail, and accelerated back to Edo City.

'The end of the line,' Mancuso said softly. He turned and led the way through the only door on the platform. It opened into another carpeted passageway that stretched thirty metres before ending at an elevator.

Inside, Weatherhill nodded at the Arabic numerals on the control buttons. 'Up or down?'

'How many floors and which one are we on?' inquired Stacy.

'Twelve. We're on two.'

'Hanamura's sketches only indicated four,' said Mancuso.

'They must have been preliminary drawings that were altered later.'

Stacy stared at the lighted panel pensively. 'So much for the hub and spoke layout.'

'Without exact directions to the computerized electronics sections,' said Weatherhill, 'we'll have to scratch our original plan and go for the power generating station.'

'If we can find it before arousing suspicion,' complained Mancuso.

'It's all we've got going. Tracing electrical wiring to the source will take less time than trying to stumble onto the control centre.'

'Twelve floors of rooms and passageways,' murmured Stacy uneasily. 'We could wander around lost for hours.'

'We're here and we have no alternatives,' said Mancuso, glancing at his watch. 'If Pitt and Giordino were successful in landing on the island's surface and diverting Suma's security systems, we should have time enough to plant the plastic and escape back through the tunnel to Edo City.'

Weatherhill looked at Stacy and Mancuso, then looked at the elevator panel. He knew exactly how they felt – nerves tense, minds alert, their bodies honed and ready to act. They had come this far and now it all depended on their decisions in the next few minutes. He punched the button marked 6.

'Might as well try the middle floor,' he said with practical logic.

Mancuso raised the briefcase that camouflaged two automatic weapons and clutched it under his arm. Immobile, he and Stacy and Weatherhill stood quietly in uneasy apprehension. A few seconds later there was an audible bong, the digital light for the sixth floor flashed, and the doors spread apart.

Mancuso went through with Stacy and Weatherhill at his heels. When he stopped dead after two steps, he hardly felt the others bump into him. They all stood and stared like village idiots on a space journey to Mars.

Everywhere inside a vast domed gallery there was a bustling purposeful confusion one would expect from an army of efficient assembly line workers, except there were no spoken orders or shouts or group conversations. All of the specialists, technicians, and engineers working on a great semicircle of computers and instrument consoles were robots in myriad different sizes and shapes.

They'd struck gold on the first try. Weatherhill had unwittingly pushed the floor button that took them directly to the electronic brains of Suma's nuclear command centre. There were no human helpers anywhere in the complex. The entire work force was totally automated and made up of sophisticated high-tech machines that worked twenty-four hours a day without coffee breaks, lunch, or sick leave. An operation inconceivable to an American union leader.

Most rolled on wheels, some on tractor treads. Some had as many as seven articulated arms sprouting like octopus tentacles from wheeled carts, a few could have passed as the familiar multipurpose units found in a dentist's office. But none walked on legs and feet, or remotely resembled C3PO from *Star Wars* or Robby from *Forbidden Planet*. The robots were immersed in their individual work programmes and went about their business without taking notice of the human intruders.

'Do you get the feeling we've become obsolete?' whispered Stacy.

'Not good,' said Mancuso. 'We'd better get back inside the elevator.'

Weatherhill shook his head. 'Not a chance. This is the complex we came to destroy. These things don't even know we're here. They're not programmed to interfere with humans. And there are no robotic security guards around. Pitt and Giordino must have saved our ass by distracting them. I say we send this automated anthill to the moon.'

'The elevator has moved on,' said Stacy, pressing the 'down' button. 'For the next minute we've got nowhere else to go.'

Mancuso wasted no more time in discussion. He set the briefcase on the floor and began tearing the packets of C-8 plastic explosives attached by tape from around his lower legs. The rest did the same from under their jumpsuit uniforms.

'Stacy, the computer section. Tim, the nuclear bomb prime systems, I'll tackle the communications gear.'

They had moved less than five steps toward their given targets when a voice boomed and echoed through the concrete walls of the chamber.

'Remain where you are! Do not move or you will surely die!' Perfect English, with barely a trace of a Japanese accent, and the voice cold, menacing.

The surprise was complete, but Mancuso bluffed it out, trying to find a target for the automatic weapons inside his briefcase.

'We are test engineers on an inspection and test programme. Do you wish to see and hear our pass code?'

373

'All human engineers and inspectors along with their codes were discontinued when the fully autonomous vehicles could perform their programmes without intervention and human supervision,' the disembodied voice rumbled.

'We were not aware of the change. We were instructed by our superior to inspect the fibre optic communications,' Mancuso persisted as his hand pressed a button disguised as a cleat on the bottom of his briefcase.

And then the elevator door opened and Roy Orita stepped out onto the control centre floor. He paused for a moment, his eyes staring with a certain respect at his former MAIT team members.

'Spare the bravado,' he said with a triumphant smile. 'You've failed. Your cover operation to stop the Kaiten Project has failed, totally and absolutely. And you're all going to die for it.'

Jordan and Sandecker shared a light breakfast with the President at the executive retreat at Camp David. They sat at a table in a small cottage in front of a crackling hickory log fire. Jordan and the admiral found the room uncomfortably warm, but the President seemed to enjoy the heat, sipping a cup of Southern chicory-flavoured coffee while wearing an Irish wool knit sweater.

The President's special assistant, Dale Nichols, came in from the kitchen with a glass of milk. 'Don Kern is outside,' he reported, addressing Jordan.

'I believe he has an update on Soseki Island,' said Jordan.

The President gestured at Nichols. 'By all means, send him in.' And as an afterthought, 'Get him a cup of coffee and see if he'd like anything to eat.'

Kern only accepted the coffee and took a seat on a nearby sofa. The President stared expectantly at him, but Jordan gazed emptily into the fire.

'They're in,' Kern announced.

'They're in,' echoed the President. 'Every one of them?'

Kern nodded. 'All three.'

'Any problems?' asked Jordan.

'We don't know. Before our British contact's signal was mysteriously cut off, he said they'd made it safely through the tunnel.'

The President reached out and shook Jordan's hand. 'Congratulations, Ray.'

'A bit premature, Mr President,' said Jordan. 'They still have hurdles to clear. Penetrating the Dragon Centre is only the first step in the plan.'

'What about my men?' demanded Sandecker testily.

'They signalled a safe landing,' answered Kern. 'We have no reason to believe they were injured or harmed by Suma's security guards.'

'So where do we go from here?' inquired the President.

'After placing their explosives and putting the Dragon Centre temporarily out of commission, our people will attempt to effect a rescue of Congresswoman Smith and Senator Diaz. If all goes according to plan, we'll have breathing space to nail Hideki Suma to the nearest cross and send in our military for a wholesale destruction operation.'

The President's face took on a concerned look. 'Is it possible for two men and a woman to accomplish all that in the next thirty-six hours?'

Jordan smiled tiredly. 'Trust me, Mr President, my people can walk through walls.'

'And Pitt and Giordino?' Sandecker pressured Kern.

'Once our people signal they're ready, a submarine will surface and launch a Delta One team to evacuate them from the island. Pitt and Giordino will be brought out too.'

'Seems to me you're taking an awful lot for granted,' said Sandecker.

Kern gave the admiral a confident smile. 'We've analysed and fine-tuned every phase of the operation until we're certain it has a ninety-point-seven-percent chance of success.'

Sandecker shot Kern a withering stare. 'Better make that a ninety-nine-point-nine percentage factor.'

Everyone looked at Sandecker questioningly. Then Kern said uncertainly, 'I don't follow you, Admiral.'

'You overlooked the capabilities of Pitt and Giordino,' Sandecker replied with a sharp edge to his voice. 'It wouldn't be the first time they bailed out a fancy intelligence agency carnival.'

Kern looked at him strangely, then turned to Jordan for help, but it was the President who answered.

'I think what Admiral Sandecker is referring to are the several occasions Mr Pitt has saved the government's ass. One in particular hits close to home.' The President paused for effect. 'You see, it was Pitt who saved my life along with that of Congresswoman Smith four years ago in the Gulf.'

'I remember.' Jordan turned from the fire. 'He used an old Mississippi River paddle steamer to do it.'

Kern refused to back down. He felt his reputation as the nation's best intelligence planner was on the line. 'Trust me, Mr President. The escape and evacuation will go as planned without help from NUMA. We've taken into account every possible flaw, every contingency. Nothing but an unpredictable act of God can prevent us from pulling it off.'

46

It wasn't an act of God that prevented Mancuso, Weather-hill, and Stacy from carrying through with Kern's exacting plan. Nor were they lacking skill and experience. They could and occasionally did open any bank vault in the world, escape from the tightest security prisons, and penetrate the KGB headquarters in Moscow or Fidel Castro's private residence in Cuba. There wasn't a lock built or a security system created that would take them more than ten minutes to circumvent. The unpredictability of attack dogs could present a troublesome obstacle, but they were expert in a variety of methods to leave snarling hounds either dead or docile.

Unfortunately their bag of well-practised tricks did not include escaping from prison cells with no windows or doors that could only be opened from the floor when the stainless steel ceiling and walls were lifted by a mechanical arm. And after being stripped of all weapons, their martial arts training was useless against sentry robots who felt no pain and whose computerized reaction time was faster than humans'.

Suma and Kamatori considered them extremely dangerous and confined them in separate cells, that held only a Japanese tatami mat, a narrow hole in the floor for a toilet, and a speaker in the ceiling. No lights were installed, and they were forced to sit alone and totally enclosed in pitch darkness, void of all emotion, their minds seeking direction, no matter how small or remote, toward escape.

Then came a bitter realization that the cells were escape-proof. Then numbed disbelief and chagrin that despite their almost superhuman skills there was no way out. They were absolutely and hopelessly trapped.

Positive identification of Pitt and Giordino was made by Roy Orita after studying videotapes of their capture. He immediately reported his revelation to Kamatori.

'Are you certain?'

'Yes, there is no doubt in my mind. I sat across a table from them in Washington. Your security intelligence staff will bear me out after a genetic code check.'

'What is their purpose? They are not professional agents.'

'They were simply diversionary decoys for the team given the assignment of destroying the control centre.'

Kamatori couldn't believe his luck in finding the man he'd been ordered to assassinate appear out of the blue into his own backyard.

He dismissed Orita and went into solitary meditation, his mind meticulously planning a cat-and-mouse game, a sport that would test his hunting skills against a man like Pitt, whose courage and resourcefulness were well known, and who would make a worthy competitor.

It was a contest Kamatori had played with men who had opposed Suma many times, and he had never lost.

Pitt and Giordino were heavily guarded around the clock by a small crew of sentry robots. Giordino even struck up a friendship of sorts with one of the robots who had captured them, calling it McGoon.

'My name is not McGoon,' it spoke in reasonable English. 'My name is Murasaki. It means purple.'

'Purple,' Giordino snorted. 'You're painted yellow. McGoon fits you better.'

'After I became fully operational, I was consecrated by a Shinto priest with food offerings and flower garlands and given the name Murasaki.'

Giordino turned to Pitt. 'Is he putting me on?'

'So you're an independent free agent,' said Giordino, astounded at speaking to a mechanism that could carry on a conversation.

'Not entirely. There *are* limits to my artificial thought processes, of course.'

Giordino turned to Pitt. 'Is he putting me on?'

'I have no idea.' Pitt shrugged. 'Why don't you ask him what he'd do if we made a run for it.'

'I would alert my security operator and shoot to kill as I have been programmed,' the robot answered.

'Are you a good shot?' Pitt asked, intrigued with conversing with artificial intelligence.

'I am not programmed to miss.'

Giordino said succinctly, 'Now we know where we stand.'

'You cannot flee the island and there is no place to hide. You would only die by drowning, eaten by sharks, or be executed by beheading. Any escape attempt would be illogical.'

'He sounds like Spock.'

There was a knock from the outside, and a man with a permanently scowling face pushed the *fusuma* sliding door with its shoji paper panes to one side and came in. He stood silent as his eyes travelled from Giordino standing beside the robot to Pitt, who was comfortably reclining on a triple pile of tatami mats.

'I am Moro Kamatori, chief aide to Mr Hideki Suma.'

'Al Giordino,' greeted the stocky Italian, smiling grandly and sticking out his hand like a used car salesman. 'My friend in the horizontal position is Dirk Pitt. We're sorry to drop in uninvited but –'

'We are quite knowledgeable of your names and how you came to be on Soseki Island,' Kamatori interrupted Giordino. 'You can dispense with any attempt at denials, self-defeating tales of misdirection, or counterfeit excuses of innocence. I regret to inform you that your diversionary

379

intrusion was a failure. Your three team members were apprehended shortly after they exited the tunnel from Edo City.'

There was a hushed quiet. Giordino gave Kamatori a dark look, then turned to Pitt expectantly.

Pitt's face was quite composed. 'You wouldn't happen to have anything to read around here?' He spoke boredly. 'Maybe a guide to the local restaurants.'

Kamatori looked at Pitt with pure antagonism in his eyes. After a lapse of nearly a minute he stepped forward until he was almost leaning over Pitt.

'Do you like to hunt game, Mr Pitt?' he asked abruptly.

'Not really. It's no sport if the prey can't shoot back.'

'You abhor the sight of blood and death then?'

'Don't most well-adjusted people?'

'Perhaps you prefer to identify with the hunted.'

'You know Americans,' Pitt said conversationally. 'We're suckers for the underdog.'

Kamatori stared at Pitt murderously. Then he shrugged. 'Mr Suma has honoured you with an invitation for dinner. You will be escorted to the dining room at seven o'clock. Kimonos can be found in the closet. Please dress appropriately.' Then he spun about briskly and strode from the room.

Giordino stared after him curiously. 'What was all that double-talk about hunting?'

Pitt closed his eyes in preparation to doze. 'I do believe he intends to hunt us down like rabbits and lop off our heads.'

It was the kind of dining room the most palatial castles of Europe still have to entertain royal and celebrity guests. It was of vast proportions, with an open heavy-beamed ceiling twelve metres high. The floor was covered by a bamboo carpet interwoven with red silk, and the walls were panelled in highly polished rosewood.

Authentic paintings by Japanese masters hung precisely

spaced as though each was in harmony with the other. The room was lit entirely with candles inside paper lanterns.

Loren had never seen anything to match its beauty. She stood like a statue as she admired the startling effect. Mike Diaz walked around her. He also came to a halt as he gazed about the richly adorned walls.

The only thing that seemed oddly out of place, that was not distinctly Japanese, was the long ceramic dining table that curled halfway across the room in a series of curves and appeared to have been fired in one giant piece. The matching chairs and place settings were spaced so that guests were not elbow to elbow but sitting partially in front of or in back of one another.

Toshie, dressed in a traditional blue silk kimono, came forward and bowed. 'Mr Suma begs your forgiveness for being late, but he will join you shortly. While you wait, may I fix you a drink?'

'You speak very good English,' Loren complimented her.

'I can also converse in French, Spanish, German, and Russian,' Toshie said with eyes lowered as if embarrassed to tout her knowledge.

Loren wore one of several kimonos she found in the closet of her guarded cottage. It beautifully draped her tall lithe body, and the silk was dyed a deep burgundy that complemented the light bronze of her fading summer tan. She smiled warmly at Toshie and said, 'I envy you. I can barely order a meal in French.'

'So we're to meet the great yellow peril at last,' muttered Diaz. He was in no mood to be polite and went out of his way to be rude. As a symbol of his defiance he had refused offered Japanese-style clothing and stood in the rumpled fishing togs he wore when abducted. 'Now maybe we'll find out what crazy scheme is going on around here.'

'Can you mix a Maiden's Blush?' Loren asked Toshie.

'Yes,' Toshie acknowledged. 'Gin, curaçao, grenadine, and lemon juice.' She turned to Diaz. 'Senator?'

'Nothing,' he said flatly. 'I want to keep my mind straight.'

Loren saw that the table was set for six. 'Who will be joining us besides Mr Suma?' she asked Toshie.

'Mr Suma's right-hand man, Mr Kamatori, and two Americans.'

'Fellow hostages, no doubt,' mutterd Diaz.

Toshie did not answer but stepped lightly behind a polished ebony bar inlaid with gold tile and began mixing Loren's drink.

Diaz moved over to one wall and studied a large painting of a narrative scene drawn in ink that showed a bird's-eye view onto several houses in a village, revealing the people and their daily lives inside. 'I wonder what something like this is worth?'

'Six million Yankee dollars.'

It was a quiet Japanese voice in halting English with a trace of a British accent, courtesy of a British tutor.

Loren and Diaz turned and looked at Hideki Suma with no small feeling of nervousness. They identified him immediately from pictures in hundreds of magazine and newspaper articles.

Suma moved slowly into the cavernous room, followed by Kamatori. He stared at them benignly for a few moments with a slight inscrutable smile on his lips. ' "The Legend of Prince Genji", painted by Toyama in fourteen eighty-five. You have excellent commercial taste, Senator Diaz. You chose to admire the most expensive piece of art in the room.'

Because of Suma's awesome reputation, Loren expected a giant of a man. Not, most certainly, a man who was slightly shorter than she.

He approached, gave a brief bow to both of them, and shook hands. 'Hideki Suma.' His hands were soft but the grip firm. 'And I believe you've met my chief aide, Moro Kamatori.'

'Our jailer,' Diaz replied acidly.

'A rather disgusting individual,' said Loren.

'But most efficient,' Suma came back with a sardonic inflection. He turned to Kamatori. 'We seem to be missing two of our guests.'

Suma had no sooner spoken when he felt a movement behind him. He looked over his shoulder. Pitt and Giordino were being hustled through the dining-room entrance by two security robots. They were still clad in their flying suits, both with huge garish neckties knotted around their necks that were obviously cut from the sashes of kimonos they'd declined to wear.

'They do not show respect for you,' Kamatori growled. He made a move toward them, but Suma held out a hand and stopped him.

'Dirk!' Loren gasped. 'Al!' She rushed over and literally leaped into Pitt's arms, kissing him madly over his face. 'Oh, God, I've never been so happy to see anyone.' Then she hugged and kissed Giordino. 'Where did you come from? How did you get here?'

'We flew in from a cruise ship,' Pitt said cheerfully, hugging Loren like the father of a kidnapped child who had been returned.

'We heard this place was a four-star establishment and thought we'd drop in for some golf and tennis.'

Giordino grinned. 'Is it true the aerobics instructors are built like goddesses?'

'You crazy nuts,' she blurted happily.

'Well, Mr Pitt, Mr Giordino,' said Suma. 'I'm delighted to meet the men who have created an international legend through their underwater exploits.'

'We're hardly the stuff legends are made of,' Pitt said modestly.

'I am Hideki Suma. Welcome to Soseki Island.'

'I can't say I'm thrilled to meet you, Mr Suma. It's difficult not to admire your entrepreneurial talents, but your methods of operation fall somewhere between Al Capone and Freddie from Elm Street.'

Suma was not used to insults. He paused, staring at Pitt in puzzled suspicion.

'Nice place you've got here,' said Giordino, boldly appraising Toshie as he edged toward the bar.

For the first time, Diaz smiled broadly as he shook Pitt's hand. 'You've just made my day.'

'Senator Diaz,' Pitt said, greeting the legislator. 'Nice to see you again.'

'I'd have preferred meeting you with a Delta team at your back.'

'They're being held in reserve for the finale.'

Suma ignored the remark and lowered himself into a low bamboo chair. 'Drinks, gentlemen?'

'A tequila martini,' ordered Pitt.

'Tequila and dry vermouth,' answered Toshi. 'With orange or lemon peel?'

'Lime, thank you.'

'And you, Mr Giordino?'

'A Barking Dog, if you know how to make it.'

'One jigger each of gin, dry vermouth, sweet vermouth, and a dash or two of bitters,' Toshie elaborated.

'A bright girl,' said Loren. 'She speaks several languages.'

'And she can make a Barking Dog,' Giordino murmured, his eyes taking on a dazed quality as Toshie gave him a provocative smile.

'To hell with this social crap!' Diaz burst out impatiently. 'You're all acting like we were invited to a friendly cocktail party.' He hesitated and then addressed himself to Suma. 'I demand to know why you've brazenly kidnapped members of Congress and are holding us hostages. And I damn well want to know now.'

'Please sit down and relax, Senator,' Suma said in a quiet but iceberg tone. 'You are an impatient man who wrongly believes everything worth doing must be done immediately,

384

on the instant. There is a rhythm to life you people in the West have never touched. That is why our culture is superior to yours.'

'You're nothing but an insular race of narcissists who think you're a super race,' Diaz spat. 'And you, Suma, are the worst of the lot.'

Suma was a classic, thought Pitt. There was no anger in the man's face, no animosity, nothing but a supreme indifference. Suma seemed to look upon Diaz as little more than an insolent toddler.

Kamatori, though, stood there, his hands clenched at his sides, face twisted in hatred of the Americans, of all foreigners. His eyes were almost closed, his lips taut in a straight line. He looked like a maddened jackal about to spring.

Pitt had earlier sized up Kamatori as a dangerous killer. He moved casually to the bar, picked up his drink, and then eased subtly between Kamatori and the senator with a you've-got-to-get-past-me-first look. The ploy worked. Kamatori turned his anger from Diaz and stared at Pitt through circumspect eyes.

With timing near perfection, Toshie bowed with her hands between her knees, the silk of her kimono rustling, and announced that dinner was ready to be served.

'We shall continue our discussion after dinner,' said Suma, cordially herding everyone to a place at the table.

Pitt and Kamatori were the last ones to sit down. They paused and gazed at each other unblinkingly, like two boxers trying to stare each other down during the referee's instructions before a fight. Kamatori flushed at the temples, his expression black and malevolent. Pitt poured oil on the fire by grinning contemptuously.

Both men knew that soon, very soon, one would kill the other.

47

The dinner was begun by an ancient form of culinary drama. A man Suma described as a *shikibocho* master appeared on his knees beside a plain board holding a fish that Pitt correctly identified as a bonito. Wearing a costume of silk brocade and a tall pointed cap, the *shikibocho* master displayed steel chopsticks and a wooden-handled long straight knife.

With hands moving the implements in a dazzling blur, he sliced up the fish using a prescribed number of slashes. At the conclusion of the ritualistic performance, he bowed and withdrew.

'Is he the chef?' asked Loren.

Suma shook his head. 'No, he is merely a master of the fish-slicing ceremony. The chef who specializes in the epicurean art of seafood preparation will now reassemble the fish, which will be served as an appetizer.'

'You employ more than one chef in your kitchen?'

'I have three. One, as I mentioned, who is expert in fish dishes, one who is a master at cooking meats and vegetables, and one who concentrates his talents on soups only.'

Before the fish was served, they were given a hot salty tea with sweet cookies. Then steaming *oshibori* towels were passed out for everyone to cleanse their hands. The fish was returned, the slices delicately replaced in their exact position, and eaten raw as sashimi.

Suma seemed to enjoy watching Giordino and Diaz struggle with their chopsticks. He was also mildly surprised to see Pitt and Loren eat with the twin ivories as though they were born to them.

Each course was served ably and smoothly by a pair of

robots whose long arms picked up and set dishes with incredible swiftness of movement. Not a particle of food was dropped nor the sound heard of a dish clatter as it met the hard tabletop. They only spoke when asking if the diners were through with a particular course.

'You seem to be obsessed with an automated society,' Pitt addressed Suma.

'Yes, we take pride in our conversion to a robotic empire. My factory complex in Nagoya is the largest in the world. There, I have computerized robotic machines building twenty thousand fully functioning robots every year.'

'An army producing an army,' said Pitt.

Suma's tone became enthusiastic. 'Unwittingly, you've touched a chord, Mr Pitt. We have already begun Japan's new robotic military forces. My engineers are designing and constructing completely automated warships without human crews, aircraft flown entirely by robots, robotic-operated tanks that drive and fight by remote command, and armies composed of hundreds of thousands of armoured machines armed with powerful weaponry and long-range sensors that can leap over fifty metres and travel at sixty kilometres an hour. Their ease of repair and their high-level sensory capabilities make them nearly invincible. In ten years, no superpower military force will be able to stand against us. Unlike your Pentagon generals and admirals, who rely on men and women to fight, bleed, and die in combat, we'll be able to fight large-scale battles without a single human casualty.'

A solid minute passed as the Americans at the table attempted to imagine the magnitude of Suma's revelation. The concept seemed so vast, so futuristic that they all had trouble accepting the fact that robotic armies were about to become a here and now proposition.

Only Giordino appeared indifferent to the immense scope of cyborg warfare. 'Our mechanical chaperon claims he was consecrated,' he said, casually picking at the fish.

'We combine our religion, Shintoism, with our culture,' answered Suma, 'believing that inanimate, as well as animate, objects are blessed with a soul, an advantage we have over you in the West. Our machines, be they industrial tools or a samurai's sword, are revered as humans. We even have machines that teach many of our workers to behave as machines.'

Pitt shook his head. 'Sounds self-defeating. You're taking jobs away from your own people.'

'An archaic myth, Mr Pitt,' replied Suma, tapping his chopsticks on the table. 'In Japan, men and machines have developed a close relationship. Shortly after the turn of the century, we'll have a million robots doing the work of ten million people.'

'And what happens to the ten million people who are laid off?'

'We export them to other countries, just as we export our manufactured goods,' said Suma quietly. 'They become good law-abiding citizens of their adopted nation, but their loyalty and economic connections will still be tied to Japan.'

'A kind of worldwide brotherhood,' said Pitt. 'I've seen how it works, I recall watching a Japanese bank being built in San Diego by Japanese architects, Japanese developers, Japanese construction workers, all using Japanese equipment and Japanese building supplies imported aboard Japanese ships. The local contractors and suppliers were cut out completely.'

Suma gave an uncaring shrug. 'Economic conquest has no rules. Our ethics and morals come from a different breeding ground than yours. In Japan, honour and discipline are knotted tightly to loyalties – to the Emperor, family, and the corporation. We are not bred to venerate democratic principles or charitable generosity. The United Way, volunteer work, charity events to raise money for starving people in Africa, and organizations for providing aid to foster children in third-world nations are virtually unheard of in my country. We concentrate our benevolent efforts on taking care of our own.' He paused and then motioned to the robots as they re-entered the room balancing trays. 'Ah, here comes the next course.'

The bonito was followed by individual wooden trays that held unpeeled ginkgo nuts threaded with pine needles and a pyramid of sliced abalone. Then came a flower soup, a clear broth with single orchids floating in the bowls.

Loren closed her eyes as she savoured it. 'It tastes as wonderful as it looks,' she said.

Suma nodded. 'Japanese haute cuisine is created to delight the eye as well as the palate.'

'A successful attempt at visual and taste perfection,' Pitt observed.

'Are you a bon vivant, Mr Pitt?' asked Suma.

'I enjoy the pleasure of a gourmet meal, yes.'

'Are your tastes varied?'

'If you mean, do I eat most everything, the answer is affirmative.'

'Good.' Suma clapped his hands. 'Then you're in for an exciting and harmonious treat.'

Loren thought the dinner was half over, but it had barely begun. A truly exceptional display of tasty dishes, their ingredients artistically arranged, arrived in a steady stream. Figs in sesame sauce; rice with basil; another soup with egg yolk, neatly sliced conger eel, radish, and mushrooms accompanied by roe of sea urchin; several kinds of fish, including turbot, snapper, pike, and squid wrapped in a collage with varied types of seaweed; and lotus root mixed with intricately cut mussels, cucumber, and zucchini. A third soup was served with pickled vegetables, rice, and sesame. At last, dessert was presented, consisting of several sweet fruits, and the feast concluded with the inevitable cup of tea.

'A final meal for the condemned?' Diaz asked harshly.

'Not at all, Senator,' Suma replied in a congenial voice.

'You and Congresswoman Smith will be returning to Washington within twenty-four hours on board my private jet.'

'Why not now?'

'You must be instructed of my goals first. Tomorrow I will personally conduct you and Congresswoman Smith on a tour of my Dragon Centre and demonstrate the source of Japan's new might.'

'A Dragon Centre,' repeated Diaz curiously. 'For what purpose?'

'You don't know, Senator, about the nuclear bomb cars our host has spread around half the world?' Pitt asked provokingly.

Diaz was uncomprehending. 'Bomb cars?'

'Suma, here, wants to play hardball with the big boys, so he's dreamed up a blue-ribbon extortion plot. As soon as his highly touted Dragon Centre is completed, he can push a button and cause the detonation of a nuclear bomb at any location his robots park a car with a built-in bomb.'

Loren's eyes went wide with shock. 'Is that true? Japan has secretly built a nuclear arsenal?'

Pitt nodded at Suma. 'Why don't you ask *him*?'

Suma stared at Pitt like a mongoose eyeing a cobra. 'You're a very astute man, Mr Pitt. I'm told it was you who put Mr Jordan and his intelligence people onto our method of smuggling the warheads into your country.'

'I freely admit that hiding them in automobile air-conditioning compressors was a cagey act of genius on your part. You almost got away with a clean operation, that is, until a bomb accidentally exploded aboard your auto transport ship.'

Frowning, baffled, Loren asked, 'What do you hope to gain?'

'Nothing deep and unfathomable,' answered Suma. 'Using your slang, Japan has always been on the short end of the stick. Raw universal anti-Japanese prejudice is deeply ingrained in the white West. We have been looked down on as an odd little Oriental race for three hundred years. The time has come to grasp the dominance we deserve!'

An angered flush crept into Loren's face. 'So you'd launch a war that would slaughter millions of people for nothing but false pride and greed. Didn't you learn anything from the death and destruction you caused in the nineteen-forties?'

'Our leaders went to war only after the Western nations strangled us to death with trade embargoes and boycotts. What we lost then in lives and destruction, we've since surpassed in expansion of economic power. Now we are being threatened again by international ostracism and world enmity merely due to our diligent efforts and dedication to efficient trade and industry. And because our great economy is dependent on foreign oil and minerals, we can never again allow ourselves to be dictated to by Washington politics, European interests, or Middle East religious conflict. With the Kaiten Project we have the means to protect ourselves and our hard-won economic gains.'

'The Kaiten Project?' Diaz repeated, never having heard of it before.

'His sordid plan to blackmail the universe,' Pitt explained caustically.

'You're flirting with fire,' Loren said to Suma. 'The United States, the Soviet Union, and Europe will band together to destroy you.'

'They will back off when they see what it will cost them,' Suma said confidently. 'They'll do little but hold press conferences and declare they will solve the problem through diplomatic means.'

'You don't give a damn about saving Japan!' snapped Diaz suddenly. 'Your own government would be horrified if they were aware of this monster you've created. You're in this for yourself, a personal power grab. You're a power-mad maniac.'

'You are right, Senator,' Suma said in quiet control. 'In your eyes I must appear as a maniac intent on supreme power. I won't hide it. And like all the other maniacs of history who were driven to protect their nation and its sovereignty, I won't hesitate to use my power to guide expansion of our race around the globe while protecting our culture from the corruptions of the West.'

'Just what do you find so corrupting about the Western nations?' demanded Diaz.

A look of contempt came into Suma's eyes. 'Look to your own people, Senator. The United States is a land of drug addicts, Mafia gangsters, rapists and murderers, homeless and illiterates. Your cities run rampant with racism because of your mixed cultures. You are declining as did Greece and Rome and the British Empire. You've become a cesspool of deterioration, and the process is unstoppable.'

'So you think America is undermined and finished as a superpower,' said Loren in an annoyed voice.

'You do not find such decay in Japan,' Suma repied smugly.

'God but you're hypocritical.' Pitt broke out laughing, turning every head at the dining table. 'Your quaint little culture is rife with corruption in the highest political levels. Reports of scandals fill your newspapers and TV stations on a daily basis. Your underworld is so powerful it runs the government. Half your politicians and bureaucrats are on the take, openly receiving money for political influence. You sell highly secret military technology to the Communist Bloc for profit. Living costs are ridiculously out of sight for your own people, who pay twice what Americans pay for goods manufactured by Japanese corporations. You steal high-tech advancements wherever you can find them. You have racketeers who regularly disrupt company meetings to extract payoffs. You accuse us of racism when your best-selling books promote anti-Semitism, your department stores display and sell black Sambo manikins and dolls, and

392

you sell magazines on street newsstands depicting women in bondage. And *you* have the gall to sit there and claim you have a superior culture. That's garbage.'

'Amen, my friend,' said Diaz, raising his teacup. 'Amen.'

'Dirk is one hundred percent right,' Loren added proudly. 'Our society isn't perfect, but people to people, our overall quality of life is still better than yours.'

Suma's face altered into a mask of wrath. The eyes were as hard as topaz on the satin-smooth face. His teeth were set. He spoke as if cracking a whip. 'Fifty years ago, we were a defeated people, reviled by the United States! Now, all of a sudden, *we* are the winners, and *you* have lost to us. The poisoning of Japan by the United States and Europe has been stopped. Our culture will prevail. We will prove to be the dominant nation in the twenty-first century.'

'You sound like the warlords who prematurely counted us out after Pearl Harbor,' Loren reminded him curtly. 'The United States treated Japan far better after the war than we'd have expected if you were victors. Your armies would have raped, murdered, and pillaged America just as you did China.'

'Besides us, you still have Europe to contend with,' warned Diaz. 'Their trade policies are not nearly as tolerant and patronizing as ours toward Tokyo. And if anything, the new European community market is going to dig in against your economic penetration. Threatened by nuclear blackmail or not, they'll close their markets to Japanese exports.'

'Over the long term, we will merely use our billions of cash reserves to slowly buy up their industries until we have a base that is impregnable. Not an impossible operation when you consider that the twelve largest banks in the world are Japanese, constituting almost three quarters of the total market value of all the rest of the foreign banks. That means we rule the world of big money.'

'You can't hold the world hostage forever,' said Pitt. 'Your own government and people will rise up against you when they discover the world's warheads are aimed at the Japanese islands instead of the United States and the Soviet Union. And the possibility of another nuclear attack becomes very real should one of your car bombs accidentally detonate.'

Suma shook his head. 'Our electronic safeguards are more advanced than yours and the Russians'. There will be no explosions unless I personally program the correct code.'

'You can't really start a nuclear war,' Loren gasped.

Suma laughed. 'Nothing as stupid and coldblooded as what the White House and Kremlin might attempt. You forget, we Japanese know what it's like to suffer the horror of atomic warfare. No, the Kaiten Project is far more technically sophisticated than masses of missile warheads aimed at cities and military installations. The bombs are designed to be set off in remote strategically unpopulated areas to create a massive electromagnetic force with the potential of destroying your entire economy. Any deaths or injuries would be minimal.'

'You really plan to do it, don't you?' said Pitt, reading Suma's mind. 'You really intend to set off the bombs.'

'And why not, if circumstances warrant it. There is no fear of immediate retaliation, since the electromagnetic force will effectively close down all American, NATO, and Soviet communications and weapons systems.' The Japanese industrialist stared at Pitt, the dark eyes cool and tyrannical. 'Whether I take that step or not, you, Mr Pitt, won't be around to find out.'

A frightened look swept Loren's face. 'Aren't Dirk and Al flying back to Washington with Senator Diaz and me?'

Suma exhaled his breath in a long silent sigh and shook his head very slowly. 'No . . . I have made them a gift to my good friend Moro Kamatori.'

'I don't understand.'

'Moro is an expert hunter. His passion is tracking human game. Your friends and the three intelligence operatives who were captured during their attempt to destroy the centre will be offered a chance to escape the island. But only if they can elude Moro for twenty-four hours.'

Kamatori gave Pitt a sub-zero stare. 'Mr Pitt will have the honour of being the first to make the attempt.'

Pitt turned to Giordino, the trace of a grin on his saturnine face. 'See, I told you so.'

48

'Escape,' muttered Giordino, pacing the small cottage under the watchful eye of McGoon, 'escape where? The best long-distance swimmer in the world couldn't make it across sixty kilometres of cold water swept by five-knot currents. And even then, Suma's hoods would be waiting to gut you the minute you crawled onto a mainland beach.'

'So what's the game plan?' asked Pitt between push-ups on the floor.

'Stay alive as long as possible. What other options do we have?'

'Die like stouthearted men.'

Giordino raised an eyebrow and stared at Pitt suspiciously. 'Yeah, sure, bare your chest, refuse the blindfold, and puff a cigarette as Kamatori raises his sword.'

'Why fight the inevitable.'

'Since when do you give up in the first inning?' Giordino said, beginning to wonder if his old friend had suffered a brain leak.

'We can try to hide somewhere on the island as long as we can, but it's a hopeless cause. I suspect Kamatori will cheat and use robotic sensors to track us down.'

'What about Stacy? You can't stand by and let that moonfaced scum murder her too.'

Pitt rose from the floor. 'Without weapons, what do you expect? Flesh can't win against mechanical cyborgs and an expert with a sword.'

'I expect you to show the guts you showed in a hundred other scrapes we've been through together.'

Pitt favoured his right leg as he limped past McGoon and stood with his back to the robot. 'Easy for you to say, pal.

You're in good physical shape. I wrenched my knee when I crash-landed into that fish pond and can barely walk. I stand no chance at all of eluding Kamatori.'

Then Giordino saw the wily grin on Pitt's face, and a dawning comprehension settled over him. Suddenly he felt a complete fool. Besides McGoon's sensors, the room must have had a dozen listening devices and video cameras hidden in and around it. He figured Pitt's drift and played along.

'Kamatori is too much a samurai to hunt an injured man. If there's a morsel of sporting blood in him, he'd give himself a handicap.'

Pitt shook his head. 'I'd settle for something to ease the pain.'

'McGoon,' Giordino hailed the sentry robot, 'is there a doctor in the house?'

'That data is not programmed in my directive.'

'Then call up your remote boss and find out.'

'Please stand by.'

The robot went silent as its communications system sent out a request to its control centre. The reply came back immediately. 'There is a small staff in a clinic on the fourth level. Does Mr Pitt require medical assistance?'

'Yes,' Pitt answered. 'I'll require an injection of a painkiller and a tight bandage if I'm to provide Mr Kamatori with a challenging degree of competition.'

'You did not appear to limp a few hours ago,' McGoon flagged Pitt.

'My knee was numb,' Pitt lied. 'But the pain and stiffness have increased to where I find it difficult to walk.' He took a few halting steps and tensed his face as though experiencing a mild case of agony.

As a machine that was completely adequate for the job, Murasaki, alias McGoon, duly relayed his visual observation of Pitt's pathetic display to his directorate controller somewhere deep within the Dragon Centre and received permission to escort his injured prisoner to the medical clinic. Another roboguard appeared to keep a video eye on Giordino, who promptly named the newcomer McGurk.

Playing his fake condition as though an Academy Award was in the offing, Pitt shuffled awkwardly through a labyrinth of corridors before being hustled into an elevator by McGoon.

The robot pressed a floor button with a metal finger, and the elevator began to quietly descend, although not as silently as the one in the Federal Headquarters Building.

Too bad the MAIT team didn't have intelligence on an elevator that dropped from the island's surface to the underground centre, Pitt thought during the ride. Penetration from the resort might have been carried off with a higher chance of success. A few moments later the doors spread and McGoon prodded Pitt into a brightly lit passageway.

'The fourth door on your left. Take it and enter.'

The door, like every piece of flat surface in the underground facility, was painted white. A small red cross was the only indication of a medical centre. There was no knob, only a button set in the frame. Pitt pushed it and the door noiselessly slid open. He limped inside. An attractive young lady in a nurse's uniform looked up from a desk through serious brown eyes as he entered. She spoke to him in Japanese, and he shrugged dumbly.

'Sorry,' he said. 'I only speak English.'

Without another word she stood and walked across a room with six empty beds and disappeared into an office. A few seconds later a young smiling Japanese man wearing jeans and a turtleneck sweater under the standard white coat with a stethoscope hanging from his neck approached with the nurse at his heels.

'Mr Pitt, Mr Dirk Pitt?' he inquired in West Coast American.

'Yes.'

'I was informed you were coming. Josh Nogami. This is a real honour. I've been a real fan of yours since you raised the *Titanic*. As a matter of fact, I took up scuba diving because of you.'

'My pleasure,' Pitt said almost bashfully. 'You don't sound like a local boy.'

'Born and raised in San Francisco under the shadow of the Bay Bridge. Where are you from?'

'I grew up in Newport Beach, California.'

'No kidding. I served my internship at St Paul's Hospital in Santa Ana. I used to surf at Newport every chance I got.'

'You're a long way from your practice.'

'So are you, Mr Pitt.'

'Did Suma make an offer you couldn't refuse?'

The smile went cool. 'I'm also an admirer of Mr Suma. I joined his employ four years ago without being bought.'

'You believe in what he's doing?'

'One hundred percent.'

'Pardon me for suggesting that you're misguided.'

'Not misguided, Mr Pitt. Japanese. I'm Japanese and believe in the advancement of our intellectual and aesthetic culture over the contaminated society America has become.'

Pitt was in no mood for another debate on lifestyle philosophies. He pointed to his knee. 'I'm going to be needing this tomorrow. I must have twisted it. Can you deaden the pain enough so I can use it?'

'Please roll up your pant leg.'

Pitt did so and made the required grimaces and quick expulsions of breath to simulate hurt as the doctor felt about the knee.

'Doesn't appear swollen or bruised. No indication of a torn ligament.'

'Hurts like hell, though. I can't bend it.'

'Did you injure it when you crashed into Mr Suma's retreat?'

'News travels fast here.'

'The robots have a grapevine that would make San Quentin prison inmates proud. After I heard of your arrival, I went up and viewed the remains of your airplane. Mr Suma wasn't happy that you killed over four hundred thousand yen worth of his prized carp.'

'Then you know I'm the opening act for the massacre tomorrow,' said Pitt.

The smile left Nogami's face and his eyes went dark. 'I want you to know, though I may follow Mr Suma's commands, I don't favour Kamatori's murderous hunting games.'

'Any advice for a condemned man?'

Nogami motioned around the room. 'The walls have more eyes and ears than a theatre audience. If I dared cheer for your side, I'd be forced to join you out on the field. No thanks, Mr Pitt. I'm greatly saddened by your predicament, but you have nobody to blame but yourself for dipping your oars in dangerous waters.'

'But you *will* see what you can do for my knee.'

'As a doctor I'll do my best to ease your pain. I'm also under orders by Kamatori to see that you're fit for the chase tomorrow.'

Nogami shot Pitt's knee with some unpronounceable drug that was supposed to deaden the pain and wrapped it with athletic tape. Then he gave Pitt a small bottle of pills. 'Take two of these every four hours. Don't overdose, or you'll become groggy and make an easy mark for Kamatori.'

Pitt had carefully watched as the nurse went back and forth into a small supply room for the tape and pills. 'Do you mind if I borrow one of your empty beds and relax for a while? Those Japanese sleeping mats aren't built for these bones.'

'Okay by me. I'll notify your guard robot that I'm keeping you under observation for an hour or two.' Nogami looked at him steadily. 'Don't even think of trying to escape. There are no windows or rear exits in here, and the robots would be all over your ass before you took two steps toward the elevator.'

'Not to worry,' Pitt said with a friendly smile. 'I fully intend to save my strength for tomorrow's fun.'

Nogami nodded. 'Take the first bed. It has the softest mattress. I use it myself. The one Western vice I refuse to give up. I can't stand those damn tatami mats either.'

'The bathroom?'

'Through the supply room to your left.'

Pitt shook the doctor's hand. 'I'm grateful to you, Dr Nogami. A pity we see things through a different lens.'

After Nogami returned to his office and the nurse sat back down at her desk with her back to him, Pitt hobbled to the bathroom, only he didn't enter but merely opened and closed the door with the required sounds to allay any suspicions. The nurse was busy filling out papers at her desk and did not turn to observe his actions through the door of the supply room.

Then he quietly searched the drawers and shelves of medical supplies until he found a box of plastic bags attached to thin tubes with eighteen-gauge needles on their ends. The bags were marked CPDA-1 Red Blood Cells with anticoagulant solution. He removed one of the bags from the box and shoved it inside his shirt. It didn't make even the slightest bulge.

A mobile X-ray unit stood in one corner of the room. He stared at it briefly, an idea forming in his mind. Using his fingernails, he worked free a plastic manufacturer's nameplate and used it to unscrew the rear panel. He rapidly twisted off the connectors to a pair of six-volt dry-cell rechargeable batteries and removed one, slipping it down the front of his trousers. Then he ripped out as much of the electrical wiring as he could without an excess of suspicious sound and wrapped it around his waist.

Finally he stepped softly into the bathroom, used it, and

flushed the toilet. The nurse didn't even look up as he settled onto the bed. In his office, Nogami seemed absorbed, talking in hushed tones on the phone.

Pitt stared at the blank ceiling, his mind at ease. It wasn't exactly what Jordan and Kern would call an earth-shattering master plan, but it was all he had, and he intended to play it to the hilt.

49

Moro Kamatori didn't merely look evil, he was evil. The pupils of his eyes never changed from the violent black poisonous stare, and when the tight lips parted in a smile, which was seldom, they revealed a set of teeth laced with more gold than the Comstock Lode.

Even at that early hour – at five o'clock the sky was still dark – he had a fastidious arrogance about him. He was immaculately dressed in a *hakama*, baggy trousers that were almost a divided skirt, and an Edo-period *kataginu*, a brocaded silk style of sleeveless hunting jacket. He wore only sandals on his feet.

Pitt, on the other hand, looked like a refugee from a rag picker's bin. He was clad only in a T-shirt and a pair of shorts cut off from the bottoms of his flying suit. His feet were clad in a pair of white sweat socks.

After being awakened and escorted to Kamatori's personal study, he stood shivering in the unheated room, taking in every detail of the walls that were filled with antique weapons of every historic era from around the world. Suits of armour, European and Japanese, stood like soldiers at attention in the middle of the room. Pitt felt a wave of revulsion in his stomach at the trophies neatly spaced between hundreds of swords, spears, bows, and guns.

He counted thirty mounted heads of Kamatori's hapless human victims staring sightlessly into space from unblinking glass eyes. Most were Asian, but four had Caucasian features. His blood iced as he recognized Jim Hanamura's head.

'Come in, Mr Pitt, and have a cup of coffee,' invited

Kamatori, motioning Pitt to a vacant cushion beside a low table. 'We'll talk a few minutes before —'

'Where are the others?' Pitt interrupted.

Kamatori stared coldly. 'They are seated in a small auditorium next door, where they will view the hunt on a video screen.'

'Like an audience watching a bad late-night movie.'

'Perhaps the last to run the hunt will profit by the mistakes of those who go before.'

'Or perhaps they'll close their eyes and miss the show.'

Kamatori sat very still, the barest hint of a smile touching the corner of his taut lips. 'This is not an experiment. The procedure has been refined through experience. The prey wait their turn tied to chairs, and if need be, with their eyes taped open. They have every opportunity to witness your demise.'

'I trust you'll send my residuals from the reruns to my estate,' Pitt said, seemingly gazing at the heads adorning the walls, fighting to ignore the horrifying display while concentrating on a rack of swords.

'You put up a very good façade of courage,' Kamatori observed. 'I'd have expected no less from a man of your reputation.'

'Who goes next?' Pitt asked abruptly.

The butcher shrugged. 'Your friend Mr Giordino, or maybe the female operative. Yes, I think hunting her down will raise the others to a furious pitch, inciting them to become more dangerous as prey.'

Pitt turned. 'And if you cannot catch one of us?'

'The island is small. No one has eluded me for more than eight hours.'

'And you give no quarter.'

'None,' said Kamatori, the evil smile widening. 'This is not a child's game of hide-and-seek with winners and losers. Your death will be quick and clean. That's a promise.'

Pitt stared the samurai in the eye. 'Not a game? Seems to me I'm to play Sanger Rainsford to your General Zaroff.'

Kamatori's eyes squinted. 'The names are not familiar to me.'

'You've never read *The Most Dangerous Game* by Richard Connell? It's a classic story of a man who hunts his fellow man for sport.'

'I do not taint my mind by reading Western literature.'

'Glad to hear it,' Pitt said, mentally adding a slight edge to his chances of staying alive.

Kamatori pointed toward the door. 'The time has come.'

Pitt held his mark. 'You haven't explained the ground rules.'

'There are no ground rules, Mr Pitt. I generously give you an hour start. Then I begin to hunt you armed only with my sword, an ancestral weapon that has been in my family for several generations and has seen much enemy blood.'

'Your samurai ancestors must be real proud of a descendant who stains their honour by murdering unarmed and defenceless people.'

Kamatori knew Pitt was deliberately provoking him, but he could not contain his growing rage with the American who showed no trace of fear. 'There is the door,' he hissed. 'I begin the pursuit in one hour.'

The act of uncaring indifference was shaken off the minute Pitt cleared the gate through the electrified fence. Ungoverned fury swept him as he ran past the line of trees surrounding the resort and into the shadows of the stark, barren rocks. He became a man outside himself, cold and cunning, his perceptions abnormally heightened, driven by one overpowering thought.

He had to save himself to save the others.

The gamble on running free in his stocking feet rather than the heavy boots he'd worn when flying off the deck of the *Ralph R. Bennett* was paying off. Thankfully the rocky ground was covered with several centimetres of damp soil eroded over the centuries from the lava rock.

He ran with deadly purpose, spurred on by anger and fear he might fail. His plan was simple enough, ridiculously simple, though the chance of pulling the wool over Kamatori's eyes seemed slightly less than impossible. But he was dead certain the ploy had not been tried by the other hunted men. The unexpected was on his side. The others had only tried to put as much distance between them and the resort as possible before frantically finding a hiding place to stall off discovery. Desperation breeds genius, but they had all failed, and with gruesome finality. Pitt was about to attempt a new wrinkle in the escape game that was just crazy enough to work.

He also had another advantage over those who had gone before. Thanks to Penner's detailed model of the island, Pitt was familiar with the general landscape. He recalled in his mind the dimensions and heights with exacting clarity, knowing precisely where he had to go, and it was not toward the highest point on the island.

People who run in terror during a chase inexplicably head upward, up stairs in a building, up a tree to hide, up to the rocks crowning the summit of a hill. All dead ends with no possibility of successful escape.

Pitt branched off and descended toward the eastern shoreline, executing a meandering trail as if he was undecided which way to turn, occasionally doubling back to make his pursuer think he was wandering lost in circles. The uneven moonlike ground and the dim light hindered any sharp sense of direction, but the stars had yet to fade, and he could still read north from Polaris. He stopped for a few minutes, resting to conserve his strength, and took stock.

He realized that Kamatori, tracking his victims in sandals, could never have brought them to bay in only eight hours. An amateur woodsman, with a small amount of luck, should have avoided capture for one or two days, even if tracked by dogs . . . unless his trail was followed by someone with the advantage of electronic body sensors.

There was no question in Pitt's mind that he was being hunted by a robot festooned with sensors. He moved off again, still cold but feeling no strain or exhaustion.

The end of the hour found Pitt skirting the cliffs above the sea. The scattered trees and underbrush grew to the very edge of the palisades. He had slowed to an easy jog as he searched for a break in the surf-pounded rocks nearly twenty metres below. At last he came to a small clearing sheltered by large rocks. A small pine with several of its roots exposed by erosion hung precariously over the restless water far below.

His eyes intently searched the nearby area for signs of a video camera or body heat sensors and came up empty.

Reasonably certain he was unobserved, he tested the trunk of the tree with his weight. It sagged, and the pine-needled top leaned another five centimetres outward and down. He calculated that if he climbed far enough into its branches, his added weight would pull the bare root system from the earth, sending both Pitt and the tree hurtling down the side of the cliff and into the sea.

Then he studied the dark and swirling water as do the divers atop the cliffs at Acapulco. He judged the depth of a narrow slot between the rocks at three metres in depth, four when a breaker roared in. No one in their right mind would consider the thought churning in Pitt's brain as he examined the backwash and the directional sweep of the current. Without either a dry or a wet suit, a swimmer wouldn't survive twenty minutes in the cold water before hypothermia set in, providing he survived the fall.

He sat down on a rock and removed the plastic blood bag from under the waistband of his shorts and laid it on the ground at his feet. He extended his left arm and squeezed his fist, probing with his right hand until he located the vein in the flat opposite the elbow. He paused a few moments, fixing the vein in his mind, picturing it as a hose. Then he took the needle that was attached to the blood bag's hose and pushed it into the vein on an angle.

He missed and had to try again. It finally slipped inside the vein on the third try. Now he sat there and relaxed as his blood flowed into the bag.

A dog's faint howl in the distance caught his ear. What seemed an obvious truth at the moment struck him with numbing force. He couldn't believe how he'd overestimated Kamatori. He didn't speculate, didn't guess he'd be tracked by a flesh and blood hound. He'd blindly accepted as fact his pursuer would use electronic or robotic means to discover his prey. He could only imagine the leering face of the cutthroat samurai as he found Pitt treed by a vicious dog.

With incredible patience, Pitt sat and waited for his blood to fill the plastic bag as he listened to the yelping draw closer. The dog was hard on his trail and less than two hundred metres away when the blood volume reached 450 millilitres, and Pitt jerked the needle from his arm. He quickly stuffed the blood-filled bag under a pile of rock, covering all sight of it with loose dirt.

Most of the men decapitated by Kamatori, ravaged by terror and panic, had foolishly tried to outrun the hound until dropping from exhaustion and being run to ground. Only the braver ones had stopped and attempted to fight off the dog with whatever weapon they could lay a hand on, in most cases a heavy stick. Still unaware of the surprise about to pounce on him, Pitt went one step further. He found a long, thick tree limb but also collected two heavy rocks. As a final defence, he threw his meagre weapons on top of a large rock and then climbed up.

His feet had only barely left the ground when the baying hound dashed through the trees and onto the cliff edge.

Pitt stared in dumb astonishment. The pursuit dog wasn't the furry kind at all. It had to be the weirdest nightmare of a robot Pitt had laid eyes on.

The Japanese engineers at Hideki Suma's robotic laboratories had outdone themselves on this one. The tail, standing straight into the air, was an antenna, and the legs rotated like spokes of a wheel with the ends bent on a ninety-degree angle to grip the ground. The body was a complex of electronics clustered around an ultrasonic ranging sensor. It was the ultimate in tracking machines, able to detect human scent, heat, and sweat, and able to navigate around or over obstacles at a rate of speed matching a Doberman pinscher.

The only similarity between a real dog and the robomutt, if Pitt stretched his imagination and ignored the recorded howls, was a nasty jaw system with teeth that circulated instead of gnashed. Pitt shoved one end of his tree limb at the metallic snout only to have it torn out of his hands and shredded in a cloud of splinters.

It was a wonder any bodily members of Kamatori's victims were left to mount on a wall after this monstrosity got through with them, Pitt thought. But the artificial dog made no effort to move in for the kill. It partially climbed the rock Pitt stood on and kept its distance, the miniature video camera recording Pitt's movements and location. Its purpose, Pitt recognized, was to corner and locate the quarry so Kamatori could home in and perform the ritual murder.

Pitt lifted one of the rocks over his head and threw it. The robomutt was too agile, it easily leaped to its right as the rock missed and struck the ground several centimetres away.

Pitt raised the other rock, the only weapon left to him, and made as if to hurl it, but he stopped in midlaunch and observed the dog again jump to his right. Then, as if he was a bombardier, he made an adjustment and let fly. The timing was good and his aim true. The dog, apparently pro- grammed only to veer on a starboard tack during an assault, dodged directly beneath the falling rock.

There was no bark or whine, no sizzle of shorted electronics or sparks. The mechanical canine just sort of sagged sluggishly on its spoke legs without falling over, its computer and monitoring systems smashed. Pitt almost felt sorry for it as it slowly went inert like a mobile toy whose batteries faded and died – but not too sorry. He came down off his rock and kicked the thing in its electronic gut, knocking it over on its side. Pitt made certain the video camera was non-functioning, and then he retrieved the blood bag from under its cover of rotted wood and leaves.

He fervently hoped the blood he'd drained from his vein had not weakened his system. He was going to need every bit of his strength for the job ahead.

Kamatori became apprehensive when the image on his tiny wrist TV monitor suddenly faded. His last reading from the robot-tracking dog's sensor put Pitt approximately a hundred and seventy-five metres in a southeasterly direction toward the palisades along the shore. He was amazed that Pitt had allowed himself to be cornered so early in the hunt. He hurried in that direction, initially thinking the system had suffered an electronic malfunction. As he rushed toward the final contact position, it began to seep into his brain that possibly the quarry was the cause of the problem.

This never happened with the earlier prey. None of them came close to defeating the robot or inflicting any damage. If Pitt had managed to do what the others couldn't, Kamatori decided he must be very cautious in his approach. He slowed his pace, no longer concerned with speed. Time was a commodity he could easily afford.

He used nearly twenty minutes to close the gap and arrived at the small clearing above the cliffs. He vaguely saw the outline of the robodog through the underbrush. He feared the worst as he realized it was lying on its side.

Staying in the trees, he made a wide sweep around the open pile of rocks. Cautiously, Kamatori crept toward the dog that lay still and motionless. He drew his sword and lifted it high above his head, the hilt clutched in both hands.

A practised user of *kiai*, the motive power to raise himself to a fighting fury and a fiery resolve to overwhelm his

opponent, Kamatori deeply inhaled a breath, gave a
bansheelike cry, and leaped, hoping to fall upon his hated
foe at the exact moment Pitt exhaled *his* breath.

But there was no Pitt.

The small clearing looked like the aftermath of a
massacre. Blood was splattered everywhere, on the robodog, the rocks, and tiny splotches ran down the cliff face. He
studied the ground. Pitt's footprints were deep and scattered
in convulsive disorder, yet no drenched trail of blood led
away from the clearing. He peered down at the sea and
rocks below and saw a tree pulled out by the receding water
only to be swept in again by an incoming wave and thrown
onto the rocks. He also studied the ragged hole and torn
root system on the edge of the drop.

For several minutes he regarded the scene, examining the
chewed tree limb, the rock lying next to the tracking robot.
The robodog was not designed to destroy, only to pursue
and locate. Pitt must have turned and fought, damaging his
pursuer and somehow altering its computer programming
and turning it into a vicious killer.

The robodog had then gone on the attack and savagely
slashed at Pitt's flesh. With nowhere to run and no way to
fight the horror, Pitt must have tried to escape by climbing
out on the tree. But his weight was too much and together
they fell onto the rocks below. There was no sign of Pitt's
body, but no man could have survived. He had either been
swept away by an undertow or finished by sharks attracted
to the bleeding body.

Kamatori exploded in blind rage. He picked up the
mechanical dog and flung it over the cliff. Pitt had defeated
him. The adventurer's head would not be mounted on the
walls with the other grisly trophies. The samurai butcher felt
shame at being cheated. No one had ever escaped his sword.

He would take his revenge on the other American
hostages. He decided Stacy was to be his next prey,
imagining with great delight the horrified faces of Giordino,

Weatherhill, and Mancuso as they viewed him hacking her to pieces in vivid colour.

He held his sword blade up in front of his eyes, experiencing a feeling of euphoria as the new sun glinted on the blade. Then he flourished it over his head in a circle and slipped it into its scabbard in one smooth instantaneous motion.

Still angered and disappointed at losing the one man he desperately hoped to kill, he headed back into the craggy landscape toward the resort, his mind already relishing the next chase.

50

The President stood on the green grass of the Congressional Country Club engaged in a late afternoon round of golf. 'You're sure about this? There is no mistake?'

Jordan nodded. He sat in a golf cart watching as the President studied a fairway from the fourteenth tee. 'The bad news is confirmed by the fact the team is four hours behind their scheduled contact time.'

The President took an offered five iron from his caddie, who rode in another cart with a Secret Service agent. 'Could they have been killed?'

'The only word we have from the British agent inside the Dragon Centre is that they were captured soon after exiting the undersea tunnel into the command centre installation.'

'What went wrong?'

'We didn't take into consideration Suma's army of robotic security forces. Without the budget to place intelligence operatives in Japan, we were ignorant of their advancement in robotics. Their technology in developing mechanical systems with human intelligence, vision, and superphysical movement came as a surprise.'

The President addressed the ball, swung, and stroked it to the edge of the green. Then he looked up at Jordan. He found it difficult if not impossible to comprehend a mechanical security force. 'Actual robots that walk and talk?'

'Yes, sir, fully automated and highly mobile and armed to the teeth.'

'You said your people could walk through walls.'

'There are none better at what they do. Until now there was no such thing as a foolproof security system. But Suma's vast technology created one. Our people met a computerized intelligence they weren't trained to bypass, that no operative in the world is trained to overcome.'

The President slipped behind the wheel of the cart and pressed the accelerator pedal. 'Any hope of a rescue mission to save your people?'

There was a moment's silence as Jordan hesitated before continuing. 'Doubtful. We have reason to believe Suma intends to execute them.'

The President felt a wave of pity for Jordan. It had to be a bitter pill for him to swallow, losing almost an entire MAIT team. No operation in national security history had suffered from such incredibly rotten luck.

'There'll be hell to pay when Jim Sandecker hears that Pitt and Giordino are going down.'

'I don't look forward to briefing him.'

'Then we must blow that damn island under the sea, and the Dragon Centre with it.'

'We both know, Mr President, the American public and world opinion would come down on you like a ton of bricks despite your attempt to stop a nuclear disaster in the making.'

'Then we send in our Delta Forces, and quick.'

'Special Force teams are already standing by their aircraft at Anderson Air Force Base on Guam. But I advise we wait. We still have time for my people to accomplish their planned mission.'

'How, if they have no hope of escape?'

'They're still the best, Mr President. I don't think we should write them off just yet.'

The President stopped his cart beside the ball that sat only a few centimetres from the green. The caddie ran up with a nine iron. The President looked at him and shook his head. 'I can putt better than I can chip. You better let me have a putter.'

Two putts later the ball dropped in the cup. 'I wish I had

the patience for golf,' said Jordan as the President returned to the cart. 'But I keep thinking there are more important things to devote my life to.'

'No man can go continuously without recharging his batteries,' said the President. He glanced at Jordan as he drove to the next tee. 'What do you want from me, Ray?'

'Another eight hours, Mr President, before you order in the Special Forces.'

'You really think your people can still pull it off?'

'I think they should be given the chance.' Jordan paused. 'And then there are two other considerations.'

'Such as?'

'The possibility Suma's robots might cut our Delta Forces team to pieces before they could reach the command centre.'

The President grinned dryly. 'A robot may not go down under the assault of a martial arts expert, but they're hardly immune to heavy weapons fire.'

'I give you that, sir, but they can lose an arm and still come at you, and they don't bleed either.'

'And the other consideration?'

'We have been unable to uncover the whereabouts of Congresswoman Smith and Senator Diaz. We suspect there is a strong case to be made for them being at Suma's retreat on Soseki Island.'

'You're stroking me, Ray. Brogan over at Langley is certain Smith and Diaz are under guard in Edo City. They were seen and identified at Suma's guest quarters.' There was a long pause. 'You know damned well I can't afford to give you eight hours. If your team hasn't resurfaced and completed their operation in four, I'm sending in the Delta Forces.'

'Suma's island is bristling with defence missile systems. Any submarine attempting to land men within twenty kilometres of the shore would be blown out of the water and any aircraft dropping parachutes shot out of the sky. And should the Delta Forces somehow gain a foothold on Soseki, they'd be slaughtered before they could get inside the Dragon Centre.'

The President gazed out on the course as the sun was settling into the treetops. 'If your team has failed,' he said pensively, 'then I'll have to doom my political career and launch a nuclear bomb. I see no other way to stop the Kaiten Project before Suma has a chance to use it against us.'

In a room deep in Building C of the National Security Agency at Fort Meade, Clyde Ingram, the Director of Science and Technical Data Interpretation, sat in a comfortable chair and studied a giant television screen. The imagery detail from the latest advance in reconnaissance satellites was unbelievable.

Thrown into space on a secret shuttle mission, the Pyramider satellite was far more versatile than its predecessor, the Sky King. Instead of providing only detailed photos and video of the land and sea surface, its three systems also revealed subterranean and subocean detail.

By merely pushing buttons on a console, Ingram could manoeuvre the Big Bird into position above any target on earth and aim its powerful cameras and sensors to read anything from the fine print of a newspaper lying on a park bench and the layout of an underground missile complex to what the crew of a submarine lurking under an ice floe was having for dinner.

This evening he was analysing the images showing the sea around Soseki Island. After picking out the missile systems hidden in the forested land around the retreat, he began to concentrate on finding and positioning underwater sensors placed by Suma's security force to detect any submarine activity and guard against a clandestine landing.

After close to an hour, his eyes spotted a small object resting on the seafloor thirty-six kilometres to the northeast and three hundred and twenty metres deep. He sent a message to the computer mainframe to enlarge the area

416

around the object. The computer in turn gave the co-ordinates and instructed the satellite's sensors to zero in.

After the signal was received and locked in, the satellite sent an enlarged image to a receiver on a Pacific island that was relayed to Ingram's computer at Fort Meade, where it was then enhanced and thrown on the screen.

Ingram rose and walked closer to the screen, peering through his reading glasses. Then he returned to his chair and pressed a number on a telephone and called his Deputy Director of Operations, who was in his car stuck in the horrendous homeward traffic crush of Washington.

'Meeker,' came a weary voice from a cellular phone.

'This is Ingram, boss.'

'Don't you ever get tired of peeking at the world's darkest secrets all night? Why don't you go home and make love to your wife?'

'I admit sex is best, but staring at these incredible pictures is a close second.'

Curtis Meeker sighed with relief as the traffic opened up and he made it through the last intersection light signal before turning down his street. 'You see something?' he asked.

'I have an aeroplane in the sea off Soseki Island.'

'What model?'

'Looks like a World War Two B-Twenty-nine, or what's left of it. Appears heavily damaged but otherwise in pretty good shape after sitting on the seabed for fifty years.'

'Any details?'

'A clear picture of numbers and letters on the side of the fuselage and the tail. I can also make out a small figure on the bow beneath the cockpit.'

'Describe it.'

'Not a perfect image, mind you, when you consider that we're looking through four hundred metres of water. But I'd say it looks like a devil with a pitchfork.'

'Make out any wording?'

'Pretty vague,' answered Ingram. 'The first word is covered by undersea growth.' He paused and gave the command to the computer for further enhancement. 'The second word looks like "Demons".'

'A little off the beaten path for the Twentieth Air Force during the war,' said Meeker.

'Think there's any importance attached to it?'

Meeker shook his head to himself as he turned into his driveway. 'Probably just an aircraft that went missing after it flew off course and crashed like the *Lady Be Good* in the Sahara Desert. Better have it checked out, though, so any living relatives of the crew can be notified of their final resting place.'

Ingram set down the receiver and stared at the shattered picture of the old aircraft buried under the sea, and found himself wondering how it came to be there.

51

There had been no need to tape their eyes open. Stacy, Mancuso, and Weatherhill had watched the viewing screen in horrified fascination just before the picture went black during Pitt's fight with the robodog. Then sadness and shock flooded their emotions as Kamatori fiendishly aimed another camera at the blood-drenched ground.

The four of them sat chained to metal chairs grouped in a small semicircle around a huge high-resolution video screen set into the wall. The two robots Giordino called McGoon and McGurk stood guard with the latest in Japanese automatic rifles aimed at the back of their prisoners' heads.

The unexpected defeat of their plans and total helplessness had stunned them worse than the virtual sentence of death. A hundred plans to salvage their predicament rushed through their minds. None had the slightest hope of getting off the ground. They were conscious now of little but approaching death.

Stacy turned and looked across at Giordino to see how he was taking the crushing blow of his friend's loss. But his face was completely composed and thoughtful, with no trace of sorrow or rage. Giordino sat there in icy calm, his eyes curiously staring at the action on the screen as if it was an adventure serial at a Saturday matinee.

A short time later, Kamatori entered the room, sat down cross-legged on a mat, and poured a cup of saki. 'I trust you watched the results of the hunt,' he said between sips. 'Mr Pitt did not play by the rules. He attacked the robot, altered its programming, and died through his own stupidity.'

'He would have died by your hand anyway!' spat Mancuso. 'At least he cheated you of that piece of butchery.'

Kamatori's lips curled downward briefly and then up in a sinister smile. 'I assure you, there will be no repeat of your friend's performance. A new robodog is presently being reprogrammed so that any unexpected damage to his system will not result in an attack on his quarry.'

'That's a break,' grunted Giordino.

'You scumbag,' hissed Mancuso, red-faced and straining against his chains. 'I've seen the brutalities men like you did to allied prisoners of war. You delight in the torture of others, but can't stand the thought of suffering yourself.'

Kamatori observed Mancuso with the same expression of haughty distaste he might have displayed at observing a rat baring its teeth from a sewer. 'You shall be the last I run to ground, Mr Mancuso. You will suffer at watching the agony of the others until your turn.'

'I volunteer to be next,' said Weatherhill calmly. His mind skipped over escape schemes and began concentrating on one act. He figured if he did nothing else, killing Kamatori would be worth dying for.

Kamatori slowly shook his head. 'Miss Stacy Fox has that honour. A professional female operative will make an interesting challenge. Far better than Dirk Pitt, I hope. He was a shocking disappointment.'

For the first time Weatherhill felt a trace of nausea run through him. He had never been afraid of death. Half his life had been spent on the brink between living or being killed. But sitting helplessly while a woman was brutally murdered, a woman he knew and respected, made him sick.

Stacy's face was pale as Kamatori rose to his feet and ordered the robotic guards to release her chains, but she glared at him with icy contempt. The locks were opened by an electronic signal, and she was roughly pulled to her feet free of the chair.

Kamatori pointed toward the door that opened to the outside of the room. 'Go,' he commanded in a sharp voice. 'I will begin the pursuit in one hour.'

Stacy took what she thought was her last look at the others. Mancuso seemed stricken, while Weatherhill stared back at her with great sorrow in his eyes. But it was Giordino who caused her to do a double take. He gave a wink, a nod, and a smile.

'You're wasting time,' Kamatori said coldly.

'No need to dash off,' came a voice from behind the two robotic guards.

Stacy turned, certain her eyes were deceiving her.

Dirk Pitt stood in the threshold, leaning negligently against the door frame gazing past her at Kamatori. Both his hands rested on the hilt of a long sabre whose tip stabbed the polished floor. His deep green eyes were set, an anticipatory grin was on his rugged face.

'Sorry I'm late, but I had to take a dog to obedience school.'

52

Nobody moved, nobody spoke. The robots stood motion-less, waiting for a command from Kamatori, their data processors not fully programmed to react at Pitt's sudden appearance. But the samurai was in the opening moments of shock at seeing Pitt standing there without a scratch on his body. His lips parted and his eyes spread, and then slowly the beginning of a forced smile twisted the lines on his curious face.

'You did not die,' he said as his mind pushed through the curtain of surprise and his face became a dark cloud. 'You faked your death, and yet the blood –'

'I borrowed a few things from your hospital,' Pitt explained casually, 'and performed a bloodletting on myself.'

'But you had nowhere to go but into the surf or onto the rocks below the cliff. And if you survived the fall and dropped into the water, you would have been swept away by the vicious undercurrents. You could not have survived.'

'I used the tree you saw floating in the surf to cushion my fall into the water. Then I floated with the current until it released me a few hundred metres from shore. After drifting a short distance, I caught the incoming tide and swam until I reached a small cove and climbed the palisades below the resort.'

The surprise in Kamatori's eyes transformed to intense curiosity. 'The security perimeter, how was it possible for you to slip through the robotic guards?'

'Speaking figuratively, I knocked them out.'

'No good.' Kamatori shook his head. 'Their detection systems are flawless. They are not programmed to let an intruder pass.'

'Bet me.' Pitt lifted the sabre, rammed its point into the wooden floor, and released his grip, leaving it quivering in the polished wood. He took the small object from under his arm that could now be seen as a sock with something wrapped inside it. He moved unobtrusively toward one of the robots from the rear. Before it could turn, he pressed the thing inside the sock against the plastic wall surrounding the computerized midsection. The roboguard immediately went rigid and immobile.

Realizing too late what Pitt was doing, Kamatori shouted, 'Shoot him!'

But Pitt had ducked under the muzzle of the second robot's automatic rifle and shoved the strange object against its processor. Like the first, it became inert.

'How did you do that?' Stacy gasped.

Pitt pulled the sock off a small 6-volt dry cell from the portable X-ray machine and an iron pipe wrapped with two metres of copper wire. He held the package up for all to see.

'A magnet. It erased the programs from the disks inside the robots' computer processors and fouled up their integrated circuits.'

'A temporary reprieve, nothing more,' commented Kamatori. 'I badly miscalculated your ingenuity, Mr Pitt, but you have accomplished little but prolonging your life by a few more minutes.'

'At least we're armed now,' said Weatherhill, nodding at the stationary guns held by the robots.

Despite the turn of events, Kamatori could not conceal the expression of triumph on his face. He was back in total control. Pitt's near-miraculous resurrection had been for nothing. 'The guns are tightly moulded to the flexible arms of the robots. You cannot remove them with anything less than a cutting grinder. You are as helpless as before.'

'Then we're in the same boat now that your bodyguards have been unplugged,' said Pitt, tossing the magnet to Stacy.

'I have my *katana*.' Kamatori's hand raised and touched

the hilt of his native Japanese ancestral sword that rested in the sheath that stuck out behind his back. The sixty-one centimetre blade was forged from an elastic magnetic iron combined with a hard steel edge. 'And I also carry a *wakizashi*.' He slipped a knife about twenty-four centimetres in length from a scabbard inside his sash, displaying its blade before resheathing it.

Pitt stepped back toward the doorway leading to Kamatori's antique arsenal and yanked the sword from the floor. 'Not exactly Excalibur maybe, but it beats swinging a pillow.'

The sword that Pitt had taken from a wall of Kamatori's study was a nineteenth-century Italian duelling sabre with a blade ninety centimetres from hilt to tip. It was heavier than the modern fencing sabre Pitt had used during his days at the Air Force Academy and not as flexible, but in the hand of a skilled fencer it could be used with great effect.

Pitt had no illusions of what he was plunging into. He didn't doubt for an instant that Kamatori was a practising expert at the Japanese sword sport of *kenjutsu*, while he hadn't swung a blade in a practice match for over two years. But if he could just stay alive while Stacy somehow freed Mancuso and Weatherhill, or distracted Kamatori so Pitt might gain an advantage, there was a slim chance they could still escape the island.

'You dare to challenge me with that?' Kamatori sneered.

'Why not?' Pitt shrugged. 'In truth samurai warriors were little more than overblown toads. I figure you were bred from the same slime pond.'

Kamatori brushed off the insult. 'So you're to wear a halo and play Sir Galahad against my black knight.'

'Actually I had Errol Flynn against Basil Rathbone more in mind.'

Kamatori closed his eyes and in an unexpected movement sank to his knees and went into a meditating trance. He became immersed in the art of *kiai*, an inner force or power attributed with accomplishing miracles, especially among the samurai class. Mentally, long practice in uniting the soul and conscious mind and bringing them into a kind of divine realm supposedly raises the practitioner to a subconscious level that aids him in performing superhuman feats in the martial arts. Physically, it involved the art of deep and prolonged breathing, the reasoning being the man who has a full load of air in the lungs has it all over the opponent who has exhaled.

Pitt sensed a quick attack and flexed his legs and body in the on-guard position.

Nearly two full minutes passed, and then suddenly, with lightning-like speed, Kamatori leaped to his feet and pulled his *katana* from its scabbard with both hands in a long sweeping motion. But instead of losing a microsecond by lifting the blade over his head for a downward stroke, he continued the motion in an upward diagonal cut in an attempt to slash Pitt open from the hip to the shoulder.

Pitt anticipated the move and narrowly parried the wicked slice, then made a quick thrust, penetrating Kamatori's thigh before jumping backward to avoid his opponent's next savage attack.

The tactics of *kenjutsu* and olympic sabre were wildly different. It was as if a basketball player was pitted against a football halfback. Traditional fencing had linear movements with thrusting strokes, while *kenjutsu* had no limitations, the *katana* wielder wading in to cut down his opponent in a slashing assault. But they both relied on technique, speed, and the element of surprise.

Kamatori moved with catlike agility, knowing that one good cut against Pitt's flesh would quickly end the contest. He moved rapidly from side to side, uttering guttural shouts to throw Pitt off balance. He rushed fiercely, his two-handed strokes beating aside Pitt's thrusts with relative ease. The wound in his thigh went seemingly unnoticed and caused no obstacle to his nimble reactions.

Kamatori's two-handed *katana* strokes cut the air slightly faster and carried more power than the sabre in Pitt's single hand.

But in the hands of a skilled fencer, the old duelling blade could reverse angle a fraction more quickly. It was also nearly thirty centimetres longer, a benefit Pitt used to keep Kamatori's slashing attack out of range of a mortal injury. The sabre combined the point with the stroke, while the *katana* was all slash and cut.

Kamatori also had the advantage of experience and constant practice with his blade. Pitt was rusty, but he was ten years younger than the *kenjutsu* expert and, except for the loss of blood, was in top physical condition.

Stacy and the others were spellbound by the spectacular display of leaping, thrusting, and running attacks as the blades glinted like strobe lights and clattered as their edges struck. Occasionally Kamatori broke off the attack and retreated, altering his position to stay between Stacy, Mancuso, and Weatherhill to prevent her from freeing them, and to satisfy himself that she wasn't attempting to attack him from the rear or flank. Then he shouted a guttural curse and resumed the slashing onslaught against the hated American.

Pitt was holding his own, lunging when an opening presented itself, parrying the explosive power of Kamatori's strokes, and evading the incredible ferocity of the attacks. He tried to work Stacy clear, but his opponent was too shrewd and shut down every opportunity. Though Stacy was an expert at judo, Kamatori would have cut her down before she came within two metres of him.

Pitt fought hard and silently, while Kamatori came on savagely, yelling with every stroke, slowly forcing Pitt to retreat across the room. The Japanese smiled faintly as a fierce swipe grazed Pitt's extended sword arm and drew a thin line of blood.

The sheer force of Kamatori's assault kept Pitt on the

defensive warding off the chopping blows. Kamatori swept from side to side, attempting to fight in a circle.

Pitt easily saw through the ploy and steadily fell back a step at a time, then suddenly lunged, relying on his dexterous use of the point and controlled fencing style to keep alive and frustrate Kamatori's timing.

One thrust caught Kamatori in the forearm but didn't slow down the *kenjutsu* master for an instant. Lost in the *kiai*, striking when he thought Pitt exhaled his breath, he felt no pain, nor seemingly noticed when Pitt's sabre point pierced his flesh. He hurtled back and came inexorably after Pitt, swishing his *katana* in a blur of whirling steel with short brutal back-and-forth strokes almost faster than the eye.

Pitt was tiring, his arm felt leaden, like a prizefighter's after the fourteenth round of a toe-to-toe slugging match. His breath was coming faster now, and he could feel the increased pounding of his heart.

The ancient sabre was showing signs of wear too. Its edge was no match for the fine steel of the Japanese *katana*. The tarnished old blade was deeply nicked in fifty places, and Pitt knew that one solid blow on the flat side could very well break it in two.

Kamatori amazingly showed no hint of weariness. His eyes seemed glazed with bloodlust, and the power behind his strokes was as strong now as at the beginning of the duel. It was only a matter of another minute or two before he would wear Pitt down and cut away his life with the proud sword of Japan.

Pitt leaped backward for a quick breather to take stock as Kamatori paused to catch Stacy's movements out of the corner of his eye. She stood suspiciously still with her hands behind her back. The Japanese sensed something and moved toward her, but Pitt advanced again, stretching forward on one knee with a rapid thrust that caught the *katana* and slid down the hilt, the sabre's tip just fanning the knuckles of Kamatori's forward hand.

Pitt suddenly changed tactics and pressed forward, seeing an opportunity that he had missed. Unlike the shorter hilt of the old duelling sabre, with its shell enclosing the hand, Kamatori's *katana* had only a small round guard at the base of the longer hilt. Pitt began aiming his thrusts, using a wrist-snapping circular motion. Feinting toward his assailant's midsection during a lunge, Pitt flicked the tip of the blade to the left and caught Kamatori's hand during a vicious upswing, slicing fingers to the bone.

Incredibly, Kamatori simply cursed in Japanese and came on again, blood spraying whenever he whipped his sword. If he felt the cold grip of defeat in his gut, he didn't show it. Immune to pain and injury by his immersion into his *kiai*, he resumed the attack like a madman.

Then his head snapped back and to one side as a steel object struck him in the right eye. With unerring aim, Stacy had thrown the lock that had fastened her chains. Pitt snatched the moment and lunged, ramming the point of his sabre into his opponent's rib cage and puncturing a lung.

Kamatori faltered momentarily and insanely continued to fight. He moved against Pitt, shouting with each stroke as blood began to foam from his mouth. But his speed and power were diminished, and Pitt had no problem fending off the weakened cuts.

Pitt's next thrust laid open Kamatori's right biceps. Only then did the highly burnished steel of the *katana* waver and droop.

Pitt stepped in and swung the sabre as hard as his strength would allow, knocking the *katana* free of Kamatori's hand. The blade clattered to the floor, and Stacy snapped it up.

He kept the sabre pointed at Kamatori and stared at him. 'You lose,' Pitt said with controlled courtesy.

It was not in Kamatori's samurai bones to acknowledge surrender so long as he still stood on his feet. His face underwent a curious change. The mask of hatred and ferocity melted away and his eyes assumed an inward look.

He said, 'A samurai takes no honour in defeat. You can cut out a dragon's tooth, but he grows a thousand more.' Then he snatched the long knife from its sheath and leaped at Pitt.

Pitt, though weak and panting for breath, easily stepped aside and parried the slashing knife. He swung the faithful old sabre for the last time and severed Kamatori's hand at the wrist.

Shock flooded Kamatori's face, the shock of disbelief, then pain, then the full realization that for the first time in his life he had been subdued by an opponent and was going to die. He stood and glowered at Pitt, his dark eyes filled with uncontrolled rage, the empty wrist hanging by his side, blood streaming to the floor.

'I have dishonoured my ancestors. You will please allow me to save face by committing *seppuku*.'

Pitt's eyes half closed in curiosity. He looked at Mancuso. '*Seppuku?*'

'The accepted and more stylish Japanese term for what we crudely call hari-kari, which actually translates as belly cutting. He wants you to let him have a "happy dispatch".'

'I see,' Pitt said, a tired but maddened understanding in his voice. 'I see indeed, but it's not going to happen. He's not going to get his way. Not with his own hand. Not after all the people he's murdered in cold blood.'

'My dishonour at having been defeated by a foreigner must be expunged by offering up my life,' Kamatori muttered through clenched teeth, the mesmeric force of *kiai* quickly fading.

'His friends and family will rejoice,' explained Mancuso. 'Honour to him is everything. He considers dying by his own hand beautiful and looks forward to it.'

'God, this is sickening,' murmured Stacy disgustedly as she stared at Kamatori's hand on the floor. 'Tie and gag him. Let's finish our job and get out of here.'

'You're going to die, but not as you hope,' said Pitt,

staring at the defiant face darkened in hate, the lips drawn back like a dog baring its teeth. But Pitt caught a slight look of fear in the dark eyes, not a fear of dying, but a fear of not joining his ancestors in the prescribed manner of honoured tradition.

Before anyone knew what Pitt was about to do, he grabbed Kamatori by the good arm and dragged the samurai into the study containing the antique arms and the gruesome collection of mounted human heads. Carefully, as if he was aligning a painting, he positioned Kamatori and rammed the sabre blade through the lower groin, pinning him upright to the wall beneath the heads of his victims.

Kamatori's eyes were filled with unbelief and the fear of a miserable and shameful end. The pain was there too.

Pitt knew he was looking at a near corpse and got in the last word before the eyes went sightless in death.

'No divine passing for a killer of the helpless. Join your prey and be damned.'

53

Pitt removed a Viking battle-axe from its brackets on a wall and returned to the video monitor room. Stacy had already picked the locks on the chains confining Giordino and Mancuso and was working to free Weatherhill.

'What did you do with Kamatori?' Giordino asked, peering curiously around Pitt's shoulder into the trophy room.

'Mounted him with the rest of his collection.' He handed the axe to Giordino. 'Break up the robots so they can't be repaired anytime soon.'

'Break up McGoon?'

'And McGurk.'

Giordino looked pained, but he took the axe and smashed it into McGoon. 'I feel like Dorothy trashing the Tin Man from Oz.'

Mancuso shook Pitt's hand. 'You saved our asses. Thank you.'

'A nice bit of swordplay,' said Weatherhill. 'Where'd you learn it?'

'That will have to wait,' Pitt said impatiently. 'What's Penner's grandiose scheme for our rescue?'

'You don't know?'

'Penner didn't deem us worthy of his confidence.'

Mancuso looked at him and shook his head. 'There is no plan for a rescue mission,' he said with an embarrassed expression. 'Originally we were to be evacuated by submarine, but Penner ruled that out as too risky for the sub and its crew after reviewing a satellite photo of Suma's sea defences. Stacy, Tim, and I were to make our way back through the tunnel to Edo City and escape to our embassy in Tokyo.'

Pitt nodded at Giordino. 'And the two of us?'

'The State Department was alerted to negotiate with Suma and the Japanese government for your release.'

'The State Department?' Giordino moaned between chops. 'I'd sooner be represented by Monty Python's Flying Circus.'

'Jordan and Kern didn't take into account Suma and Kamatori's nasty dispositions,' said Mancuso cynically.

Pitt's mouth tightened in a hard bitter line. 'You people are the experts. What's the next move?'

'Finish the job as planned and hot-foot it through the tunnel,' answered Weatherhill as Stacy opened the lock and his chains fell away.

'You still aim to destroy the Dragon Centre?'

'Not completely, but we can put a dent in it.'

'With what?' inquired Giordino. 'A homemade magnet and an axe?'

'No sweat,' Weatherhill replied airily, massaging his wrists. 'Suma's security forces may have taken our explosives kit during our capture and subsequent search, but we still have enough for a minor bang.' He sat down and pulled off his shoes, prying off the soles and incredibly kneading them into a ball. 'C-Eight plastic,' he said proudly. 'The very latest in explosives for the discriminating spook.'

'And the detonators are in the heels,' muttered Pitt.

'How'd you know?'

'Positive thinking.'

'Let's move out,' said Mancuso. 'The robot's controllers and Kamatori's human pals will wonder why his private hunt has been shut down and come running to investigate.'

Stacy stepped to the door leading outside Kamatori's personal quarters, opened it slightly, and peered around the garden outside. 'Our first hurdle is to find the building with the elevator to the underground centre. We were led up here from our cells blindfolded and didn't get a feel of its exact location.'

'I'll lead you to it,' said Pitt.

'You know the location?'

'I should. I rode it down to the hospital.'

'Your magnet won't be of much help if we run into a squad of robots,' Mancuso said grimly.

'Then we'll have to expand our bag of tricks,' said Pitt. He moved over beside Stacy and looked through the cracked door. 'There's a garden hose just under that bush to your left. See it?'

Stacy nodded. 'Beside the terrace.'

He gestured at the *katana* she still held in her hand. 'Sneak out and slice off a few feet.'

She stared at him quizzically. 'May I ask why?'

'Cut up the hose in short lengths, rub one against a piece of silk, and you strip out the negative electrons,' Pitt explained. 'Then touch the end of the hose against a robot's integrated circuits, making the electronic jump and destroying the delicate components.'

'An electrostatic discharge,' murmured Weatherhill thoughtfully. 'Is that it?'

Pitt nodded. 'You could do the same thing by rubbing a cat or dragging your feet across a carpet.'

'You'd make a good high school physics teacher.'

'What about the silk?' asked Giordino.

'Kamatori's kimono,' Weatherhill said over his shoulder as he hurried into the trophy room.

Pitt turned to Mancuso. 'Where do you intend to set off your firecrackers where they'll do the most damage?'

'We don't have enough C-Eight to do a permanent job, but if we can place it near a power supply, we can set back their schedule for a few days, maybe weeks.'

Stacy returned with a three-metre section of garden hose. 'How do you want it sliced?'

'Divide it into four parts,' Pitt answered. 'One for each of you. I'll carry the magnet as a back-up.'

Weatherhill came back from the trophy room carrying

433

torn shreds of Kamatori's silk kimono, some showing bloodstains, and began passing them out. He smiled at Pitt. 'Your placement of our samurai friend made him a most appropriate piece of wall decor.'

'There is no sculpture,' Pitt said pontifically, 'that can take the place of an original.'

'I don't want to be within a thousand kilometres when Hideki Suma sees what you've done to his best friend.' Giordino laughed, throwing the broken remains of the two roboguards into a pile in a corner of the room.

'Yes,' Pitt said indifferently, 'but that's what he gets for pissing off the dark side of the force.'

Loren, her face still and angered, observed in mounting shock the awesome technical and financial power behind Suma's empire as he led her and Diaz on a tour through the complex that was far more vast than she could ever imagine. There was much more to it than a control centre to send prime and detonate signals to a worldwide array of nuclear bombs. The seemingly unending levels and corridors also contained countless laboratories, vast engineering and electronic experimental units, a fusion research facility, and a nuclear reactor plant incorporating designs still on the drawing boards of the Western industrialized countries.

Suma said proudly, 'My primary structural engineering and administration offices and scientific think tank are housed in Edo City. But here, safe and secure under Soseki Island, is the core of my research and development.'

He ushered them into a lab and pointed out a large open vat of crude oil. 'You can't see them, but eating away at the oil are second-generation genetically engineered microbes that actually digest the petroleum and multiply, launching a chain reaction and destroying the oil molecules. The residue can then be dissolved by water.'

'That could prove a boon for the clean-up of oil spills,' commented Diaz.

'One useful purpose,' said Suma. 'Another is to deplete a hostile country's oil reserves.'

Loren looked at him in disbelief. 'Why cause such chaos? For what gain?'

'In time, Japan will be almost totally independent of oil. Our total generating power will be nuclear. Our new technology in fuel cells and solar energy will soon be incorporated in our automobiles, replacing the gasoline engine. Deplete the world's reserves with our oil-eating microbes, and eventually all international transportation – automobiles, trucks, and aircraft – grinds to a halt.'

'Unless replaced by Japanese products,' Diaz stated coldly.

'A lifetime,' Loren said, becoming sceptical. 'It would take a lifetime to dry up the billion-gallon oil reserves stored in our underground salt mines.'

Suma smiled patiently. 'The microbes could totally deplete United States strategic oil reserves in less than nine months.'

Loren shook her head, unable to absorb the horrible consequences of all she'd learned in the past few hours. She could not conceive of one man causing such a chaotic upheaval. She also could not accept the awful possibility that Pitt might already be dead.

'Why are you showing us all this?' she asked in a whisper. 'Why aren't you keeping it a secret?'

'So you can tell your President and fellow congressmen that the United States and Japan are no longer on equal terms. We now have an unbeatable lead, and your government must accept our demands accordingly.' Suma paused and stared at her. 'As to generously giving away secrets, you and Senator Diaz are not scientists or engineers. You can only describe what you've seen in vague layman terms. I have shown you no scientific data but merely an overall view of my projects. You will take home nothing that can prove useful in copying our technical superiority.'

'When will you allow Congresswoman Smith and I to leave for Washington?' asked Diaz.

Suma looked at his watch. 'Very soon. As a matter of fact, you will be airlifted to my private airfield at Edo City within the hour. From there, one of my executive jets will fly you home.'

'Once the President hears of your madness,' Diaz snapped, 'he'll order the military to blow this place to dust.'

Suma gave vent to a confident sigh and smiled. 'He's too late. My engineers and robotic workers are ahead of schedule. You did not know, could not have known, the Kaiten Project was completed a few minutes after we began the tour.'

'It's operational?' Loren spoke in a shocked whisper.

Suma nodded. 'Should your President be foolish enough to launch an attack on the Dragon Centre, my detection systems will alert me in ample time to signal the robots to deploy and detonate the bomb cars.' He hesitated only long enough to flash a hideous grin. 'As Buson, a Japanese poet, once wrote, "With his hat blown off the stiff-necked scarecrow stands there quite discomfited."

'The President is the scarecrow, and he stands stymied because his time is gone.'

54

Lively, but not hurriedly, Pitt led them into the building of the retreat that housed the elevator. He walked in the open while the others dodged from cover to cover behind him. He met no humans but was halted by a robotic security guard at the elevator entrance.

This one was programmed only to speak in Japanese, but Pitt had no trouble in deciphering the menacing tone and the weapon pointing at his forehead. He raised his hands in front of him with the palms facing forward and slowly moved closer, shielding the others from its video receiver and detection sensors.

Weatherhill and Mancuso stealthily closed in from the flanks and jabbed their statically charged hoses against the box containing the integrated circuits. The armed robot froze as if in suspended animation.

'Most efficient,' Weatherhill observed, recharging his length of hose by rubbing it vigorously against the silk.

'Think he tipped off his supervisory control?' Stacy wondered.

'Probably not,' Pitt replied. 'His sensory capability was slow in deciding whether I was a threat or simply an unprogrammed member of the project.'

Once inside the deserted elevator, Weatherhill opted for the fourth level. 'Six opens onto the main floor of the control centre,' he recalled. 'Better to take our chances and exit on a lower level.'

'The hospital and service units are on four,' Pitt briefed him.

'What about security?'

'I saw no sign of guards or video monitors.'

'Suma's outside defences are so tight he doesn't have to concern himself with interior security,' said Stacy.

Weatherhill agreed. 'A rogue robot is the least of his problems.'

They tensed as the elevator arrived and the doors slid open. Fortunately it was empty. They entered, but Pitt hung back, head tilted as if listening to a distant sound. Then he was inside, pressing the button for the fourth level. A few seconds later they stepped out into a vacant corridor.

They moved quickly, silently, following Pitt. He stopped outside the hospital and paused at the door.

'Why are you stopping here?' Weatherhill asked softly.

'We'll never find our way around this complex without a map or a guide,' Pitt murmured. 'Follow me inside.' He pushed the door button and kicked it back against its stops.

Startled, the nurse-receptionist looked up in surprise at seeing Pitt burst through the doorway. She was not the same nurse who aided Dr Nogami during Pitt's earlier visit. This one was as ugly and ruggedly constructed as a road grader. Even as she recovered, her arm snapped out toward an alarm button on an intercom communications unit. Her finger was a centimetre away when Pitt's flattened palm struck her violently on the chin, catapulting her in a backward somersault onto the floor unconscious.

Dr Nogami heard the commotion and rushed from his office, stopping abruptly and staring at Pitt and the MAIT team as they flooded through the door before pushing it closed. Oddly, the expression on his face was one of curious amusement rather than shock.

'Sorry for intruding, Doc,' Pitt said, 'but we need directions.'

Nogami gazed down at his nurse who was lying on the floor out cold. 'You certainly have a way with women.'

'She was about to set off an alarm,' Pitt said apologetically.

'Lucky you caught her by surprise. Nurse Oba knows

438

karate like I know medicine.' Only then did Nogami take a few seconds and study the motley group of people standing around the prostrate nurse. He shook his head almost sadly. 'So you're the finest MAIT team the US can field. You sure don't look it. Where in hell did Ray Jordan dig you people up?'

Giordino was the only one who didn't stare back at the doctor in mute surprise. He looked up at Pitt. 'Do you know something we don't?'

'May I introduce Dr Josh Nogami, the British deep cover operative who's been supplying the lion's share of information on Suma and his operation.'

'You figured it out,' said Nogami.

Pitt made a modest hands-out gesture. 'Your clues made it elementary. There is no St Paul's Hospital in Santa Ana, California. But there *is* a Saint Paul's Cathedral in London.'

'You don't sound British,' said Stacy.

'Though my father was raised as a British subject, my mother came from San Francisco, and I attended medical school at UCLA. I can do a reasonable American accent without too much effort.' He hesitated and looked Pitt in the eye, his smile gone. 'You realize, I hope, that by coming back here you've blown my cover.'

'I regret throwing you in the limelight,' Pitt said sincerely, 'but we have a more immediate problem.' He nodded toward the others. 'Maybe only another ten or fifteen minutes before Kamatori and three of his security robots are discovered . . . ah . . . incapacitated. Damned little time to set off an explosive charge and get out of here.'

'Wait a minute.' Nogami raised a hand. 'Are you saying you killed Kamatori and zapped three roboguards?'

'They don't come any deader,' Giordino answered cheerfully.

Mancuso was not interested in cordial conversation. 'If you can please provide us with a diagram of this complex, and quickly, we'll be on our way and out of your hair.'

'I photographed the construction blueprints on micro-film, but had no way of smuggling them out to your people after I lost my contact.'

'Jim Hanamura?'

'Yes. Is he dead?' Nogami asked, certain of the answer.

Pitt nodded. 'Cut down by Kamatori.'

'Jim was a good man. I hope Kamatori died slowly.'

'He didn't exactly enjoy the trip.'

'Can you please help us?' Mancuso asked urgently, insistently. 'We're running out of time.'

Nogami didn't seem the least bit rushed. 'You hope to get out through the tunnel to Edo City, I suppose.'

'We had thought we might take the train,' said Weather-hill, his eyes aimed through the door into the corridor.

'Fat chance.' Nogami shrugged. 'Since you guys pene-trated the complex, Suma ordered the tube guarded by an army of robots on the island side and a huge security force of specially trained men at the Edo City end. An ant couldn't get through.'

Stacy looked at him. 'What do you suggest?'

'The sea. You might get lucky and be picked up by a passing ship.'

Stacy shook her head. 'That's out. Any foreign ship that came within five kilometres would be blown out of the water.'

'You have enough on your minds,' Pitt said calmly, his eyes seemingly fixed on one wall as if seeing something on the other side. 'Concentrate on planting the explosives. Trust the escape to Al and me.'

Stacy, Weatherhill, and Mancuso all looked at each other. Then Weatherhill nodded in agreement. 'You're on. You've saved our lives and got us this far. Be downright rude not to trust you now.'

Pitt turned to Nogami. 'How about it, Doc, care to tag along?'

Nogami shrugged and gave a half smile. 'Might as well.

Thanks to you, my usefulness here is finished. No sense in hanging around for Suma to have my head lopped off.'

'Any suggestions for a place to set explosives?' asked Weatherhill.

'I'll show you an access hole to the electrical cables and fibre optics that feed the entire complex. Set your charge there and you'll put this place out of business for a month.'

'What level?'

Nogami tilted his head toward the ceiling. 'The level above, the fifth.'

'Whenever you're ready,' Weatherhill said to Pitt.

'Ready now.' Cautiously, Pitt slipped into the corridor and dogtrotted back to the elevator. They all followed and piled in and stood silent as it rose to the fifth level, tensed for any trouble they might face when the doors opened. Suddenly the elevator dropped down instead of going up. Someone had beat them to it by pressing the button on the level below.

'Damn,' Mancuso swore bitterly. 'That's all we need.'

'Everybody!' Pitt ordered. 'Push the doors together to keep them from opening. Al, lean on the "door close" button.'

The elevator stopped and they all pressed their hands on the doors and pushed. The doors tried to spread apart but could only jerk spasmodically without opening.

'Al!' Pitt said softly. 'Now hit *five!*'

Giordino had kept one finger pressed against the 'door close' button so tightly the knuckle went white. He released it and pushed the button marked 5.

The elevator shuddered for a few moments as if torn in two directions, then it gave an upward jerk and began rising.

'That was close, too close,' Stacy sighed.

'Going up,' Giordino announced. 'Housewares, kitchen utensils, dishes, and hardware –' Abruptly he broke off. 'Oh, oh, we haven't tagged home base yet. Someone else wants on. The light on five just blinked.'

441

Again alerted, every eye unconsciously rotated toward the panel and the small indicator light that was flashing for the fifth level. Then, as if activated by the same set of gears, they turned and crouched, ready to spring into action.

A white-coated engineer was standing there wearing a hard hat, intently studying notations on a clipboard. He didn't even look up as he entered the elevator. Only when it began to seep through to him that the elevator wasn't moving did he gaze around into the Occidental faces. None that he observed were smiling.

He opened his mouth to shout, but Pitt clamped one hand over the engineer's mouth and squeezed the carotid arteries with the other. Even before the eyes rolled back in the head and the body went limp and sagged to the elevator floor, Nogami was out and leading the others into a passageway.

Weatherhill was the last to go. He paused and looked at Pitt. 'When and where do you want us to join up?' he asked.

'Topside in twelve minutes. We'll hold the cab.'

'Good luck,' Mancuso muttered, hurrying after the others, wondering what the man from NUMA had on his canny mind.

Giordino looked down at the unconscious engineer. 'Where do we stash *him*?'

Pitt pointed at the access door in the ceiling of the elevator. 'Tear his lab coat into strips, then tie and gag him. We'll park him on the elevator roof.'

As Giordino pulled off the white lab coat and began ripping it apart, he gave Pitt a half-crooked grin. 'I heard it too.'

Pitt grinned back. 'Ah, yes, the sweet sound of freedom.'

'If we can snatch it.'

'Optimism, optimism,' Pitt muttered cheerfully as he launched the elevator upward. 'Now let's show some speed. It's twelve minutes to show time.'

55

The MAIT team deep in the Dragon Centre could not have been under heavier stress than the two men sweating out the minutes in the communications room of the Federal Headquarters Building. Raymond Jordan and Donald Kern sat watching a huge clock and listening anxiously for the team call sign to be beamed from a satellite in a fixed synchronous position over Japan.

As if triggered by the sudden buzz of a telephone sitting on the table between them, their eyes met, their faces drawn. Jordan picked up the receiver as if it carried the plague.

'Yes, Mr President,' he answered without hesitation.

'Any word?'

'No, sir.'

The President went quiet for a moment, then said solemnly, 'Forty-five minutes, Ray.'

'Understood, sir. Forty-five minutes until the assault.'

'I've called off the assault by the Delta Forces. After a conference with my other security advisers and the Joint Chiefs, I've come to the decision that we cannot afford the time for a military operation. The Dragon Centre must be destroyed before it becomes operational.'

Jordan felt as though his world was slipping away. He threw the dice one more time. 'I still believe that Senator Diaz and Congresswoman Smith may be on the island.'

'Even if you're right, their possible deaths would have no bearing on my decision.'

'You won't change your mind and give them another hour?' Jordan pleaded.

'I wish I could find it in my heart to let you have more time, but our national security is at high risk. We cannot allow Suma the opportunity to launch his campaign of international blackmail.'

'You're right, of course.'

'At least I'm not alone. Secretary of State Oates has briefed the leaders of the NATO nations and Soviet President Antonov, and they have each agreed that it's in all our mutual interest to proceed.'

'Then we write off the team,' said Jordan, his frustration showing in his tone, 'and perhaps Diaz and Smith.'

'I deeply regret compromising the lives of dedicated Americans, some of whom were good friends. Sorry, Ray, I'm faced with the age-old quandary of sacrificing a few to save many.'

Jordan set the receiver in its cradle. He seemed strangely hunched and shrunken. 'The President,' he said vacantly.

'No reprieve?' asked Kern grimly.

Jordan shook his head. 'He's scrubbed the assault and is sending in a nuclear warhead.'

Kern went ashen. 'Then it's down to the wire.'

Jordan nodded heavily as he looked up at the clock and saw only forty-three minutes remaining. 'Why in God's name can't they break free? What happened to the British agent? Why doesn't he communicate?'

Despite their fears, Jordan and Kern were not remotely prepared for an even worse disaster in the making.

Nogami guided the MAIT team through a series of small side passageways filled with heating and ventilating pipes, skirting heavily populated offices and workshops, keeping as far out of the mainstream of activity as possible. When confronted by a roboguard, Nogami engaged it in conversation while one of the others slowly angled in close and shut down its circuits with a charge of static electricity.

They came to a glass-enclosed room, a large expansive area filled with electrical wiring and fibre optic bundles, all branching out into narrow tunnels leading throughout the

Dragon Centre. There was a robot standing in front of a huge console of various dials and digital instruments.

'An inspector robot,' said Nogami softly. 'He's programmed to monitor the systems and report any shorts or disconnects.'

'After we queer his circuits, how long before his supervisor sends someone to check on him?' asked Mancuso.

'From the main telepresence control, five or six minutes.'

'Plenty of time to place the charge and be on our way,' said Weatherhill casually.

'What do you figure for the timer setting?' Stacy asked him.

'Twenty minutes. That should see us safely to the surface and off the island if Pitt and Giordino come through.'

Nogami pushed open the door and stepped aside as Mancuso and Weatherhill entered the room and approached the robot from opposite sides. Stacy remained in the doorway, acting as lookout. The mechanical inspector stiffened at his console like a metal sculpture as the statically charged hoses made contact with his circuit housing.

Smoothly, skilfully, Weatherhill inserted the tiny detonator into the plastic explosive and set the digital timer. 'In amongst the cables and optical fibres, I think.'

'Why not destroy the console?' said Nogami.

'They've probably got back-up units in a supply warehouse somewhere,' explained Mancuso.

Weatherhill nodded in agreement as he moved up a passageway a short distance and taped the charge behind several bundles of heavily insulated cable and optical fibres. 'They can replace the console and reconnect new terminal leads in twenty-four hours,' he lectured, 'but blow a metre out of the middle of a thousand wires and they'll have to replace the whole system from both ends. It will take them five times as long.'

'Sounds fair,' Nogami acquiesced.

'Don't make it obvious,' said Mancuso.

Weatherhill looked at him reproachfully. 'They won't be looking for something they don't know exists.' He gave a love pat to the timer and exited the passageway.

'All clear,' Stacy reported from the doorway.

One at a time they moved furtively into the corridor and hurried toward the elevator. They had covered nearly two hundred metres when Nogami suddenly halted and held up his hand. The sound of human voices echoed along the concrete walls of a side passage followed by the soft whirr of an electric motor. Nogami furiously gestured for them to move ahead, and they darted across the opening and rushed around a corner before the intruders came into sight of the main corridor.

'I misjudged their efficiency,' Nogami whispered without turning. 'They're early.'

'Investigators?' Stacy asked him.

'No,' he answered quickly. 'Telepresence supervisors with a replacement for the robot you put out of commission.'

'You think they might be onto us?'

'We'd know if they were. A general alarm would be sounded and a horde of Suma's human security forces along with an army of roboguards would have swarmed through every corridor and blocked all intersections.'

'Lucky someone hasn't smelled a rat from all the robots we've wasted,' grunted Mancuso as he rushed along the corridor in Nogami's trail.

'Without obvious signs of damage, the telepresence supervisors will think they suffered from simple electronic malfunctions.'

They reached the elevator and lost a full two minutes as they waited for it to rise from a lower level. After what seemed half a lifetime, the doors finally opened to an empty interior. Weatherhill was the first in, and he pressed the button for the surface level.

The elevator, with the three men and one woman standing grimly and silently, rose with excruciating slowness. Only Nogami had a watch, the others having lost theirs when they were captured. He peered at the dial.

'Thirty seconds to spare,' he informed them.

'Out of the fire,' murmured Mancuso. 'Now let's hope there's no frying pan.'

All that mattered now was their escape. What plan did Pitt have circulating inside his head? Had anything happened to him and Giordino? Had Pitt miscalculated and was he recaptured or dead? If he was, then all hope had vanished and they were left with nothing, no direction for freedom, their only hope of escape struck down.

They had lost track of the number of times they'd prepared for the worst, crouched ready to spring at whatever or whoever stood outside the elevator. They stiffened as the doors pulled apart.

Giordino stood there as big as life, grinning like he'd won the lottery. When he spoke it was as though he was standing at the gate of an airport. 'May I see your boarding passes, please?'

Ubunai Okuma and Daisetz Kano were top-level robotic engineers, highly trained in the teleoperation of computer vision and artificial intelligence, as well as the maintenance and trouble-shooting of sensory malfunctions. In the tele-presence control room they had received a signal that robot electrical inspector Taiho, whose name meant 'big gun', was non-functioning, and they immediately moved to replace him for repair.

Sudden breakdown from myriad problems was not uncommon. Robotics was still a new science, and bugs cropped up with maddening frequency. Robots often stalled abruptly for reasons that became readily apparent only after they were returned to a reconditioning centre and probed.

Kano circled inspector Taiho, making a quick visual

check. Seeing nothing obvious, he shrugged. 'Looks like a faulty circuit board.'

Okuma glanced at a chart on a clipboard that he carried. 'This one has a history of problems. His vision imaging has caused trouble on five different occasions.'

'Strange, this is the fourth unit to be reported as failed in the past hour.'

'It always runs in streaks,' muttered Okuma.

'His systems need updating and modifying,' agreed Kano. 'No sense in giving him a quick fix. I'll schedule him for a complete rebuild.' He turned to the replacement robot. 'Ready to assume inspection duties, Otokodate?'

An array of lights flashed and Otokodate, a term for a sort of Robin Hood, spoke in slow but crisp words. 'I am ready to monitor all systems.'

'Then begin.'

As the replacement robot took its place at the monitor, Okuma and Kano hoisted the malfunctioning robot onto a motorized dolly with a small crane. Then one of them programmed a code word into the dolly's computer and it began to move automatically toward the conditioning area without human control. The two engineers did not accompany the injured robot but made their way toward the workers' comfort room to indulge in a brief cup of tea.

Left alone Otokodate concentrated his vision system on the dials and blinking digital readings and routinely began to process the data in his computer. His high-level sensing ability, incredibly advanced over a human's, caught an infinitesimal deviation of measurement.

The laser pulse rate through an optic fibre is measured in millions of beats per second. Otokodate's sensors could read the instrument measurements far more accurately than a human, and he recognized a minuscule drop in the pulse rate from the standard 44.7 million beats per second to 44.68 million. He computed the refractive index profile and determined that the light transmitting its waves through two of the strands inside a ribbon containing thousands of optic fibres was temporarily zigzagging at some point.

He signalled telepresence command that he was leaving the console for an inspection of the fibre bundles inside the passageways.

56

Suma was growing more angry and impatient by the moment. Diaz and Smith never seemed to tire of quarrelling with him, giving vent to their hatred of his achievements, threatening him as if he was a common thief off the street. He came to welcome the chance to wash his hands of them.

Abducting Senator Diaz, he felt, was a mistake. He took him only because Ichiro Tsuboi was confident that Diaz carried substantial influence in the Senate and held the President's ear. Suma saw the man as petty and narrow minded. After a medical discharge from the Army, Diaz had worked his way through the University of New Mexico. He then used the traditional road to power by becoming a lawyer and championing causes that brought headlines and support from the majority state party. Suma despised him as an obsolete political hack who harped on the monotonous and tiresome harangue of taxing the rich for welfare programmes to feed and house non-working poor. Charity and compassion were traits Suma refused to accept.

Congresswoman Smith, on the other hand, was a very astute woman. Suma had the uncomfortable feeling she could read his mind and counter any statement he tossed at her. She knew her facts and statistics and could quote them with ease. Loren came from good western stock, her family having ranched the western slope of Colorado since the 1870s. Educated at the University of Colorado, she ran for office and beat an incumbent who had served for thirty years. She could play hardball with any man. Suma suspected that the only soft spot was Dirk Pitt, and he was closer to the truth than he knew.

Suma stared across the table from them, sipping saki and

regrouping for another exchange of harsh words. He was about to make another point when Toshie came into the room and whispered softly in his ear. Suma set his saki cup on the table and stood.

'It's time for you to leave.'

Loren elegantly came to her feet and locked eyes with Suma. 'I'm not moving from here until I know Dirk and Al are alive and treated humanely.'

Suma smiled indulgently. 'They covertly came onto foreign soil, my soil, as intelligence agents of a foreign country –'

'Japanese law is the same as ours in regards to espionage,' she interrupted. 'They're entitled to a fair trial.'

Suma gloated with malicious satisfaction. 'I see little reason to carry this discussion further. By now, Mr Pitt and Mr Giordino, along with the rest of their spy team, have been executed by my friend Moro Kamatori. Make of it what you will.'

Loren felt as if her heart had been crushed in ice. There was a stunned silence, made even more shocking at knowing it must be true. Her face went white and she swayed on her feet, her mind suddenly void.

Toshie grabbed Loren's arm and pulled her toward the door. 'Come, the aircraft that will take you to Edo City and Mr Suma's private aircraft is waiting.'

'No ride through your amazing tunnel beneath the sea?' asked Diaz without a hint of disappointment.

'There are some things I don't wish you to see,' Suma said nastily.

As if walking through a nightmare, Loren uncaringly allowed Toshie to drag her through a foyer that opened onto a stone path that crossed over a small pond. Suma bowed and motioned for Diaz to accompany the women.

Diaz shrugged submissively and limped with his cane ahead of Suma while the two roboguards brought up the rear.

Beyond the pond, a sleek tilt-turbine aircraft sat in the middle of a lawn surrounded by a high, neatly trimmed hedge. The jet engines were turning over with a soft whistling sound. Two crewmen in red nylon flight suits and brimmed caps stood at attention on each side of the steps leading inside the main cabin. Both were short, one slim, the other fairly bursting the stitched seams over his shoulders. They respectfully bowed their heads as Suma's party approached.

Diaz stopped suddenly. 'When I return to Washington, I'm going to hold a news conference and expose you and your monstrous plans. Then I'll fight you with every means at my command in both houses of Congress, until every asset you have in the United States is confiscated and nationalized. I won't rest until you pay for your crimes.'

Suma made an infuriating grin. 'Our Washington lobbyists are more than strong enough to dilute your pathetic efforts. We own too many of your fellow legislators, who have a weakness for hidden wealth, for you to influence. Your voice will ring hollow, Senator Diaz. Your government, whether you like it or not, corrupt and mired in emotional programmes instead of technology and science, has become a wholly owned Japanese subsidiary.'

Loren leaned toward Suma, her eyes narrowing in scorn. 'You underestimated American guts fifty years ago, and once again you've awakened a sleeping giant and filled him with terrible resolve.'

'Admiral Yamamoto's words after December seventh do not apply now,' Suma said contemptuously. 'Your people have lost the fortitude to make sacrifices for the good of the nation. You must face reality, Congresswoman Smith. America's greatness is gone. I have nothing more to say except to urge you to warn your President of Japan's intentions.'

'Don't you mean *your* intentions,' said Loren bravely, the colour coming back to her face. 'You don't represent the Japanese people.'

'A safe journey home, Congresswoman Smith. Your visit has ended.'

Suma turned and began to walk away, but he'd only taken one step when the two crewmen grabbed his arms from each side, lifted him off his feet and hurled him backwards through the open door into the aircraft's cabin, where he seemingly vanished. It all happened so fast that Loren and Diaz stood in blank-minded shock. Only Toshie reacted, lashing out with her foot at the heavier-built crewman.

'Is this any way to begin an intimate relationship,' laughed Giordino, grabbing Toshie's foot, sweeping her up in his arms, and hoisting her through the door to Weatherhill and Mancuso's waiting hands as easily as if she was filled with air.

Loren gasped and started to mutter something to Giordino, but Stacy brusquely pushed her up the short stairs. 'No time to waste, Ms Smith. Please step lively.' With Loren on her way, she pulled at Diaz. 'Get a move on, Senator. We've worn out our welcome.'

'Where . . . where did you all come from?' he stammered as Mancuso and Weatherhill hauled him through the hatch.

'Just your friendly neighbourhood hijackers,' Weatherhill answered conversationally. 'Actually, it was Pitt and Giordino who got the drop on the crew and tied them up in the cargo compartment.'

Giordino lifted Stacy into the cabin and scrambled up the stairs after her. He threw a smart salute at the two roboguards that aimed their weapons at him but stood in stationary bewilderment.

'Sayonara roboturkeys!'

He yanked the door shut and locked it. Then he turned and shouted one brief word in the direction of the cockpit.

'Go!'

The soft whistle of the two turbine engines increased to an earsplitting shriek, and their thrust flattened the grass under the stubby wings. The wheels lifted from the damp ground and the aircraft rose straight into the air, hung there for a few moments as the engines slowly twisted to a horizontal position, and then it shot off in a wide bank that took it over the sea toward the east.

Loren hugged Giordino. 'Thank God you're all right. Is Dirk with you?'

'Who do you think is driving the bus?' Giordino smiled broadly as he nodded toward the cockpit.

Without another word, Loren ran up the aisle and threw open the cockpit door. Pitt sat in the pilot's seat, heavily concentrating on flying an aircraft that was new to him. He didn't blink or turn his head as she slipped her hands around his neck and down inside his borrowed Suma Corporation flight suit and kissed him at least a dozen times.

'You're alive,' she said joyfully. 'Suma said you were dead.'

'It hasn't exactly been a fun-filled day,' Pitt managed between her kisses. 'Does this mean you're glad to see me?'

She lightly dragged her nails over his chest. 'Can't you ever get serious?'

'Lady, right now I'm about as serious as I can get. I've got eight people depending on me to fly an aircraft I've never touched before. And I better get the hang of it real quick or we're all going body surfing.'

'You can do it,' she said confidently. 'Dirk Pitt can do anything.'

'I wish people wouldn't say that,' Pitt groaned. He gave a quick tic of his head to his right. 'Take the co-pilot's seat and play with the radio. We've got to call the cavalry before the samurai air force takes up the chase. No way we can outrun jet fighters.'

'Suma doesn't own the Japanese military.'

'He owns everything else around here. I'm not taking any chances. Switch on the radio; I'll give you the frequency.'

'Where are we going?'

'The *Ralph R. Bennett*.'

'A boat?'

'A ship,' Pitt corrected her. 'A US Navy detection and tracking ship. If we get to her before we're intercepted, we're home free.'

'They wouldn't dare shoot us down with Hideki Suma on board.'

Pitt's eyes flickered from the instrument panel to the water rushing by below. 'Oh, how I hope you're right.'

Behind them, Giordino was trying but failing to soothe Toshie, who was hissing and striking out like a hysterical cat. She spat at him but narrowly missed his cheek, catching him on the ear. Finally he grabbed her from the rear and held her in a tight vice grip.

'I realize I don't make a good first impression,' he said happily, 'but to know me is to love me.'

'You Yankee pig!' she cried.

'Not so, my Italian ancestors would never admit to being Yankees.'

Stacy ignored Giordino and the struggling Toshie and tightly bound Suma to one of several plush leather chairs in the luxurious executive main cabin. Disbelief was written all over his face.

'Well, well, well,' said a happy Mancuso. 'Surprise, surprise, the big man himself came along for the ride.'

'You're dead. You're all supposed to be dead,' he muttered incredulously.

'Your buddy Kamatori is the one who's dead,' Mancuso sadistically informed him.

'How?'

'Pitt stuck him on the wall.'

Pitt's name seemed to act as a stimulant. Suma came back on keel and he said, 'You have made a disastrous mistake. You will unleash terrible forces by taking me hostage.'

'Fair is fair. Now it's our turn to act mean and nasty.'

The human voice can't exactly imitate the hiss of a viper, but Suma came pretty close to it. 'You are too stupid to understand. My people will launch the Kaiten Project when they have learned what you've done.'

'Let them try,' Weatherhill fairly purred. 'In about another three minutes your Dragon Centre is going to have its lights put out.'

The robotic electrical inspector Otokodate soon found the explosive charge taped to the ribbon of fibre optics. He deftly removed it and rolled it back to his console. He studied the package for several moments, recognizing the timer for what it was, but his memory had not been programmed to analyse plastic explosives, and he had no concept of its purpose. He transmitted a signal to his superior in robotic control.

'This is Otokodate at power centre five.'

'Yes, what is it?' answered a robot monitor.

'I wish to communicate with my supervisor, Mr Okuma.'

'He is not back from tea yet. Why are you transmitting?'

'I have found a strange object attached to the primary fibre optical bundle.'

'What sort of object?'

'A pliable substance with a digital timing device.'

'Could be an instrument left behind by a cable engineer during installation.'

'My memory does not contain the necessary data for a positive identification. Do you wish me to bring it to control for examination?'

'No, remain at your station. I'll send a courier down to collect it.'

'I will comply.'

A few minutes later a courier robot named Nakajima that was programmed to navigate every passageway and corridor and pass through the doors to all office and work areas in the complex entered the power centre. As ordered, Otokodate unwittingly turned over the explosive to Nakajima.

Nakajima was a sixth-generation mechanical rover that could receive voice commands but not give them. It silently extended its articulated gripper, took the package, deposited it in a container, and then began the trip back to robotic control for inspection.

Fifty metres from the power centre door, at a point well removed from humans and critical equipment, the C-8 plastic detonated with a thundering roar that rumbled throughout the concrete passageways of level five.

The Dragon Centre was designed and built to withstand the most severe earthquakes, and any structural damage was minimal. The Kaiten Project remained intact and operational. The only result of Weatherhill's explosive charge was the almost total disintegration of courier rover Nakajima.

57

The roboguards alerted their security command to the strange drama in the garden before Pitt had lifted the tilt-turbine clear of the hedged confine. At first the robots' warning was discounted as a malfunction of visual perception, but when an immediate search failed to turn up Suma, the security command offices became a scene of frenzied confusion.

Because of his monumental ego and fetish for secrecy, Hideki Suma had failed to groom a top-level executive team to act in an emergency if he was beyond reach. In panic, his security directors turned to Kamatori but quickly discovered all private phones and pages went unanswered, nor were signals to his personal roboguards acknowledged.

A special defence team, backed by four armed robots, rushed to Kamatori's quarters. The officer in charge knocked loudly, but receiving no reply, he stepped aside and ordered one of the robots to break in the locked door. The thick etched glass partition was quickly smashed into fragments.

The officer cautiously stepped through the empty video viewing room and advanced slowly into the trophy room, his jaw dropping in stunned disbelief. Moro Kamatori hung, shoulders hunched over, in an upright position, his eyes wide open and blood streaming from his mouth. His face was contorted in pain and rage. The officer stared vacuously at the hilt of a sabre protruding from Kamatori's groin, the blade running through his body and pinning him to the wall.

Like a man in a daze, the officer could not believe he was dead and gently shook Kamatori and talked to him. After a minute it finally broke through that the born-too-late samurai warrior wasn't going to speak again, ever. And then, for the first time, the officer realized the prisoners were gone and Kamatori's roboguards were frozen where they stood.

The confusion was magnified by the news of Kamatori's killing and the almost simultaneous explosion on level five. The ground-to-air missiles installed around the island rose from their hidden bunkers, poised and ready for launch but put on hold due to the uncertainty of Suma's presence on the plane.

But soon the action became purposeful and controlled. The remote video recordings of the roboguards were replayed, and it was clearly seen that Suma was forced aboard the aircraft.

The ageing leader of the Gold Dragons, Korori Yoshishu, and his financial power force, Ichiro Tsuboi, were in Tsuboi's offices in Tokyo when the call came from Suma's security director. The two partners of Suma immediately assumed full command of the situation.

Within eight minutes after the explosion, Tsuboi used his considerable influence with the Japanese military to scramble a flight of jet fighters to chase the fleeing tilt-turbine. His orders were to intercept and attempt to force the plane back to Soseki Island. Failing in this, they were to destroy the craft and everyone on board. Tsuboi and Yoshishu agreed that, despite their long friendship with Suma, it was better for the Kaiten Project and their new empire that he should die than become a tool for foreign policy blackmail. Or worse, scandalized as a criminal under the American justice system. And then there was the frightening certainty that Suma would be forced to reveal details of Japan's secret technology and plans for economic and military surpremacy to US intelligence interrogation experts.

Pitt took a compass heading of the position where the ship

was cruising when he'd taken off for Soseki Island. He pushed the engines dangerously past their limit as Loren tried desperately to make contact with the *Bennett*.

'I can't seem to raise them,' she said in frustration.

'You on the right frequency?'

'Sixteen VF?'

'Wrong band. Switch to sixteen UF and use my name as our call sign.'

Loren selected the ultra high frequency band and dialled the frequency. Then she spoke into the microphone attached to her headset.

'Pitt calling USS *Bennett*,' she said. 'Pitt calling the *Bennett*. Do you hear me? Do you hear me? Please answer.'

'This is the *Bennett*.' The voice replied so loud and clear it nearly blasted out Loren's eardrums through the headset. 'Is that really you, Mr Pitt? You sound as if you had a sex change since we last saw you.'

The aircraft had been scanned by the *Bennett*'s super-sensitive detection systems from the moment it left the ground. Once it was perceived as heading over the sea to the east, it was tracked by a tactical electronic warfare and surveillance receiver system. Within minutes of being alerted, Commander Harper was pacing the deck in the situation room. He stopped every few seconds and peered over the shoulders of the console operators who stared into the radar screens and the computer monitor that analysed and measured the signals and enhanced the approaching target into a recognizable classification.

'Can you distinguish – ?'

'Either a tilt-rotor or a new tilt-turbine,' the operator anticipated Harper. 'It lifted like a helicopter, but it's coming on too fast for rotor blades.'

'Heading?'

'One-two-zero. Looks to be on a course toward the position where we launched the two Ibises.'

Harper swung to a phone and picked it up. 'Communications.'

'Communications, sir,' a voice answered instantly.

'Any radio signals?'

'None, sir. The airwaves are quiet.'

'Call me the second you receive anything.' Harper slammed down the phone. 'Any course change?'

'Target still flying on a one-two-zero heading slightly south of east, Captain.'

It had to be, but it couldn't be Pitt, Harper thought. But who else would fly toward that particular position? A coincidence, he wondered? Not one to run on idle, he barked an order to his executive officer, who was standing at his side.

'Turn on a course toward the position where we launched the Ibises. Full speed until I tell you different.'

The officer knew Harper preferred efficiency to traditional protocol, so he turned without acknowledging and speedily relayed the orders to the bridge.

'Communications for you, Captain,' announced a seaman.

Harper snatched the phone. 'This is the captain.'

'I have a signal from a woman claiming to be Congresswoman Loren Smith. She also claims Mr Pitt is at the controls of an aircraft hijacked from Soseki Island, carrying eight passengers including Senator Michael Diaz and Mr Hideki Suma.'

Too far down the chain of command to be informed of the abductions of Loren and Diaz, Harper could not be blamed for a lack of credence. 'They hijacked an airplane and snatched Suma? And where in hell did Pitt dig up a pair of politicians on Soseki Island?' He paused to shake his head in wonderment, then gave an order over the phone. 'Tell whoever you're in contact with that I require more concrete identification.'

The communication specialist came back within half a

461

minute. 'The woman swears she's Congresswoman Loren Smith of Colorado, and if we don't guide them in and provide protection in the event they're pursued, she's going to lunch with Roy Monroe and demand you're put in command of a tugboat in the Arctic. I'm not one to offer advice to the captain, sir, but if she's friendly with the Secretary of the Navy, she must be who she says she is.'

'All right, I'll buy her story for now.' Harper reluctantly caved in. 'Give instructions to turn twenty degrees south and continue on a westerly heading until we meet up –'

'I have two aircraft rising from Senzu Air Base,' the console operator monitoring the tactical receiver system broke in. 'Configuration and speed indicate Mitsubishi Raven interceptors of the Japanese Air Self-Defence Force. They've turned onto the same heading as the tilt-turbine and are probing with radar.'

'Damn it!' Harper burst. 'Now we've got the Jap military to deal with.' He turned to his exec again. 'Apprise Pacific Command of our situation. Inform them I am going on combat mode. I intend to fire on the pursuers if they show any indication of a hostile act. I'm taking on the responsibility of protecting those people in the tilt-turbine aircraft in the belief they're American nationals.'

His executive officer hesitated. 'Aren't you going out on a limb, sir?'

'Not too far out.' Harper smiled shrewdly. 'Do you seriously think I'll be court-martialled for shooting down hostile aircraft to save the lives of two members of Congress?'

Harper's logic was unarguable. The executive officer smiled back. 'No, sir, I don't guess you would.'

Pitt took the aircraft up to four thousand metres and held it there. The time for hugging the surface of the sea was past. He was out of range of the island's missile systems and now had a straight shot at the *Ralph R. Bennett*. He relaxed and donned the radio headset and microphone that was hanging on the arm of his seat.

'Eighty kilometres to go,' he said quietly. 'She should be coming into sight dead ahead.'

Giordino had relieved Loren in the co-pilot's seat and was studying the fuel gauges with a bemused eye. 'Suma's ground crew was pretty stingy with the gas. We'll be on fumes in another ten minutes.'

'They only needed to partially fill the tanks for the short hop from Soseki and back from Edo City,' said Pitt. 'I've pushed her hard and used up fuel at an extravagant rate.'

'You better take it easy and conserve.'

There was a click in their earphones and a deep voice came through. 'This is Commander Harper.'

'Nice to hear from you, Commander. This is Dirk Pitt. Go ahead.'

'I hate to be the bearer of grim tidings, but you've got a pair of Japanese mosquitoes chasing your tail.'

'What next?' muttered Pitt in exasperation. 'How soon before they intercept?'

'Our computers say they'll be sitting in your lap twelve to fifteen kilometres before we rendezvous.'

'We're dead meat if they attack,' Giordino said, tapping the fuel gauges.

'You're not as bad off as you think,' Harper said slowly. 'Our electronic countermeasures are already jamming their radar missile guidance systems. They'll have to be almost on top of you to go on visual.'

'Got anything you can throw at them to spoil their aim?'

'Our only weapon is a thirty-millimetre Sea Vulcan.'

'Not much better than a peashooter,' Giordino complained.

'I'll have you know that peashooter, as you call it, can spit forty-two hundred rounds a minute as far as eight kilometres,' Harper shot back.

'A good five kilometres too short, too late,' said Pitt. 'Got any other ideas?'

'Hang on.' Two full minutes passed before Harper spoke. 'You might make it under our fire cover if you put your craft into a dive and pull out on the deck. The increased speed during your descent will give you an extra four minutes of lead time.'

'No advantage I can see,' said Giordino. 'Our pursuers will dive too.'

'Negative,' Pitt replied to Harper. 'We'll be like a helpless duck gliding over the waves. Better to remain at an altitude where I still have air space to manoeuvre.'

'They're pretty smart fellas,' retorted Harper. 'They've planned ahead. We track them closing at an altitude of twelve hundred metres, twenty-eight hundred metres below you. Looks to me like they figure to cut you off at the pass.'

'Keep talking.'

'If you use the tactics created by our computers, you increase your odds of making it under our umbrella of fire. Also, and this is a vital issue, once they come within range of our Vulcan we'll have an open field of fire above you.'

'I'm persuaded,' said Pitt. 'Will begin descent in forty seconds.' He turned to Loren, who was sitting in the seat directly behind the cockpit door. 'See that everyone straps in good and tight. We're going to rock and roll for a little while.'

Loren quickly made the rounds of the cabin, checking on Suma and Toshie, alerting the others. Any joy shared among the survivors of the MAIT team quickly faded as a dark mood settled over the cabin. Only the Japanese industrialist looked suddenly happy. Suma smiled the smile of a carved Buddha.

In the cockpit, Pitt briefly went through a stretching routine to relieve muscle tension and loosen his joints. He took a series of deep breaths and then he massaged his hands and fingers as if he was a concert pianist about to attack Liszt's Second Hungarian Rhapsody.

'Eighteen kilometres and closing fast,' came Harper's voice.

464

Pitt grabbed the wheel on the control column and nodded at Giordino. 'Al, read out the airspeed and altitude readings.'

'My pleasure,' Giordino said without the slightest note of excitement. His faith in Pitt was total.

Pitt pressed the transmit button on his radio. 'Commencing dive,' he said in the tone of a pathologist announcing an incision on a corpse. Then he took a firm grip on the wheel and eased the control column forward, wondering what he would say when he met the devil. The aircraft nosed over and down, its jet engines screaming as it hurtled toward the vast blue sea that filled the entire expanse of the cockpit's windscreen.

58

Tsuboi put down the phone and stared dolefully across his desk at Korori Yoshishu. 'Our fighter aircraft have reported Hideki's plane has taken evasive action. They have no time for an attempt to force it back to Soseki Island before it reaches the American naval ship. Their flight commander requests confirmation of our order to shoot it down.'

Yoshishu replied thoughtfully. Already he had mentally accepted Suma's death. He inhaled a cigarette and nodded. 'If there is no other way, Hideki must die to save what we have all struggled so long to build.'

Tsuboi looked into the old dragon's eyes but saw only a flinty hardness. Then he spoke into the phone. 'Order to destroy confirmed.'

As Tsuboi set down the phone, Yoshishu shrugged. 'Hideki is only one of a long line who sacrificed their lives for the new empire.'

'That is so, but the American government won't be happy over sacrificing two of their legislators in the same incident.'

'The President will be pressured by our lobbyists and friends in his government to say little and do nothing,' Yoshishu said with shrewd certainty. 'The uproar will swirl around Hideki. We will remain in the shadows, free of the storm.'

'And very quietly assume control of Hideki's corporations.'

Yoshishu nodded slowly. 'That is a law of our brotherhood.'

Tsuboi looked at the older man with renewed respect. He understood how Yoshishu had survived when countless other underworld leaders and Gold Dragons had fallen by the wayside.

He knew Yoshishu was a master at manipulating others, and no matter who crossed him, no matter how strong his enemies, he was never defeated. He was, Tsuboi had come to realize, the most powerful man in the world who did not hold public office.

'The world news media,' Yoshishu continued, 'is like a voracious dragon that devours a scandal. But quickly tiring of the taste, it moves on to another. Americans forget quickly. The death of two of their countless politicians will soon fade.'

'Hideki was a fool!' Tsuboi lashed out sharply. 'He began to think he was a god. As with most men, when they become too powerful and self-worshipping, he made grave mistakes. Kidnapping American congressional members from their own soil was idiotic.'

Yoshishu did not immediately reply but looked across Tsuboi's desk. Then he said quickly, 'You are like a grandson to me, Ichiro, and Hideki was the son I never had. I must bear the blame. If I had kept a tighter rein on him, this disaster would not have happened.'

'Nothing has changed.' Tsuboi shrugged. 'The attempt by American intelligence agents to sabotage the Kaiten Project was checked. We are as powerful as before.'

'Still, Hideki will be sorely missed. We owe him much.'

'I would have expected no less if our positions were reversed.'

'I'm sure you wouldn't hesitate to throw yourself on the sword if necessary,' Yoshishu said with a condescending smile.

Tsuboi was too sure of his abilities to even consider failing. He was of the new breed and would never have the slightest intention of stepping aside by sticking a knife in his gut. 'Our financial and industrial empire will continue to expand without Hideki,' he said without remorse. 'We must harden our hearts and push forward.'

Yoshishu saw the look of ambition in Tsuboi's eyes. The

young financial wizard was too anxious to step into Suma's shoes. 'I leave it to you, Ichiro, to arrange a fitting ceremony for our friend when we enshrine his spirit at Yasakuni,' said Yoshishu, referring to Suma as if he had been dead for days.

Tsuboi dismissed this with a wave of one hand. He rose to his feet and leaned across the desk. 'Now, Korori, with the Kaiten Project operational, we must seize the moment to undermine European and American economic independence.'

Yoshishu nodded, his white hair falling forward over his brow. 'I agree, we cannot allow Hideki's death to delay our timetable. You must return to Washington immediately and dictate our demands to the President for the extension of our financial ventures in America.'

'And if he doesn't accept our *demands*?'

'I've studied the man for years. He's a realist. He will see that we are throwing a rope to his dying country. He knows of our Kaiten Project and what it can do. Have no fear, the President of the United States will deal, and so will Congress. What choice do they have?'

'Twenty-two hundred,' Giordino droned as he read aloud the altitude in metres and the airspeed in knots. 'Speed five-twenty.'

The ocean was rising rapidly, the scattered whitecaps growing larger. They darted through a wisp of cloud. There was almost no sensation of speed except for the screaming engines that Pitt held on full power. It was next to impossible to judge height above water. Pitt put his faith in Giordino, who in turned relied on the instruments to warn him when to pull level.

'Where are they?' he asked into his microphone.

'This is Ray Simpson, Dirk,' came the voice of the commander who had briefed them on the Ibis. 'I'll talk you in.'

'Where are they?' Pitt repeated.

'Thirty kilometres and closing fast.'

'I'm not surprised,' said Pitt. 'They can't be more than a thousand knots faster than this bus.'

'Fifteen hundred,' read Giordino. 'Speed five-ninety.'

'I wish I'd read the flight manual,' Pitt muttered under his breath.

'Twelve hundred metres. Speed six-fifty. Looking good.'

'How do you know?'

'It seemed the thing to say.' Giordino shrugged.

At that instant, an alarm gong began sounding in the cockpit. They had taken the aircraft beyond its safety limits into the realm of the unknown.

'One thousand metres. Speed seven-forty. Wings, don't fail us now.'

Now within visible range, the lead Japanese aircraft's pilot centred the red dot that appeared in his targeting system's TV monitor on the diving tilt-turbine. The optical computer took over the firing sequence and launched the missile.

'Air-to-air missile on the way,' Simpson warned them in an ominous voice.

'Alert me when it's closed to within one kilometre,' ordered Pitt quickly.

'Six hundred metres,' Giordino warned Pitt. 'Speed eight hundred. Now is the time.'

Pitt did not waste his breath on a reply but pulled back on the control column. The tilt-rotor responded as if it was a glider gripped by a giant hand. Smoothly, in a perfectly curved arc, it swooped into level flight perilously low, less than seventy metres above the water.

'Missile closing, three kilometres,' Simpson said, his voice flat and empty.

'Al, begin maximum tilt to engines.' Pitt hesitated.

Almost instantly, it seemed, Simpson called out, 'One kilometre.'

'Now!'

Giordino shoved the levers that tilted the engines from horizontal to full vertical.

The aircraft seemed to shoot from level flight into a near ninety-degree angle upward. The tilt-turbine shuddered as everyone was thrown forward under the sudden change in momentum and the skyward pull of the engines still turning on full power.

The missile streaked beneath, missing the aircraft's belly by less than two metres. And then it was gone, flashing away and eventually falling into the sea.

'Nice work,' complimented Simpson. 'You're coming within range of our Vulcan. Try to stay low so we have an open field of fire above you.'

'It'll take some time to swing this bus back to level flight on the deck,' Pitt told Simpson, frustration displayed on the furrowed lines of his face. 'I've lost my airspeed.'

Giordino returned the jet turbines to horizontal as Pitt nosed the aircraft over. It levelled and screamed a scant twenty metres over the water toward the looming outline of the ship. From Pitt's view, hurtling across the wave tops, it looked like a stationary paper ship on a plastic sea.

'Aircraft closing but no indication of a missile launch,' came Simpson's anxious voice. 'They're delaying until the last second to compensate for your next manoeuvre. You'd better hit the deck and damned fast.'

'I'm surfing the waves now,' Pitt snapped back.

'So are they. One above the other so you can't pull your flying saucer stunt again.'

'They must be reading our minds,' said Giordino calmly.

'Since you don't have a scrambler to encrypt voice transmissions, they listen to your every move,' Simpson warned them.

'Now he tells us.'

Pitt stared through the windscreen at the *Ralph R. Bennett*. He felt as if he could reach out and touch its giant radar array. 'The next play action is yours, *Bennett*. We've run out of surprises.'

'The gate to the fort is open,' came the voice of Harper suddenly. 'Swing five degrees to port and don't forget to duck when the mail goes out.'

'Missile away,' Simpson called.

'I read,' said Pitt, 'but have nowhere to go.'

Pitt and Giordino instinctively crouched in anticipation of the impact and explosion. They poised as helpless as homing pigeons under attack by a falcon. Suddenly their salvation erupted in a maelstrom of fire that flashed in front of the tilt-turbine's bow and roared overhead and to the rear.

The *Bennett*'s thirty-millimetre Sea Vulcan had cut loose. The modern Gatling gun's seven barrels rotated and spat 4,200 rounds a minute in a swath of fire so thick the shells could be followed by the naked eye. The stream cut across the sky until it met the incoming missile, blasting it into a mushroom of flame less than two hundred metres behind the fleeing tilt-turbine aircraft.

Then it walked toward the lead aircraft, caught up with it, and chewed away one wing like teeth through a potato chip. The Mitsubishi Raven jet fighter flipped into a series of contorted rollovers and smacked the water with a great splash. The seond jet went into a steep bank, barely staying ahead of the river of shells that raced relentlessly toward its exhaust, and whirled around on a course back to Japan. Only then did the Sea Vulcan fall silent as the last of its rounds swept the blue and fell, spraying the crests of the swells into white foam.

'Bring her on in, Mr Pitt.' Harper's vast relief could be clearly distinguished in his voice. 'Wind is off the starboard beam at eight knots.'

'Thank you, Commander,' said Pitt. 'And thank your crew. That was nice shooting.'

'It's all in knowing how to make love to your electronics.'

'Beginning final approach.'

'Sorry we don't have a brass band and a proper reception committee.'

'The Stars and Stripes flapping in the breeze will do nicely.'

Four minutes later, Pitt set the tilt-turbine on the *Bennett*'s helicopter pad. Only then did he take a deep breath, sag in his seat, and relax as Giordino shut down the engines.

For the first time in weeks he felt safe and secure. There was no more risk or danger in his immediate future. His part of the MAIT team operation was finished. He thought only of returning home, and then perhaps going on a dive trip to the warm waters and tropical sunshine of Puerto Rico or Haiti, hopefully with Loren at his side.

Pitt would have laughed in absolute disbelief if anyone had walked into the cockpit and predicted that within a few short weeks Admiral Sandecker would be delivering a eulogy at his memorial service.

PART FOUR
Mother's Breath

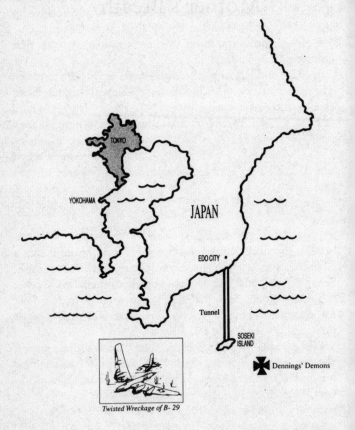

TOKYO

YOKOHAMA

JAPAN

EDO CITY

Tunnel

SOSEKI
ISLAND

Dennings' Demons

Twisted Wreckage of B-29

59

October 20, 1993
Washington, DC

'They're out!' Jordan announced exuberantly as he slammed down a telephone in the National Security Council's Situation Room deep under the White House. 'We've just received a signal that our MAIT team has escaped Soseki Island.'

Dale Nichols stared at Jordan suspiciously. 'Is that confirmed?'

Jordan nodded in tight confidence. 'Solid information. They were attacked by Japanese Self-Defence fighters, but evaded and broke clear.'

The President came forward in his chair. 'Where are they now?'

'Safely landed on board the *Ralph R. Bennett*, a naval surveillance ship stationed a hundred kilometres off the island.'

'Any casualties?'

'None.'

'Thank God for that.'

'There's more, much more,' Jordan said, wound like a clock spring. 'They brought Congresswoman Smith, Senator Diaz, and Hideki Suma out with them.'

The President and the rest stared at him in wordless astonishment. Finally Nichols murmured. 'How was it possible?'

'The details are still sketchy, but Commander Harper, skipper of the *Bennett*, said Dirk Pitt and Al Giordino hijacked the aircraft that was to carry Smith and Diaz to Edo City. Somehow they also managed to snatch Suma and his secretary and take off during the confusion.'

'Suma,' muttered CIA Director Martin Brogan in awe. 'Now there's a gift out of the blue.'

The surprise and delight in the President's eyes turned to thoughtfulness. 'This puts a whole new face on the situation.'

'Under the circumstances, Mr President,' said Defense Secretary Jesse Simmons, 'I advise we cancel the nuclear strike against the Dragon Centre.'

The President glanced at the big countdown clock on one wall of the situation room. It read nine minutes to launch. 'Good lord yes, call it off.'

Simmons simply nodded at General Clayton Metcalf, Chairman of the Joint Chiefs, who immediately picked up a phone and began issuing orders. After a brief half minute, Metcalf nodded.

'They're standing down at the launch site.'

Secretary of State Douglas Oates wore an expression of triumph. 'A near thing, Mr President. I was against a nuclear strike from the beginning.'

'The Dragon Centre and the Kaiten Project haven't gone away,' the President reminded Oates. 'They still pose a dangerous threat. The crisis has merely moved from critical to temporary hold.'

'True,' Oates argued, 'but with Suma in our hands, we're holding the snake by the head, so to speak.'

'I can't wait to hear what an expert interrogation team digs out of him,' muttered Brogan blissfully.

Oates shook his head in strong disagreement. 'Suma is not some small fish in the pond. He's one of the richest and most powerful men in the world. You can't expect to use strong-arm tactics on him without grave consequences.'

'Fair is fair.' Jordan's voice was filled with satisfaction. 'I see no reason to show mercy with a man who kidnapped two members of Congress and was planning to detonate nuclear bombs on American soil.'

'I'm with you, Ray,' said Brogan, giving Oates an acid stare. 'This guy is as rotten as they come. I'll bet dinner for everyone in the room, the Japanese government will remain silent and issue no protest.'

Oates was adamant. 'It is not in our national interest to act barbaric.'

'Nice guys finish last,' said Jesse Simmons. 'If we'd played hardball like the Russians, we wouldn't have hostages in Lebanon.'

'Jesse is right,' Nichols agreed. 'We'd be idiots to set him free to return to Japan and resume his private war against us.'

Brogan said, 'Prime Minister Junshiro and his cabinet won't dare create a fuss, or the whole sordid mess would leak to the international news media and come down on them like a ton of bricks. No, you're wrong, Doug, the next step in removing this terrible threat against our people is to twist Suma's arm until he reveals the exact locations of the bomb cars.'

The President looked around the table with an expression of weary patience. 'Mr Suma is no friend of this nation. He's all yours, Martin. Make him sing like a canary. We've got to get to those bombs and neutralize them damned quick.'

'How soon can the Navy airlift Suma off the *Bennett*?' Brogan turned and asked Simmons.

'With no aircraft carrier in that part of the ocean,' answered the Defense Secretary, 'we'll have to wait until the ship is within helicopter range of Wake Island, the nearest pick-up point.'

'The sooner we get Suma to Washington, the sooner we can extract data from him,' said Brogan.

The President nodded. 'I'd be interested in hearing what Congresswoman Smith and Senator Diaz observed as well.'

Don Kern entered the room and spoke softly to Jordan, who nodded as he listened, and then looked up at the President. 'It appears our friends from NUMA have solved another problem for us. Commander Harper has signalled that the tilt-turbine aircraft Pitt and Giordino hijacked for their flight from the island has been refuelled on board the *Bennett*. They're in the air and flying toward Wake Island as we speak.'

The President turned his attention to Metcalf. 'General, I leave it to you to arrange military transportation for Suma and our legislators to the capital as quickly as humanly possible.'

'I'll alert General Duke Mackay, commander of Anderson Air Force Base on Guam, to send his personal jet to Wake. It should be on the ground and waiting when Pitt sets down.'

The President then focused on Jordan. 'What's the status of the Dragon Centre?'

'Sorry, sir,' replied Jordan. 'Commander Harper's signals were brief. There was no word from our MAIT team on whether their operation was a success.'

'Then we won't know anything until they reach Wake.'

'No, sir.'

Oates thrust a hard stare at Jordan. 'If your people failed in their mission to halt the Dragon Centre from becoming operational, we could be facing a terrible calamity.'

Jordan stared back. 'If they escaped in one piece, they accomplished what they set out to.'

'We don't know that for certain.'

'Even so, we surely bought some breathing space, with the architect and builder of the Kaiten Project in hand,' said Simmons. 'Suma's co-conspirators will be demoralized. They won't attempt any major aggression without their leader at the helm.'

'I'm afraid your theory won't hold water,' Jordan said slowly. 'We've overlooked Harper's message from the *Bennett*.'

'What about it?' asked the President.

'The part about the aircraft surviving an attack by Japanese fighters,' Brogan pointed out.

Jordan nodded. 'They must have known Suma was on board. And yet they tried to shoot the plane down.'

Simmons doodled on a notepad as he spoke. 'Then we must assume they . . . whoever they are –'

478

'The old kingpin of the Japanese underworld, Korori Yoshishu, and his financial crony, Ichiro Tsuboi,' explained Jordan, interrupting. 'They're criminal partners in Suma's industrial empire.'

'Then we must assume,' Simmons repeated, 'that Hideki Suma is expendable.'

'It comes down to that,' said Kern, speaking for the first time.

'Which means Yoshishu and Tsuboi can step in and activate the detonation systems,' the President theorized.

Brogan's expression of optimism was slowly collapsing. 'With Suma in our hands, there's no predicting how they'll react.'

'Perhaps I should reorder the nuclear strike,' said the President halfheartedly.

Jordan shook his head negatively. 'Not just yet, Mr President. There's another way we can buy time to reassess the situation.'

'What's on your mind, Ray?'

'We let the Japanese tune in to Commander Harper's signals reporting that the plane carrying Diaz, Smith, and Suma crashed into the sea with the loss of all on board.'

Brogan looked doubtful. 'You really think Yoshishu and Tsuboi would buy that?'

'Probably not,' said Jordan with a canny look, 'but I'll bet they'll think about it until we can put the Kaiten Project out of business for good.'

60

True to his word, the Chairman of the Joint Chiefs had General Mackay's personal Air Force C-20 passenger jet sitting beside the runway that stretched across Wake Island as Pitt dropped the tilt-turbine on a marked pad in front of the small terminal building.

Mel Penner had flown up from Palau and was waiting, cupping his ears against the scream of the turbines as the wheels touched the concrete. The area was surrounded and cordoned off by nearly twenty air police. Penner moved toward the aircraft and stood expectantly at the doorway. It swung open and Weatherhill was the first out.

Penner stepped forward and they shook hands. 'Glad to see you're still in the land of the living.'

'That makes two of us,' said Weatherhill with a huge smile. He glanced around at the Air Force security ring. 'We didn't expect a welcoming committee.'

'You're the hottest topic of discussion at the White House. Is it true you made it out with Suma?'

Weatherhill nodded. 'And Diaz and Smith.'

'You made quite a haul.'

Stacy stepped down and was also surprised to see Penner and the guards. 'Somehow I get the feeling we're not going to refuel and continue to Hawaii,' she said, hugging Penner.

'Sorry, no. There's an Air Force jet waiting to fly Suma and the legislators to Washington. They'll be accompanied and guarded by a military intelligence team. The rest of us have been ordered to remain here on Wake for a meeting with a group of high-level hotshots sent by Jordan and the President.'

'I'm sorry we couldn't have sent you more data,' explained Weatherhill, 'but we thought it best if we stayed off the airwaves and made out a report in person.'

'Jordan agrees. You made the right decision.'

Weatherhill handed Penner a file folder filled with neatly typed sheets. 'A full report.'

Penner stared at the report with a blank look. 'How?'

Weatherhill gestured back inside the aircraft. 'Suma had it fully equipped to conduct business. We wrote it up during the flight on a word processor.'

Mancuso popped his head out of the door. 'Hi, Mel. Did you bring the party hats and champagne?'

'Good to see you, Frank. When can I meet your passengers?'

'Sending them out now. You'll have to wait a minute for our guests from Japan to disembark until I free them.'

'You had them under restraint?'

'They got a little testy at times.'

Loren and Diaz stepped squinting into the bright sun and were introduced to Penner, who related the flight procedure. Then Suma and Toshie were ushered out by Mancuso, his hands tightly gripping each by an arm.

Penner made a slight bow. 'Welcome to United States territory, Mr Suma, but I don't think you're going to enjoy your stay.'

Suma gave Penner the offhand glance he reserved for underlings and acted as if the intelligence operative was invisible.

Toshie looked at Penner with uncontrolled hatred. 'You will treat Mr Suma with proper respect. He demands he be freed immediately and returned to Japan.'

'Oh, he will,' Penner said mockingly. 'After he's enjoyed an all-expense paid vacation in our nation's capital, courtesy of the American taxpayer.'

'You are violating international law,' Suma said nastily. 'And if you do not release us, vengeance shall be swift and many of your countrymen will die.'

Penner turned to Weatherhill. 'Can he back up the threat?'

Weatherhill looked at Suma. 'Sorry, you can forget about the Dragon Centre. Its juice has been cut off.'

'You were successful?' asked Penner. 'Ray Jordan and Don Kern are clawing the walls, waiting to hear.'

'A temporary fix. We only had enough explosive to blow out a fibre optic bundle. They should be back in business in several days.'

Dr Josh Nogami exited the plane and was greeted by Penner. 'A real pleasure to meet you, Doc. We're grateful for your efforts in getting information out to us. Your help was invaluable.'

Nogami shrugged modestly. 'I'm sorry I couldn't have saved Jim Hanamura.'

'You might have given yourself away and been murdered too.'

'Mr Pitt did his best to prevent that.' Nogami glanced around, but saw no familiar faces. 'It looks as though I'm an agent without an assignment.'

'When our Deputy Director of Operations, Don Kern, learned you were on board, he requested that you be temporarily assigned to us. Your superior agreed. If you don't mind working with a bunch of colonials for a few days, your knowledge of the Dragon Centre's layout would be very helpful.'

Nogami nodded. 'The weather here beats rainy London any day.'

Before Penner could reply, Giordino leaped down from the tilt-turbine and ran toward a squad of air police that were herding Suma and Toshie to the waiting C-20. He rushed over to the officer in charge and asked him to hold up the procession for a moment.

Giordino was only half a centimetre taller than Toshie. He looked straight into her eyes. 'Dear heart, wait for me.'

She stared at him in angered surprise. 'What are you talking about?'

'Courtship, amorous pursuit, nestling, endearment, proposal. As soon as I can catch up to you, I am going to make you the happiest woman alive.'

'You're mad!'

'Only one of my many charms,' said Giordino engagingly. 'You'll discover lots of others in the years to come.'

Amazingly, Toshie wavered. For a strange reason she couldn't comprehend, she began to find Giordino's very un-Japanese approach appealing. She had to struggle to suppress any friendliness she felt toward him.

Giordino recognized her uncertainty and grasped her slender shoulders in his beefy hands, kissed her briefly on the lips, and smiled. 'I'll catch up to you as soon as I can.'

She was still staring at him wordlessly over her shoulder as Penner took her by the elbow and brusquely led her away.

Pitt escorted Loren to the C-20 jet after Suma, Toshie, and Diaz were seated aboard. They walked in silence, feeling the warmth from the sun and the humidity stroke their skin.

Loren stopped several metres from the aircraft and stared into Pitt's eyes. 'It seems one of us is always coming and going.'

He nodded. 'We lead busy, separate lives. Our schedules never mesh.'

'Maybe someday . . .' Her voice died softly.

'Someday,' he said in understanding.

'You're not going back?' she asked hesitantly.

He shrugged. 'I don't know. Al and I have been ordered to remain behind.'

'They can't send you back to that island. Not now.'

'I'm a marine engineer, remember? I'm the last man they'd ask to assault the Dragon Centre with six-shooters blazing.'

'I'll talk to the President and request you and Al be sent home.'

'Don't put yourself out,' he said easily. 'We'll probably be on the next flight east.'

She stood on her toes and kissed him gently on the mouth. 'Thank you for everything.'

Pitt smiled. 'Anything to please a pretty lady.'

Tears began forming in her eyes. Loren had a feeling of dread in her stomach. Somehow she knew he wouldn't be following her anytime soon. Suddenly she turned and hurried up the boarding stairs into the aircraft.

Pitt stood there looking after her. Then he waved as her face appeared in a window, but when Loren looked for him again as the plane taxied to the runway he was gone.

Tsuboi could not believe it. After leaving Yoshishu and rushing from Tokyo to Edo City and then to the Dragon Centre to take personal command, he stood in the control room tense with growing rage.

'What do you mean you cannot detonate any of the bomb cars?' he demanded.

Takeda Kurojima, the Dragon Centre's chief director, was stricken. He looked around helplessly at his small army of engineers and scientists for moral support, but they all stared at the floor as if hoping to be swallowed by it.

'Only Mr Suma knows the codes,' Kurojima answered with a patronizing hands-out shrug. 'He personally programmed the code system for the prime and detonate signals.'

'How long will it take you to reprogram the codes?'

Kurojima stared at his staff again. They began muttering rapidly between themselves. Then, seemingly agreeing on something, one stepped forward and murmured so softly Tsuboi didn't hear.

'What – what was it you said?'

Kurojima finally stared into Tsuboi's eyes. 'Three days, it will take three days minimum to erase Mr Suma's command codes and reprogram the systems.'

'That long?'

'It is not a quick and simple procedure.'

'What is the status of the robotic drivers?'

'The robot program is accessible,' replied Kurojima. 'Mr Suma did not insert the codes to set in motion their drive and destination systems.'

'Two days, forty-eight hours. That's all you have to make

the Kaiten Project fully operational.' Tsuboi tightened his mouth and clenched his jaws. He began to pace the control room of the Dragon Centre. He cursed the serpentine mastermind who had outfoxed them all. Suma had trusted no one, not even his oldest and closest friend Yoshishu.

A phone buzzed and one of the technicians picked it up. He went rigid and held out the receiver to Tsuboi. 'Mr Yoshishu in Tokyo for you.'

'Yes, Korori, Ichiro here.'

'Our intelligence people have intercepted a report from the American ship. They claim Hideki's plane was shot down. Did our pilots actually see Hideki's aircraft go into the sea?'

'Only one returned. I was informed the surviving pilot reported that he was too busy evading return fire from the ship to witness his missile strike the target.'

'It could be a bluff by the Americans.'

'We won't know if that's the case until one of our observer satellites can be programmed to pass over the ship.'

'And if it shows the plane is on board?'

Yoshishu hesitated. 'Then we know we are too late. Hideki is lost to us.'

'And under tight security by American intelligence forces,' Tsuboi finished.

'We're faced with a very grave situation. In the hands of American intelligence, Hideki can become an acute embarrassment to Japan.'

'Under drugged interrogation he will most certainly divulge the locations of the bomb cars.'

'Then we must act quickly to preserve the Kaiten Project.'

'There is another problem,' said Tsuboi grimly. 'Only Hideki knew the operational codes to activate the prime and detonate signals.'

There was a pause on the other end of the line. Then Yoshishu said slowly, 'We always knew he had a cunning mind.'

'Only too well,' agreed Tsuboi.

'Then I leave it to you to discover new directions.'

'I won't fail your trust.'

Tsuboi set down the receiver and gazed out the observation window. A silence came over the control room as everyone waited on his word. There had to be another solution for delaying any retribution by the United States and other Western nations. Tsuboi was a smart man, and it only took him a few seconds to come up with alternate plans.

'How complicated is it to set off one of the bombs manually?' he asked the assembled engineers and scientists in the control room.

Kurojima's eyebrows raised up questioningly. 'To detonate without a coded signal?'

'Yes, yes.'

The technical brain who headed the Kaiten Project from start to finish bowed his head and answered. 'There are two methods by which a mass of fissionable material can be made subcritical and forced to explode. One is to surround the mass by a ring of high explosives whose detonation will in turn set off the fissionable material. The other is to shoot together two masses by a cannon-type device.'

'How do we explode a bomb car?' Tsuboi demanded impatiently.

'Velocity,' Kurojima answered briefly. 'The impact from a high-velocity bullet through the compressor shell and into the mass should do it.'

Tsuboi glared inquiringly. 'Are you saying the bombs can be set off by nothing more than a shot from a rifle?'

Kurojima bowed his head. 'At close range, yes.'

The effect on Tsuboi was just within the limits of credibility. 'Then why don't you simply program a robot to fire a high-powered rifle into the air-conditioner shell?'

'There is the problem of time again,' replied Kurojima. 'The robots that are programmed to drive the cars to their detonation sites are not constructed or programmed for anything else.'

'One of the roboguards, could it be modified?'

'The reverse. Security robots are designed for mobility and weapons fire. They are not designed to drive a car.'

'How long to make one that can do the job?'

'Weeks, no less than a month. You must realize we have to create a very complicated piece of machinery. We do not have one in production that can drive a car, climb out on articulated legs, open a hood, and shoot a gun. A robot with these built-in movements would have to be built from the ground up, and that takes time.'

Tsuboi stared at him. 'We must detonate one within the next five hours to make the Americans think the system is operational.'

Kurojima's confidence had returned. He was in control and his fear of Tsuboi had faded. He gave the financier a long steady look. 'Well then, you'll just have to find a human to do the job.'

It was about five in the evening, and the sky to the east was turning dark blue as the C-20 winged over the Pacific toward California. They were only two hours out of a refuelling stop at Hickam Field in Hawaii. Loren looked down, straining her eyes to pick out the tiny shape and white wake of a ship, but she could see only the flat expanse of the sea and a few whitecaps.

She swivelled the executive chair she was sitting in and faced Suma. He sat arrogantly composed, sipping a glass of soda water. The shock of the hijacking and the distress at knowing Yoshishu had ordered his death had long since melted and he was now relaxed, supremely confident that he would regain the upper hand once he reached Washington.

He stared at her and smiled thinly. 'So you intend to promote legislation to close all your markets to Japanese goods.'

'In light of what I've seen and experienced in the past few days,' said Loren, 'do you blame me?'

'We Japanese have planned far into the future for just such a possibility. Our economy will survive because we have already invested heavily in the European and Asian markets. Soon we will no longer need the United States consumer. The closing of your market is merely another unfair tactic of you Americans.'

Loren laughed. 'What do you know about fair trade practices?' Then she got down to serious business. 'No foreigners can come into Japan to sell their products without being hassled to death by your trade barriers, stonewalled by your graft-ridden distribution system, and undermined by your home competition. All the while insisting that no outsider understands your culture.'

'Your behaviour, Congresswoman Smith, is obviously motivated by racist anti-Japanese sentiments. We feel no guilt over expanding our international market shares. We started with nothing after the war. And what we have built, you want to take away.'

'Take what away? Your self-proclaimed right to rule the economic world?' Loren could just detect a hint of growing frustration in Suma's eyes. 'Instead of picking you up from the ashes and helping you build an enormously successful economy, perhaps we should have treated you like you treated Manchuria, Korea, and China during your years of occupation.'

'Many of the postwar economic successes of those countries were due to Japanese guidance.'

Loren shook her head in wonderment at his refusal to acknowledge historical facts. 'At least the Germans have demonstrated regret for the atrocities of the Nazis, but you people act as though your butchery of millions of people throughout Asia and the Pacific never happened.'

'We have freed our minds of those years,' said Suma. 'The negative events were unfortunate, but we were at war.'

'Yes, but you made the war. No one attacked Japan.'

'It lies in the past. We think only of the future. Time will prove who has the superior culture,' he said with contempt. 'Like all the other Western nations since ancient Greece, you will fall by decay from within.'

'Perhaps,' said Loren with a soft smile, 'but then eventually, so will you.'

62

Penner rose from a chair, turned, and faced the surviving members of the MAIT team who were seated in an office inside one of the commercial aircraft hangars. He tapped ashes from his pipe in a bucket of sand beside a desk and nodded at two men, one sitting, the other standing along the rear wall.

'I'm going to turn the briefing over to Clyde Ingram, the gentleman in the loud Hawaiian shirt. Clyde is blessed with the fancy title of Director of Science and Technical Data Interpretation. He'll explain his discovery. Then Curtis Meeker, an old friend from my Secret Service days and Deputy Director of Advanced Technical Operations, will explain what's circulating in his warped mind.'

Ingram walked over to an easel with a blanket thrown over it. He stared from blue eyes through expensive designer glasses attached to a cord that dangled around the nape of his neck. His hair was a neatly combed brown, and he lived inside a medium-sized body whose upper works was covered by a black aloha shirt that looked as if it had been worn in a Ferrari driven around Honolulu by Tom Selleck as Thomas Magnum.

He threw the blanket off the easel and gestured a casual thumb toward a large photograph of what appeared to be an old aircraft. 'What you see here is a World War Two B-Twenty-nine Superfortress resting thirty-six miles from Soseki Island on the seabed, three hundred and twenty five metres, or for those of you who have trouble converting to metrics, a little over a thousand feet below the surface.'

'The picture is so clear,' said Stacy. 'Was it taken from a submersible?'

'The aircraft was originally picked up by our Pyramider Eleven reconnaissance satellite during an orbit over Soseki Island.'

'You can get a picture that sharp on the bottom of the sea from an orbiting satellite?' she asked in disbelief.

'We can.'

Giordino was sitting in the rear of the room, his feet propped on the chair in front of him. 'How does the thing work?'

'I won't offer you an in-depth description, because it would take hours, but let's just say it works by using pulsating sound waves that interact with very low frequency radar to create a geophysical image of underwater objects and landscapes.'

Pitt stretched to relieve tense muscles. 'What happens after the image is received?'

'The Pyramider feeds the image, little more than a smudge, to a tracking data relay satellite that relays it to White Sands, New Mexico, for computer amplification and enhancement. The image is then passed on to the National Security agency, where it is analysed by both humans and computers. In this particular case, our interest was aroused, and we called for an SR-Ninety Casper to obtain a more detailed picture.'

Stacy raised a hand. 'Does Casper use the same imagery system as the Pyramider?'

Ingram shrugged in regret. 'Sorry, all I can reveal without getting into trouble is that Casper obtains real-time imaging recorded on analogue tape. You might say that comparing the Pyramider and Casper systems is like comparing a flashlight beam to a laser. One covers a large spread, while the other pinpoints a small spot.'

Mancuso tilted his head and stared at the blown-up photograph curiously. 'So what's the significance of the old sunken bomber? What possible connection can it have with the Kaiten Project?'

492

Ingram flicked a glance at Mancuso and then tapped a pencil on the photo. 'This aircraft, what's left of it, is going to destroy Soseki Island and the Dragon Centre.'

Nobody believed him, not for an instant. They all stared at him as though he was a con man selling a cure-all elixir to a bunch of rubes at a carnival.

Giordino broke the silence. 'A mere trifle to raise the plane and repair it for a bombing run.'

Dr Nogami forced a smile. 'It'd take considerably more than a fifty-year-old bomb to make a dent in the Dragon Centre.'

Ingram smiled back at Nogami. 'Believe me, the bomb inside this B-Twenty-nine has the punch to do the job.'

'The plot thickens.' Pitt nodded glumly. 'I smell a screw coming on.'

Ingram did a neat sidestep. 'That part of the briefing will come from my partner in crime, Curtis Meeker.'

Pitt's sardonic stare went from Ingram to Meeker. 'You two and Ray Jordan and Don Kern must all play in the same sandbox.'

'We have occasion to mix it up now and then,' Meeker replied without smiling.

Ingram turned again to the easel, removed the photograph, and propped it on a chair, revealing a close-up photo of a little devil painted on the side of the aircraft's bow.

'*Dennings' Demons*,' he said, tapping a pencil on the faded letters beneath the little devil. 'Commanded by Major Charles Dennings. Please note that the little demon is standing on a gold brick marked twenty-four carat. The crew enjoyed referring to themselves as goldbrickers after they were reprimanded for tearing apart a beer hall during training in California.'

'Obviously my kind of guys,' said Giordino.

'Unknown, forgotten, and buried deep in Langley files, until a few days ago when Curtis and I dug out the facts, was

493

the story of a very courageous group of men who set out on a very secret mission to drop an atom bomb on Japan —'

'They what!' Weatherhill was incredulous, but no more so than the others.

Ingram ignored the interruption and went on. 'At about the same time as Colonel Tibbets took off in the *Enola Gay* from Tinian Island in the Pacific with the bomb known as "Little Boy", Major Dennings lifted off Shemya Island far to the north in the Aleutians with his bomb, which was code-named "Mother's Breath". What was left of the report on the mission was heavily censored, but we believe Dennings' flight plan called for him to follow a one-way course, dropping his bomb on the target, probably Osaka or Kyoto, and then continuing to Okinawa to refuel before pushing on to Tinian. As we all know from the history books, Tibbets successfully dropped his bomb on Hiroshima. Dennings, unfortunately, vanished, and the entire event was covered over by presidential orders.'

'Hold on a minute,' said Mancuso. 'Are you telling us that we built more than three bombs in nineteen forty-five?'

Stacy cleared her throat. 'Except for Little Boy, the first Trinity bomb at Los Alamos, and Fat Man, which was dropped on Nagasaki, no other bombs are recorded.'

'We still don't have the exact count, but it appears there were at least six. Most were of the implosion type like Fat Man.'

Pitt said, 'Dennings' bomb makes four. That still leaves two.'

'A bomb with the code name of Mother's Pearl was loaded aboard a superfort called *Lovin' Lil* on Guam, not too long after the island was liberated from the Japanese. *Lovin' Lil* was in the air flying toward Japan when *Bock's Car*, piloted by Major Charles Sweeney, dropped Fat Man on Nagasaki. After word was received that the drop went off as planned, *Lovin' Lil* and her crew were recalled back to Guam, where the bomb was dismantled and shipped back to Los Alamos.'

'That leaves one.'

'Ocean Mother was on Midway Island, but was never airborne.'

'Who came up with those awful names?' murmured Stacy.

Ingram shrugged. 'We have no idea.'

Pitt looked at Ingram. 'Were Dennings and the crews on Guam and Midway part of Colonel Tibbet's Five-o-ninth Bomber Squadron?'

'Again, we don't know. Eighty per cent of the records have been destroyed. We can only guess that General Groves, the director of the Manhattan bomb project, and his staff came up with a complicated back-up plan at the last moment because there was great fear the firing mechanisms on the bombs might not work. There was also the possibility, although unlikely, that the *Enola Gay* or *Bock's Car* might crash on takeoff, detonating their bombs and wiping out the entire five-o-ninth and leaving no trained personnel or equipment to deliver additional bombs. And on top of all that, there were a host of other dangers staring Groves and Tibbets in the face. The threat of Japanese bombing attacks in Tinian; mechanical failures during flight, forcing the crew to jettison their bombs in the sea; or being shot down by enemy fighters or anti-aircraft fire during the mission. Only at the last minute did Groves see the dark clouds gathering around the bomb-delivery operation. In less than a month's time, Major Dennings and the Demons, along with the crews on Guam and Midway, were given rush training and sent on their way.'

'Why was all this kept from public knowledge after the war?' asked Pitt. 'What harm could the story of *Dennings' Demons* cause nearly fifty years later?'

'What can I say?' Ingram made a baffled gesture. 'After thirty years passed and it came up under the Freedom of Information Act, a pair of political hack appointees decided on their own that the American public, who paid their salaries by the way, was too naive to be entrusted with such an earth-shaking revelation. They reclassified the event as top secret and filed it away in the CIA vaults at Langley.'

'Tibbets got the glory and Dennings got deep-sixed,' Weatherhill waxed philosophically.

'So what does *Dennings' Demons* have to do with us?' Pitt put to Ingram.

'Better you should ask Curtis.' Ingram nodded to Meeker and sat down.

Meeker stepped up to a blackboard on a side wall and took a piece of chalk in one hand. He drew a rough sketch of the B-29 and a long, uneven contour line representing the seafloor that stretched across the board's surface and ended with a sudden rise that was Soseki Island. Thankfully to all in the room, he didn't squeak the chalk. Finally, after adding in a few geological details on the sea bottom, he turned and flashed a warm smile.

'Clyde has only given you a brief peek at our satellite surveillance and detection systems,' he began. 'There are others that have the capability of penetrating through an impressive distance of solid material and measuring a vast array of different energy sources. I won't bother to get into them – Clyde and I aren't here to teach a class – but will simply reveal that the explosive device you placed inside the electrical network of the Dragon Centre did not do the job.'

'I've never laid an explosive that failed to detonate,' Weatherhill growled on the defensive.

'Your charge went off all right,' said Meeker, 'but not where you set it. If Dr Nogami was still in deep cover inside the command complex, he could tell you the explosion occurred a good fifty metres from the electrical junction centre.'

'No way,' Stacy protested. 'I watched Timothy set the charge behind a bundle of optical fibres in an access passage.'

'It was moved,' Dr Nogami said thoughtfully.

'How?'

'The inspector robot probably observed a slight drop in the power pulse, searched, and found the charge. He would have removed it and notified his robotic control. The timer must have set off the charge while it was being carried through the corridors to robotic control for investigation.'

'Then the Dragon Centre is fully operational,' Mancuso said with grave foreboding.

'And the Kaiten Project can be primed and detonated,' added Stacy, her face displaying lines of disappointment.

Meeker nodded. 'We're afraid that's the case.'

'Then our operation to knock out the centre was a bust,' Weatherhill said disgustedly.

'Not really,' Meeker explained patiently. 'You captured Suma, and without him the cars can't be detonated.'

Stacy looked confused. 'What's to stop his fellow conspirators from setting off the bombs?'

Pitt threw Nogami a bemused look. 'I suspect the good doctor has the answer.'

'A small bit of information I picked up after becoming chummy with the computer technicians,' Nogami said with a wide smile. 'They allowed me to wander freely in their data centre. On one occasion I stood behind a programmer and looked over his shoulder when he punched in data concerning the Kaiten Project. I memorized the entry code, and at my first opportunity I entered the system. It gave the bomb car locations, which you had already obtained, but I became stymied when I attempted to insert a virus in the detonation system. I discovered only Suma had the detonation codes.'

'So no one but Hideki Suma can launch the Kaiten Project,' Stacy said in relieved surprise.

'A situation his henchmen are working like hell to correct,' answered Meeker. He glanced around at the MAIT team. 'But congratulations are still in order; you pulled off a winner. Your efforts effectively shut down the Dragon

Centre, causing the Japanese to reprogram their prime and detonate systems, and giving us enough time to put together a plan to destroy it once and for all.'

'Which, if I'm not sidetracking your lecture,' said Pitt quietly, 'brings us back to *Dennings' Demons.*'

'You're quite right,' acknowledged Meeker. He hesitated while he sat on a desk. Then he began cutting toward the heart of the briefing. 'The President was willing to lay his political life on the line and sanction a nuclear strike against the Dragon Centre. But he called it off when word came of your escape. Your operation bought him some time, not much, but enough to accomplish what we've planned in the few hours we've got left.'

'You figure on setting off the bomb inside the B-Twenty-nine,' Pitt said, his eyes half closed in weariness.

'No,' Meeker sighed, 'it will have to be moved a short distance.'

'Damned if I can see what damage it will cause to an island almost forty kilometres away,' Giordino muttered.

'A group of the finest oceanographers and geophysicists in the business think that an underwater atomic blast can take out the Dragon Centre.'

'I'd like to know how,' Stacy said as she swatted at a mosquito that had found one of her bare knees.

Meeker refaced the blackboard. 'Major Dennings could not have known, of course, that his aircraft crashed into the sea and fell to the seafloor close to a perfect location to remove a serious threat to his country forty-eight years later.' He paused and drew another jagged line that travelled under the sea bottom from the plane to Soseki Island and then curved southward. 'A section of a major Pacific seismic fault system. It travels almost directly beneath the Dragon Centre.'

Nogami shook his head doubtfully. 'The centre was constructed to withstand a major earthquake and a nuclear strike. Exploding an old atomic bomb, providing it can still detonate after five decades under saltwater, to cause a shift in the fault would prove a wasted effort.'

'Dr Nogami has a sound argument,' said Pitt. 'The island is almost solid rock. It won't sway and shift during a heavy shock wave.'

Meeker said nothing for a moment, only smiled. Then he swung the axe. 'No, it won't sway and shift,' he repeated with a fiendish smile, 'but it *will* sink.'

63

About twenty-five miles north-east of Sheridan, Wyoming, as the crow flies, just south of the Montana border, Dan Keegan sat on a buckskin quarter horse searching for signs of trespassing hunters. While washing up for supper he had heard the distant rumble of two gunshots and immediately told his wife to put his fried chicken in the oven to warm. Then he gathered up an old Mauser bolt-action rifle and saddled up his favourite riding horse.

Hunters who ignored his fences and no-trespassing warning signs were a constant source of irritation to Keegan. Less than two months back a stray shot had dropped one of his herd's calves. The hunter had fired at a six point buck and missed, his bullet carrying over a slight rise and striking the calf almost two kilometres distant. Since then, Keegan wanted no part of hunters. They could just damn well shoot on somebody else's property.

Keegan followed a trail that ran along Hanging Woman Creek. He never knew where the name came from. The only woman he recalled being hanged in Wyoming was Ella Watson, known as 'Cattle Kate'. Prominent ranchers under the guise of vigilantes had strung her up for rustling in 1889. But that event occurred along the Sweetwater River, three hundred kilometres to the southwest.

The rays of the setting sun were intensified by the biting cold air, painting the surrounding hills in glowing yellow-orange tones. He came out onto a flat plain and began studying the ground. Keegan quickly picked up the tyre tracks, following them from a spent shell casing to a rash of booted footprints and a pool of blood soaking the sandy soil. The hunters and their fallen game were gone.

He was too late and mad as hell. To drive a car on his range, the trespassers must have either cut his fence or shot off the lock on the gate across his private road leading to the highway. It would be dark soon. He decided to wait until morning to send one of his ranch hands to ride fence and check the gate. He mounted up and turned the horse for home.

After riding a short distance, he reined up.

The wind carried the faint sound of an automobile engine. He cupped one ear and listened. Instead of retreating as he thought the hunters had done, the sound grew louder. Someone was approaching. He urged the horse up the slope of a small mesa and scanned the flatland below. A vehicle was speeding up the road, trailing a cloud of dust.

He expected to see a pickup truck or a four-wheel drive emerge from the brush bordering the road. When it finally came close enough to recognize, Keegan was surprised to see it was an ordinary car, a brown four-door sedan, a Japanese make.

The driver soon braked and stopped at an open spot in the road. The car sat there for a few moments as the dust drifted over the roof and settled into the range grass. The driver slipped from behind the wheel and opened the hood and leaned under for a few moments. Next he walked around to the rear of the car, raised the trunk lid, and lifted out a surveyor's transit. Keegan watched in curiosity as the intruder set the transit on a tripod and aimed the lens at several prominent landmarks, jotting down the distance readings on a clipboard and comparing them on a geological map that he spread on the ground.

Keegan was experienced with a transit himself, and he'd never seen a survey conducted like this. The stranger seemed more interested in merely confirming his location than in establishing a baseline. He watched as the man casually tossed the clipboard into the underbrush and stepped to the front of the car and stared at the engine again as if hypnotized by it. Only when he seemed to shake himself from his thoughts did he reach inside the car and pull out a rifle.

Keegan had seen enough to know the trespasser was acting too strange for a county surveyor who was out to shoot a little game on the side, and certainly not while dressed in a business suit and knotted tie. He rode his horse closer, coming up quietly behind the stranger, who was intent on trying to insert a shell into the rifle, an act that seemed foreign to him. He didn't hear Keegan approach from his rear. Any sound from the hooves of the horse was muffled by the soft earth and dry grass. Keegan reined in when he was only eight metres away and eased the Mauser from a leather case tied to his saddle.

'You know you're trespassin', mister?' he said, resting the gun in the crook of one arm.

The driver of the brown car jumped and wheeled around, dropping a shell and banging the gun barrel on the door. Only then did Keegan recognize him as an Asian.

'What do you want?' the startled man demanded.

'You're on my property. How did you get in here?'

'The gate was open.'

It was as Keegan thought. The hunters he'd missed had forced the gate. 'What are you doin' with a surveyor's transit? Who do you work for? You with the government?'

'No . . . I'm an engineer with Miyata Communications.' The English was heavily Japanese accented. 'We're scouting a site to set up a relay station.'

'Don't you fellas ever get permission before you run around private property? How in hell do you know I'll let you build one?'

'My superiors should have contacted you.'

'Damn right,' Keegan muttered. He was anxious to return home for supper before daylight faded. 'Now you better move along, mister. And the next time you want to drive on my land, you ask first.'

'I deeply regret any inconvenience.'

Keegan was a pretty good judge of character and could tell by the man's voice he wasn't the least bit sorry. His eyes warily kept focusing on Keegan's Mauser, and he seemed edgy.

'You plan on doin' any shootin'?' Keegan nodded at the high-powered rifle the man still awkwardly gripped in one hand, muzzle wavering toward the darkening sky.

'Target shooting only.'

'Well I can't allow that. I have cattle roamin' this section. I'd appreciate it if you'd pack up your gear and leave by the way you came in.'

The intruder acted agreeable. He quickly broke down the surveyor's transit and tripod, placing them in the trunk of the car. The rifle he placed in the back seat. Then he came around to the front of the car and peered under the open hood.

'The engine is not running properly.'

'Will it start?' Keegan asked.

'I believe so.' The Japanese surveyor leaned in the window and turned the ignition key. The engine fired and idled smoothly. 'I go,' he announced.

Keegan failed to notice the hood was lowered but not latched. 'Do me a favour and close and wrap the chain around the gate behind you.'

'I will gladly do so.'

Keegan threw him a wave, slipped the Mauser back in its case, and began riding off toward his ranch house, a good four kilometres away.

Suburo Miwa gunned the engine, turned the car around, and headed down the road. Meeting up with the rancher in such desolate country was unforeseen, but in no way jeopardized his mission. As soon as he put two hundred metres between the car and Keegan, Miwa suddenly slammed on the brakes, leaped out, snatched the gun from the back seat and raised the hood.

503

Keegan heard the engine revolutions die and he turned and stared over his shoulder, wondering why the car had abruptly halted.

Miwa held the gun tightly in sweating palms and aimed the muzzle until it was only a few centimetres from the compressor of the air conditioner. He had volunteered for this suicidal mission without reservation when asked because he felt it was an honour to give his life for the new empire. Other considerations were his loyalty to the Gold Dragons, the promise made by Korori Yoshishu himself that his wife would be well taken care of financially for the rest of her life and the guarantee his three sons would be accepted and funded through the finest university of their choice. The inspiring words of Yoshishu as Miwa departed for the United States ran through his mind one last time.

'You are sacrificing for the future of a hundred million of your country's men and women. Your family will honour you for untold generations. Your success is their success.'

Miwa pulled the trigger.

64

In a millisecond, Miwa, Keegan, the car, and the horse were vaporized. An enormous brilliance of yellow light flashed and then became white as it burst across the rolling ranch land. The shock wave followed like a vast invisible tidal wave. The fireball expanded and seemed to grow and lift from the ground like the sun rising over the horizon.

Once the fireball broke free of the ground and surged into the sky, it became fused with the clouds and turned purple from glowing radiation. It sucked behind a great swirling stem of radioactive soil and debris that soon formed into a mushroom cloud that soared to thirteen kilometres, only to eventually fall wherever the winds carried the pulverized dust.

The only loss of human life was Keegan and Miwa. Scores of rabbits, prairie dogs, snakes, and twenty of Keegan's cattle were killed, most of them by the shock wave. Four kilometres away, Mrs Keegan and three hired hands suffered only cuts from flying glass. The hills shielded the buildings from the worst of the blast, and except for a few shattered windows, there was little damage.

The fiery explosion left behind a huge crater a hundred metres wide and thirty metres deep. The dry brush and range grass ignited and began to spread in a great circle, adding black smoke to the brown dust cloud.

The dying shock wave echoed through the hills and canyons. It shook houses and swayed trees in the small surrounding cattle and farm towns before rumbling over the Custer battlefield at the Little Bighorn, 112 kilometres to the north.

In a truck stop outside Sheridan an Asian man stood

beside a rental car, ignoring the people talking excitedly and wildly gesturing toward the rising mushroom cloud in the distance. He peered intently through binoculars trained on the cloud that had risen out of the evening gloom and was now high enough to be illuminated by the glow of the sun fallen below the horizon.

Slowly he lowered the glasses and walked to a nearby telephone booth. He inserted a coin, dialled a number, and waited. He spoke a few soft words in Japanese and hung up. Then, without even a glance at the cloud boiling through the upper atmosphere, he got in his car and drove off.

The blast was recorded at seismograph stations located around the world. The closest to the epicentre was the National Earthquake Center on the campus of the Colorado School of Mines in Golden. The seismographic tracings abruptly bounded back and forth across the graph recorders, alerting geophysicist Clayton Morse to an earth movement as he was about to knock off for the day and drive home.

He frowned and then ran the data through a computer. While his eyes remained locked on the computer monitor, he dialled Roger Stevenson, the director of the centre, who had called in sick that day.

'Hello.'

'Roger?'

'Yes, speaking.'

'God, you sound terrible. I didn't recognize your voice.'

'The flu has really knocked me out.'

'Sorry to bug you, but we just received a strike.'

'California?'

'No, the epicentre is somewhere around the Wyoming–Montana border.'

There was a brief silence. 'Odd, that area is hardly classed as an active quake zone.'

'This one is artificial.'

'Explosion?'

'A big one. From what I can tell on the intensity scale, this one reads like it's nuclear.'

'God,' Stevenson muttered weakly, 'are you sure?'

'Who can be sure about these things?' said Morse.

'The Pentagon never held tests in that part of the country.'

'They haven't alerted us to any underground testing either.'

'Not like them to conduct testing without alerting us.'

'What do you think? Should we check it out with the Nuclear Regulatory Commission?'

Stevenson may have been laid low with the flu, but his mind was perfectly healthy. 'Leapfrog the system and go to the top. Call Hank Sauer, our mutual friend at the National Security Agency, and find out what in hell is going on.'

'And if Sauer won't tell?' asked Morse.

'Who cares? The main thing is we've dumped the mystery in his lap, and now we can go on watching for the next big one due in California.'

Sauer didn't tell what he didn't know. But he recognized a national emergency when he heard one. He asked Morse for additional data and immediately passed on the information to the Director of Central Intelligence.

The President was aboard Air Force One flying to a political fund-raising dinner in San Francisco when he received the call from Jordan.

'What's the situation?'

'We have reports of a nuclear explosion in Wyoming,' answered Jordan.

'Damn!' the President cursed under his breath. 'Ours or theirs?'

'Certainly not ours. It has to be one of the bomb cars.'

'Any word of casualties?'

'Negligible. The blast took place in a lightly populated part of the state, mostly ranch land.'

The President was fearful of posing the next question. 'Are there indications of additional explosions?'

'No, sir. At the moment, the Wyoming blast is the only one.'

'I thought the Kaiten Project was on hold for forty-eight hours.'

'It is,' Jordan said firmly. 'There hasn't been enough time for them to reprogram the codes.'

'How do you see it, Ray?'

'I've talked to Percy Nash. He thinks the bomb was detonated on site with a high-powered rifle.'

'By a robot?'

'No, a human.'

'So the kamikaze phenomenon is not dead.'

'It would seem so.'

'Why this suicidal tactic now?' asked the President.

'Probably a warning. They're reasonably certain that we have Suma, and they're hedging their bets by trying to fake us out of a nuclear strike while they desperately struggle to reprogram the detonation codes for the entire system.'

'They're doing a darn good job of it.'

'We're sitting in the driver's seat, Mr President. We now have every excuse in the world to retaliate with a nuclear strike.'

'All too true, but what solid proof do you have that the Kaiten Project isn't operational? The Japs might have pulled off a minor miracle and replaced the codes. Suppose they're not bluffing?'

'We have no hard evidence,' Jordan admitted.

'If we launch a warhead missile on Soseki Island and the Dragon Centre controllers detect its approach, their final act will be to signal the bomb cars to be detonated before the robots can drive them to isolated destinations around the country.'

'A horrible thought, Mr President. Made even more so by

the known locations of the bomb cars. Most of them are hidden in and around metropolitan cities.'

'Those cars must be found and their bombs neutralized as quickly and quietly as possible. We can't afford to have this horror leak to the public, not now.'

'The FBI has sent an army of agents out in the field to make a sweep.'

'Do they know how to dismantle the bombs?'

'Each team has a nuclear physicist to handle that job.'

Jordon could not see the worry lines on the President's face. 'This will be our last chance, Ray. Your new plan is the last roll of the dice.'

'I'm fully aware of that, Mr President. By this time tomorrow morning we'll know if we're an enslaved nation.'

At almost the same moment, Special Agent Bill Frick of the FBI and his team were converging on the vault that held the bomb cars in the underground parking area of the Pacific Paradise hotel in Las Vegas.

There were no guards and the steel doors were unlocked. A bad omen, thought Frick. His apprehension increased when his electronics men found the security systems turned off.

Cautiously he led his team through doors into what looked to be an outer supply room. On the far side was a large metal door that was rolled into the ceiling. It yawned wide and high enough to pass a highway semitrailer.

They entered a huge vaultlike space and found it completely empty, not even a scrap of trash or a cobweb was evident. It had been scrubbed clean.

'Maybe we're in the wrong area,' said one of Frick's agents hopefully.

Frick stared around the concrete walls, focused on the ventilator Weatherhill had wormed through, then looked down at the barely discernible tyre marks on the epoxy-coated floor. Finally he shook his head. 'This is the place, all right. It matches the description from Central Intelligence.'

A short nuclear physicist with a full beard pushed his way past Frick and stared at the emptiness. 'How am I supposed to disarm the bombs if they're not here?' he said angrily, as if the disappearance of the cars was Frick's fault.

Without answering, Frick walked swiftly through the underground parking area to a command truck. He entered, poured himself a cup of coffee, and then opened a frequency on the radio.

'Black Horse, this is Red Horse,' he said in a tired voice.

'Go ahead, Red Horse,' answered the Director of the FBI's field operations.

'We've struck out. The rustlers got here first.'

'Join the club, Red Horse. Most of the herd has come up dry too. Only Blue Horse in New Jersey and Grey Horse in Minnesota found steers in the corral.'

'Shall we continue the operation?'

'Affirmative. You've got twelve hours. Repeat, twelve hours to track your herd to a new location. Additional data is being faxed to you; and all police, sheriff, and highway patrol units have been alerted to stop any trucks and semitrailers matching descriptions provided by Central Intelligence.'

'I'll need a helicopter.'

'You can sign for an entire fleet if that's what it takes to find those bomb cars.'

Frick switched off his radio and stared at his coffee. 'Too bad they don't fax instructions on how to find a needle in a million square kilometres of desert in twelve hours,' he mumbled to himself.

As Yoshishu emerged from the Maglev train at the end of the tunnel from Edo City, Tsuboi was waiting on the platform to greet him.

'Thank you for coming, old friend,' said Tsuboi.

'I want to be here at your side when we are ready to play our hand,' said the old man, his steps more sprightly than Tsuboi had seen in months.

'The blast went off in a midwest state as planned.'

'Good, good, that should send a shiver of fear through the American government. Any signal of reaction at the White House?'

Tsuboi's face had a concerned expression. 'Nothing. It's as if they're trying to cover it up.'

Yoshishu listened impassively. Then his eyes brightened. 'If the President hasn't ordered a nuclear warhead against us, then he has a great fear of what he sees in his future.'

'Then we have won the gamble.'

'Perhaps, yet we cannot celebrate the enormity of our triumph until the Kaiten Project is ready.'

'Takeda Kurojima promises to have the program on-line sometime tomorrow evening.'

Yoshishu placed his hand on Tsuboi's shoulder. 'I think it's time we opened a direct line of communication to the President and informed him of our terms for the new Japan.'

'And a new America,' Tsuboi said pompously.

'Yes, indeed.' Yoshishu looked proudly at the man who had become his chief disciple. 'A new Japanese America.'

65

The Lockheed C-5 Galaxy, the largest cargo plane in the world, settled with all the awkward grace of a pregnant albatross onto the Wake Island airstrip and rolled to a stop. A car approached and braked under the shadow of one enormous wing. Pitt and Giordino left the car and entered the aircraft through a small hatch just aft of the aircraft wheel wells.

Admiral Sandecker was waiting inside. He shook hands and led them through the cavernous cargo bay that could fit six highway buses and seat a hundred passengers. They walked past a NUMA Deep Sea Mining Vehicle that was tied down on a pair of wide stainless steel tracks. Pitt paused in his stride and ran his hand over one of the great tractor treads and stared for a moment at the huge machine, recalling his narrow escape in *Big John*. This DSMV was a later model and was given the nickname of *Big Ben*.

The two big articulated arms with the excavation scoop and claw that were normally installed on the deep-sea vehicles had been removed and replaced with extensions fitted with a variety of remote manipulators for grasping and cutting through metal.

The other modification, Pitt noticed, was an immense nylon pack that rested on top of the upper body and control cabin. Heavy lines ran from the pack and were attached at numerous points around the vehicle.

Giordino shook his head sadly. 'I've got that old feeling we're about to be used again.'

'They aim to really stick it to us this time,' Pitt said, wondering how the aircraft could lift off the ground with such a massive weight in its belly.

'We'd better get forward,' said Sandecker. 'They're ready for take-off.'

Pitt and Giordino followed the admiral into an officelike compartment with a desk and chairs bolted to the floor. They were connecting the buckles on their seat belts when the pilot pushed the throttles forward and sent the great aircraft and the twenty-eight wheels of its landing gear rolling down the runway. Affectionately called the *Gentle Giant*, the huge C-5 Galaxy lifted into the tropical air with a thundering roar and slowly climbed in an easy bank toward the north.

Giordino glanced at his watch. 'Three minutes, that was a quick turnaround.'

'We haven't time to throw away,' Sandecker said seriously.

Pitt relaxed and stretched out his legs. 'I take it you have a plan.'

'The best brains in the business have put in a lot of last-minute homework on this one.'

'That's obvious by this aircraft and *Big Ben* arriving here with less than twenty-four hours' notice.'

'How much did Ingram and Meeker tell you?' Sandecker asked.

'They enlightened us on the secret history of the B-Twenty-nine resting on the seabed,' Pitt answered, 'and gave a brief lecture on the geology and seismic fault system around Soseki. Meeker also claimed that by detonating the atomic bomb still inside the aircraft, the shock waves could cause the island to sink beneath the sea.'

Giordino pulled out a cigar he'd already stolen from Admiral Sandecker by sleight-of-hand and lit it up. 'A cockamamie idea if I ever heard one.'

Pitt nodded in agreement. 'Then Mel Penner ordered Al and me to enjoy a holiday on the sandy beaches of Wake Island while he and the rest of the team flew off into the blue for the States. When I demanded to know why we were being left behind, he clammed up, revealing only that you were on your way and would explain everything.'

'Penner didn't fill in the cracks,' said Sandecker, 'because he didn't know them. Nor were Ingram and Meeker briefed on all the updated details of "Arizona".'

'Arizona?' Pitt asked curiously.

'The code name of our operation.'

'*Our* operation?' Giordino questioned guardedly.

'It wouldn't, of course,' Pitt said sarcastically, 'have anything to do with *Big Ben*, or the fact that Arizona is the name of a state, or more precisely the name of a battleship at Pearl Harbor.'

'It's as good as any. Code names never make any sense anyway.'

Sandecker stared at his friends closely. A day's rest had helped, but they looked dead tired and worn out. He felt a gnawing sense of guilt. It was his fault that they had already endured so much. And now once more he had recommended their services to Jordan and the President, knowing full well that no other two men alive could match their skills and talents in a deep-ocean environment. How terribly unfair to throw them into another deadly maelstrom so quickly. But there was no one else on God's earth he could turn to. Sandecker could taste the remorse in his mouth. And he felt guilt at knowing Pitt and Giordino would never refuse to attempt what he asked of them.

'All right, I won't hand you a lot of crap or sing "America the Beautiful". I'll be as straightforward as I can.' He broke off and laid a geological chart on the desk that showed the seafloor for fifty kilometres around Soseki Island. 'You two are the best qualified to make a last-ditch effort to finish off the Dragon Centre. No one else has much hands-on experience with a Deep Sea Mining Vehicle.'

'It's nice to feel needed,' Giordino said wearily.

'What did you say?'

'Al was wondering what exactly it is we're supposed to

do.' Pitt leaned over the chart and stared down at the cross marking the location of *Dennings' Demons*. 'Our assignment is to use the DSMV to blow up the bomb, I assume.'

'You assume correct,' said Sandecker. 'When we reach the target site, you and *Big Ben* will exit the plane and drop into the water by parachute.'

'I hate that word,' Giordino said, holding his head in his hands. 'The mere thought of it gives me a rash.'

Sandecker gave him a curt look and continued. 'After landing in the sea, you'll settle to the bottom, still using the chutes to slow your descent. Once you are mobile, you drive to the B-twenty-nine, remove the atomic bomb from inside its fuselage, carry it to a designated area, and detonate it.'

Giordino went as rigid as a man seeing a ghost. 'Oh, God, it's far worse than I thought.'

Pitt gave Sandecker a glacial stare. 'Don't you think you're asking a bit much?'

'Over fifty scientists and engineers in universities, government, and high-tech industries joined together on a crash programme to develop Arizona, and take my word for it, they've created a perfect diagram for success.'

'How can they be so sure?' said Giordino. 'No one has ever dumped a thirty-five-ton deep-sea vehicle out of an aircraft and into the ocean before.'

'Every factor was calculated and evaluated until all probability of failure was worked out,' said Sandecker, eyeing his expensive cigar in Giordino's mouth. 'You should hit the water as lightly as a falling leaf on a sleeping cat.'

'I'd feel more comfortable jumping from a diving board into a dish rag,' grumbled Giordino.

Sandecker gazed at him with forbearance. 'I am aware of the dangers, and I sympathize with your misgivings, but we can do without your Cassandran attitude.'

Giordino looked at Pitt questioningly. 'What attitude?'

'Someone who predicts misfortune,' explained Pitt.

Giordino shrugged moodily. 'I was only trying to express honest feelings.'

'Too bad we can't ease *Big Ben* down a ramp off a ship and let it drift to the bottom with variable pressure tanks, as we did with *Big John* over Soggy Acres.'

Sandecker said indulgently, 'We can't afford the two weeks it took to get your DSMV here by sea.'

'May I ask just who the hell is going to instruct us how to remove an atomic bomb from tangled wreckage and detonate it?' demanded Pitt.

Sandecker handed them both folders holding forty pages of photos, diagrams, and instructions. 'It's all in here. You'll have plenty of time to study and practise procedures between now and when we reach the drop zone.'

'The bomb has been under water inside a mangled aircraft for fifty years. How can anyone be certain it's still in any condition to be detonated?'

'The photos from the Pyramider imaging system show the fuselage of the B-Twenty-nine to be intact, indicating the bomb was undamaged during the crash. *Mother's Breath* was designed to be jettisoned in water and recovered. The armoured components of its ballistic casing were precision cast with machine finishing and fit together with tolerances that were guaranteed to keep the interior waterproof. The men still living who built it swear it could remain on the bottom of the sea and be detonated five hundred years from now.'

Giordino wore a very sour look. 'The explosion will be set with a timer, I hope.'

'You'll have an hour before detonation,' Sandecker answered. '*Big Ben*'s top speed has been increased over *Big John*'s. You should be well away from any effects of the blast.'

'What's well away?' Pitt pursued.

'Twelve kilometres.'

'What is the end result?' Pitt put to Sandecker.

'The concept is to induce a submarine earthquake with the old atomic bomb and cause a similar set of circumstances that destroyed Soggy Acres.'

'A totally different situation. The explosion on the surface may have caused a sub-bottom quake, but our habitat was wiped out by a resulting avalanche combined with thousands of kilograms of water pressure. Those forces don't apply on ground above the surface.'

'The water pressure, no. The avalanche, yes.' Sandecker tapped his finger on the chart. 'Soseki Island was formed millions of years ago by a long-extinct volcano that erupted just off the coast of Japan and spewed a river of lava far out into the sea. At one time this immense lava bed was an arm of the Japanese mainland, rising above the water to a height of two hundred metres. It rested, however, on soft layers of ancient sediment. Gradually, gravity forced it down into the softer silt until it fell beneath the water surface with only its lighter and less massive tip remaining above sea level.'

'Soseki?'

'Yes.'

Pitt studied the chart and said slowly, 'If I get this right, the bomb's shock waves and resulting submarine quake will shift and weaken the underlying sediment until the weight of the island pushes it under the sea.'

'Similar to standing in the surfline while the wave action slowly buries your feet in the sand.'

'It all sounds too simple.'

Sandecker shook his head. 'That's only the half of it. The shock waves alone aren't enough to do the job. That's why the bomb must be moved ten kilometres from the plane before it's detonated.'

'To where?'

'The slope of the deep trench that travels parallel to the island. Besides producing a subocean shock, the magnitude of the atomic explosion is expected to tear loose a section of the trench wall. The tremendous energy, as millions of tons

517

of sediment avalanche down the side of the trench in unison with the shock waves from the bomb, will create one of the most destructive forces of nature.'

'A tsunami,' Pitt anticipated the admiral. 'A seismic sea wave.'

'As the island begins to sink from the seismic shocks,' Sandecker continued, 'it will be dealt a knockout blow by the wave, which will have achieved a height of ten metres and a speed between three and four hundred kilometres an hour. Whatever is left of Soseki Island above the surface will be completely forced under, inundating the Dragon Centre.'

'*We* are going to unleash this monster?' Giordino asked suspiciously. 'The two of us?'

'And *Big Ben*. It was a rush job, no way around it, but the vehicle has been modified to do whatever is demanded.'

'The Japanese mainland,' Pitt said. 'A heavy quake followed by a tsunami smashing into the shore could kill thousands of people.'

Sandecker shook his head. 'No such tragedy will occur. Soft sediments out to sea will absorb most of the shock waves. Nearby ports and cities along the coast will feel no more than a few tremors. The seismic wave will be small on the scale of most tsunamis.'

'How can you be sure of the ten-metre crest? Tsunamis have been known to go as high as a twelve-storey building.'

'Computer projections put the wave crest that strikes the island at less than ten metres. And because Soseki is so close to the epicentre, its mass will act as a barrier and blunt the effects of the wave's momentum. By the time the first mass of water reaches the coast, at low tide I might add, its crest will have diminished to only one and a half metres, hardly enough for serious damage.'

Pitt mentally measured the distance from the bomber to the spot marked on the slope of the underwater trench for the detonation. He judged it to be about twenty-eight kilometres. An incredible distance to drag an unstable

518

forty-eight-year-old atomic bomb across rugged and un-known terrain.

'After the party,' wondered Pitt, 'what happens to us?'

'You drive *Big Ben* onto the nearest shore, where a Special Forces team will be waiting to evacuate you.'

Pitt sighed heavily.

'Do you have a problem with any part of the plan?' Sandecker asked him.

Pitt's eyes reflected an undercurrent of doubt. 'This has to be the craziest scheme I've ever heard of in my life. In fact it's worse than that. It's damn right suicidal.'

66

Running at its maximum cruising speed of 460 knots per hour, the C-5 Galaxy ate up the kilometres as darkness fell over the North Pacific. In the cargo bay, Giordino ran through a checklist of *Big Ben's* electronic and power systems. Sandecker worked in the office compartment, providing updates on information and responding to questions raised by the President and his National Security Council, who were sweating out the operation in the Situation Room. The admiral was also in constant communication with geophysicists who supplied new data on seafloor geology, along with Payload Percy, who answered Pitt's inquiries on the bomb removal from the aircraft and its detonation.

To anyone observing Pitt during the final hour of the flight, his behaviour would have seemed most peculiar. Instead of a final attempt to cram a thousand and one details into his head or inspecting the DSMV with Giordino, he collected all the box lunches he could beg and buy from the crew. He also borrowed every drop of available drinking water, thirty litres, and the entire production of the aircraft's coffee maker, four litres, and stashed it all in *Big Ben*.

He huddled with the Air Force flight engineer, who knew the C-5 better than anyone on board. Together they rigged up a cable for tying down cargo and a small electric winch above the small compartment that held the crew's toilet. Pleased with his unscrupulous handiwork, he entered the DSMV and sat in the operator's chair and silently contemplated the almost hopeless mission ahead of him.

Cutting the bomb free of the B-29 and detonating it was

bad enough, but attempting to drive twelve kilometres over unknown territory to escape the blast was a very iffy proposition indeed.

Less than a minute after the Air Force transport landed at Langley Field, Loren and Mike Diaz were quickly swept away by a limousine with an armed escort and driven to the White House, while Suma and Toshie were hustled into a bland-coloured sedan and driven to a secret destination in Maryland.

Upon arrival, Loren and Diaz were ushered down to the Situation Room. The President rose from his end of the table and came forward.

'You don't know how glad I am to see you,' he said, beaming. He gave Loren a light hug and a kiss on the cheek, then embraced Diaz as if the senator was a close relative.

The tense atmosphere lightened as everyone greeted the recently escaped hostages. Jordan moved in and softly asked them to step into an adjoining office. The President accompanied them and closed the door.

'I apologize for rushing you like this,' he said, 'and I realize you must need a good rest, but it's extremely vital for Ray Jordan to debrief you while an operation is underway to eliminate the threat of the Kaiten Project.'

'We understand,' Diaz said, happy to be back amid the tumult of political action. 'I'm sure I speak for Congresswoman Smith when I say we're only too glad to help.'

The President courteously turned to Loren. 'Do you mind?'

Loren felt in desperate need of a good soaking bath. She wore no make-up, her hair was tousled, and she was dressed in pants and slacks a size too small that she had borrowed from an aircraft maintenance man's wife on Wake Island. Despite that and the exhaustion, she still looked remarkably beautiful.

'Please, Mr President, what would you like to know?'

521

'If we can skip the details of your abductions, your treatment by Hideki Suma, and your incredible escape until later,' said Jordan with quiet firmness, 'we'd like to hear what you can tell us about Suma's operations and the Dragon Centre.'

Loren and Diaz silently exchanged tense glances that conveyed more fearfully than words the spectrum of menacing horrors that were being created in Edo City and under Soseki Island. She nodded in deference to Diaz, who spoke first.

'From what we saw and heard, I'm afraid that the threat from Suma's bomb-car programme is only the tip of the iceberg.'

'Fifteen minutes to drop, gentlemen,' the pilot's voice came over the cargo bay speakers.

'Time to mount up,' said Sandecker, his face taut.

Pitt put his hand on Giordino's shoulder. 'Let's hit the john before we go.'

Giordino looked at him. 'Why now? There's a waste system on *Big Ben*.'

'A safety procedure. No telling how hard we're going to strike the water. Formula One and Indianapolis Five Hundred drivers always drain their bladders before a race to prevent internal injury in case they're in an accident.'

Giordino shrugged. 'If you insist.' He walked over to the closetlike toilet for the crew that was stationed behind the cockpit and opened the door.

He had no sooner entered when Pitt made a gesture to the flight engineer. A brief nod in reply and several strands of cable dropped and encircled the toilet and were then winched tight, sealing the door.

Giordino sensed immediately what had happened. 'Dirk, no! God, don't do this!'

Sandecker also realized what was happening. 'You can't make it alone,' he said, grasping Pitt's arm. 'The procedures call for two men.'

'One man can operate *Big Ben*. Stupid to risk *two* lives.'
Pitt winced as Giordino's efforts to escape the privy became
more frenzied. The little Italian could have easily kicked out
the aluminium, but the wrapped steel cable bound it tight.
'Tell Al I'm sorry and that someday I'll make it up to him.'

'I can order the crew to release him.'

Pitt smiled tightly. 'You *can*, but they'd have to fight me to
do it.'

'You realize you're jeopardizing the operation. What if
you were injured during impact? Without Al, you have no
back-up.'

For a long moment Pitt stared at Sandecker. Then finally
he said, 'I don't want the fear of losing a friend on my mind.'

Sandecker knew there was no moving his Special Projects
Director. Slowly he took Pitt's hand in both of his. 'What
would you like waiting for you when you get back?'

Pitt gave the admiral a warm smile. 'A crab louis salad
and a tequila on the rocks.' Then he turned and climbed
through the DSMV's hatch and sealed it.

The C-5 had been specially modified for aerial drops. In the
cockpit the co-pilot pulled a red handle on his side of the
instrument panel, activating the electric motors that swung
open a large section of the cargo deck.

Sandecker and two crew members stood in front of the
DSMV, their bodies harnessed to safety straps that clipped
to tie-down rings. They leaned forward against the wind
that swept through the massive opening, their eyes drawn to
Pitt seated in *Big Ben*'s control cabin.

'Sixty seconds to drop zone,' the pilot's voice came over
the headsets clamped on their heads. 'Surface wind holding
at five knots. Skies clear with a three-quarter moon. Sea
maintaining a slight chop with four-foot swells. No surface
ships showing on radar.'

'Conditions acceptable,' Sandecker confirmed.

From his position in front of the DSMV, all Sandecker

could see was a yawning black hole in the cargo deck. A thousand metres below, the sea was sprinkled in silver from the moon. He would have preferred a daylight drop with no wind and a flat sea, but he felt lucky there was no typhoon.

'Twenty seconds and counting.' The pilot began the countdown.

Pitt gave a brief wave through the transparent bow of the great vehicle. If he was concerned, no trace of it showed on his face. Giordino still beat on the door of the toilet in a rage of frustration, but the sounds were drowned by the wind howling through the cargo bay.

'Five, four, three, two, one, drop!'

The forward ends of the big rails were raised suddenly by hydraulic pumps, and *Big Ben* slid backward and through the opening into the darkness in a movement lasting only three seconds. Sandecker and the crewmen were temporarily stunned at seeing the thirty-ton behemoth disappear so smoothly out of sight. They cautiously moved to the edge of the deck and gazed behind and below.

The great mass of the DSMV could just be seen in the moonlight, hurtling toward the sea like a meteor from space.

67

The multiple chute system automatically derigged, the night air tugged fiercely as three huge canopies streamed into the dark sky. Then they filled and burst open, and the monster vehicle slowed its express-train descent and began drifting at greatly reduced speed towards the waves.

Pitt looked up at the reassuring spectacle and began to breathe more easily. First hurdle behind, he thought. Now all the DSMV had to do was strike the sea on an even keel and fall through 320 metres of water without mishap before landing on the seafloor in one piece, right side up. This part of the operation, he reflected, was entirely beyond his control. He could do nothing but sit back and enjoy the ride with a small degree of trepidation.

He looked upward and easily distinguished the C-5 Galaxy under the light from the moon as it slowly circled the DSMV. He wondered if Sandecker had released Giordino from the toilet. He could well imagine his friend turning the air blue with choice expletives.

God, how long ago was it when he and the NUMA team set up housekeeping in Soggy Acres? Three months, four? It seemed an eternity. And yet the disaster that destroyed the deep-sea station seemed like yesterday.

He stared up at the parachutes again and wondered if they would provide the necessary drag through water as they did in air.

The engineers who dreamed up this insane mission must have thought so. But they were thousands of miles from where Pitt was sitting, and all they relied on were a lot of formulas and physical laws governing the fall of heavy objects. There were no experiments with models or a full-scale test drop. It was win in one quick gamble or lose at Pitt's expense if they miscalculated.

Judging distance above water is extremely difficult by day and almost impossible at night, but Pitt caught the moonlit sparkle of spray tossed from the wave crests by the light breeze. Impact was less than fifteen seconds away, he judged. He reclined his seat and settled into the extra padding some thoughtful soul had provided. He gave a final wave at the circling aircraft, stupidly he realized. They were too far away to make him out in the darkness; the pilot was maintaining a safe distance to keep Pitt's canopies free of turbulence from the plane.

The sudden jarring impact was followed by a great splash as the DSMV struck in the trough between two swells. The vehicle carved a sizeable crater in the sea, throwing up a circular wall of water in a blazing display of phosphorescence. Then it sank out of view and the sea closed over *Big Ben* as if healing a giant pockmark.

The blow was not as bad as Pitt had expected. He and *Big Ben* had survived the parachute drop without a bruise or a fracture. He returned his seat to the upright position and immediately began a check of all his power systems, considerably happy to see green lights sweep across the instrument console while the computer monitor reported no malfunctions. Next he switched on the exterior lights and swivelled them upward. Two of the parachutes had remained flared, but the third was twisted and tangled in its own shroud lines.

Pitt quickly turned his attention to the computer screen as he punched the appropriate keys to monitor his descent. The numbers travelled across the screen and flashed a warning. The DSMV was dropping into the black void at sixty-one metres per minute. The maximum descent speed had been calculated at forty-two. *Big Ben* was falling nineteen metres a minute too fast.

'Too busy to talk?' Sandecker's voice came slurred through Pitt's earphones.

'I have a small problem,' Pitt replied.

'The parachutes?' Sandecker asked, fearful of the answer.

'One of the chutes tangled and I've lost drag.'

'What's your descent speed?'

'Sixty-one.'

'Not good.'

'Tell me about it.'

'The event was considered. Your landing site was selected because the geology is flat and layered with soft sediment. Despite your excessive rate of descent, impact will be less than what you encountered on the water surface.'

'I'm not worried about impact,' Pitt said, warily eyeballing the TV monitor whose camera was aimed below the rapidly sinking DSMV. 'But I am worried about a thirty-ton machine burying itself in ten metres of ooze. Without a scoop *Big Ben* can't dig its way out of the muck like *Big John*.'

'We'll get you out,' Sandecker promised.

'And what of the operation?'

Sandecker's voice dropped off so low that Pitt could hardly hear him. 'We close the play –'

'Hold on!' Pitt snapped abruptly. 'The bottom has come into viewing range.'

The ugly brown of the seabed rose up out of the blackness. He watched apprehensively as the desolate terrain burst up toward the camera. The DSMV struck and sank into the silt like a fist into a sponge cake. A huge cloud billowed into the cold black water and curtained off all visibility.

On board the aircraft, as if triggered by a mutual fear, the eyes of Giordino and Sandecker lifted and met across the top of the communications equipment. Their faces were taut and grim as they waited for Pitt's next voice contact.

All anger had vanished from Giordino after he was released from his latrine prison. Now there was only intense concern as he waited for news of his friend's fate in the depths of the sea.

Far below, Pitt could not immediately tell if the DSMV had buried itself under the seabed. His only sensation was of being pressed into his chair by a firm weight. All vision was gone. The cameras and exterior lights only recorded brownish ooze. He had no way of knowing whether the control cabin was covered by a thin coating of silt or entombed by five metres of quicksand-like muck.

Fortunately the parachute canopies were caught in a three-knot current and drifted off to the side of the DSMV. Pitt pulled a switch releasing the hooks attached to the chutes' thick lines.

He engaged nuclear power systems and shifted *Big Ben* into 'forward'. He could feel the vibration as the great tractor belts dug their cleats into the silt and began to turn. For close to a full minute nothing happened. The belts seemed to spin on their gear wheels with no indication of forward traction.

Then *Big Ben* lurched to starboard. Pitt adjusted the controls and turned the DSMV back to port. He could feel it edge ahead slightly. He repeated the process, careening the great vehicle back and forth until centimetre by centimetre it began to gain headway, picking up momentum and increasing its forward movement.

Suddenly it broke the suction and lunged up and ahead, travelling over fifty metres before breaking out of the silt cloud into clear visibility.

Long seconds passed and a vague feeling of triumph began to seep into Pitt's body. He sat there quietly relaxed, allowing the DSMV to travel across the seafloor under its own control. He switched on the automatic drive and set a computerized navigational course to the west, then waited a few moments to be certain the DSMV was operating smoothly. Thankfully, *Big Ben* soon reached its maximum speed and was rolling over the barren underwater plain as effortlessly as if it were ploughing under a cornfield in Iowa.

Only then did Pitt contact Sandecker and Giordino and report that he was on his way toward *Dennings' Demons*.

68

It was mid-morning in Washington when Jordan took the message from Sandecker, ten time zones to the west. The President had returned to his bedroom in the upstairs White House for a shower and a change of clothes. He was standing in front of a mirror knotting his tie when the call came from the Situation Room.

'Sorry to interrupt you, Mr President,' said Jordan respectfully, 'but I thought you'd like to know the drop was successful. Pitt and the Deep Sea Mining Vehicle are in motion.'

'Nice to start the day with some good news for a change. How soon before they reach the bomber?'

'An hour, less if the seafloor is flat and doesn't hold any geological surprises.'

'And detonation?'

'Two hours to remove the bomb and another three to reach the explosion site, set the detonators, and give the DSMV enough time to get safely out of the area.'

'There were no problems?' asked the President.

'Admiral Sandecker reported the fall through water was a bit hairy for a while, but the DSMV survived the impact in good shape. The only other hitch, if you want to call it that, is Pitt somehow arranged to leave Giordino behind and is conducting the operation on his own.'

The President was secretly pleased. 'That doesn't surprise me. He's the kind of man who would sacrifice himself before endangering a friend. Any late developments on the bomb cars?'

'The task force engaged in the search have turned up twenty-seven.'

'Yoshishu and Tsuboi must know we're breathing down their necks. If they had the code to explode the bombs, we'd have heard from them.'

'We'll know shortly if we've won the race or not,' Jordan said soberly.

The President's special assistant, Dale Nichols, rushed up to the President as he stepped out of the elevator. The President immediately recognized a look of urgency on Nichols's face.

'You look like you're standing barefoot on an anthill, Dale. What's going down?'

'You'd better step into the communications lounge, Mr President. Ichiro Tsuboi has somehow entered our safe system and opened up communications on the video entry.'

'Is he on view now?'

'Not yet. He's on hold, demanding he talk only to you.'

'Alert the Situation Room so they can tune in the conversation.'

The President entered a room down the hall from the Oval Office and sat in a leather chair on one end of a small stage backed by a giant rectangular opening in the far wall. He pressed a button on a console in the armrest and waited. Suddenly time and space melted into one place, one moment, as a life-sized three-dimensional image of Ichiro Tsuboi materialized on the other side of the stage.

Thanks to the magic technology of photonics – fibre optic transmission – and computer wizardry, the two men could sit and converse as though they were in the same room. The detail was so incredible that Tsuboi's image appeared sharply defined and solid without the faintest indication of fuzzy transparency.

Tsuboi was kneeling stiffly on his knees on a bamboo mat, his hands loosely clenched and resting on his thighs. He was dressed in an expensive business suit but wore no shoes. He bowed slightly as the President's image appeared on his end of the transmission.

'You wish to establish dialogue, Mr Tsuboi?' said the President for openers.

'That is correct,' replied Tsuboi, rudely refusing to address the President by title.

The President decided to shoot from the hip. 'Well, you certainly got my attention with that nuclear blast in Wyoming. Was that supposed to constitute a message?'

The impact of the President's words was heightened by his seeming indifference. The consummate politician, the President was a shrewd judge of human character. He quickly detected a perceptible tenseness in Tsuboi's eyes and deduced the Japanese was not dealing from a solid power base.

The international financial wizard and heir apparent to Suma's underworld and industrial empire tried to appear calm and in control, but the President's prior silence on the explosion had produced an unsettling effect. He and Yoshishu could not understand why the chief executive had virtually ignored it.

'We can save many words, Mr President,' said Tsuboi. 'You know of our technical advances and superiority in defensive technology, and by now Senator Diaz, Congresswoman Smith, and your intelligence people have provided you with information on our facility on Soseki Island.'

'I'm quite aware of your Dragon Centre and the Kaiten Project,' the President countered, mindful that Tsuboi failed to mention Hideki Suma. 'And if you believe I won't order massive retaliation should you insanely detonate any more of your bomb cars, you're sadly mistaken.'

'Our original intent was not to kill millions of people,' Tsuboi insisted.

'I know what you intended, Mr Tsuboi. Try it and Armageddon is yours.'

'If you wish to go down in history as the greatest monster since Adolf Hitler for a totally irrational act, then there is little more to say.'

532

'You must have wanted to say something, or why else did you contact me?'

Tsuboi paused, then pressed on. 'I have certain proposals to throw on the table.'

'I'm willing to hear them.'

'You will call off your search for the cars. If any more are seized, the signals will be sent to detonate. And since you once dropped such a weapon on my people, I assure you I will not hesitate to explode the remaining bombs in populated cities.'

The President fought hard to suppress his growing anger. 'A standoff then. You kill a few million of us, we decimate your entire population.'

'No, you won't do that. The people of the great White Christian American nation will not condone such butchery.'

'We're not all white or Christian.'

'The minorities that undermine your culture will never back your stand.'

'They're still Americans.'

'Nevertheless, my people are committed and prepared to die for the new empire.'

'That's a damned lie,' the President shot back. 'Until now, you and Suma and the rest of your gangland mob have operated in secret. The Japanese people have no idea you've placed their lives on the line for world economic dominance. They won't risk the devastation of their nation for a cause based on greed by a few criminals. You don't speak for them or your government.'

The barest trace of a smile crossed Tsuboi's face, and the President knew he had been sucked in. 'You can avoid this horrible holocaust on both our countries by simply accepting my proposals.'

'You mean demands.'

'As you wish.'

'State your case,' said the President, his voice beginning to sound strained. He'd lost his edge and was angry with himself.

'There will be no nationalization or takeover of Japanese-owned companies, nor judicial interference with any of our projected corporate or real estate buy-outs.'

'That's no big deal. Nationalization has never been in the interests of the United States. No legislation has ever been considered on such an unconstitutional premise in our two hundred years. As to the latter, no Japanese firm that I know of has been barred by law from purchasing a business or land in the United States.'

'Japanese citizens will not be required to present visas when entering the United States.'

'You'll have to battle Congress on that one.'

Tsuboi coldly continued. 'No trade barriers or increased tariffs on Japanese products.'

'What about your end?'

'Not negotiable,' said Tsuboi, obviously prepared for the question. 'There are sound reasons why many of your products are not welcome in Japan.'

'Go on,' ordered the President.

'The State of Hawaii becomes a territory of Japan.'

The President had been forewarned of that unreasonable demand. 'The good people of the island are already madder than hell over what you've done to their real estate prices. I doubt if they'd be willing to exchange the Stars and Stripes for the rising sun.'

'Also the State of California.'

'Impossible and outrageous are words that come to mind,' the President said cynically. 'Why stop now? What else do you want?'

'Since our money keeps your treasury afloat, we expect representation in your government, which includes a seat on your cabinet and our people highly placed in your State, Treasury, and Commerce departments.'

'Who makes the selection of your people, you and Yoshishu or the leaders of your government?'

'Mr Yoshishu and myself.'

The President was aghast. It was like inviting organized crime to participate in government at the highest levels. 'What you ask, Mr Tsuboi, is absolutely unthinkable. The American people will never allow themselves to become economic slaves to foreign nationals.'

'They'll pay a heavy price if you ignore my terms. On the other hand, if we have a say in the operation of the American government and business community, your whole economy will turn around drastically and provide a higher standard of living for your citizens.'

The President's teeth clenched. 'With a monopoly, prices and profits on Japanese products would skyrocket.'

'You'd also have lower unemployment, and the national debt would diminish,' Tsuboi went on as if the President was impotent.

'I don't have it in my power to make promises that Congress won't keep,' said the President, his anger stilled, his mind jockeying for an upper hand. He lowered his eyes to appear perplexed. 'You know your way around Washington, Mr Tsuboi. You have an understanding of how our government works.'

'I am quite aware of your executive limits. But there is much you can do without congressional approval.'

'You must excuse me for a few moments while I digest the enormity of your demands.' The President paused to gather his thoughts. He could not lie and pretend to cave in to all of Tsuboi's ridiculous demands. That would indicate an obvious ploy, a stall for time. He had to put up a brusque front and appear agitated. He looked up and stared directly at Tsuboi. 'I cannot in good conscience accept what has to be unconditional terms of surrender.'

'They are better terms than you offered us in nineteen forty-five.'

'Our occupation was far more generous and benevolent than your people had any right to expect,' the President said, his nails digging into the armrests of his chair.

'I am not here to discuss historic differences,' Tsuboi stated bluntly. 'You've heard the terms and know the consequences. Indecision or procrastination on your part will not delay tragedy.'

There was no sign of a bluff in Tsuboi's eyes. The President well realized the threat was made more horrible by the cars hidden in heavily populated cities and the suicidal maniacs waiting for the signal to set off the bombs.

'Your extortion demands don't leave much room for negotiation.'

'None whatsoever,' Tsuboi replied in a tone that defied debate.

'I can't just snap my fingers and produce a miracle of cooperation with the political opposition,' said the President, feigning exasperation. 'You damned well know I can't dictate to Congress. Senator Diaz and Congress-woman Smith carry heavy weight in both houses, and they're already inflaming their fellow legislators against you.'

Tsuboi shrugged indifferently. 'I fully realize the wheels of your government grind in a swamp of emotions, Mr President. And your elected representatives vote along party lines, irrespective of the national good. But they will be persuaded to accept the inevitable once you inform them that two of the bomb cars are being driven around Washington as we talk.'

Not good. The ball was back on the President's side of the court. He made a monumental effort to remain impassive and show strains of anger. 'I'll need time.'

'You have until three o'clock this afternoon, your time, to appear on national television with your advisers and the leaders of Congress standing behind you in a show of support as you announce the new cooperation agreements between Japan and the United States.'

'You're asking too much.'

'That is the way it must be,' said Tsuboi. 'And one more

thing, Mr President. Any indication of an attack on Soseki Island will be answered with the bomb cars. Do I make myself clear?'

'As crystal.'

'Then, good morning. I shall look forward to watching you on television this afternoon.'

Tsuboi's image swiftly dissolved and vanished.

The President looked up at a clock on one wall. Nine o'clock. Only six hours remained. The same time sequence Jordan projected for Pitt to set off the old atomic bomb and launch the submarine quake and tsunami.

'Oh, God,' he whispered to the empty room. 'What if it all goes wrong?'

69

Big Ben moved across the vast seascape at fifteen kilometres an hour, almost lightning speed for an immense vehicle travelling underwater through the abyssal mud. A great cloud of fine silt swirled in its wake, blossoming into the yawning blackness before dissipating and slowly settling back to the bottom.

Pitt studied a viewing screen connected to a laser-sonar unit that probed the seafloor ahead and enhanced it into three dimensions. The submarine desert held few surprises, and except for a detour around a narrow but deep rift, he was able to make good time.

Precisely forty-seven minutes after he detached the parachutes and set *Big Ben* in motion, the hard outline of the B-29 appeared and grew until it filled the monitor. The coordinates from the Pyramider satellite that were programmed into the DSMV's navigation computer had put him right on the target.

Pitt was close enough now to see the wreckage creeping under the far edges of the exterior lights. He slowed *Big Ben* and circled the bleak and broken aircraft. It looked like a cast-off toy on the bottom of a backyard pond. Pitt stared at it with the rapture experienced by divers the first time they approach a manmade object in the sea. To be the first to see or touch a sunken automobile, a missing plane, or a lost shipwreck is a fearful yet melancholy experience, only shared by those who daringly walk through a haunted house after midnight.

Dennings' Demons had sunk a little over a metre in the silt. One engine was missing and the starboard wing was twisted backward and up like a grotesque arm reaching for the surface. The blades of the remaining three propellers had folded back from the impact with the water like drooping petals on a dying flower.

The three-storey-high tail section showed the effects of shell fire. It had broken away and lay several metres behind the main fuselage and slightly off to one side. The tail gunner's section was shattered and riddled, the rusting barrels of the 20-millimetre cannons dipped into the mud.

The aluminium surfaces of the 30-metre-long tubular fuselage were covered with slime and encrustations, but the framed glass windows encircling the bow were still clear. And the little demon painted under the pilot's side window was surprisingly clean and free of scale and growth. Pitt could have sworn the beady little eyes stared back at him and the lips pulled back in a satanic grin.

He knew better than to let his imagination run wild and envision skeletons of the crew still at their stations, skulls with jaws dropped in deathly silence, eye sockets empty and unseeing. Pitt had spent enough time under the sea swimming through sunken vessels to know the soft organic substances of the human body were the first to go, quickly consumed by bottom-dwelling sea creatures. Then the bones, eventually dissolving in the icy cold of saltwater. Strange as it seems, clothing would be the last to disintegrate, especially leather flight jackets and boots. In time, even those would disappear, as well as the entire aircraft.

'I have visual on the target,' he announced to Sandecker in the C-5, flying overhead in the night.

'What is the condition?' Sandecker's disembodied voice came back quickly.

'One wing is heavily damaged. The tail is broken off, but the main fuselage is intact.'

'The bomb is in the forward bomb bay. You'll have to position *Big Ben* at an angle where the leading edge of the wing joins the fuselage. Then make your cut across the aircraft's roof.'

'Luck was a lady tonight,' said Pitt. 'The starboard wing is torn back, offering easy access. I can move into perfect position to slice the bulkheads from the side.'

Pitt manoeuvred the DSMV until its manipulator arms reached over the forward bomb bay of the aircraft. He inserted his hand into a glovelike actuator that electronically controlled the mechanical arms and selected a multidirectional metal-cutting wheel from one of three tools coupled to the wrist of the left manipulator. Operating the system as if it was an extension of his hand and arm, he laid out and measured the cut on a monitor that projected interior cutaway views of the aircraft's structural components. He could perform the difficult operations by observing it on video from several close-up angles instead of relying on direct sight through the transparent bow. He positioned the wheel against the aluminium skin of the plane and programmed the dimensions and the depth of the cut into the computer. Then he switched on the tool and watched it attack the body of *Dennings' Demons* as precisely as a surgeon's scalpel.

The fine teeth of the whirling disc sliced through the aged aluminium of the airframe with the ease of a razor blade through a balsa-wood model glider. There were no sparks, no heated glow from friction. The metal was too soft and the water too icy. Support struts and bundled wiring cables were also efficiently severed. When the cut was finally completed fifty minutes later, Pitt extended the opposite manipulator. The wrist on this one was fitted with a large gripper assembly sprouting pincerlike fingers.

The gripper bit through the aluminium skin and into a structural bulkhead, the pincers closed, and the arm slowly raised up and back, ripping away a great piece of the aircraft's side and the roof. Pitt carefully swung the manipulator on a ninety-degree angle and very slowly lowered the torn wreckage into the silt without raising a blinding cloud of silt.

Now he had an opening measuring three by four metres. The Fat Man-type bomb, code-named Mother's Breath, was clearly visible from the side, hanging securely and eerily from a large shackle and adjustable sway braces.

Pitt still had to carve his way through sections of the crawl tunnel that travelled above the bomb bay, connecting the cockpit with the waist-gunner compartment. Part of it had already been partially removed, as were the bomb-bay catwalks, so the immense bomb could be squeezed inside the bowels of the plane. He also had to cut away the guide rails that were installed to ensure the bomb's fin didn't snag during the drop.

Again the operation went smoothly. The remaining barriers were soon dropping in a pile on top of the wreckage already sliced away. The next part of the bomb's removal was the trickiest.

Mother's Breath seemed festered with death and destruction. Nine feet in length and five feet in diameter, the dimensions given when it was built, it looked like a big fat ugly egg dyed in rust with boxed fins on one end and a zipper around its middle.

'Okay, I'm going for the bomb,' Pitt reported to Sandecker.

'You'll have to use both manipulators to remove and transport it,' said Sandecker. 'She weighed close to five tons by the old weight measurement.'

'I need one arm to cut away the shackle and sway braces.'

'The stress is too great for one manipulator. It can't support the bomb without damage.'

'I'm aware of that, but I have to wait until after I sever the shackle before I can replace the cutting disc with a gripper. Only then do I dare attempt the lift.'

'Hold on,' Sandecker ordered. 'I'll check, and be right back to you.'

While he waited, Pitt put the cutting tool in place and clamped the gripper on the lifting eye beneath the shackle.

'Dirk?'

'Come in, Admiral.'

'Let the bomb drop.'

'Say again.'

'Cut through the shackle cables and let the bomb fall free. Mother's Breath is an implosion-type bomb and could survive a hard shock.'

All Pitt saw as he stared at the horrific monstrosity dangling only a few metres away was the erupting fireball repeated constantly in documentary films.

'Are you there?' Sandecker inquired, the nervousness detectable in his voice.

'Is that a fact or a rumour?' Pitt came back.

'Historical fact.'

'If you hear a big underwater boom, you'll know you spoiled my day.'

Pitt took a long breath, exhaled, unconsciously closed his eyes, and directed the cutting disc to slash the shackle cables. Half rusted through after nearly fifty years beneath the sea, the strands quickly parted under the onslaught of the disc's teeth, and the great bomb fell onto the closed bomb-bay doors, the only explosion coming from the silt that had seeped in and accumulated.

For an eerie, lonely minute Pitt sat there numb, almost feeling the silence as he waited for the sediment to fade and the bomb to reappear.

'I didn't hear a boom,' Sandecker notified him with infuriating calm.

'You will, Admiral,' Pitt said, catching up and corralling rational thought, 'you will.'

70

Hope was hanging in and rising. Slightly less than two hours to go, and *Big Ben* was barrelling over the seabed with Mother's Breath securely gripped in the pincers of its manipulators. Like the final minutes of a ball game when the outcome and score are still in doubt, the tension inside the C-5 Galaxy and in the White House was becoming heavier as the operation approached its peak.

'He's eighteen minutes ahead of schedule,' said Giordino softly, 'and looking good.'

' "Like one that on a lonesome road doth walk in fear and dread," ' Sandecker quoted absently.

Giordino looked up quizzically. 'What was that, Admiral?'

'Coleridge.' Sandecker smiled apologetically. ' "The Ancient Mariner". I was thinking of Pitt down there, alone in the deep with millions of lives riding on his shoulders, centimetres away from instant cremation —'

'I should have been with him,' Giordino said bitterly.

'We all know you'd have locked *him* up if only you'd thought of it first.'

'True.' Giordino shrugged. 'But I didn't. And now he's staring at death while I sit here like a store-window dummy.'

Sandecker gazed at the chart and the red line showing Pitt's course across the seafloor to the B-29, and from there to the detonation site. 'He'll do it and come out alive,' he murmured. 'Dirk is not the kind of man to die easily.'

Masuji Koyama, Suma's expert technician in defence detection, stood behind the operator of a surveillance radar display and pointed out a target to Yoshishu, Tsuboi, and Takeda Kurojima, who were grouped around him.

'A very large American Air Force transport,' he explained. 'Computer enhancement shows it as a C-Five Galaxy, capable of carrying an extremely heavy payload for great distances.'

'You say it is acting most strangely?' said Yoshishu.

Koyama nodded. 'It approached from the south-east along a course towards the American Air Force Base at Shimodate, an air traffic corridor used by their military aircraft that passes within seventy to a hundred kilometres of our island. While tracking it, we observed an object detach itself and fall into the ocean.'

'It dropped from the aircraft?'

'Yes.'

'Could you identify it?' asked Tsuboi.

Koyama shook his head. 'All I can tell you is it appeared to fall slowly, as if attached to a parachute.'

'An underwater sensing device perhaps?' mused Kurojima, the Dragon Centre's chief director.

'A possibility, although it looked too large for a sonic sensor.'

'Most odd,' mused Yoshishu.

'Since then,' Koyama continued, 'the aircraft has remained over the area in a circular holding pattern.'

Tsuboi looked at him. 'How long?'

'Almost four hours.'

'Have you intercepted voice transmissions?'

'A few brief signals, but they were electronically garbled.'

'Spotter plane!' Koyama snapped as if seeing a revelation.

'What,' inquired Yoshishu, 'is a spotter plane?'

'An aircraft with sophisticated detection and communications equipment,' Koyama explained. 'They're used as flying command centres to coordinate military assaults.'

'The President is a vicious liar!' Tsuboi hissed suddenly. 'He laid a smokescreen and falsified his position to stall for time. It is clear now, he intends to launch a manned attack on the island.'

544

'But why be so obvious?' Yoshishu said quietly. 'The American intelligence knows well our capacity to detect and observe targets of interest at that range.'

Koyama stared at the reflection of the plane on the radar display. 'Could be a mission to electronically probe our defences.'

Tsuboi's face was hard in anger. 'I will open communications with the President and demand he remove it from our waters.'

'No, I have a better plan.' Yoshishu's lips parted in a bleak, wintry smile. 'A message the President will understand.'

'Your plan, Korori?' Tsuboi inquired respectfully.

'Quite simple,' answered Yoshishu with emotionless candour. 'We destroy it.'

Within six minutes, two Toshiba infrared surface-to-air missiles spewed from their launchers and homed in on the unsuspecting crew of the C-5. The defenceless, frighteningly vulnerable aircraft did not carry attack warning systems. It went about its business of monitoring *Big Ben*'s progress, circling the sea in blissful ignorance of the destructive terror streaking toward its great bulk.

Sandecker had stepped into the communications compartment to send a status report to the White House while Giordino remained in their office. Giordino stood hunched over the desk studying the marine geologist's report on the undersea trench Pitt had to cross to reach the safety of the Japanese coast. He was plotting the distance for perhaps the fifth time when the first missile struck the aircraft and burst with a great roar. The shock and pressure wave knocked Giordino to the deck. Stunned, he had barely hoisted himself to his elbows when the second missile smashed into the lower cargo hold and tore a huge gaping hole in the belly of the fuselage.

The end should have been swift, spectacular, but the first

missile did not explode on immediate contact. It passed through the upper waist of the aircraft between bulkheads and shot across the cargo bay, bursting as it penetrated the airframe ribs on the opposite wall. The major force of the explosion was thrust into the night air outside, saving the aircraft from tearing apart.

Even as he fought off the shock, Giordino thought, She must go down now. She can't stay in the air. But he was wrong on both counts. The big Galaxy was not about to die easy. She was miraculously free from flames, and only one of her flight control systems was damaged. Despite her gaping wounds, she remained solidly in the air.

The pilot had put the crippled aircraft into a shallow dive before levelling out less than thirty metres above the sea on a southern course away from Soseki Island. The engines were running normal, and except for the vibration and restraining drag from the holes in the fuselage, the pilot's primary concern was the loss of the elevator control.

Sandecker came aft, accompanied by the flight engineer, to assess the damage. They found Giordino picking his way gingerly on his hands and knees across the cargo bay. Clutching a bulkhead support for dear life, he cast a jaundiced eye out the gaping opening at the sea that swept past like quicksilver.

'I'll be damned if I'll jump,' he shouted over the roar of the chaotic wind that pounded through the aircraft.

'I don't fancy it either,' Sandecker shouted back.

The flight engineer stared in frightened awe at the damage. 'What in hell happened?'

'We took a pair of hits from ground-to-air missiles,' Giordino yelled at him.

Giordino motioned to Sandecker and pointed forward to get out of the wind blast. They made their way to the cockpit while the flight engineer began a damage inspection of the shattered lower belly. They found the pilots calmly struggling with the controls, quietly conversing as though they were conducting a textbook emergency in a flight simulator.

Giordino sank wearily to the floor, thankful to still be alive. 'I can't believe this big bird is still flying,' he mumbled gladly. 'Remind me to kiss the designers.'

Sandecker leaned over the console between the pilots and gave a brief accounting of the damage. Then he asked, 'What's our chances?'

'We've still got electrical and some hydraulic power and enough control to manoeuvre,' answered the chief pilot, Major Marcus Turner, a big ruddy-featured Texan, usually cheerful and humorous but now tense and grim. 'But the blast must have cut the lines running from the main fuel tank. The needles on the gauges have made a drastic drop in only two minutes.'

'Can you stay on station beyond the range of the missiles?'

'Negative.'

'I can make that an order from the chief executive,' said Sandecker gruffly.

Turner did not look happy, nor did he cave in. 'No disrespect, Admiral, but this aircraft may come apart at the seams any second. If you have a death wish, that's your business. My duty is to save my crew and my aircraft. As a professional Navy man, you know what I'm talking about.'

'I sympathize, but my order stands.'

'If she'll stick together and we nurse the fuel,' said Turner unperturbed, 'we might make it to Naha Airfield on Okinawa. That's the nearest long runway that isn't in Japan proper.'

'Okinawa's out,' Sandecker announced curtly. 'We get clear of the island's defence systems and we stay within communication range with my man on the bottom. This operation is too vital to national security to abandon. Keep us in the air as long as you can. If worse comes to worse, ditch her in the sea.'

Turner's face was red, and perspiration was beginning to drip from it, but he managed a taut smile. 'All right, Admiral, but you'd better plan on a long swim to the nearest land.'

Then, as if to add insult to injury, Sandecker felt a hand on his shoulder. He turned quickly. It was the communications operator. He looked at Sandecker and shook his head in a helpless gesture that signalled bad news.

'I'm sorry, Admiral, but the radio's knocked out. We can't transmit or receive.'

'That tears it,' said Turner. 'We can't accomplish anything by flying around with a dead radio.'

Sandecker gazed at Giordino, sorrow and anguish showing clearly in every deeply etched line in the admiral's face. 'Dirk won't know. He'll think he's been abandoned.'

Giordino looked impassively through the windscreen to a point somewhere between black sea and black sky. He felt sick at heart. This was the second time in the past few weeks he felt he had failed his closest friend. At last he looked up, and strangely he was smiling.

'Dirk doesn't need us. If anyone can damn well explode that bomb and park *Big Ben* on the shore, he will.'

'My money is on him too,' Sandecker said with total conviction.

'Okinawa?' Turner asked, his hand tightly gripping the controls.

Very slowly, with much difficulty, as if he were fighting the devil for his soul, Sandecker looked at Turner and nodded. 'Okinawa.'

The big aircraft banked on a new course and limped into the darkness. A few minutes later the sound of its engines faded, leaving behind a silent sea, empty but for one man.

71

With the bomb hanging grotesquely from its manipulators, *Big Ben* sat poised on the edge of the great submarine trench that yawned ten kilometres wide and two deep. Inside, Pitt stared grimly down the slope that trailed off into the gloom.

The geophysicists had selected a point about twelve hundred metres below the rim of the trench wall as the optimum location for the blast to set off a landslide that would in turn launch the seismic sea wave. But the grade was a good five percent steeper than the satellite photos had suggested. And worse, much worse, the upper layer of sediment that formed the sides of the trench was the consistency of oily clay.

Pitt had activated a telescoping probe into the silt and was far from overjoyed at the geological test results that read across the computer screen. He realized the danger of his position. It would be a battle to prevent the heavy vehicle from slithering through the slick muck all the way to the bottom of the trench.

And once he was committed and plunged *Big Ben* over the edge, there was no turning back. The cleats on the drive tracks could never gain a grip solid enough to pull the DSMV back up the slope and over the ridge to safety before the explosion. After priming the bomb, he decided to continue on a diagonal course downward along the side of the slope, much like a skier traversing a snow-packed hill. His only chance, and a slightly less than non-existent one, was to use gravity to increase his speed and push *Big Ben* beyond the clutches of the avalanche before they were both caught up in its force, swept away, and buried for the next ten million years.

Pitt appreciated how narrow the fine dividing line was between survival and death. He thought wryly that Murphy's Law never took a holiday. He missed not having Giordino at his side and wondered why all communications had ceased from the C-5 Galaxy. There had to be a good reason. Giordino and Sandecker would never desert him without cause. It was too late now for explanations and too early for final farewells.

It was eerie and lonely with no human voice to prop up his morale. He felt the fatigue sweeping over him in great woolly waves. He slumped in his seat, any optimism drained away. He examined the coordinates for the detonation site and peered at his watch for the last time.

Then he took manual control of *Big Ben*, engaged the forward drive, and plunged the huge tractor vehicle down the steep slope.

The momentum rapidly increased after the first hundred metres, and Pitt began to doubt he could stop DSMV before it barrelled to the bottom of the trench. He quickly discovered that braking the treads failed to check his speed. Friction did not exist between the cleats and the slick mud. The great mechanical beast began to slide over the slick surface like a runaway truck and semitrailer hurtling down a steep road grade.

The rotund bomb swung wildly in the grip of the manipulators. Because it hung directly in front of his forward view, Pitt could not avoid glancing at the evil thing without conceding it in his mind's eye as the instrument of his own impending death.

Suddenly another terrifying thought mushroomed in his mind. If it broke free and rolled down the slope, he might never be able to retrieve it. He stiffened in desperate fear, not of death, but that he might falter in the home stretch.

Pitt moved quickly now, uncaring that he had taken a risk no sane man would ever have contemplated. He slipped the drive into reverse and applied extra power. The cleats wildly thrashed through the slippery ooze backward, and *Big Ben* sluggishly slowed to a crawl.

A wall of silt engulfed the vehicle as he brought it to a full stop. He waited patiently for visibility to return before easing forward for fifty metres, then engaging reverse and drawing the DSMV to a halt again. He continued this series of manoeuvres until he regained firm control and had a feel for the interaction between the drive track and the mire.

His movements at the controls became hurried now. Each passing minute increased his desperation. At last, after nearly thirty minutes of intense effort to move the big DSMV where he directed it, the navigational computer signalled that he had reached his destination. Thankfully, he found a small level shelf protruding from the slope. He disengaged the power systems and parked.

'I have arrived at the detonation site and will begin to arm the bomb,' he announced through his communications phone in the forlorn hope Sandecker and Giordino might still be listening in somewhere above.

Pitt lost little time in lowering the manipulator arms and setting the bomb in the soft sediment. He released the grippers and interchanged the pincers for working tools. Once more he inserted his hand into the manipulator control and very carefully used a sheet-metal shear to cut away the panel on the tapered tail assembly that covered the main fusing compartment.

The housing inside contained four radar units and a barometric pressure switch. If the bomb had been dropped as planned, the radar units would have bounced their signals off the approaching ground target. Then, at a predetermined altitude, an agreed reading by two units would send the firing signal to the fusing system mounted on the front of the implosion sphere. The second arming system was the barometric switch that was also set to close the firing circuit at a preset altitude.

The firing signal circuits, however, could not be closed

while the plane was in flight. They had to be triggered by clock-operated switches that were not bypassed until the bomb had dropped well clear of the bomb bay. Otherwise *Dennings' Demons* would have gone up in a pre-detonated fireball.

After the panel was removed, Pitt swivelled a miniaturized video camera on the end of the left manipulator. He quickly found the barometric arming switch and focused on it. Constructed of brass, steel, and copper, it showed signs of corrosion but was still intact.

Next, Pitt coupled a slender three-pincer hand to one manipulator. The arm was flexed back toward the front of the DSMV, where the pincers opened the heavy mesh lid of a tool crib and removed a strange ceramic object that looked like a small deflated soccer ball. A copper plate was embedded in the concave bottom, surrounded by a pliable bonding material. The appearance was deceiving. The object was actually a very sophisticated pressurized container filled with an inert puttylike compound composed of plastic and acid. The ceramic cover surrounding the caustic substance had been contoured to fit snugly over the barometric firing switch and form a watertight seal.

Pitt worked the manipulator hand and positioned the container around the switch. Once it was firmly in place, he delicately pulled a tiny plug that allowed the sea to seep very slowly into the container. When the inert compound inside came in contact with saltwater, it chemically turned active and became highly caustic and corrosive. After eating through the copper plate – the thickness governed a delayed sequence of one hour – the acidic compound would then attack the copper in the barometric switch, eventually creating an electrical charge that would set off the firing signal and detonate the bomb.

As Pitt retracted the manipulators and gently backed *Big Ben* away from the hideous monstrosity lying like a fat, slimy bulge in the mud, he stole a quick glance at the digital clock on his instrument console.

He had run a tight race. Mother's Breath would explode forty-eight years late but within a new deadline in another time.

'Any word?' asked the President anxiously from the Oval Office.

'We have an unexplained communications breakdown,' Jordan reported from the Situation Room.

'You've lost Admiral Sandecker?'

'I'm afraid so, Mr President. We've tried every means at our disposal but have been unable to re-establish contact with his aircraft.'

The President felt a numbing fear spread through him. 'What went wrong?'

'We can only guess. The last pass of the Pyramider showed the aircraft had broken off with the Deep Sea Mining Vehicle and was headed on a course towards the island of Okinawa.'

'That doesn't make any sense. Why would Sandecker abort the mission after Pitt had successfully removed the bomb from *Dennings' Demons*?'

'He wouldn't, unless Pitt had a serious accident and was unable to complete the detonation.'

'Then it's over,' the President said heavily.

When Jordan replied, there was the hollow ring of defeat in his voice. 'We won't know the full story until the admiral makes contact again.'

'What is the latest on the search for the bomb cars?'

'The FBI task force has uncovered and neutralized another three, all in major cities.'

'And the human drivers?'

'Every one a diehard follower of Suma and the Gold Dragons, ready and willing to sacrifice their lives. Yet they put up no resistance or made any attempt to detonate the bombs when FBI agents arrested them.'

'Why so docile and accommodating?'

'Their orders were to explode the bombs in their respective vehicles only when they received a coded signal from the Dragon Centre.'

'How many are still out there hidden in our cities?'

There was a tense pause, and then Jordan answered slowly, 'As many as ten.'

'Good God!' The wave of shock was followed by an intolerable fear and disbelief.

'I haven't lost my faith in Pitt,' said Jordan quietly. 'There is no evidence that he failed to prime the firing systems in the bomb.'

A small measure of hope returned to the President's eyes. 'How soon before we know?'

'If Pitt was able to adhere to the timetable, the detonation should occur sometime within the next twelve minutes.'

The President stared at his desktop with an empty expression. When he spoke, it was so softly Jordan could barely make out the words.

'Keep your fingers crossed, Ray, and wish. That's all that's left for us.'

72

As the acid compound reacted on contact with the salt-water, it slowly ate through the timing plate and attacked the barometric pressure switch. The action of the acid on the copper switch soon created an electrical charge that shorted across the contacts and closed the firing circuit.

After waiting nearly five decades, the detonators at thirty-two different points around the core of the bomb then fired and ignited the incredibly complicated detonation phenomenon that resulted in neutrons penetrating sur-rounding plutonium to launch the chain reaction. This was followed by fission bursting in millions upon millions of degrees and kilograms of pressure. The underwater gaseous fireball bloomed and shot upward, breaking the surface of the sea and spearheading a great plume of water that was sprayed into the night air by the shock wave.

Because water is incompressible, it forms an almost perfect medium for transmitting shock waves. Travelling at almost two kilometres a second, the shock front caught and overtook *Big Ben* as the vehicle forged across the trench slope only eight kilometres distant, a good four kilometres short due to the vehicle's agonizingly slow passage through the mud. The pressure wave pounded the huge DSMV like a sledgehammer against a steel drum, but it took the blow with the unyielding toughness of an offensive lineman for the Los Angeles Rams blocking a tackler.

Even then, as the energy shock and raging wall of swirling silt washed over the DSMV, shuttering all visibility, Pitt felt only jubilation. Any fear of failure was swept aside with the explosion. Relying blindly on the sonar probes, he drove through the maelstrom of sediment on a juggernauting course into the unknown. He was running on a long ledge that ran midway down the long slope, but his progress was only a few kilometres faster than it had been on the steeper grades. Adhesion between the tractor belts and the mud was only marginally improved. Any attempt to drive the great mechanical monster in a straight line became impossible. It skidded all over the slope like a truck on an icy road.

Pitt fully realized his life hung by an unravelling thread, and that he was in a losing race to escape the path of the coming landslide. The chance of his being overtaken was a bet no self-respecting bookmaker would turn down. All fear was detached, there was only his stubborn determination to survive.

On the surface, unseen in the darkness, the plume of spray rose to 200 metres and fell back. But deep in the fault zone below the bottom of the trench, the shock waves forced a vertical slippage of the earth's crust. Shock followed shock as the crustal fracture rose and fell and widened, creating a high-magnitude earthquake.

The many layers of sediment laid down for millions of years shifted back and forth, pulling the heavy lava of Soseki Island downward as though it was a rock in quicksand. Cushioned by the soft, yielding sediment, the great mass of the island seemed to be immune to the initial shock waves during the first minutes of the quake. But then it began to sink into the sea, the water rising up the palisade walls.

Soseki Island continued to fall until the underlying layers of silt compressed, and the floating rock mass slowed its descent and gradually settled on a new level. Now the waves no longer crashed against the base of the cliffs, but broke over the jagged edges and lapped into the trees beyond.

Seconds after the explosion and the ensuing seismic blows, an enormous section of the eastern trench wall shuddered and bulged menacingly. Then with a great thundering roar, hundreds of millions of tons of mud slid away and plunged to the bottom of the trench. An incredible pressure wave of energy was generated that rushed toward the surface, forming a mountainous wall of water below the surface.

The indestructible tsunami was born.

Only a metre in height on the open surface of the sea, it quickly accelerated to a speed of 500 kilometres an hour and rolled westward. Irresistible, terrifying in its destructive power; there is no more destructive force on earth. And only twenty kilometres away, the sinking Soseki Island stood directly in its path.

The stage was set for disaster.

The death of the Dragon Centre was imminent.

Tsuboi, Yoshishu, and their people were still in the defence control room tracking the southerly course of the crippled C-5 Galaxy.

'Two missile strikes, and it's still flying,' Yoshishu said in wonder.

'It may crash –' Tsuboi suddenly broke off as he sensed rather than heard the distant rumble as Mother's Breath exploded. 'Do you hear that?' he asked.

'Yes, very faintly, like the faraway sound of thunder,' said Koyama without turning from the radar display. 'Probably from a lightning storm echoing down the ventilators.'

'You feel it too?'

'I feel a slight vibration,' replied Yoshishu.

Kurojima shrugged indifferently. The Japanese are no strangers to earth movement. Every year more than a thousand seismic quakes are recorded on the main islands, and a week never passes when Japan's citizens do not notice the ground tremble. 'An earth tremor. We sit near a seismic fault. We get them all the time. Nothing to worry about. The island is solid rock, and the Dragon Centre was engineered to be earthquake resistant.'

The loose objects in the room rattled faintly as the bomb's dying energy passed through the centre. Then the shock wave from the shift in the subocean fault slammed into the island like a gigantic battering ram. The entire Dragon Centre seemed to shake and sway in all directions. Everyone's face registered surprise, then the surprise gave way to anxiety, then the anxiety to fear.

'This is a bad one,' Tsuboi said nervously.

'We've never felt one this intense,' Kurojima uttered in shock as he pushed his back and outstretched arms against a wall for support.

Yoshishu was standing quite still as if angered by what was happening. 'You must get me out of here,' he demanded.

'We are safer here than in the tunnel,' Koyama shouted above the growing tumult.

Those who were not holding on to something were thrown to the floor as the shock wave tore beneath the lava rock, undulating the deep sediment below. The control centre was jolted more savagely now as the island shifted back and forth during its descent into the mud. Equipment that wasn't bolted down began to topple over.

Tsuboi pushed himself into a corner and stared numbly at Kurojima. 'It feels like we're falling.'

'The island must be settling,' Kurojima cried in fright.

What the horrified men in the Dragon Centre did not know, could not have known, was that the titanic bulk of the tsunami was only two minutes behind the shock waves.

With Pitt on manual drive, *Big Ben* slugged tortuously through the mud, sliding ever closer towards the floor of the trench. The tractor belts constantly lost their hold, sending the DSMV sideways down the grade until their leading edges piled up the silt, dug in, and regained their grip.

Pitt felt like a blind man driving the tractor in a blind world, with only a few dials and gauges and a screen with little coloured words to guide him. He weighed his chances, sizing up the outside situation as it was revealed by the sonar-laser scanner, and came to the conclusion that so long as he was still mired in sediment his only escape was by a miracle. According to the calculations by the geophysicists, he had not travelled nearly far enough to escape the predicted reaches of the landslide.

Everything depended on finding firm ground or rock structure that was stable and would resist tearing away from the wall of the trench. Even then, his toughest hurdle was the trench itself. He was on the wrong side. To reach the safety of the Japanese shore, he would have to drive the great vehicle down into the bottom and up the opposite slope.

He did not see, his scanner could not tell him, that there was no hard ground or shallow slopes for the DSMV to claw its way up to the flat terrain. If anything, the great fracture in the seabed deepened and curved south-east, offering no chance of escape for over eight hundred kilometres. And too late, his scanner revealed the mighty seismic landslide flaring out across the eastern bank of the trench, much as sand spreads when falling through an hourglass, and closing on him at an incredible rate of speed.

Big Ben was still battling through the soft ooze when the avalanche caught up to it. Pitt felt the ground slipping away under the vehicle and knew he'd lost the race. The sound of it came like the roar of a cataract in a tiled room. He saw death's finger reaching out to touch him. He just had time to tense his body before a great wall of mud engulfed the DSMV and swept it end over end into the black void far below, concealing it under a burial shroud of featureless ooze.

The sea looked as if it had gone insane as the mighty bulk of the tsunami towered into the night, forming a raging frenzy of destruction. It sped out of the darkness, rising ever higher as it came in contact with the island's shoals, the sheer magnitude of its power beyond human belief.

As its front slowed from friction at meeting the rising

bottom, the water in its rear piled up, lifting with fantastic speed to the height of an eight-storey building. Blacker than the night itself, its crest bursting like fireworks with the fire of phosphorescence, its roar slashing across the sea like a sonic boom, the mammoth nightmare reared up like a mountain summit and flung itself against the defenceless island's already sunken palisades.

The stupendous wall of death and devastation crushed and swept away every tree, every stick of organic growth, and the resort buildings above the island like toothpicks in a tornado. Nothing made by man or nature resisted the catastrophic force longer than an eye blink in time. Trillions of litres of water obliterated everything in their path. The island was pushed under even further as if by a giant hand.

Much of the tsunami's astronomical power was sapped from the onslaught against the land mass. A counter surge was created in a kind of backlash that sent the major force of the wave back into the vastness of the ocean. What energy was left of the westward thrust passed on and struck Japan's main island of Honshu, the wave having dropped to a one-metre coastal surge that caused some damage to several fishing ports but no deaths.

In its wake the tsunami born of Mother's Breath left Soseki Island and its Dragon Centre drowned under a turbulent sea, never to rise above the surface again.

From deep under the island the aftershocks went on. They sounded like the rumblings of heavy gunfire. At the same time, countless tons of black water gushed through the air vents and elevator shaft, pressured by the enormous weight from above. Rivers spurted from fractures opened in the concrete roof and by widening fissures in the overhead lava rock from the stress forces brought on by the sinking island.

The entire Dragon Centre was suddenly filled with the

noise of water cascading from above. And behind that noise was the heavier, deeper thunder of water exploding into the rooms and corridors of the upper levels. Impelled by fantastic pressure, the flood plunged into the heart of the complex, shoving a great blast of air ahead of it.

All was confusion and panic now. The full realization by the hundreds of workers that they all faced certain death came with strickening suddenness. Nothing could save them, there was no place to run to escape the inundation. The tunnel had been split apart as the island shifted downwards, sending the sea pouring through the tube toward Edo City at the other end.

Tsuboi's ears rang from the air pressure. A great roaring sound came from outside the control room, and he recognized it as a wall of water ramming its way towards the defence control room. He had no more time for his mind to create another thought. In that instant, a sudden torrent of water burst into the room. There was no time to run, to even shout. In his final moments he saw his mentor, the evil old archcriminal Yoshishu, shot away from the column he was clinging to like a fly from the spurt of a garden hose. With a faint cry he disappeared in a rush of water.

Rage dominated all of Tsuboi's other emotions. He felt no fear of pain or death, only a rage directed against the elements for denying him the leadership of the new empire. With Suma and Yoshishu gone, it would have all belonged to him. But it was only the fleeting hallucination of a dying man.

Tsuboi felt himself being sucked out and swept into the flow of water rushing through the corridor. His ears stabbed with agony from the pressure. His lungs were squeezed to the bursting point. And then he was thrust against a wall, his body crushed.

Only eight minutes had elapsed since Mother's Breath had exploded, no more. The destruction of the Dragon Centre was terrifyingly complete. The Kaiten Project no longer existed, and the island the ancients knew as Ajima was now only a mound beneath the sea.

73

For the President and the vastly relieved advisers on his National Security Council, the news of the total elimination of the Dragon Centre was greeted with tired smiles and a quiet round of applause. They were all too exhausted for any display of unrestrained celebration. Martin Brogan, the CIA chief, compared it to waiting all night at the hospital for his wife's first baby.

The President came down to the Situation Room to personally congratulate Ray Jordan and Don Kern. He was in a jubilant mood, and fairly beamed like an airport beacon.

'Your people did one hell of a job,' said the President, pumping Jordan's hand. 'The nation is in your debt.'

'The MAIT team deserves the honours,' said Kern. 'They truly pulled off the impossible.'

'But not without sacrifice,' Jordan murmured softly. 'Jim Hanamura, Marv Showalter, and Dirk Pitt; it was a costly operation.'

'No word on Pitt?' asked the President.

Kern shook his head. 'There seems to be little doubt that he and his Deep Sea Mining Vehicle were swept away by the seismic landslide and buried.'

'Any sign of him from the Pyramider?'

'During the satellite's first pass after the explosion and upheaval, there was so much turbulence the cameras couldn't detect any image of the vehicle.'

'Maybe you can spot him on the next pass,' the President said hopefully. 'If there is even the slightest chance he may still be alive, I want a full-scale rescue mission mounted to save him. We owe Pitt our butts, and I'm not about to walk away from him.'

'We'll see to it,' Jordan promised. But already his mind was turning to other projects.

'What news of Admiral Sandecker?'

'His surveillance aircraft was struck by missiles launched from the Dragon Centre. The pilot managed to make a safe wheels-up landing at Naha Air Field on Okinawa. From initial reports, the plane was shot up pretty badly and lost all communications.'

'Casualties?'

'None,' answered Kern. 'It was a wonder they survived with little more to show than a few cuts and bruises.'

The President nodded thoughtfully. 'At least we know now why they broke off contact.'

Secretary of State Douglas Oates stepped forward. 'More good news, Mr President,' he said, smiling. 'The combined Soviet and European search teams have uncovered almost all of the bomb cars hidden in their territories.'

'We have MAIT team to thank for stealing the locations,' explained Kern.

'Unfortunately, it didn't help much on our end,' said Jordan.

Kern nodded. 'The United States was the main threat to the Kaiten Project, not the European alliance or the Eastern Bloc countries. We were sidetracked when Tsuboi and Yoshishu became certain Suma was in our hands and ordered the cars rehidden on our end.'

The President looked at Jordan. 'Have any more been found?'

'Six.' The Central Intelligence Director grinned slightly. 'Now that we have some breathing space, we should track down the rest without further risk to national security.'

'Tsuboi and Yoshishu?'

'Believed drowned.'

The President looked pleased, and he felt it. He turned and faced everyone in the room. 'Gentlemen,' he announced, 'on behalf of a grateful American people, who

564

will never know how narrowly you saved them from disaster, I thank you.'

The crisis was over, but already another had erupted. Later that afternoon, fighting broke out along the border of Iran and Turkey, and the first reports came in of a Cuban military Mig-25 shooting down a United States commercial airliner filled with tourists returning from Jamaica.

The search for one man quickly became lost in the shuffle. The imaging technology on board the Pyramider satellite was shifted toward world events of more importance. Nearly four weeks would pass before the satellite's eyes were turned back to the sea off Japan.

But no trace of *Big Ben* was found.

PART FIVE

Obituary

74

November 19, 1993
The Washington Post

It was announced today that Dirk Pitt, Special Projects Director for the National Underwater and Marine Agency, is missing and presumed dead after an accident in the sea off Japan.

Acclaimed for his exploits on land and under the sea that include his discoveries of the Pre-Columbian Byzantine shipwreck *Serapis* off Greenland; the incredible cache from the Library of Alexandria; and the *La Dorada* treasure in Cuba, among others, Pitt also directed the raising of the *Titanic*.

The son of Senator George Pitt of California and his wife, Susan, Pitt was born and raised in Newport Beach, California. He attended the Air Force Academy, where he played quarterback on the Falcon football team, and graduated twelfth in his class. Becoming a pilot, Pitt remained in active service for ten years, rising to the rank of major. He then became permanently attached to NUMA at the request of Admiral James Sandecker.

The admiral said briefly yesterday that Dirk Pitt was an extremely resourceful and audacious man. During the course of his career, he had saved many lives, including those of Sandecker himself, and the President during an incident in the Gulf of Mexico. Pitt never lacked for ingenuity or creativity. No project was too difficult for him to accomplish.

He was not a man you can forget.

Sandecker sat on the running board of the Stutz in Pitt's hangar and stared sadly at the obituary in the newspaper.

'He did so much, it seems an injustice to condense his life to so few words.'

Giordino, his face expressionless, walked around the Messerschmitt ME-262A-1a Luftwaffe jet fighter. True to his word, Gert Halder had looked the other way when Pitt and Giordino had smuggled the aircraft out of the bunker, hauled it on a truck under canvas, and arranged for it to be hoisted on board a Danish cargo ship bound for the States. Only two days earlier the ship had arrived in Baltimore, where Giordino had waited to transport the aircraft to Pitt's hangar in Washington. Now it sat on its tricycle landing gear amid the other classic machinery of Pitt's collection.

'Dirk should have been here to see this,' Giordino said heavily. He ran his hand across the nose of the mottled green fuselage with its light grey underbelly and stared at the muzzles of the four thirty-millimetre cannon that poked from the forward cowl. 'He'd have loved to get his hands on it.'

It was a moment neither of them had foreseen, could never imagine. Sandecker felt as though he'd lost a son, Giordino a brother.

Giordino stopped and stared at the apartment above the classic autos and aircraft. 'I should have been in the DSMV with him.'

Sandecker looked up. 'Then you would be missing and maybe dead too.'

'I'll always regret not being with him,' Giordino said vaguely.

'Dirk died in the sea. It's the way he'd have wanted it.'

'He might be standing here now if one of *Big Ben*'s manipulators had been fitted with a scoop instead of cutting tools,' Giordino persisted.

Sandecker gave a weary shake of his head. 'Allowing your imagination to run riot won't bring him back.'

Giordino's eyes lifted to Pitt's living quarters. 'I keep

thinking all I have to do is yell for him, and he'll come down.'

'The same thought has crossed my mind,' Sandecker admitted.

Suddenly the door of the apartment opened, and they momentarily stiffened, then relaxed as Toshie emerged carrying a tray with cups and a teapot. With incredible supple grace, she delicately wound down the iron circular stairway and glided towards Sandecker and Giordino.

Sandecker wrinkled his brows in puzzlement. 'A mystery to me how you sweet-talked Jordan into having her committed into your custody.'

'No mystery,' Giordino grinned. 'a trade-off. He made her a present to me in return for keeping my mouth shut about the Kaiten Project.'

'You're lucky he didn't encase your feet in cement and throw you in the Potomac.'

'I was bluffing.'

'Ray Jordan is no dummy,' Sandecker said dryly. 'He knew that.'

'Okay, so she was a gift for services rendered.'

Toshie set the tray on the running board of the Stutz next to the admiral. 'Tea, gentlemen?'

'Yes, thank you,' Sandecker said, rising to his feet.

Toshie smoothly settled to her knees and performed a brief tea ceremony before passing the steaming cups. Then she rose and admiringly stared at the Messerschmitt.

'What a beautiful aeroplane,' she murmured, overlooking the grime, the flattened tyres, and the faded paint.

'I'm going to restore it to its original state,' said Giordino quietly, mentally picturing the dingy aircraft as it looked when new. 'As a favour to Dirk.'

'You talk like he's going to be resurrected,' Sandecker said tightly.

'He's not dead,' Giordino muttered flatly. Tough as he was, tears were welling in his eyes.

'May I help?' asked Toshie.

Giordino self-consciously wiped his eyes and looked at her curiously. 'I'm sorry, pretty lady, help me what?'

'Repair the aeroplane.'

Giordino and Sandecker exchanged blank glances. 'You're a mechanic?' asked Giordino.

'I helped my father build and maintain his fishing boat. He was very proud when I mended his ailing engine.'

Giordino's face lit up. 'A match made in heaven.' He paused and stared at the drab dress Toshie was given when she was released from Jordan's custody. 'Before you and I start to tear this baby apart, I'm going to take you to the best boutiques in Washington and buy you a new wardrobe.'

Toshie's eyes widened. 'You have much, much money like Mr Suma?'

'No,' Giordino moaned sorrowfully, 'only lots of credit cards.'

Loren smiled and waved over the lunch crowd as the maitre d' of Washington's chic restaurant Twenty-One Federal led Stacy through the blond wood and marble dining room to her table. Stacy had her hair tied back in a large scarf and was more informally dressed in an oatmeal cashmere turtleneck sweater under a grey wool shawl with matching pants.

Loren wore a plaid wool checked jacket over a khaki blouse with a taupe wool faille skirt. Unlike most women, who would have remained seated, she rose and offered her hand to Stacy. 'I'm glad you could come.'

Stacy smiled warmly and took Loren's hand. 'I've always wanted to eat here. I'm grateful for the opportunity.'

'Will you join me in a drink?'

'That cold wind outside stings. I think I'd like a manhattan straight up to take the chill off.'

'I'm afraid I couldn't wait. I already went through a martini.'

'Then you'd better have another to fight the cold when we leave.' Stacy laughed pleasantly.

Their waiter took the order and went off toward the elegant bar.

Loren replaced her napkin in her lap. 'I didn't have a proper chance to thank you on Wake Island; we were all so rushed about.'

'Dirk is the one we all owe.'

Loren turned away. She thought she had cried herself out after hearing the news of Pitt's death, but she still felt the tears behind her eyes.

Stacy's smile faded, and she looked at Loren with sympathy. 'I'm very sorry about Dirk. I know you two were very close.'

'We had our ups and downs over the years, but we never strayed very far from each other.'

'Was marriage ever considered?' asked Stacy.

Loren gave a brief shake of her head. 'The subject never came up. Dirk wasn't the kind of man who could be possessed. His mistress was the sea, and I had my career in Congress.'

'You were lucky. His smile was devastating, and those green eyes. God, they'd make any woman melt.'

Suddenly Loren was nervous. 'You'll have to forgive me. I don't know what's come over me, but I have to know.' She hesitated as if afraid to continue and fidgeted with a spoon.

Stacy met Loren's eyes evenly. 'The answer is no,' she lied. 'I came to his place late one night, but it was on orders from Ray Jordan to give Dirk instructions. Nothing happened. I left twenty minutes later. From that moment until we parted on Wake Island it was strictly business.'

'I know this must sound silly. Dirk and I often went our own way when it came to seeing other men and women, but I wanted to be sure I was the only one near the end.'

'You were more deeply in love with him than you thought, weren't you?'

Loren gave a little nod. 'Yes, I realized it too late.'

'There will be others,' Stacy said in an attempt to be cheerful.

'But none to take his place.'

The waiter returned with their drinks. Stacy held up her glass. 'To Dirk Pitt, a damned good man.'

They touched glasses.

'A damned good man,' Loren repeated, as the tears formed. 'Yes … he was that.'

75

In the dining room of a safe house somewhere in the Maryland countryside, Jordan sat at a table having lunch with Hideki Suma. 'Is there anything I can do to make your stay more comfortable?' asked Jordan.

Suma paused, savouring the delicate flavour of a noodle soup with duck and scallions accented by radish and gold caviar. He spoke without looking up. 'There is one favour.'

'Yes?'

Suma nodded at the security agent standing guard by the door and at his partner who served the meal. 'Your friends will not allow me to meet the chef. He is very good. I wish to offer him my compliments.'

'*She* apprenticed at one of New York's finest Japanese restaurants. Her name is Natalie, and she now works with the government on special assignments. And no, I'm sorry but you cannot be introduced.'

Jordan examined Suma's face. There was no hostility in it, no frustration at being isolated in heavily guarded confine-ment – nothing but a supreme complacency. For a man who had been subtly drugged and then forced to endure long hours of interrogation over four weeks, he showed almost no sign of it. The eyes were still as hard as onyx under the shock of greying hair. But that was as it should have been. Through post-hypnotic suggestion from Jordan's expert interrogators, Suma did not recall, nor did he realize he had provided a team of curious engineers and scientists a wealth of technical data. His mind was probed and scrutinized as neatly as by professional thieves, who after searching a house left everything as they found it.

It had to be, Jordan mused, one of the few times American

intelligence actually obtained foreign industrial secrets that could prove profitable.

'A sadness.' Suma shrugged. 'I would have liked to hire her when I leave.'

'That won't be possible,' Jordan said frankly.

Suma finished the soup and pushed the bowl aside. 'You cannot continue holding me like a common criminal. I am not some peasant you arrested out of the gutter. I think you would be wise to release me without further delay.'

No hard demand, merely a veiled threat from a man who was not informed that his incredible power had vanished with his announced death throughout Japan. Ceremonies had been performed, and already his spirit was enshrined at Yasukuni. Suma had no idea that as far as the outside world was concerned, he no longer existed. Nor was he told of the deaths of Tsuboi and Yoshishu, and the destruction of the Dragon Centre. For all he knew the Kaiten Project's bomb cars were still safely hidden.

'After what you attempted,' said Jordan coldly, 'you're lucky you're not up before an international tribunal for crimes against humanity.'

'I have a divine right to protect Japan.' The quiet, authoritative voice came to Jordan as if it was coming from a pulpit.

Irritation flushed Jordan's temples. 'Besides being the most insular society on earth, Japan's problem with the rest of the world is that your business leaders have no ethics, no principles of fair play in the Western sense. You and your fellow corporate executive officers believe in doing unto other nations as you would not allow others to do unto you.'

Suma picked up a teacup and drained it. 'Japan is a highly honourable society. Our loyalties run very deep.'

'Sure, to yourselves, at the expense of outsiders, such as foreign nationals.'

'We see no difference between an economic war and a military war,' Suma replied pleasantly. 'We look upon the

576

industrial nations merely as competitors on a vast battlefield where there are no rules of conduct, no trade treaties that can be trusted.'

The lunacy combined with the cold reality of the situation suddenly seemed ridiculous to Jordan. He saw it was useless trying to make a dent in Suma. Perhaps the madman was right. America ultimately *would* become divided into separate nations governed by race. He brushed the uncomfortable thought from his mind and rose from the table.

'I must go,' he announced curtly.

Suma stared at him. 'When can I return to Edo City?'

Jordan regarded him thoughtfully for a moment. 'Tomorrow.'

'I would like that,' said Suma. 'Please see that one of my private planes will be waiting at Dulles Field.'

The guy had gall, Jordan thought. 'I'll make arrangements through your embassy.'

'Good day, Mr Jordan.'

'Good day, Mr Suma. I trust you will forgive me for any inconvenience you've suffered.'

Suma's lips compressed in a thin menacing line and he squinted at Jordan through half-closed eyes. 'No, Mr Jordan, I do not forgive you. Please rest assured you will pay a stiff price for my captivity.' Then Suma seemingly dismissed Jordan and poured another cup of tea.

Kern was waiting as Jordan stepped past the armoured doors separating the entry hall from the living room. 'Have a nice lunch?'

'The food was good but the company was lousy. And you?'

'I listened in while eating in the kitchen. Natalie made me a hamburger.'

'Lucky you.'

'What about our friend?'

'I told him he would be released tomorrow.'

'I heard. Will he remember to pack?'

Jordan smiled. 'The thought will be erased during tonight's interrogation session.'

Kern nodded slowly. 'How long do you think we can keep him going?'

'Until we know everything he knows, unlock every secret, every memory in his grey matter.'

'That could take a year or two.'

'So?'

'And after we've sucked him dry?'

'What do you mean?'

'We can't keep him hidden from the world forever. And we'd be cutting our own throats if we set him free and allowed him to return to Japan.'

Jordan stared at Kern without a flicker of change in his expression. 'When Suma has no more left to give, Natalie will slip a little something extra into his noodle soup.'

'I'm sorry, Mr President, but in your Western idiom, my hands are tied.'

The President looked across the cabinet room conference table at the smiling little man with the short-trimmed white hair and defiant brown eyes. He seemed more a military commander of a tough infantry battalion than the political leader of Japan.

Prime Minister Junshiro, who had come to Washington on an official state visit, sat flanked by two of his ministers and five staff aides. The President sat opposite with only his interpreter by his side.

'I'm sorry too, Prime Minister, but if you think you're simply going to sweep the tragedies of the past weeks under the rug, you've got another think coming.'

'My government was not responsible for the alleged actions of Hideki Suma, Ichiro Tsuboi, and Korori Yoshishu. If, as you accuse, they were indeed behind the nuclear bombs that exploded in your State of Wyoming and on the high sea, they acted for their own ends in secret.'

This meeting between the heads of state was not going to be pleasant. Junshiro and his cabinet had stonewalled any investigation and had indignantly reacted as if the Western intelligence services had fabricated the entire tragedy.

The President's hard stare swept the other side of the table. The Japanese could never negotiate without a committee. 'If you would be so kind as to ask your ministers and staff, with the exception of your interpreter, to leave the room, I would be grateful. Considering the delicate nature of our talk, I believe it will prove more beneficial if we hold it in private.'

Junshiro's face darkened as the request was translated. He clearly did not like what he heard. The President was smiling, but there was no humour in his eyes. 'I must ask you to reconsider. I'm certain we can accomplish more with my advisers present.'

'As you can see,' the President replied, gesturing around the kidney-shaped mahogany table, 'I have no advisers.'

The Prime Minister was confused, as the President expected. He conversed in rapid-fire Japanese with the men who huddled around him voicing their objections.

The President's interpreter smiled ever so slightly. 'They don't like it,' he murmured. 'It's not their way of doing business. They think you're being unreasonable and very undiplomatic.'

'How about barbaric?'

'Only in their tone, Mr President, only in their tone.'

At last Junshiro turned back to the President. 'I must protest this unusual protocol, Mr President.'

When he heard the translation, the President replied, his voice cold, 'I'm through playing games, Prime Minister. Either your people leave or I do.'

After a moment of thought, Junshiro made a deep nod of his head. 'As you wish.' Then he motioned his advisers to the door.

After the door closed, the President looked at his

interpreter and said, 'Translate exactly as I speak, no niceties, no syrup over the harsh words.'

'Understood, sir.'

The President fixed a hard stare on Junshiro. 'Now then, Prime Minister, the facts are that you and members of your cabinet were fully aware and informally approved of Suma Industries' manufacture of a nuclear arsenal. A project funded in part by an underworld organization known as the Golden Dragons. This programme in turn led to the Kaiten Project, a hideous international blackmail plan, conceived in secrecy and now veiled by lies and phony denials. You knew of it from the beginning, and yet you condoned it by your silence and non-intervention.'

Once he heard the translation, Junshiro pounded the table with angered indignation. 'This is not true, none of it. There is absolutely no foundation for these absurd charges.'

'Information from a variety of intelligence sources leaves little doubt of your involvement. You secretly applauded while known underworld criminals were building what they called the "new empire". An empire based on economic and nuclear blackmail.'

Junshiro's face paled, but he said nothing. He saw the handwriting on the wall, and it spelled out political disaster and great loss of face.

The President kept his eyes locked on him. 'What we don't need here is a lot of self-righteous crap. There will always be a basic conflict between American and Japanese interests, but we can't exist without each other.'

Junshiro recognized that the President had thrown him a rope, and he snatched at it. 'What do you propose?'

'To save your nation and your people the shock and shame of scandal, you resign. The trust between your government and mine is shattered. The damage is irreparable. Only a new prime minister and a cabinet of honest, decent people with no connections to your underworld will bring about a renewed state of mutual cooperation between our two countries. Hopefully, we can then work in close partnership to resolve our cultural and economic differences.'

'The event will remain secret?'

'I promise all data on the Dragon Centre and the Kaiten Project will remain classified from this end.'

'And if I do not resign?'

The President leaned back and spread his hands. 'Then I'd have to predict that Japanese businessmen should prepare for a recession.'

Junshiro came to his feet. 'Am I to understand, Mr President, that you are threatening to close the United States market to all Japanese goods?'

'I don't have to,' the President answered. His face took on a curious change. The blue eyes lost their glint of anger and assumed a pensive look. 'Because if word leaks out that a Japanese nuclear bomb was smuggled into the United States and exploded where the deer and the antelope roam . . .' He paused for effect. 'I doubt seriously the American consumer will look kindly on buying your products ever again.'

76

November 21, 1993
Marcus Island

Far off the beaten tourist track, 1,125 kilometres southeast of Japan, Marcus Island lies in pristine isolation. A coral atoll tucked away without island neighbours, its shores are formed in an almost perfect triangle, each measuring approximately one and a half kilometres in length.

Except for brief notoriety while being bombed by American naval forces during World War II, few people had ever heard of Marcus Island until a Japanese developer just happened to stumble upon its desolate beaches. He visualized its potential as a select destination for winter-weary Japanese and promptly constructed a luxury resort.

Designed in a contemporary Polynesian style, the villagelike atmosphere included a championship golf course, a casino, three restaurants with cocktail lounges and dance floors, a theatre, a vast lotus-shaped swimming pool, and six tennis courts. The sprawling complex, along with the golf course and the airfield, covered the entire island.

When the resort was completed and fully staffed, the developer flew in an army of travel writers, who soaked up the free material comforts and returned home to report. The resort immediately proved popular with adventurous tourists who collect exotic and faraway locations. But instead of an influx of Japanese, the reservations flowed in from other areas of the Pacific rim, and soon the island's satiny milk-white sands were littered with Australians, New Zealanders, Taiwanese, and Koreans.

The resort island also quickly became a playground for romance and a mecca for honeymooners, who indulged in the many sporting activities or simply lolled around and made love in their village bungalows scattered among the palm trees.

Brian Foster from Brisbane came out of the ice-blue water inside the outer reef and walked across the beach towards his bride, Shelly, who was dozing in a lounge chair. The fine sand felt hot against his naked feet, and the late afternoon sun glistened on the water drops streaming from his body. As he towelled away the dampness, he glanced back over the water.

A Korean couple, Kim and Li Sang, who stayed in the next bungalow, were taking windsurfing lessons from one of the resort's attentive guest hosts. Beyond them, Edward Cain from Wellington snorkelled on the reef while his new bride, Moira, floated on a mat in his wake.

Foster gave his wife a light kiss and patted her tummy. He lay in the sand beside her, put on a pair of sunglasses, and idly watched the people in the water.

The Sangs were having a difficult time mastering the technique and coordination it took to pilot a sailboard. They seemed to be spending an inordinate amount of time regaining the board and pulling up the sail after losing their balance and spilling in the water.

Foster turned his attention to the Cains, admiring Moira, who had rolled over on her back without falling off the mat. She was wearing a one-piece gold bathing suit that did very little to hide her lush contours.

Suddenly something caught Foster's eye in the entrance of the channel that cut through the coral reef and led to the open ocean. Something was happening under the water. He was sure some *thing* or some sea creature was making a disturbance beneath the surface. He couldn't see what it was, only that it appeared to be moving through the reef towards the lagoon.

'There's something out there!' he snapped to his wife as he jumped to his feet. He ran to the water and began shouting and pointing towards the channel. His shouts and wild gesturing quickly drew others, and soon a crowd from the nearby pool and restaurants gathered on the beach.

The Sangs' windsurfing instructor heard Foster, and his eyes followed the Australian's pointing finger. He saw the approaching commotion in the water and swiftly herded the Sangs toward shore. Then he leaped on a sailboard and flew across the lagoon to warn the Cains, who were leisurely drifting into the path of the unknown apparition that was seemingly intent on invading the lagoon.

Edward Cain, with his wife floating close to him, swam blissfully unaware of the danger, viewing the sculptured garden of coral through his dive mask, enthralled by the vivid colours and the swarming schools of luminous fish.

He heard a humming sound in the distance but thought it was probably one of the guests bobbing over the water on a Jet Ski. Then, as if in a practised precision movement, the surrounding fish abruptly darted away and vanished. Cain felt the breath of fear on his skin. The first thought that ran through his mind was that a shark had entered the lagoon.

Cain raised his head above the surface, searching for a telltale fin slicing the water. Thankfully, none was in sight. All he saw was a sailboard gliding in his direction and his wife dozing on the floating pad. He heard the shouting from the beach, turned, and spied the crowd of resort guests and employees frantically motioning towards the channel.

A rumbling vibration seemed to agitate the water, and he ducked his head back under the surface. What in God's name was it? he wondered. Through the turquoise void, no more than fifty metres away, a great shapeless thing covered with green and brown slime crawled into view.

He grabbed a corner of his wife's float and began madly paddling towards a rise in the coral where it broke through the surface of the water. She had no idea of what he was doing and hung on, thinking he was simply in a playful mood and wanted to roll her into the water.

The awesome thing ignored them and rolled past the reef

into the lagoon and headed directly for the beach. Like some unspeakable monster out of a deep-sea horror movie, it slowly rose from the lagoon. The dumbfounded crowd of resort guests parted as the immense thing, water pouring down its sides, the sand trembling beneath its weight, pulled up between two palm trees and stopped dead.

In total silence they all stood rooted and stared. They could see now that it was a huge mechanical vehicle that travelled on wide tracks, with a large, cigar-shaped housing on top. Two mechanical arms rose into the air like mutated antennae on a giant insect. Colonies of crustaceans clung to crevices of the exterior that was coated with hardened brown ooze and slime, shrouding any view through the normally transparent bow.

There was a soft clunk sound as a hatch on the roof was unsealed and thrown back.

A head with a shag of black hair and a beard slowly rose into view. The face was gaunt and thin, but the eyes that were sunken in dark hollows sparkled with green intensity. They gazed around the stunned audience and picked out a young man who was gripping a round tray in both hands.

Then the lips spread in a great flashing smile and the voice rasped hoarsely. 'Am I right in thinking you're a waiter?'

'Yes . . . sir.'

'Good thing too. After a diet of mouldy bologna sandwiches and coffee for the past month, I'm ready to kill for a crab louis salad and a tequila on the rocks.'

Four hours later, his stomach supremely sated, Pitt was sleeping the most enjoyable and satisfying sleep he had ever known.

Sahara

Clive Cussler

HIS SPECTACULAR INTERNATIONAL NO.1 BESTSELLER

Clive Cussler's peerless hero Dirk Pitt in his most gripping and action-packed adventure yet.

Deep in the African desert, Pitt discovers that a top-secret scientific installation is leaking a lethal chemical into the rivers, threatening to kill thousands of people – and to destroy all life in the world's seas.

To warn the world of the catastrophe, Pitt must escape capture and death at the hands of a ruthless West African dictator and French industrialist, and undertake a long, perilous journey across the merciless Sahara . . .

'The ultimate Dirk Pitt tale. Nobody does it better than Clive Cussler, America's finest adventure writer.'
STEPHEN COONTS, author of *Under Siege*

'A cram course in rip-roaring action . . . a sizzling yet thoughtful thriller.' *Chicago Tribune*

'Amazing feats of derring-do . . . non-stop action . . . refreshing escapist entertainment.' *Washington Post*

ISBN 0 586 21766 5

Inca Gold

Clive Cussler

A desperate call for help from a stricken archaeological expedition brings Dirk Pitt to a sacred well high in the Andes. What he discovers as he attempts to rescue two divers lost in its perilous depths leads him into deadly confrontation with a ruthless band of international art-thieves, who plunder ancient sites for their precious arte-facts.

Dirk Pitt's extraordinary adventures take him to the fabled Lost City of the Dead, lead him in search of a Spanish galleon washed miles inland by a giant tidal wave centuries before, and eventually set him on the trail of a fabulous hoard of Inca Gold. But Pitt will need all his skills and tenacity simply to survive as he races to track down the sacred site – before the richest prize known to man is lost to the world for ever. . .

'Clive Cussler's hero Dirk Pitt is made of strong stuff, handling the improbable with nerves of steel . . . he is one of the best adventure heroes around.'   *Today*

'Clive Cussler is the guy *I* read.'   TOM CLANCY

ISBN 0 00 647909 X

Treasure
Clive Cussler

THE HIGH EXPLOSIVE
SECRET OF THE AGES

AD 391: Fanatics destroy the greatest storehouse of knowledge and treasure in the ancient world – the great library and museum of Alexandria. But a few conspirators secretly remove the most precious items and ship them to a distant, desolate land, hiding them deep in a specially excavated stronghold...

AD 1991: A UN plane, with the Secretary General aboard, crashes in the icy wastes of Greenland, brought down by a monstrously cunning terrorist conspiracy. Troubleshooter supreme Dirk Pitt, in the area on an undercover search mission for a crippled Soviet submarine, finds himself caught up in an even more dangerous vortex of complex intrigue. And with a beautiful, sensual female archaeologist who has found an ancient gold coin nearby – far further north than it should be...

Dirk Pitt's quest for the Alexandrian treasure combines with his battle against the forces of murderous international terrorism in an outstanding story of razor's-edge suspense, hair-trigger international intrigue and all-out action and excitement.

'If you like your action fast, your prose faster and your plot unexpected, then Mr Cussler is the man for you.'

Manchester Evening News

'Clive Cussler is the guy *I* read.'

TOM CLANCY

ISBN 0 00 720559-7